For Harry and Mason

Lorna Gray's relationship with the rugged beauty of the West Wales coastline began when she studied Fine Art (BA Hons) at Aberystwyth University. Lorna's subsequent training as an archaeological illustrator led her to Cirencester where she's been exploring her love of history, adventure and romance ever since.

Her first post-war novel *In the Shadow of Winter* was published in 2015. She lives in the Cotswolds with her husband.

# Also by Lorna Gray

*In the Shadow of Winter*

# *The*
# WAR
# WIDOW

# LORNA GRAY

A division of HarperCollins*Publishers*
www.harpercollins.co.uk

Harper*Impulse* an imprint of
HarperCollins*Publishers*
The News Building
1 London Bridge Street
London SE1 9GF

www.harpercollins.co.uk

This paperback edition 2018

First published in Great Britain in ebook format by
HarperCollins*Publishers* 2018

Copyright © Lorna Gray 2018

Lorna Gray asserts the moral right to
be identified as the author of this work

A catalogue record for this book
is available from the British Library

ISBN: 9780008279578

Printed and bound by CPI Group (UK) Ltd, Croydon, CR0 4YY

MIX
Paper from
responsible sources
FSC™ C007454
www.fsc.org

# Chapter 1

Thursday 20 November 1947

I might have done things differently had I had known today that I only had four more days of glorious solitude. That in four short days they would find me at last. That four short days would carry my race to the limit of this sea-ravaged coastline. That here I would feel the nauseating pull and draw of the waves and above it all, hear the darker overtone of footsteps as they strolled inescapably towards me.

I wouldn't be thinking about myself at that moment. I would simply be waiting, defeated, quivering on the wooden harbour jetty and looking down into the murky water as it heaved beneath. Thinking about *him* and what he had done; and finally and absolutely admit that despite all my determined efforts to the contrary, I had lost control over both my mind and my freedom, with no hope left of ever regaining it.

But that would be four days from now. Today there were still four more days ahead of wonderful optimism. Today I was feeling the tug of the waves too, but in an altogether more peaceful way.

I had come to Aberystwyth in November two years after the war. I was climbing down from a rough little hilltop that overlooked the town a little after dawn and the view was glorious. The wide bay of terraces clung bravely to the curve where sweeping cliffs met dark granite seashores and today, as ever, it called to the artist in me.

I probably shouldn't have been up there. The doctors had prescribed rest after my accident and I knew even the walk back to my hotel would have drawn their united disapproval. But at least it was quiet and calming in its way because very few people were about. Those that were cared little for a woman in a beige trench coat with the collar turned up who was walking briskly past shops declaring fresh stocks of corned beef and offal – a novelty in this time of rationing. Nobody noticed me walking past the shuttered tearooms either. These were papered with posters bearing the information that the cinema would be showing the full coverage of the Princess Elizabeth's wedding just as soon as the newsreels got here. It was all wonderfully like being invisible. It was just unfortunate that the illusion abandoned me just as soon as I climbed the steps to my hotel.

"Good morning, Miss Word."

The lady in the wood-panelled reception booth in the foyer was excessively genteel and her grey hair was done up in a neat bun. Her greeting was dignified and gracious but slightly marred by the fact that Word wasn't actually my name. It was *Ward* but I didn't tell her that. Just as I had been too embarrassed to correct her late last night when she'd said it after watching me sign my name on the registration form, and again after she'd taken custody of my ration book and handed me my key...

So this morning I repeated the peculiar habit of feeling guiltily responsible for having the wrong name and only stated warmly that it was indeed a good morning and moved bravely towards the dining room. It was the sort of room that belonged a largely imaginary bygone era that had never known the war. The requirement to be brave came from my reluctance to interact with the other guests. I didn't want conversation today. And besides, the pages of the hotel's guestbook bore the signatures of an intimidatingly large scattering of high society grandees, which I certainly wasn't. It had prices to match. I never would have chosen to stay here at all if I hadn't remembered it from a brief visit many years ago during my honeymoon and the fact that I couldn't have faced any more decisions last night after such a day and such a long journey.

As it was, when I took my seat it was only to be reassuringly greeted and then ignored by two elderly ladies who were deep in an animated discussion. They were worrying about the danger of introducing unbridled enjoyment – embodied by the recently lifted embargo on foreign travel I think – to a generation that had been brought up knowing only wartime excursions to the respectable English seaside. I think they were unaware that they were, in fact, at present in Wales.

I hid my head in a book. I had borrowed it from the tiny library in the lounge next door and it was a battered copy of *Jane Eyre*. It was supposed to keep my mind from working while I finished my breakfast but it wasn't doing very well since I had read the book more times than I could count.

Then I discovered a more modern effort abandoned on the table next to me. It promised *'A Sterling Mystery!!!'* – a weak pun on the name of the principle character I think – and bore the name A. E. Woolfe emblazoned across the cover like a banner. Sceptical purely on the grounds of too many exclamation marks, I picked it up and read the first few pages easily enough but when the first character died in a grisly fashion at the wheel of his car, I felt my head begin to swim and had to put it down.

"Not to your taste?" A male voice.

Looking up, I discovered that the surrounding tables were now packed with a different set of people and the comfortable Miss Bartlemans had miraculously transformed into a dark-haired gentleman who was now sitting in the chair opposite, with a newspaper spread over the table between us. His eyes were a mild pale blue and were watching me benignly and at least they had the relatively harmless excuse that I had been thoroughly absorbed in my book. Anonymity and similar ambitions aside, I tend to be like that when reading. It used to drive my husband wild, along with a great number of other things.

Swiftly suppressing that sobering thought, I lifted my head properly and slipped the paperback back onto the table to sheepishly retrieve the tattered classic. A faint curve was showing at one corner of his mouth. It made me tell him with a foolish beam, "It seems very well written actually but I need something gentle that won't tax my brain. At least with *Jane Eyre*, I know the book so well I can start at an easy bit. Even if it does feel a little like sacrilege to discard the childhood section without so much as a glance."

4

I stopped. He was sitting with his forearms resting upon his paper and he was the sort of man who wore reasonably good clothes as if they didn't matter at all. I think he belonged in this hotel rather more than I did. I also think my light reply made him feel he had just made an awkward social error. Those eyes blanked of all expression as he tried to hide it and I cringed inwardly. I cursed myself for breaking my silence so soon after all my good intentions and quickly buried my head in the book before the more alert part of my mind could find another explanation for the barely definable stiffness that had come over his posture as soon as I had begun to speak.

Some other people arrived, noisily. This was the truly fashionable contingent of the hotel's residents. They were a Dr Alderton and wife and her younger sister followed by a capable-looking gentleman who settled with his paper at the table behind. He had arrived shortly after me the night before and he had, from what I had overheard, found something wrong with his original hotel, had almost cut short his business and made for home but then had decided to give Aberystwyth another try. I had a vague recollection of his name being Brighton. Or perhaps it was Brinnington, or something like that. I couldn't quite remember.

"Adam Hitchen, by the way." The man sitting at my table interrupted just as my heroine was exploring Thornfield for the first time. His manner of speaking seemed shorter now. "We've met before."

"We have?" I looked up, startled all over again. Then I recalled the walker, complete with notebook and innocent binoculars, whose arrival earlier this morning on that hilltop had sent me scurrying away with my half-finished painting back down to the town. He'd seemed middle-aged in that blurry dawn light but this man wasn't. But he certainly was the same man. When standing, he'd been reasonably tall and well-built but slim in the way men are when they have a natural enjoyment of the outdoors. Since this was consistent with the taking of lonely hilltop walks of the sort that I liked, I added easily enough, "Of course we have. You identified those little birds in the gorse for me. I'm Kate Ward; and pleased to meet you again, naturally."

I smiled at him just long enough to imply that I meant it and then escaped into my book again. She was about to unhorse Mr Rochester, I was sure.

"On holiday?" Another interruption. It was delivered in that new oddly abrupt tone that made it seem as though he barely cared to hear the answer, but was going to ask the question anyway.

"Something like that," I said, turning a page. There at last was the vital exchange of words between governess and master. But then manners roughly asserted themselves and I remembered that it would be better not to be rude to the same man too many times in one day. I closed my book and smiled at him, this time genuinely. "What about you?"

But the question was lost in the sudden interest of Mrs Alderton and her sister. They turned to us, or rather him, and claimed him with a flurry of excited talking. Their casual assumption that they had the right made it clear they were already on considerably better terms with this man than I.

They were both beautifully made-up. The younger sister was perhaps five years younger than my thirty-two and had lovely big doe eyes. I suspected that she knew full well the effect they had. She had also achieved the near-impossible in the form of perfect satin curls. This was something my hair would never do, which was why mine was now cropped short and left to its own devices in a woolly version of the style seen everywhere in recent years curling neatly around the base of a WREN's cap.

The older sister, Mrs Alderton, was adhering to the new severely girdled style and she was so smart that even to a cynic it must have seemed a little odd that she had been united with a slightly moth-eaten if wealthy husband. Perhaps she thought the same because she paid the doctor about the same amount of attention as she did me; although in theory I was more relieved than otherwise to be permitted to retreat once more into the comparative sanctuary of my book.

It wasn't a sanctuary for long. I heard the walker speak; a light response to the younger woman's extraordinary brand of banter and I noticed that she was receiving even less than the bland sentences he had used on me. Now his replies were actually painfully flat. They made his whole person seem very dull indeed and, to be quite frank, I just couldn't quite believe him. It made me suspect he was deliberately trying to seem insignificant here. Though it also occurred to me that perhaps he was just a little shy.

Or perhaps he simply liked to be awkward. The sister, Mary James, said something – she made an unashamed joke at her fellow guest's expense I think; she certainly leaned in closer to deliver it – and I must have made the mistake of glancing up from my book because I suddenly found myself catching a brief and most definitely unexpected flash of wry intelligence in her victim's eyes as he calmly countered this new attack with yet another very bland reply. They were actually grey and, disconcertingly, very alert indeed.

Mrs Alderton must have seen his glance. She certainly turned towards me with a very odd expression on her elegant face. I had already moved to gather together my things, but I felt her gaze as it took in my taste in clothes, my age and my figure before dismissing it all just as rapidly. Then it ran onto the table beside me.

"Oh. *Here's* your book, Mary."

From the distance of several feet, I felt Mary James turn like a puppet to her sister's command. She immediately snatched up the modern paperback. She drew me helplessly away from my book again as she murmured silkily, "Thank heavens it isn't lost after all; I've read it a thousand times, haven't I, Alice? It has to be one of my all-time favourites."

Mrs Alderton only inclined her head. Then I saw her follow it with one of those swift, calculating glances beneath lowered lashes which only ever seem necessary for married women when there is a potentially available man around; particularly if she has an unmarried sister on hand and that man should happen to be passably attractive. In Adam Hitchen's case, he was certainly passable and I suspected that the crinkle at the corner of his eyes when he smiled very possibly qualified him for the next tier above that. Not that he was smiling now though.

"Haven't I?" Mary's prompt was faintly urgent. Mrs Alderton took her cue, theatrically, saying, "You really should be more careful, dear. Who knows who might try to borrow it? Not everyone has read them *all* you know."

There was quite some emphasis on the 'all'.

My gaze touched the walker's eyes again but there was no betraying flash of character this time. They seemed in fact, if it were possible, to now be devoid of any personality whatsoever.

It was the goad I needed to lever me out of my seat and across the foyer into the mild November day.

---

The town was busier now that its residents had emerged to undertake their morning scurry to offices and shops. The thick traffic was a bizarrely confused mixture of old carts and aged horses that should probably have been retired after the war, and lorries in the crisp painted liveries of the bigger firms who had the advantage now that the basic petrol ration was being withheld from the public. There were few cars on the road. It probably explained why the vast town centre train station was absolutely crowded with people again just as it had been last night.

My destination was the Vale of Rheidol railway, a narrow gauge line tucked in a modest corner away from its larger black cousins. It was a lifeline for the remote villages dotted picturesquely along the steeply rising mountains and it gave me an odd moment when the train gave a jolting shudder and began the slow ascent.

Many years of my life had been spent in paying dutiful visits to my husband's family in this seaside town. Then a war had been declared and he had gone away, with the result that opportunities for sightseeing of any sort had ceased for the duration. So I ought to have been thrilled now that it was peacetime and a crowded seat in a tiny carriage was gifting me a fresh glimpse of that once much loved scenery. But I wasn't. The past minutes had been occupied by an unceasing surveillance of the platform and now I was able to only stare blankly as the valley slopes closed steadily in.

It was a fiercely controlled air of calm. I wished that I'd managed to achieve something like this yesterday during the long journey south from Lancaster. Yesterday's hours between waking and dinner had been consumed by an exhaustion of crowded stations and carriages until the deafening rattle shook me out of logical thought. Sometime after Crewe I had convinced myself that an elderly gentleman was making notes about me and his neighbour was excessively interested in the stops along my route. All of which had, of course, later been embarrassingly – and publicly – proved false.

Today though, I was rested and defiant in the face of yet another journey. No silliness was permitted to accompany me here, not even when my neighbour smiled at me and urged me to precede him into the jostling herd of disembarking passengers at the bare levelled ground that made up the station at Devil's Bridge.

This was a tiny place. It was situated at the narrow head of a steeply wooded gorge and spanned only by the bridge that lent the hamlet its name. A few buildings straggled along the winding road and the sole hotel peeped out over the treetops, seeming incapable of supporting the sheer volume of tourists that were descending from the train. In summer this place was darkly leafy but now, when the autumn had already struck the dead leaves from the mossy boughs, the grazing land above was like a crown above the wild sweep downhill into bleak wooded valleys.

I'd expected it to be quiet here today. Instead it was as busy as summer and I could feel the excitement growing in the crowd around me long before we swept in a sort of united disorientation of hats, handbags and raincoats around a bend lined with high metal railings towards the low parapet that signalled our first glimpse of the natural spectacle that made this place famous.

I handed my shilling to the man at the turnstile. He took my money in a greasy hand and the mechanical clanking as the turnstile's metal arms turned was stiff and unwelcoming. But then I was through and stepping down into the sudden wilderness of dormant woodland. It was no quieter inside; it seemed as though the crowd's chatter was magnified in here and I stood for a moment, gathering my bearings before trailing after them down the steps towards the first viewpoint.

For a while there was no view at all. The trees grew sinuously, twisted old oaks clinging to any piece of ground they could. Even leafless, the damply rusting branches still strained vigorously to reclaim the scene. They acted like a ruthless blind; for a while I could see nothing and it seemed as though the cluster of tourists might never grow bored enough to move on and leave me to take in the view in peace. But then, finally, the last of them turned away and bustled past on their own private mission to tackle the waymarked path so I could step forwards and reach out a hand to take sole possession of the cold metal barrier. Here I was at last.

It felt like a lifetime had passed since I'd first begun this journey to this place where I would mark my husband's death.

But this was no agonised pilgrimage of the sort undertaken by a bewildered war widow. The sort where a grief-stricken wife hopes to achieve some kind of comprehension of the cruelty that stole her beloved husband's life. This was peace-time, he was my ex-husband after our divorce thirteen months ago and he had been a stranger to me for far longer than that. This was no respectful farewell to former happiness at all.

Before me rose the bridge like a stark monument to past centuries. It held two older bridges cocooned beneath its arch. They lay one on top of the other, each bridge built at a slightly different angle to the older stonework that had gone before and each squatting over a wider gap. Somewhere far below, the fierce waters of the Mynach roared blind into the chasm; folklore claimed that the devil himself had built the first narrow crossing and today, for the first time, I could have almost believed it.

Because about eight days ago, my ex-husband had taken himself to that selfsame spot and looked down into the raging depths. And had then decided to follow the look with his body.

Whatever else had happened in the days since then and now, this part of my story at least was not a creation. The police had confirmed it. The river had been in spate; it had been swollen beyond all normal bounds by heavy rain in the hours before and there was no hope of anyone surviving that. No hope even of a decent funeral. His body had never been recovered. This river's current was the sort that was strong enough to move rocks and trees, and a human body had been a mere speck of dirt in the stream. The only fragments the torrent had left us as proof of a man's passing were a broken camera, a few traumatised passers-by and a ruined sock recovered from an eddy half a mile downstream.

It was insane. And worse, it was insufferably sad to have to hear polite judgements about his character, as if this could have ever had anything to do with his usual state of mind. I hadn't received so much as a note from him in the year since our divorce but still it was incomprehensible; impossible to imagine Rhys, my stubbornly individual ex-husband, ever meaning to end it like this.

And yet he had. And somehow, now, whatever it was that had brought him to this desperate extreme had since turned its gaze upon my life and my mind. And I still didn't have the faintest idea why.

# Chapter 2

I wasn't going to find my answers here. Abruptly my silent vigil was broken. Oblivious to the recent history of this place, the next group of tourists appeared noisily on the viewpoint beside me to exclaim in their turn, and my bitter enjoyment of my half-angry grief was destroyed in an instant. Casting a last glance at the bridge and its forbidding heights, I swallowed the wealth of unanswered questions and found myself leaving room for sorrow instead. It came with a bolt that rocked me. One doesn't expect to feel grief in company and there is a certain shame inherent in feeling a flood of emotion that is at odds with the laughter of all your fellows. Somehow it felt a little like seeking attention despite the fact that attention was the very last thing that I could possibly want. And yet he was the man I had spent years of my life with – had loved once and probably still did – and this was where he had died.

And then in the next breath I had myself under control again and emotion of any sort was swept aside with about as much resolution as the sheer strength of will that had brought me here in the first place. It was the same willpower that had seen me leave him all those months ago and the same steel that had helped me build my new life in the north. Now it helped me set my feet to the empty path downhill. There was a distant whistle from a departing train.

It was echoed by a deep voice saying my name. My proper one I mean; Miss Ward. As a question. I span round. My solemn descent had led me far beyond the reach of the nearest tourist chatter and it was hard to contain the urge to curse at this resounding proof of my stupidity. How could I have imagined fear would give me room to breathe here?

My first line of defence rested on politeness. "Yes, it is. Hello, Mr ...?"

"Bristol. Jim Bristol."

Suspense transformed into an urge to laugh as he solved the little mystery of his name, but then mirth evaporated as the suave businessman from the hotel stepped lightly down the immensely steep stone staircase to join me. He was wearing a well-made suit in one of the customary shades of grey – because the variety afforded by clothing coupons limited men just as much as women – and he stopped on the step above and turned to lean his elbows easily on the barrier there before throwing an appreciative glance around him. He was perhaps six foot tall and broad shouldered to match and standing on that step he positively towered over me. The twisting fingers of bare branches cast lines across his jaw. He was one of those men whose muscular fitness made him very handsome. I thought he was also one of those men who knew it. His gaze settled on me.

"Beautiful spot, isn't it?"

I tried not to feel crowded by him or by the white flood of water travelling down the black rock face, the stunted overhanging trees and the impossible sweep below of the near-vertical staircase descending into deeper darkness. My fingers knotted in the straps of my bag while I smiled. "Yes. Yes, it is."

He was probably in his late thirties but it was difficult to be precise. His toned physique perhaps indicated that he had recently returned from his duties in foreign climes, although his hair wasn't cropped short in the military style and his suit wasn't the standard shapelessness of the Government Issue demob suit. Anywhere else he might have been impressive or even beautiful but here, far from any other voices, he definitely was not. I swear I saw something lodged within those friendly brown eyes that hinted at a harder mind behind.

Superficially, however, he was only warm and I was only useless at saying no. He said, "Do you mind if I keep you company for a while? I'm trying to find a nice spot to sit down with a sandwich. You won't mind if I go first?"

I let him move past me. I concentrated on the tricky steps and not glaring fiercely at the back of his head. The woodland smelled of wet things down here and rot and moss. A wren snapped past with the speed of a rifle shot but oblivious to the dramatic comparisons my mind was making between small birds and weaponry, my companion only turned back once more and fixed me with a mischievous grin. "You know, you looked very picturesque back there framed by all those trees and rocks."

"How very ..." I searched for the word, "gratifying."

"Oh definitely." He was negotiating another narrow step and pointing out a broken section. "Makes me wish I could paint – you know the sort of thing, all blobs of paint and drama entitled 'Girl in Raincoat by Waterfall' or something equally unimaginative. But I shouldn't be telling you this. You actually are an artist I gather?"

"How on earth did you discover that?"

Jim Bristol cast a captivatingly handsome smile over his shoulder that made a mockery of my tone. He also didn't seem to notice that I had stopped dead with one hand gripping the metal rail. "Among other things, you put it on your registration form last night when you were collecting your key. I'm unashamedly nosey, you see – an occupational hazard you might say – so I noticed. What sort of things do you paint?"

"People mainly. What's your occupation? If it makes you curious, I mean?"

"Have you got your sketchbook here? You do carry one, I presume? All artists do."

He turned his head briefly to note that I had resumed walking – where else could I go, really, when the alternative was to run back up these lethal stone steps – and I shook my head in a lie. "Not today."

"That's a shame. I should have liked to see it – I'm sure you must be very gifted. Perhaps you can show me when we get back later. You'll be having dinner at the hotel of course?"

I only gave a deliberately ambiguous, "I imagine so."

He returned my smile with a more generous one of his own and stepped down off the last flight onto the narrow platform that marked the base of the gorge. It was surprisingly sunlit after the dank brown shade of our descent through autumnal trees. A narrow bridge was the only exit on the far side, spanning the surprisingly tame outflow from the final plunge pool. A yellow wagtail flew in to land bobbing on an outcrop on the towering cliff only to notice us and dart away again. It was the perfect place for a trap. He only said harmlessly, "I'd like that."

Doubt rekindled, and this time with a vengeance.

I think he might have been intending to help me down off the last step but I kept my fingers firmly entwined in the straps on my bag. And even if his gesture wasn't the sinister action I was watching for, the look he gave me as I stepped past him was almost certainly that of one who was checking whether his much-exercised charm was having its customary effect. It meant that, now, there was no need to wonder why I should be feeling so untrusting. Since attempting to travel quietly, it was, I suppose, inevitable that I would instantly find myself attracting attention from all sorts of quarters who would have normally let me pass unnoticed. But no one can pretend that ordinary men deal out this sort of unsolicited flirtation to perfect strangers. And certainly not when the setting is beyond isolated and the woman in question frequently feels that the stain of her failed marriage is written all over her like a marker to steer well clear. This might all seem like a plea to be contradicted, but the facts were there all the same.

The wagtail sauntered by, letting out a sharp *tic tic* of annoyance as it flashed away again. I put a pathetically unsteady hand on the rail of the footbridge but his voice called me back. "What do you plan to do with your day now?"

I made myself tear my gaze away from the both forbidding and inviting prospect of the towering ascent. Somewhere far, far above, a buzzard was calling. I turned to face him. He was crouching over his pack and focussed on attempting to draw out the tin that bore his sandwiches. He spared only one brief glance for me as he added, "Now that you've seen the sights here, I mean?"

"I don't know. What exactly is it that you do, Mr Bristol? You said your job requires you to be inquisitive."

If he noticed the brusqueness in my question he didn't show it. He paused in his task, elbow resting easily on one grey-clad knee. "It's not as exciting as I made it sound, I'm afraid. I'm just a civil servant; local government dogsbody – you know the sort, endlessly running around following up other people's loose ends. Quite tedious really."

I stared at him sideways beneath lowered lashes while pretending to examine the flowing water, trying to decide whether I could fit this person wearing the standard camouflage of the businessman-at-large with a vision of the same man, starched, collared and ensconced in any kind of bland office tedium. Somehow I really could not.

I watched as he lifted out the first neat triangle of his lunch, declining the tilt of a hand that offered another to me. The close walls of the gorge towered above us. Even now, eight days on, there were signs of the recent heavy rain. Truly sizeable branches and bits of rubbish had jammed themselves on this the lowest of the various steps of the waterfall's descent and just beyond the little bridge I could see where a green furred boulder had been crudely thrust aside to reveal fresh stone underneath. For a moment something red flickered beneath the current and my heart turned over. It wasn't his body. It was a fragment of different coloured stone and that was all.

That was all. It made me wonder how far down the treacherous course of this river the rescue team had dared to climb. And how much danger they must have encountered working hastily beside a river in spate purely because some hope still remained. This rough terrain would continue for some miles before the river widened into the easier floodplains that led to the sea. It seemed clear to me now that perhaps the buzzards might find him, but no one else would.

"Are you catching the train back later?" Jim Bristol's voice was jarringly cheerful. I must have been hiding the desolation in my heart very well because he was oblivious. He had moved his bag to one side and was now leaning comfortably against the flat plane of the towering rock. He was about five yards away.

"The train?" I had to moisten my lips.

"I saw you on it this morning. I was wondering which one you would be taking back."

"The last one," I said smoothly, stepping onto the bridge. "I want to explore a little first."

"Ah. I might see you on it." He moved to take a bite from his last sandwich, seeming pleased with the information, and then paused with it inches from his mouth. "I'd like to talk more, if you don't mind?"

That sense of alarm intensified sharply. He seemed innocently intent on enjoying his lunch but the quick glance I saw him cast before taking that next bite seemed to my heightened senses to contain far more than purely casual interest. And I was sure he couldn't possibly have missed the fact that I couldn't wait to get away from him. It suddenly occurred to me that if I didn't hurry up and take my leave, he'd have finished his lunch and I'd find myself accepting his company for the ascent.

"I'll look forward to it," I lied.

He let me go. "Excellent. Enjoy the rest of your day." The smile he gave was simply one of open friendliness but I must have climbed about two hundred steps before I allowed myself to slow down.

---

At least that's what it felt like. The ascent rose in short aggressive bursts from pool to pool with the black cliffs of the narrow gorge towering above. My heart was pounding and my leg muscles were complaining to the point of nausea, but I almost enjoyed the sensation as a relief from the panic I was experiencing because a man from the hotel had drawn me into conversation. Because that, after all, was all it had been.

Now I was free of him, I even had time to feel the irony; I knew full well that I wouldn't have felt the need to break into a run just as soon as I had climbed out of his sight, had my companion been a woman from the hotel instead.

It was all very predictable, of course, that the divorcee should have developed an aversion to men, but that didn't diminish the inner debate that was roaring away in my head. The one that didn't care about my romantic history and was simply waiting to find proof, either in this man's favour or against it; and all the while knowing with a grim sort of certainty that with the usual pattern of this thing I never would.

I finally faltered at the viewpoint that jutted out over the largest of the swirling steps in the waterfall. I was very hot. I knew I should feel tired too, I knew I must, but adrenalin held it at a determined distance. It held foresight at a stubborn distance too. I removed my coat simply for the sake of doing something that might bring some relief and laid it over the cool metal barrier that was designed to protect the unwary from the drop. And unfortunately that, perfectly predictably, led me to look down at the rushing water crashing into the pool below. The sight did me no good at all.

That chattering herd of holidaymakers finally laboured into view; the pack that had driven me on from my lonely examination of the head of the waterfall but lagged too far behind to save me from the distress of a private interview with Jim Bristol. Their breathless voices were filled with the excitement of the view. A family with a teenage girl and a younger brother in short trousers leaned over the barrier beside me, exclaiming and pointing as the whirlpool sucked and dragged at a few small branches caught in the flow. The girl was teasing the boy and threatening to throw him in, or worse still, leave him there as a test for whether the devil really did stalk the bridge at night. His half-laughing half-fearful pleas for help as she tugged on his arm made my mind flinch. They crashed carelessly past me, wrestling and completely ignoring the routine complaint from their mother and the boy, laughing giddily, pretended to fall.

I found that I had turned quickly away to the comparative safety of the path and then had to turn back again when I remembered my coat. I was flustered now and angry with myself and with Jim Bristol, and other people were coming so I pushed myself onwards. I was determined to keep ahead of them, I don't know why. The steps were crude and very steep, and I had to concentrate hard on simply keeping my footing. And all the while I was focussing on the vision of the hotel at the top, the refreshing tea I would take, and the time I would find there to adjust to the realisation that now I almost craved the company of a crowd more than I dreaded it.

"Careful!"

A hand flashed out. I stumbled clumsily against it. I flinched as it steadied me. No jacket at all on this one; only the practical woollen jumper of a hiker and my eyes travelled from the hand to his face as I was thinking *I shouldn't have come here*. I really shouldn't have come.

I had the horrible impression I might have said that out loud.

Adam Hitchen released me and I made to hurry on only to discover that he had changed his mind and put out his hand again. His grip was warm through my clothing. My frock was a handmade belted affair in red that wrapped around with a tie above my left hip – my treasured coupons always went on fabric – and the thick winter sleeves were no barrier to the sense of his touch. I was suddenly very conscious indeed of how close we were to the lip of the drop; how easy it would be to have a little slip, an unfortunate accident. To go tumbling over the edge to the same inevitable end that had met my husband…

I found myself falling again into the trap of that first line of defence by apologising hastily: "So sorry, I wasn't looking where I was going." Then, brittle, "I must get on. Goodbye."

If only I didn't keep thinking politeness would save me. He didn't let me go. He didn't acknowledge my distress either. But at least the first words that interrupted the pounding of my heart were not unnaturally admiring. When he spoke, it was not pitched to match the visions that stalked my dreams, but in his distinctive tone that was perfectly level. "I've found something you might find interesting, do you want to see?"

I stopped trying to work out how I would force my way past for a moment and blinked up at him. If anything he seemed to be fighting a private battle with his own embarrassment. "That came out sounding a little strange, didn't it? It really is nothing untoward, I promise you. Are you prepared to take a chance?"

*Quite frankly, no* I thought fiercely but didn't say it. Instead I waited for his odd manner to run to an explanation. It didn't come and he simply fixed his attention upon a tree standing a short distance away from the path. I would have judged his behaviour truly disturbing, except for the faintest disarming impression, given by the way a muscle in his jaw tightened, that he was in fact cringing from his own oddness and hoping very profoundly that I hadn't noticed.

The latest cluster of holidaymakers – one that might have been my salvation – puffed past but still that hand kept a firm grip upon my arm, both shielding me from their breathless jostling and preventing me from getting away. Jim Bristol was following them and he eyed us curiously as he climbed the path but then he too rounded the turn and it was just me and the walker alone in the woodland. Allowing him to keep me here, I realised sharply as the silence closed in around us, could well prove to have been a very, very stupid mistake.

My companion seemed oblivious to the shivers running under my skin and simply ducked his head towards my ear. "Look there; above that broken branch."

His hand dropped from my arm. The release of his grip seemed to unleash surprise so that it washed over my over-burdened brain like the floodwaters in the pools below. With it came a surge of relief that made me want to both laugh and cry at the same time.

There was an owl. Just an owl, resplendent in his mottled plumage, pretending to be part of the bark of a tree. It was a repeat of the momentary connection that this man had instigated very early this morning on top of the isolated hilltop behind Aberystwyth. Then it had been a jolly little bird that I had been both seeing and not seeing as I took in the view, oblivious to the man's approach. This bird was perched in the curve where the heavy limb of a gnarled and twisted oak joined the main trunk and he was perfectly confident that he had succeeded in assuming the identity of a rather stunted branch growing from the larger bough beneath his feet.

"You see?" said my companion softly. He was laughing a little. "Well worth taking a chance."

It was then that I discovered that the sudden release into something unexpectedly like happiness had made me pass my hand across my body to meet the warm wool of his sleeve instead. It had been an instinctive gesture. It meant appreciation, gratitude. I don't believe he had noticed; or at least he didn't until the sound of approaching voices made me snatch my hand away and turn swiftly towards the path. My heart was pounding in a different way, high and nervous, and I felt a fool. I felt a fool because my touch to his sleeve was nothing, and yet, it was also a marker of a deeper emotion that I had no right to share; not now; not when every sign of weakness was a forerunner to making a mistake again and I was finding it so hard these days to temper my reactions to within normal bounds. Whether dealing with fear, friendliness or some other sudden expression, in the end I always made a mistake and embarrassment crept close enough to wreak its own damage.

Now I was wrestling with a giddy sense of exhilaration in that way one does when, in a moment of severe distress, someone does something that reminds you that humanity is sometimes beautiful after all. Adam didn't seem particularly keen to capitalise on the feeling though. He left me in peace to regain my composure and he even let me feel like I was managing to behave quite normally when he followed me up the last flight of steps towards the exit. And in return, I suppose for the first time, my usual gnawing readiness to find him suspicious slunk to the back of my mind.

The turnstile was there and then we were stepping out onto the sweeping curve of the road barely yards from the hotel. I waited, calm once more, while he slipped through the gate behind me. He stooped under the low archway. The air was fresher up here away from the dense gloom of the gorge, and the breeze was cool through the sleeves of my frock. I slung my coat around my shoulders and as I did so I spotted Jim Bristol through a small swarm of people moving towards the bridge. The rest were all wearing excitement on their cheery faces and all pointing delightedly over the edge. But not Jim Bristol. I had the very strong suspicion that only lately had he bent forward to peer over someone's shoulder. I turned my head aside and found Adam Hitchen meeting my gaze instead.

He said, "Do you think our luck will hold long enough to get us a table in the tearooms?" His voice held that unsmiling reserve again.

It ought to have made me decline but somehow, before I knew it, I was walking with him towards the grandly over-bearing frontage of the hotel. Then I was allowing myself to be ushered towards the comfort of a plush upholstered seat in the crowded room almost before the previous occupant had left it. If this was a fresh assault on my nerves, so be it. At least I would be fed at the same time.

Dining out was a restricted affair when nearly every morsel of food was regulated by rationing. Patrons irrespective of wealth could enjoy two courses, either a starter and a main, or a main and sweet, with tea or coffee to follow. I think I must have been rather too quick to state a preference for the latter. It made his eyebrows lift but he didn't disagree.

The reason for my decisiveness was that the main was only a standard offering of some kind of stew but the dessert was a neat little plate of Welsh cakes, freshly made and warm still. I think they were the dish that first made me realise that I too had been entirely unsmiling for the duration of our meal.

"Thank you, Mr Hitchen." He was handing me the plate bearing my share of our second course. Taking it was like awakening after an unsettled sleep and finding daylight more cheerful than you had thought.

"Adam, please." He poured the tea that had accompanied the dessert. "Assuming you don't mind my calling you Kate?"

The first of my pair of Welsh cakes was simply heavenly. I will forever remember that moment as a brief peaceful island in the sea of all that fear, and in all honesty I don't think my companion can take all the credit. That gentle scone-like delicacy was a little touch of much needed comfort and it acted like a restorative upon my entire mind.

My companion was being reassuringly harmless too as he prompted, "It is Kate, isn't it? Not Katherine?"

I leaned back in my seat with the teacup cradled in my hands. I was ready at last to attempt the part of civilised luncheon partner. "No," I said, "definitely Kate. It's short for Katarina, which I hate."

"You're from Russia? Your English is very good, if you don't mind my saying."

I couldn't tell whether he was teasing or not. I really couldn't

28

tell. It made me say drily, "Yes. I mean; no I don't mind your saying. And yes, as if you haven't already guessed: my accent is boring and English through and through. My mother just has an active imagination and an unhealthy obsession with the Ballets Russes, that's all. My older sister is called Ludmilla, so I count myself lucky."

An eyebrow lifted. "And does she abbreviate her name too?"

"Millie," I said with a faint smile. "Much more pronounceable."

"You're an artist, aren't you?"

Again that abrupt delivery that made his question seem somehow like an accusation. With a little sickening swoop from confidence into restraint, I wondered if this was working up to being a parody of my recent conversation in the gorge after all. He must have noticed the sudden tightening of my mouth because by way of explanation he added more gently, "You were painting when I stumbled across you this morning."

I swallowed the sour taste of suspicion and admitted the truth. "Lovely up there, isn't it? I might have gone further if I had thought to bring a more useful wardrobe of clothes."

"No slacks or gumboots?"

He *was* teasing me. I nodded. "Precisely. I reached the point where the path turns into a very dirty sheep track and then stalled. Painting was my excuse – or camouflage if you will – and at least honour was saved by the fact that the view up there ranks as beyond inspirational."

"Yes. It does. There's quite some atmosphere around that hilltop."

There was a deeper ring of sincerity in his tone. Then I

saw him blink at me across the brim of his teacup. I saw his mouth dip as he set the teacup down. There was something in the action that was a familiar kind of self-reproach; like a guilty realisation he'd said too much. I recognised the feeling because I was constantly doing it myself. My attention sharpened abruptly. I said quickly, "You were making notes – are you a writer?"

Then a sudden thought struck me as he looked at me – that sort where you get a rare glimpse of the real person for the first time and it comes with a kind of kick that feels like shock but might just as easily be care. I found myself staring. "You go by the name of A. E. Woolfe ..."

"Quick, aren't you?" He spoke a shade curtly. Then he conceded with a rueful smile, "This is meant to be a research trip but unfortunately I haven't been able to travel quite as incognito as I would have liked."

I laughed and saw his eyelashes flicker.

He asked "What's funny?"

"I was just thinking that it's a good job I'd said that book was well written, otherwise I'd be feeling very embarrassed at this precise moment."

Suddenly he grinned. He sat back in his chair. It was like a sudden shelving of reserve. Then he leaned in to rest his forearms upon the table with an eagerness that matched Jim Bristol's, but with an entirely different energy. An entirely different style of warmth I mean. In his person he was as physically fit as Jim Bristol, as befitted a tall man who clearly liked walking, but without Jim's excess of muscle so that the whole effect was of restrained strength rather than formidable bulk. As he leaned in his whole posture changed as if his nervousness had suddenly eased, and in a rare moment of not thinking everything was about me and my little drama, I wondered if my earlier theory had been correct and he truly was a little shy.

As if to prove the point, his attention dropped to the salt cellar, toying with it and moving it in a circle around the pepper pot. Then his hand stilled and he said carefully with his gaze resting upon the tabletop, "What about you – you're travelling incognito too, aren't you?"

"What do you mean? What makes you say that?" I demanded, thrust abruptly back into unhappy suspicion. I wondered what I would do if it turned out that this man sitting opposite in a pleasant hotel tearoom was actually a different kind of person entirely.

"No reason," he said, "just an impression I got, that's all." He was still playing with the salt cellar and he carefully set it back into its place beside its peppery companion before lifting his head again. His mouth gifted me a quick glimpse of a reassuring smile. "Natural assumption based on nothing more than solidarity between artists. If I'm in hiding then so must you be."

I gave a short laugh then and turned my head aside under the guise of being distracted by the earnest discussion between the waitress and the patrons at the next table so that he needn't see the workings of my mind. Then I dared to glance at him again and the expression on his face drew my mouth into a sheepish smile. "Comparing me with the great A. E. Woolfe? That's setting me a little high I should think – no need for incognito when you're an unknown." And then, lulled by the answering crease that touched the corners of his eyes, I foolishly added, "And this isn't really a painting trip anyway."

"No?" he asked. "What is it then?"

I hesitated. I actually wavered for a moment between sense and further stupidity. But then I heard myself only say, "I'm sorry to sound mysterious but I'd rather not speak about it, if you don't mind."

To many this would have been the perfect encouragement to pry but I was astounded to find that with this man at least, this was not the case. He simply sat back in his chair and said calmly, "Fair enough. You needn't tell me anything you don't want to. After all, why should you when—"

"—I don't know you from Adam?"

"Quite," he said. And then he smiled at me.

# Chapter 3

Adam Hitchen was as good as his word. By degrees our conversation returned to the safer ground of his books and my artwork, though given my general intention of remaining aloof from my fellow guests, it was perhaps a little startling to find myself willingly telling him about my gradual rediscovery of inspiration in the year since my divorce. I was also struck by how astute he was in his observations on the difficulty of regaining lost creativity. There was no sympathy – even on a normal day I wouldn't have wanted that – but absolute understanding that must come from a creative mind who had faced his own challenges during the turmoil of the war.

I had barely painted through the war years and hadn't particularly wanted to. I had been far too busy hosting patriotic exhibitions in the little Cotswold gallery that had been my home and putting in my hours as a married woman at the WVS canteen; and if I had painted, what would I have used as my inspiration? The bleak horror? Or would I have become one of those artists pretending that all was as it should be and beauty could be found in all the usual places?

Now though, there was hope again. I had moved away in the course of my separation and subsequent divorce and in all honesty it was an escape from the emotional barrier that had begun chipping away at my creativity long before the dramatic changes of a world war. I was of course careful to make no mention of where I had been living, or even the name of the northern gallery where I now worked and had recently had a minor exhibition and, to Adam's credit, he didn't ask.

In return he told me something of his own experiences while undertaking the research for his current novel. I tried not to feel like I was quizzing him because to be honest, it didn't feel particularly like he had been quizzing me. His first had been released before the war. His second was penned during the six months' leave after Dunkirk and the last had been a thoroughly chaotic affair jotted in note form on any scrap he could find in the lull between manoeuvres in Malta, Italy and Greece, and hastily thrashed into shape and published almost as soon as he had returned.

This one, he told me, was being allowed to take a rather less disorganised course and his research was thorough. Although that apparently still presented its own difficulties.

"Research is a problem?" I asked doubtfully. I felt like I'd missed a point.

I had. There was a trace of that smile again. "The last two were set in the area around home. It was inescapable when I was away and home was all I could think about. But I was demobbed about fifteen months ago and life has settled into something of its new rhythm and now the whole of the British

Isles is supposedly my muse. Unfortunately in a fit of optimism I've managed to set this book in the depths of Wales just for the time when it has suddenly become very socially unpopular to go tearing about the countryside racking up the miles, even if it is running on my own relatively legitimately saved cans of fuel. I've had to visit this area twice so far this year chasing threads and locations."

"You've come by car?"

"I have. This'll be my last trip for a while I think."

"What sort is it?"

"Sort of what?"

"Car. What sort of car is it?"

It was my turn to startle him by barking out my question. I hadn't meant to, but I suppose it was inevitable that the mention of the car should jerk me back into a remembrance of what I had come here for today. And it wasn't to form new friendships with travelling authors.

He made his answer while I was also remembering that I ought to have been watching the turn of the road outside the window. His car was a red Rover 10 and there was something else he told me about it that didn't matter anyway because my gaze had already run to the wide terrace outside. As it did so I caught sight of Jim Bristol yet again. Not close by; he was about forty or so yards away and I felt a sudden surge of tension when I saw that man, or rather the turn of his head as he examined the wares of a postcard seller. He appeared completely absorbed by the mundane products but I knew beyond all doubt that a moment ago he had been staring straight at me.

Then the chill of seeing him was undone by the idiotic thrill that followed in the next second. The one that made me think for a moment that the postcard seller was my husband.

He wasn't of course. This wasn't one of those moments when a person believed to be dead turns out to be alive after all and takes to turning up in all the oddest places. Instead it was like trying to convince a wounded war veteran that he'll hardly miss his left foot: impossible and the delusion can only ever last a heartbeat. Fiercely, defiantly, while the blood roared in my ears, I took a deep breath and forced myself to think. The postcard seller was dark haired, as I had known he would be, and was presumably Welsh, and that was where the resemblance ended.

"Kate?"

My companion had stopped speaking and was staring at me. We retreated into the uncertain formality of new acquaint-ances. He said again, "Kate – Miss Ward – perhaps I shouldn't ask, but are you all right?"

Finally, I felt my heart begin to beat again. I knew the sense of my ridiculousness would hit in a moment, as it had done every time I had seen my husband's image in the past days since my accident. It was a public humiliation, a cruel display of my overactive and stressed imagination timed to happen just at the precise moment when any misstep would be observed by an audience. It was a bizarre mirror of the way my life was now. Like always; a hurtful confirmation of my sheer inability to exert any control, and nothing more.

I met the stranger's concern across the table and set down

my cup with a distant hand. Now I felt alone again and glad of it. In a moment I would make my excuses and leave. But first, for the sake of formality, I said, "Sorry, I was listening really. What were you saying about May? Why didn't you bring her?"

I was impressed that I had managed to grasp the dog's name; I had barely heard the rest of what he had been saying.

"She wouldn't like all the hanging about while I write my notes." He was speaking slowly, staring at me still. "You're not all right at all. Whatever is the matter?"

I thought about my answer and what he would say if I admitted the full implausible truth. Not about seeing Rhys, but the rest of it. I could already picture the concerned looks, the hasty covering of his instinctive recoil and the rushed assurances that of course it didn't sound like fantasy, not really. This was, I observed grimly, precisely why I had decided to avoid unnecessary contact with my fellow guests.

Reluctantly, I said, "I had an accident. Just over five days ago. I banged my head and still get awfully tired." Even as I said it, I wondered what on earth had prompted me to speak. After all, any excuse would have done. Indigestion perhaps. Or a sudden alarm about the time of the next train. I gave him a watery smile. "I'm quite all right really. Please just ignore me."

He didn't even blink. I began to feel extraordinarily uncomfortable. I wasn't alone because he wouldn't let me feel it. His eyes, I realised with a jolt, were flecked with deeper hues and at this moment they were fixed on me with an intensity that seemed to be trying to bore right into my mind.

"An accident?"

His brows had furrowed, perhaps in doubt. Perhaps in disbelief. And this was just the edited version. I wasn't mad enough to tell him the truth.

I wouldn't tell him about the nightmare which claimed to be a memory of two men who had appeared beside me as I waited by the bus stop in Lancaster.

The images of that day belonged to the subsequent moments of semi-consciousness at the hospital. Moments of confusion where visits from nurses and doctors merged seamlessly with the dizzying recollection of being at one moment innocently daydreaming and in the next being steered by rough hands into the depths of a shaded doorway. The questions those men had asked there were impossible demands woven about my husband's end that I couldn't understand and certainly could never fulfil. The bewilderment I experienced that day was indescribable. They had fixed me there with a determination that was like nothing I had ever encountered before. They had left me with a desperate hope to the very limit of my being that I would never again be required to accept the utter inferiority of my will when pitted against the dominance of another. And a terrible suspicion that hoping was never going to be enough.

---

I had woken – if waking was the correct term when I had never been asleep in the conventional sense – to the busy silence of a women's ward where fresh questions began just as soon as I opened my eyes. These questions in their turn had brought their own confusion but at least the doctors and nurses hadn't minded at first if I didn't know the answers. But those men, the pair on the foggy shopping street, had acted decisively when I failed to give them the response they wanted. There had been no violence from them. There had been no need. I had found myself being bustled with grasping fingers beneath each elbow towards the flank of a waiting car. I can vividly recall that moment. The memory is filled with the sheer debilitating agony of experiencing all that in a crowd and learning that that not one of the labourers, shopkeepers or besuited office workers scurrying by was even going to notice.

It was like a very bitter repeat of an old lesson that I had tried very hard to forget.

It had ended at the moment the car door was dragged open and I somehow slithered free and dashed round the rear to make my escape. Only to run slap bang into the path of the oncoming traffic.

Adam was still waiting for my explanation so I gave him a carefully edited version. "I stepped out in front of a bus." My lips formed a hapless smile. "Don't worry; it was coming to a stop anyway."

"Good grief—"

I added, "Oh, the bus wasn't the problem. It was the rapid collision between my head and the pavement as I fell that did the damage."

"Good grief," he said again. He stared at me for a moment. I watched the disbelief fade into other calculations as he read the proof in my face, in my manner and my general bearing. Then he was saying in an altogether harder tone, "And this was barely even a week ago? What on earth are you doing here? Why did I see you strolling about on the crown of a hill at the crack of dawn when you should be at home in bed being fussed over and generally well looked after?"

I was hastily making calculations of my own. This was the most I had confessed yet to a stranger. Every other time that I had been drawn into speaking about my injury, the explanation had been forced out of me. It had been required by such people as the cab driver who had carried me away from the hospital, those people on the train and lastly the station master at Shrewsbury. Always, it had formed part of the aftermath of a dreadfully uncontrolled slide into panicked accusations. Now, for once, suspicion wasn't directed at the person I was speaking to and I was, nominally at least, a willing participant in this conversation. It left me utterly unprepared.

Finally, I said as mildly as I could, "My parents are abroad – in Paris in fact, as a kind of homage to the Ballets Russes who are disbanding or relocating or something like that, and I couldn't possibly go to my sister." I caught his look and added quickly, "She has far better things to do with her time than worry about me when she already has a hard-working husband and two very young children to care for."

It was easier to let him see that I was tired. It was the better part of my defence to play the hand of feebleness. Experience had taught me that much at least. It was after all a perfectly real symptom of a severe concussion and it was a wise fraudster who filled her excuses and explanations with something that passed as plausible truth.

Because whatever else I said, I knew now beyond all doubt that I mustn't let him see that I was frightened. That I mustn't give anyone else the opportunity to encounter the same bare-faced distrust that I had levied at about half a dozen people in the past two days and even now was trying to fix itself anew upon the dubiously friendly Jim Bristol after our strange conversation at the base of the waterfall.

By contrast, this man wasn't looking particularly friendly at all. He was asking, or rather demanding tersely, "Why aren't you in hospital then? You can't tell me your doctor willingly let you take yourself off like this?"

I tried to think of a convincing lie, but I couldn't. He wasn't impressed.

"This is downright insane, Kate. Why the devil—" He stopped when he saw my chin lift. I wasn't helpless here. I had, I know, had a stiff lesson that sometimes people will do things that I can't stop and can't control, but that didn't mean that I had to give up the fight.

Besides, the people on the next table were listening in. They were pretending to be reading the menu but I could tell they were eavesdropping. The tilt of the nearest person's head gave them away. Adam seemed to perceive this too. He leaned in with a lowered voice to say more earnestly, "Sorry. No wonder you look pale."

His was the one new voice in the sea of all the memories. I swear it was new. It didn't fit the helplessness of that time when two male voices growled questions about my husband, followed by the doctors' whispered consultations over my head with the police while my self-belief bled away into the stiff white sheets of my hospital bed.

Because I *had* told the police. I wasn't foolish enough to omit that sensible step. And besides they could see for themselves that I cringed in my hospital bed every time a door opened and I heard a man's heavy tread approaching. But those passers-by at the bus stop had been thoroughly blind to my plight. No witnesses could recall my two men and the bus driver was adamant that he had seen nothing untoward until a lone woman had lurched into the road. And what did it matter that I could describe those two men, when there was no real proof that they even existed?

All the same, the police had been very thorough. Their questions had begun in the usual way but very gradually even a person in my state had to notice that the kindly constables seemed to be pursuing something else, chasing an altogether different line of investigation which was perhaps even more dangerous than the incident by the bus stop had been. The tone of the policemen's questions barely changed as they drew me to talk about my grief at my husband's passing. I had mentioned it earlier myself so couldn't claim it was unrelated now. In any case, they said, this particular event wasn't actually decisive enough to count as *unstable*. Clearly I was perfectly sound in mind now. But wasn't it possible I had experienced a momentary bleakness? An upsurge of desolation just as the bus had made its final approach? Apparently I should find it reassuring that the doctors didn't think there was enough evidence for true instability; because suicide was illegal and therefore liable to end, if not in an untimely grave, then certainly with a spell in prison.

If that hadn't been awful enough, I had to lie there patiently while they tested a second theory in the course of their questions. And I fought it even more violently than the first. They asked me why I accepted so fully that my husband was dead. They were probing for a different kind of delusion, the sort where blind hope meets reality and the collision drives a person crazy. They needn't have worried. It was impossible for me to believe that my husband was still alive. Because if he were; if this should have been unleashed on me because he was making some devious play of his own, it meant he had knowingly sent these men after me without even so much as a note of warning and I couldn't believe my worth ranked so low with him as that. I didn't dare. I was even more afraid of that idea taking root than all the rest put together.

I was used to his indifference. I had in fact worked very hard since my divorce to teach myself that indifference was all it had been and grow wise enough to share some of the responsibility for that. I was even able to apply the same reasonableness to the fact that strangers had passed by the scene of my abduction without a glance. But this wasn't an act of indifference. This was a man I had been married to. And he *had* loved me once.

If Rhys should have willingly staged his disappearance and passed this violence on to me, this was something so indescribably evil it must question the very meaning of everything I thought he was, and everything I was too. It would shatter all my values, all ideas I'd nurtured of rediscovering empowerment and freedom since my divorce. It meant my sense of self-worth really did belong to other people – those men in the bus stop, the doctors, the police and more particularly my husband. And it was theirs to take away again.

I couldn't believe that. I wouldn't. I'd left hospital that same day and given myself the only hope I could. I set myself the task of unpicking Rhys's last movements. I'd come to Aberystwyth.

---

This day, Adam was waiting for my answer. I pulled myself together and began working towards a peaceful exit.

"Anyway," I told him cheerfully. It wouldn't help to overdo the weariness. "I do have something to be thankful for."

"Really? And that is ..."

"That the bus didn't live up to the old adage: You wait half an hour and then two come along at once."

He relaxed at that, clearly relieved that for the moment I was sounding perfectly normal once more. Then there was a sudden sharp clatter as a car passed beyond the window and although I fought bitterly against the instinct that prompted me to turn and look, I saw something form in his face that might have been a reflection of my underlying obsession. Sure enough I watched helplessly as his brows lowered.

"Kate?" he began, leaning in and watching me closely. In that unsmiling gaze was something more than concern.

Suddenly our comfortable conversation over tea and Welsh cakes might never have been. All the wise strategies for dealing with this conversation were nothing. His mouth was not forming a new question about my general welfare. It began to form something unanswerable. It only remained to discover whether the question was designed to continue the work of those men in that bus stop, or to exert control over the precarious strength of my mind.

"Do you really not recall—?" he began but was interrupted this time by an extraordinarily prolonged clanging of bells and blowing of whistles from the station. I took the chance. I began hastily gathering my things together.

"Oh, goodness; that's my train." I ignored his surprise – the perfectly authentic surprise that undid rather too many of my concerns – and set about scrabbling in my bag. "Here, let me give you my share of the bill. Did you come by train too?"

"No, by car. You know that." He waved aside my money with an air of intense irritation. Then I felt his hand close over my wrist as I moved to stand up. "Don't think for one minute that I'm letting you go."

I felt something cold stab inside at this new tone. His hand was there upon mine. I demanded sharply, "Why ever not?"

It was his touch that hardened me. It swung the pendulum back towards distrust. Although he was being stern it might have been meant as a joke between us. By rights the gesture ought to have belonged to someone who knew me. A friend, perhaps, who might have the right. Only he didn't and it made me afraid to test the power of his grip and measure it against the rough grappling of those two men. Fear hinted that he wanted me to try.

Only he didn't. He must have felt my recoil. I saw him

make a rapid reassessment, a jerked withdrawal of his hand, and watched his mind dismiss the moment as nonsense. He was already saying impatiently like a perfectly normal man might, "*Why not?* Because you've just told me you have lately sustained a severe concussion; that you haven't been resting properly and that you're absolutely exhausted. That's why."

I struggled out of my seat and past him, dragging my unwieldy coat and bag through the gap behind me, unable to recall any more if this rough attempt at reasonableness really did stand apart in my memory from all the other angry voices that were lodged there now. It felt like something he'd said was an echo of something familiar, something much older than this recent stress, which drifted out of reach almost at the instant that I reached for it. But there was no memory there. It was nothing more than a fresh trick of the tiredness that stalked behind the fear in my mind.

Because I *was* tired. I was tired of pretending to be nice. I snapped, "Don't be silly, Mr Hitchen. I'm quite capable of looking after myself."

I saw his lips release from their tight line. They parted slightly. Disbelief, stupefaction, injury; they were all here. I had to pretend I didn't care. I had to make such a drama out of my exit even when we had just shared such a civilised lunch because the alternative was even worse. The alternative was to cling to him in the way that a lifetime of conditioning urges any frightened female to cling to the first unwitting male who happens to present himself for the part of prospective hero. But I didn't need the vision of those men at the bus stop to remind me that reality didn't mirror imagination and

I certainly wasn't going to truly put chivalry to the test by actually getting into a car with one.

I shuffled out of my seat and past him with a simple farewell as my only concession. He didn't return it. I hadn't got many yards down the road, however, before he'd changed his mind and caught up with me. I stopped at the entrance to the station, turning to face him and trying not to bristle, not to give in to weary frustration, and most of all trying not to notice how very forbidding he seemed.

"Thank you for the lovely meal," I said with a brightness that jarred. "I truly am very grateful for your offer, but I'd really rather take the train."

"Never accept lifts from strangers, eh?"

His wry perceptiveness shook me more than any temper could. I gave a jerky nod and turned my eyes fiercely to the oblivion of the waiting carriages before doubt could transform into guilt and from there into a confession.

He stood there, saying nothing and frowning down at me, waiting for my attention to return to him again with perfectly genuine disbelief etched across his face. The frown softened to something closer to his natural level of seriousness and abruptly I realised, conditioning or not, just how much I wished to dare go with this kindly man with whom I'd shared a pleasant lunch instead of hurrying for the crowded train.

But before I could formulate the thought into words, he was saying heavily, "All that steam whistling, by the way, was to mark the end of the Royal Wedding. But all the same you'd better get on. Looks like it's about to leave. If you change your mind, I'll be the one wrestling with the starter handle of that draughty relic of a geriatric car over there."

I followed the line of his hand and saw, amongst the modest cluster of blue Morrises and black Austins that still had enough fuel for a scenic outing, a sweet red touring car with soft canvas roof and deep leather seats. It was battered and worn and might have been splendid in summer but was really not very suitable for a November excursion, even when it was a dry day like this one.

It struck me then, just how sorry I was.

"Thank you," I said, very sincerely indeed. He only inclined his head in a short nod of farewell that somehow communicated everything that needed to be said about fiercely independent women and their lunatic decisions, and turned away to find his car. Its plates showed that it had been registered in Brighton.

Feeling both the wonder and shame of my release in equal measures, I hurried down the platform into the fug of coal smoke with the other passengers. I expected a rush for the seats but they seemed to be all standing about exchanging merry congratulations on the successful conclusion of a state wedding rather than queuing to get on.

"Miss Ward." A quick step and a man's voice appeared just behind me. "We get to have our chat after all. What luck."

I was a fool. A complete and utter fool. In my urge to get away I had forgotten about this irrepressible source of cheerfulness.

Trying to be discreet, I cast a desperate glance at the waiting carriages ahead and then back down the platform past Jim

Bristol to the dirty gravel near the road. I could just make out Adam as he rummaged beneath the dashboard for the starter handle. No more than a moment later, he had it in his hand. I looked up to Jim Bristol's face. He was still smiling, honest, handsome and open; and yet again peculiarly thrilled by the prospect of spending more time with me.

I blinked at him for a moment and then looked away. In the car park, the engine must have rattled into life because Adam was climbing in behind the wheel.

"Sorry, Mr Bristol." I stepped out of the crowd and smiled guilelessly. "I've just realised I've forgotten something. Would you mind being very kind and seeing if you can find me a seat?"

I left him nodding eagerly into the space where I had been and hurried back down the platform. I reached the end just as the car roared into life. For a moment I thought I had left it too late and my heart fell as I saw the car swing in a great arc towards the road. But then I was stepping heedlessly out onto the smooth tarmacadam and lifting a hand.

I thought he hadn't seen me; I wondered whether to actually place myself in his path. But then, with a hiss of brakes, the car slowed and drew to a smooth halt so that the driver's door was about a yard from my feet. Adam turned his head; he looked up at me with a mixture of surprise and badly concealed impatience and something else that was obscurely like a quickening into relief.

I gave a silly flustered smile and spoke through the glass. "I'm sorry, Mr Hitchen, I've changed my mind. Might I come with you after all?"

"I thought we'd settled on Adam."

"Adam, then."

He hesitated. But then, without another word, he reached across and tugged on the handle to the passenger door. In the time that it took to swing open, I had stepped around the car and then I was climbing in beside this irritated stranger, just as the train gave a formal whistle to indicate that the party was over.

With a rather less elegant chuckle, the car's engine rose to match it, smothered it, and then we were away in this Rover 10 that came from Brighton and accelerating along the high winding ridge towards Aberystwyth.

# Chapter 4

The reason it mattered so much that the car was from Brighton was that it wasn't from Gloucestershire – or, to be precise, the market town of Cirencester. It meant they hadn't found me again. And it meant that I hadn't made a terrible mistake in getting into this car.

Cirencester had been my home until my divorce and it housed the gallery where Rhys had still been living and working until those final few hours that had ended here. At least one of the demands levied by those two men had tenuously referenced the gallery and, although the details had grown muddier through the course of my bewildered wanderings in that hospital bed, they had certainly decided to take me somewhere. Reason told me it was the gallery. The alternative was that they'd simply decided to carry me away to some secluded spot where they might dispose of me, but I didn't dare think about that for long.

Either way, this car mattered. And so did the risk I was taking now. Aberystwyth gave me hope. In Aberystwyth I stood a chance of uncovering a few meagre hints about Rhys's last movements and through them a glimpse of what awaited me at the gallery. It could all vanish in a heartbeat if it turned out I'd made the wrong choice by tentatively deciding to believe this man beside me was what I thought he was.

We were at least heading in the right direction; west towards the coast where the sun was already dipping. Adam was driving smoothly but with a degree of seriousness that implied conversation would be unwelcome, even if I could have made myself heard over the noise from the road. He was wearing driving gloves. This was perhaps an alarming development since it meant he would leave no fingerprints. But actually, on the assumption he wasn't planning to throttle me, even I could understand why he should want them. The view northwards to the foothills of Snowdonia was glorious but the car was immensely draughty, the canvas roof thrummed overhead and I was grateful when he reached one of those gloved hands onto the back seat and drew forward a thick woollen blanket for me to drape across my knees.

The road ran high along a ridgetop. Every turn offered a fresh spectacular panorama of the wide glacial valley below, filled with leafless trees and pasture fields and sparse hills turned the colour of burgundy by old heather. I caught sight of the distinctive spread wings of a buzzard once and I lifted my hand to point it out to my companion but he only gave it a cursory acknowledgement now that he didn't feel the need to disarm me. That is to say, he glanced upwards and nodded his appreciation and then returned his attention to the curling road. It was actually quite pleasant to be travelling with a man who understood the value of companionable silences.

Then the worst happened. The car suddenly checked as if to stop.

We were passing through a small hamlet; a little plain cluster of five or so workman's cottages typical of the area. They meant nothing to me; at least nothing beyond the vague familiarity of having travelled this road once or twice in the course of my marriage. Now I turned to my driver. He wasn't looking at me. He was peering beyond me at a set of two grey cottages that squatted a short distance away from the road. Quite automatically, I pressed back in my seat to give him a better view, and it was barely acknowledged before he identified the one he wanted and steered the car to a halt on the verge.

Now he turned to me. He looked very different in this dull light. He wouldn't have known it but the cold had ruffled his hair and drawn his features into dramatic relief. It hardened him and made him a stranger all over again. He was drawing off the leather gloves with measured tugs on long fingers. They would have dwarfed mine. The cold must have been working on my face too and making my eyes very large because when his gaze found mine, it seemed to throw him for a moment. Then he covered it by reaching past me into the cramped space of the back seat for a jacket and a discarded hat.

He said, "Are you in a hurry to get back?" His gaze was angled into the footwell; his posture held that air of distance which for a time had disappeared.

My voice wasn't working very well. "N—no?"

"Good," he said. "You won't mind then if I just nip in there for a few minutes? You can come if you'd like? Or stay in the car; it's up to you."

He was already pushing open his door. I stayed in the car. It seemed to be what he wanted and politeness was acting as my defence again. I do believe if he'd asked if I minded a spot of abduction I probably would have given him a tactful reply to that too.

As he climbed out, I asked in a voice made even more rapid by the shadow of his own tension, "What are you doing?"

He paused in the act of shutting the door. "Research," he said.

Then, by way of an afterthought, his head ducked below the doorframe. He added, "Here, put these on. Your hands will thaw in a moment. It's not that cold out here now that the car's stationary, I promise."

He'd dared to glance at me at last. The swift gleam of those grey eyes was shy but the humour there was genuine. He was bemused by his own brusqueness and by my reaction to it. It was a sudden simple reassurance. He knew he'd confused me and he meant me to know everything was fine with this little act of kindness. I took the gloves. Then he shut the door.

I watched as, shrugging his way into the coat and conventionality, he stepped across the grassy verge towards the nearest of the low run-down cottages. The unkempt door with its peeling red paint and the dilapidated coal shed certainly fitted my idea of what constituted sinister. Adam rapped lightly on the wood, waited, then peered through the glass at the side before knocking again. Someone must have seen him because with a change to his posture he waited until the door finally opened and then, with a quick unsmiling glance back at me, he stepped inside. The other man had been ordinary and old and crabbed.

I sat there for about ten minutes, watching the road behind in the single driver's side wing mirror in case it should turn out that this was a simple way of arranging an exchange with those men, but no other car appeared. A pony-cart crossed the road ahead from one field into another with a lean sheepdog trailing dutifully behind, but nothing else happened that could possibly be an excuse for alarm and finally I was forced to admit that his stop was exactly as he implied – nothing to do with me.

With a grimace at what amounted to yet another painfully unnecessary display of doubt, I rummaged in my bag to drag out the little sketchbook. I waited a while longer but then, laying the gloves upon his seat and clutching my pencil and pad like a shield, I decided firmly that if he could do research, so could I. I climbed out of the car and drifted artlessly around the wide curve of the road.

Beyond the corner I found a gateway overlooking a promising field where broken hedges and ancient trees straggled down the tussock-strewn slopes. The solitude was glorious. But I wasn't alone. A sheep gave a surprised grunt and lumbered quickly to her feet as I appeared and I quickly sketched her head before she could decide to run away. She had half a bramble thicket trailing from her fleece and I sketched that too before slowly but surely moving onto the hints and touches for the field's other occupants as they rolled gently downhill to the floodplain at the bottom.

"I thought you must have given up and had decided to walk back."

A now familiar voice broke my all-absorbing peace of concentration. I'd heard his step on the gravel behind but it hadn't frightened me this time. I turned my head as Adam appeared next to me to contemplate the view, faintly perfumed with pipe smoke and inoffensively comparing my work with the scene below. He had reverted to his more usual habit of looking like a relaxed companion, although his voice was not fully restored to the ease of our tea in the hotel. He asked, "Are you ready to go, or do you want to stay a while?"

I shut my sketchbook with a snap and smiled at him.

"I'm finished, thank you. I was only passing the time while you paid your visit, and my model has very rudely walked away without so much as a by-your-leave anyway ..." And then, because I knew that was, to all intents and purposes, exactly what I had done to him at Devil's Bridge, I followed it with a hastily mumbled, "Sorry. I am very glad, you know, that you let me tag along on this drive."

"Think nothing of it." His quick dismissal was meant to reassure. We were already walking back around the bend to the car.

I waited until we were out of the hamlet before trying to make a fresh beginning by asking, "Did you get what you needed?"

He had to incline his head towards me to be heard over the shrill wail of the old engine and he made me think his tension over the past minutes had been because he'd been waiting for that apology because that old stiffness wouldn't quite leave his voice and he barked out, "Very useful interview actually." Then he grimaced a little before adding in a less stilted tone, "In case you haven't guessed, that meeting was the conclusion of one of the threads I've been following for some time. It's taken me all week to set up this visit and it was worth the effort. My latest work will be – or I should say *is* – based around a small mining community. Old Mr Hughs worked in the local lead mine before it shut so was able to give me all sorts of useful insights on the mechanics of that kind of life."

"How interesting," I said. I suspect my own efforts to sound more normal were lost in the noise from the road because I saw his eyes flick left twice to read my face before apparently being reassured that I wasn't trying to mock. His doubt was valuable to me in its way though. It gave me the chance to realise once and for all that it wasn't temper that had been colouring his manner on this drive; he hadn't been trying to punish me for my rudeness. He'd simply been nervous about his meeting. And the realisation was like a glimpse of a far less justifiable tragedy than the one that was presently stalking me. The one that had made a kind, normal, safe man like him shy.

It made me say in a sudden urgency of honesty because I knew now that it mattered, "I didn't mind staying in the car just now, you know. If I'd been in your position I'd have wanted to go in alone too. I know what it's like when you're steeling yourself to do an interview. You don't need anyone else muscling in and disrupting your thoughts when you just need a few quiet seconds to think of everything you want to say.

You know I had to do it all the time with the clients at the gallery." I stumbled a little then. I'd slipped into talking about my old life at the Cirencester gallery where I'd handled the business for Rhys. In fact, invariably Rhys would have been the source of the distraction that had put me off my stride. But Adam wasn't going to know that and he couldn't have known that I wasn't talking about my present placement at the Lancaster gallery, certainly not when I hastily tacked on, "I mean I still *do* have to talk to people. I told you that at lunch earlier."

I faltered. I'd seen his initial surprise as I'd sympathised. That had been natural enough perhaps, but then it appeared again as I rushed into adding those last words. I'd meant to make him comfortable and he was in a way but his swift sideways glance also bore a hint of incredulity, like the rhythm of his thoughts had experienced a momentary sharpening of concentration, followed by an anticlimax when the growing feeling was dismissed as an error. Then I felt his gaze briefly touch my face again and saw him register the curiosity there, and in an instant his expression was wiped clean.

When he spoke, it was only to assure me that I wouldn't have been in the way.

"But thank you," he added, contradicting himself. "Thank you all the same."

And then we were safely stowing his car on a backstreet where the salty sea-spray couldn't cement itself onto the precious paintwork before winding our way back through the town.

He stopped as we were about to cross the main shopping street onto the road that ran down to meet the seafront and turned to me. Behind him, someone stepped out of a red telephone box and I heard the quick murmur of apology as they made him step aside.

He was himself again. He tipped his head at the box as an indication of what he intended to do next. It obviously required privacy since there was a telephone at the hotel. He knew I'd noticed, and he also clearly appreciated that I made no remark. Then he asked with his faintly mocking smile, "Do you think you can cope with walking all the way back to the hotel on your own?"

He'd obviously read my thoughts too. I'd been running an eye downhill towards the frontage of the pier that stood at the bottom and telling myself sternly that the gauntlet of terrors – imagined or otherwise – between me and the hotel was all of about four hundred yards long. Adam meant his comment as a joke. He didn't really think I was worried. I gave him a slanting smile in return. And was still smiling when I said something vague about it nearly being time for dinner and he broke in to say rather abruptly, "I'm sorry, this is going to sound strange but since you said in the car a moment ago that you know me, I'm going to take you up on it. Can you not mention to the other guests that I drove you back just now?"

"I, er ... Yes. Of course, if you like."

His brows lowered. "Now I've confused you and that isn't what I meant, I promise. I just don't want to attract any more attention to myself than I already have. You've seen how it is;

if I become the subject of idle chatter about a fellow guest, my cover really will be blown ..."

"Absolutely," I agreed heartily. I could tell I was beaming like a mad thing. Inside I was cold. I was rapidly thinking that he was right; I was confused and if he thought I knew him, he was mistaken. I was trying to absorb the unpalatable truth that my attempt at ordinary friendliness with this man was an even bigger disaster than paranoia. I had the horrible feeling he thought I was meaning to turn our quiet lunch at the hotel into a public dinner together at the hotel and this was his way of tactfully curbing it. Only if he was he was mistaken there too. And now I was rushing into giving him blind sympathy and I could tell from the way those grey eyes were scrutinising my face that this wasn't the response he wanted. He drew breath and I knew he was going to try to change it, soften it and steer me into not minding the misunderstanding, and it was all going to get even more excruciatingly tangled than ever.

So I took control in the only way I knew how and paved the way for an easy – and permanent – conclusion to this ridiculousness for both of us by wrapping the moment in yet more layers of politeness. I gave him a broad smile and said brightly, "Actually, I understand perfectly. No, really I do. Fame and fortune is all very well, but not when you want a bit of peace in which to get on with the day job?"

I saw him nod. "Exactly," he said. "Thank you."

There didn't seem much to say after that. I thought he would be glad to have it so easily laid out that I understood and he would get the privacy he required but I found instead that my smile had made his brows furrow again. Apparently he'd read my withdrawal beneath its cheerful mask and he was puzzled by it. Quite simply, I couldn't get away from him today without causing some upset first.

Instinct made me slide hastily into a firm utterance of goodbye and then things went from bad to worse because he seemed determined to end things on a friendlier note after all and in the midst of the confusion of awkwardness and platitudes we ended with a swift step in to touch cheek to cheek.

I don't honestly know who initiated it. I thought he had but there was that briefest telltale hesitation from him as I automatically reciprocated that gave me time to realise that I really had got it wrong this time. Or perhaps I hadn't. Perhaps he'd done it in that awful impulsive way people have of assuaging their conscience when they're a little bit ashamed that you've guessed they really just want to be shot of you and end up accidentally lurching into warmth instead. Perhaps it was simply a reasonably appropriate way to mark the end of a social outing as new acquaintances might do.

Whichever way it was, it didn't exactly warrant the reaction I had. After all, I'd made this gesture all the time at home both in greeting and farewell with clients at the various events in the gallery. At the Cirencester gallery I mean. In the north, women simply shook hands like sensible creatures and saved themselves the trouble of getting it wrong. In Cirencester, this would have all just been an embarrassingly mishandled version of a familiar social norm. The feel of his touch to my arm, the automatic lift upwards to draw closer, that brief ordinary moment of confusion as one or other of us had to dictate which cheek was presented, even the accidental little intake of breath at the moment of contact and with it drawing in the faintest hint of the scent of his skin, followed by the oddly prolonged sense of suspense before one or other of us finally withdrew ... It was all so familiar.

In a way this was the problem. We might have done this before. This all told me that this was a man who was used to observing this kind of social etiquette too. And yet even this needn't have really been a cause for alarm. After all, logically speaking, I already knew this. His accent was non-descript and could have originated from anywhere vaguely southern. His car was from Brighton. He had as much right to belong to that cultural tradition as I did.

When I drew away with the beginning of embarrassment that must verge on laughter because it was funny how this latest bit of confusion really had crowned all the rest, I saw his face. His eyes lifted. He was embarrassed too but in a different way. He saw my shock. Instantly my mind was tripped into trying to match his dimly lit features to the pattern of some inconsistent memory. In its way, this was the same infuriating trick that daylight persisted in playing with visions of my husband. But if this was an echo of the past, it was a puzzling one. He wasn't wearing a scowl to match the harsh demands of those men who stalked every shadow in my mind. He was looking like an attractive, capable man who had just seen his mask exposed and was calculating how best to explain the joke.

And above it all, like a persistent tone playing a darker

note that had for a while slipped by unnoticed, I discovered that his hand was still gripping my arm.

Firmly so.

I felt the moment that he registered the shift in my attention. I felt the tightening in his concentration too and the faintest echo of his heartbeat transmitting from his fingertips through the layers of my sleeve. His grip held me sternly on the spot before him. I could only stare, fascinated, as that mouth hardened. It slid on towards speech. As it twisted from there inexorably to frame a question, I knew that this was the point where it became a demand. It would be the same one I had experienced in that Lancaster shop doorway. And this time I would have to fight for my soul as well as my body.

Adam's voice said roughly, "What on earth have I said to make you look like that?"

---

*Oh.* That most certainly was not the question I had been expecting.

This one belonged to a man who was only entirely wounded by whatever he saw written on my face.

*Oh no.*

Whatever offence I had given him earlier, this crime was worse. Mortification rose far beyond the shame of repeatedly mishandling the consequences of a bad exit from a tearoom. *That* was humbling enough but regardless of what had come before and what must certainly come after, I couldn't imagine anything would ever again be as crippling as this moment;

this instant of finally having to accept that the police and the doctors and everyone were right. Reality was not a fixed mark for me. I truly could not rely on the accuracy of my own mind.

This day had been exhausting. My voice was a taut rush. "You've done nothing." I'd broken contact with his hand a moment before. Now I was blinking rapidly and backing away. "Nothing at all. I'm so sorry. I must get on. Goodbye."

And I left him standing there at the telephone box. I could feel him staring after me all the way to the corner by the pier.

# Chapter 5

It wouldn't exactly be surprising if I found it distressing to discover this question mark hanging over my sanity. But actually, I did still have my wits enough to know that it wouldn't be unusual for anyone in my circumstances to be reacting a little nervously, particularly coming as it did after a day spent braced to meet the terrors of my first tentative steps towards uncovering Rhys's last actions only to discover nothing but my personal grief. And in truth, this wasn't why I was upset.

I was distressed because I'd wounded an innocent man and there was in my history a very small, very insignificant part of me that nursed an insecurity far older than abrupt encounters with moving buses. It was a part that had instead everything to do with that old lack of faith in my value to the world.

Sometimes I feel that the belief I am generally found to be harmless is my most durable merit. Only today I hadn't been harmless at all. I'd taken what ought to have been a pleasantly peaceful afternoon for a fellow guest and ruined his day with my own irrational anxieties. The experience humbled me, and it brought me face to face with an uglier aspect of myself. And now I was ruining his evening too.

This was because it became very swiftly became clear to me almost as soon as I entered the lounge after dinner that our resident famous person had completely wasted his time asking me to keep our shared journey a secret. The other guests already knew. I'd seen Jim's smirk. They knew it hadn't merely been a kindly passerby who had taken pity on me when I'd missed the last train. And what's more, the fact that this information had been deliberately omitted from Adam's own description of his day wasn't simply taken as a reflection on me and left to rest at that. They were delighted to have the excuse to tease him about it.

I was reading the same paragraph for the fifth time when I overheard Mrs Alderton drawing Adam out from behind his newspaper long enough to confirm that he had driven to Devil's Bridge today and that yes indeed he still had fuel for his car. Then Mary said something about it being a long way to go and that good company might have made all the difference. I don't think she was really making a jibe at me, at least not completely; I imagine she was merely hinting that Adam should invite her and her sister along with him next time but her challenging manner of asking was more than a little intimidating. Her bold way of talking belonged to a woman who was in the habit of confronting what she wanted. Since her recent past must have been not entirely dissimilar to mine and by that I mean it must have featured war, I thought she was, if it wasn't unkind to say it, the sort of woman for whom the war had meant liberty, frivolity and adventure; and she hadn't yet decided whether peace was going to rank on the whole as an improvement.

I already knew what peace meant for her older and colder sister, Mrs Alderton. It meant a tearing race to snare Mary a wealthy husband. And at present that meant steering the room away from a discussion on Jim's experiences on manoeuvres in Burma and back onto the subject of Devil's Bridge with delicious details of the site's awful heights.

She did it because she thought Adam might join in. Instead she had Jim's account of nauseating plunges, relentlessly roaring water and crushing swoops onto the rocks. Now he was sharing the spectacle of the first viewpoint that looked out at the falls beneath the three bridges. Mrs Alderton was disappointed because while Adam clearly ranked as a desirable conversational partner, Jim Bristol, only a lowly civil servant and an infantryman before that, very definitely did not.

I distracted myself from it all by talking to the little boy who was kicking the leg of the chair beside me. He was tired and wishing he hadn't been lured in here by the Miss Bartlemans since they were now being old and boring. His mother seemed to be desperately praying that no one would say anything about certain guests being better fitted for boarding houses before she managed to get him away to bed. They were the perfect distraction for me. I was just in the throes of discovering young Samuel was a fellow artist and quietly attempting to interest him, rather unsuccessfully I might add, in the gift of a few bits and pieces I kept at the back of my sketchbook when I noticed that Jim was watching me.

He watched me slip the sketchbook back into my bag and then he very deliberately turned back to Mary and began revisiting every dip, every plunge of the crashing waters in vivid, untamed detail. It made my head spin but not because of his passion for the waterfalls. It was because it felt horribly like Jim was punishing me for the lie over the sketchbook; the one where I'd told him that I didn't have it with me today. It felt like he blamed me for leaving him on the train and that he must have enjoyed betraying this second lie to these two woman because he knew what they would do with it. It felt like he must know too what the endless revisits to the scene of that awful drop would mean to me so was describing them deliberately.

My distress came also from fearing that I was being unkind in my present judgements about him and he was as blameless here as the last man had been.

It was then that Adam abruptly decided to speak. He dropped his newspaper to say loudly, "Yes Mary, it *was* a long way to go by car."

His interjection was rough. It burst onto the room like it was wrenched out of him against his better judgement as his resistance was finally eroded by their incessant probing on the subject of that fated decision to allow me along on his drive. The truth is it actually came when he might have just as easily remained silent. They weren't talking about him any more. They had been distracted by a longer, more delightfully detailed account from Jim of the claustrophobic depths of the gorge and the weight of the falling water and the branches and debris being soundly shattered in the roaring maelstrom at the base.

Then Adam added this rather helplessly, "And indeed you were right about the other bit too."

He meant the part about good company being a useful addition.

I knew I deserved it, but somehow I'd never have expected this man to be intentionally cruel.

I stayed just a few seconds more, long enough to hear the wireless silence everyone with a report on the Royal Wedding and to observe the solemn toast to the newlyweds as instigated by the Miss Bartlemans, and then I retreated to my room.

The only truly disconcerting element that followed me from the lounge was that the dignity of my quiet exit didn't stop me from accidentally leaving my borrowed library book behind as I hurried away.

---

The loss of *Jane Eyre* was the real punishment for my mistakes that day. I felt it particularly at three o'clock in the morning when I gave up on sleep just as I had the night before and the night before that. It was proof of why I ought to have been grateful to Adam for his interjection. No one here can have known – with the exception perhaps of Jim Bristol – about Rhys's fall from that bridge. They didn't know that every fresh mention of those branches churning in the depths hurt my mind and flooded it with visions of my husband's broken limbs doing precisely the same thing. They wouldn't know that I would have traded almost anything not to be driven from the lounge to my room with that image in my head. It had been hard enough getting to sleep of late without the stresses of that place stalking me in my dreams.

As it was, I ended up climbing out of bed to wrap a housecoat over my unnecessarily elegant nightdress for a prowl about the darkened corridors back down to the lounge. The nightdress was an unhelpfully extravagant birthday present from my mother designed to reawaken my femininity after the divorce – thoughtful, generous and, in that way only mothers can achieve, it had the dispiriting effect of making me feel like I must routinely look like a shapeless sack where I had thought myself quietly sophisticated.

The lounge opened off the marble-clad entrance hall. It was an ornate box with no windows that was tucked in the space between the wide sweep of the staircase, the long range of the kitchens at the back and the dining room that overlooked the seafront. It had a deep carpet and heavy plasterwork framing the ceiling and a very grand arch that let patrons through to the dining room. The pictures on the wall harked back to the time when the educated classes were getting particularly excited about imaginary classical ruins. The furniture was equally antiquated and smelled faintly of stale potpourri. In the dim light cast from the reception desk everything was a grey shapeless clutter, which unfortunately didn't include my book.

A burst of tired frustration hit me hard then. It served me right, I thought viciously, for presuming that the century since its publication would protect *Jane Eyre* from the same interest excited by the work of a Mr A. E. Woolfe. *That* book, I could see, was lying abandoned on a footstool where I suspected it would remain until the next time it was required for the ongoing campaign to impress the author. I was tempted to take it, but realised that as well as being tantamount to open warfare with Mary, the act would be bound to give the other guests the delight of deciding that I too was vying for his attention. So instead I took the well-thumbed remains of a newspaper and climbed the darkened stairs again.

It was when I put the key in the lock that I happened to notice *Jane Eyre* lying innocently outside my door. It was propped against the doorframe where some kind soul had placed it and I had simply missed it before.

At least that was what I realised about five ludicrous minutes later, once I'd finished worrying that someone was playing tricks on me and had scoured the shadowy doorways for their presence.

I read for a while, blinking through the eternal sparring of its heroine with her will, her hardship and indeed her master, wondering whether a book filled with heartache and loneliness was really the right kind of reading matter for someone on the brink. But then, lulled by its comfortingly familiar tones, I actually managed to doze a little and when I stepped out of my room for an early breakfast, I was surprisingly rested. It was a good job too because this morning promised to be just as difficult as the last; although at least it wasn't expected to involve yet another cramped train ride.

"Good morning."

Adam had stepped out of a room two removed from mine. He was dressed in the same style as the day before; a pair of tough-looking trousers that had probably been very expensive once and a warm jumper that on any other man might have been purposefully chosen to enhance the colour of his eyes. Clearly today was expected to involve more walking.

"Morning," I returned formally and shrugged off the impulse that made me think to wait while he set his key to its lock.

But today it seemed he thought I should because I heard a short mention of my name as he stepped quickly down the carpeted corridor to join me and then a brief uneasy quirk at the corner of his mouth followed by: "I think you must have—"

The revelation of what I must have done now was interrupted by the unusually disorderly arrival of Mrs Alderton and her sister as they clattered down the stairs from the upper floor. Judging by the younger woman's urgent hushing movement with her hands and the few words that drifted down the length of the corridor, we'd met them at the end of a fierce lecture. Mrs Alderton only seemed to be satisfied by Mary pursuing us down the stairs, across the foyer and flinging herself down into the spare seat at the breakfast table that Adam was claiming. Once there, she promptly helped herself to a portion of his paper. I saw him shrug and take his seat. Then he quietly offered to exchange a different part of the paper for the piece she'd taken, which had consisted of dry numbers from the stock exchange, and it made her smile.

My breakfast became isolation then, wonderful and tranquil isolation. No one cared about me. Whatever had been building in the undercurrents in last night's conversation appeared to have been miraculously relegated to the status of old news today. No one was going to be required to drive me anywhere and none of the guests had any cause to speak to me, alarm me or otherwise disturb my peace when I then took my walk through town. I was free to think only of the rhythm of my footsteps and how they had carried me many times before to this familiar secluded street.

# Chapter 6

The houses in this part of town were set in steep terraces that must have originally sheltered the town's shipwrights. My sharp rap on the metal door knocker was lost in the musical jingling as boats and their yards shivered in the light breeze at the nearby harbour. Those two men and their demands might never have existed. The only footsteps I heard were the muffled ones that approached in the passage behind the blue front door.

They belonged to the aproned figure of Sue Williams. My ex-mother-in-law.

Rhys's mother was pretty and plump in the manner of the quintessential housewife in an advert for baking powder and she stared at me from an armchair that was well-hung with doilies. It was placed in the corner of a small room made dark by heavy burgundy wallpaper and thick curtains that might have easily been blackout curtains left over from the war. I suppose she must have been in her late-sixties by now. She looked younger. "Well," she said finally. "It's a long time since I last set eyes on you."

"It is," I said and settled on the settee, wondering if the

stuffy shadows replayed the old scenes as vividly for her as they did for me. It took bravery of many different sorts to come here. "It is. How are you?" Then I felt like an utter fool. How exactly should she be, given what had happened.

"Well enough," she said, and reached for a half-drunk cup of tea. It seemed she did recall those old scenes.

I smiled one of those sympathetic smiles that are nothing to do with happiness and made some stilted offerings of regret, which were received graciously but coolly, and tried to remember what I had come here for. I was glad at least that her husband was not present. That man was like a cumbersome caricature of his son; the same forceful personality and strong features, but without the brightness of mind which marked his son. *Had* marked his son.

Seeing her like this abruptly brought it home to me. If there had been any lingering doubts about whether or not he had really died that day, they couldn't survive this visit. Rhys would never have let her suffer like this. It came as a violent little shock somehow. Perhaps I really had never quite accepted it before now.

Her softly accented voice covered my stumbling halt. "So, you're here to read the condolence messages?" She swept a collection of cards off a gloomy dresser and passed them to me without leaving time to demur. I had to carry them to the small shaded window to make them out. They were a varied bunch, some inclined towards mourning and some treading a fine line nearer disbelief. All expressed sympathy and care to the parents of a lost man and they did not remotely make for easy reading.

One in particular caught in my hand. It was written in elegant curls and it read; *'We each want to make our mark, to stand out a little from the rest and Rhys did just that. He always will. I will miss him.'* and an indecipherable scrawl that I knew must read *'Gregory Scott'*.

"What is it?"

I turned in the light from the window to find Mrs Williams staring at me. "Oh, Sue," I said, shaken into a guilty realisation of what this visit must mean for her. "Gregory called me the day after I heard the news. He wondered if I would help him go through the prints Rhys had kept for him from that project they did together but I said I couldn't. I wouldn't."

I stopped short when I registered the hurt that had passed over his mother's face. Gregory was one of Rhys's oldest patrons. When he, Rhys and I had first been introduced I had still been a young painter studying classical lighting techniques under the tutelage of my long-suffering uncle at the old man's gallery in Cirencester. That had been twelve years ago. Six months after that, Gregory had been signing his name as the witness on my marriage certificate. And a year after *that*, Gregory had performed the next in a long line of introductions by bringing a famous critic to the launch of Rhys's one-man show. This critic had promptly dubbed Rhys the Most Promising Photographer to Emerge from the Depths of Wales and I might add that Rhys had mildly resented this title. He hadn't particularly liked being considered only promising.

"Oh, Sue," I repeated. "I'm so sorry. I'm letting you think the unforgivable." I moved back to my seat before adding firmly, "Gregory didn't mean that I should march over the gallery threshold as if I'd never left. He wasn't thinking about retrieving his old sporting photographs; he was thinking that we should do our utmost to honour the work that Rhys had done with him. Whatever else happened between Rhys and me, however our marriage ended, I could never forget the sheer beauty of his talent and the important part that Gregory played in it."

This determined eulogy did far more to smooth the waters than any wild outpourings of emotion could. Her demeanour transformed and she showed the bright cheerfulness of the truly bereaved. "I know. And you're right; Gregory was the friend Rhys needed. I remember the rows when Rhys first told his father he was going to pursue photography rather than engineering."

I also remembered the other rows, like the one in this house that last summer before Rhys left us all for the war and the other one in our Cirencester home when he came back again. Looking back now, it amazes me that I had let his creative impulses dictate my life for so long. If I was looking for proof my judgement was poor, this was it. Not, it must be said, that I mean to imply that I call his going off to war one of his impulses.

His decision to lend his considerable skills to the Army Film and Photographic Unit was a raw opportunity to test his talent against the grittiest subject matter of all. The war was the muse to end all muses, and even I can admit that he had never lacked the kind of resolve a person must need to face the long years of hard work and utter bravery of sustained conflict. It could have changed him like many other men, but it didn't. When he came back he only brought with him a new muse, a revitalised urge to create and the expectation that his wife would once again give way to the weight of his point of view and compromise as she always had; which really meant redrawing every fresh line, reforming every fragile emotional boundary that previously had been the last one I'd thought would never be crossed.

The surprise I think was for him, because he came home to a wife who understood herself a little more clearly. The war for me had come as a glorious respite. The hardships and terrors of bombing were nothing. War gave me the solitude I needed to rediscover a sense of balance and to break the old patterns so that by the time Rhys came back again I was a little more capable of perceiving where I was right and a little less wedded to the idea of sacrificing everything for the sake of his art.

Or perhaps I was still shackled. He came back as demanding as ever. I won my little victory by divorcing him. But he got to stay in our beautiful home while I scuttled meekly away to the north of England and my parents like the dreary little cast off I'd always played. And yet, feeble as it might sound, it had seemed right at the time. Even before the war I must have had opinions. After all, our rows were always pretty heated affairs. But this wasn't an argument I would have even attempted to win, for my own sake rather than his. Anything else would have felt painfully like revenge.

"He left a note, you know," his mother suddenly announced.

Before the divorce she had liked me well enough I think – though without children, what was the point of me? – but Sue Williams was a woman who was fiercely committed to the idea that it was a woman's duty to maintain the appearance of happiness even when it was absent. I think I'd offended her more than anyone by suddenly deciding to set my own desires above the luxury of continuing to care for her flawless, incomparable son.

Today the acrimony of my sudden departure was like a shadow that faded in and out of her manner as she wavered, quite reasonably, between despising me for being the woman who had walked away from her son, and treating me as the only other woman who had known him intimately enough to appreciate the full horror of his loss. Her lightness of tone now was so far along on the scale of control that it practically met devastation coming the other way. She told me, "He left a note but the police have it so you can't see it. He just said sorry. No explanation or anything. Just *sorry*."

Behind it all, I think her voice cracked and I nearly put my hand out to her but she raced on. Her eyes were held wide open and they glittered in the dim light as she rushed into saying, "He only visited us a few weeks before, and he seemed fine, absolutely fine. He'd just opened an exhibition in the gallery so he was tired of course but nothing that ..." Her voice suddenly deepened. "Nothing that could imply he was thinking of—" Devastation really did show itself this time.

It was beginning to tell on me too. Rhys belonged to that set of artistic temperaments that verge upon genius. He had been prone to bleak periods of self-doubt and foul moods, and the run-up to a new exhibition had always been our most fraught time. But stubborn, beautiful, magnetic, inspiring and exacting though he was, no one could ever pretend that the stress of a new exhibition would have been sufficient to drive him to this lonely end.

Instead, this dark heavy room was filled with the echoes of his presence. His personality lingered in the gramophone in the corner and in the terrible prints his mother kept on the wall in a kind of merry defiance of his lectures on taste. He lurked in the desk where I knew she had written her regular fortnightly letters to tell him the news.

I asked, "In this last visit did he say anything about any kind of harassment or some sort of trouble or anything? Anything at all? I mean, are you really sure that this note meant that he was planning to ...?" I trailed off helplessly, not at all sure I could justify this crime of interrogating a recently bereaved mother and not even sure I wanted to ask any more. In the midst of all the real grief for the loss of his life, it felt intensely selfish to have come here for the sake of worrying about the difficulties of quietly going on living mine.

Her reply was a flat croak. "You mean to ask if anyone was pressurising him? No. One of the people who saw him there was Mrs Thomas from next-door's sister's girl. She was out for dinner with her new husband. She actually called in barely minutes after the police came knocking on my door. I told her she was a fool and a liar. She told me she wished she was. He was ... alone."

The way she said the word *alone* made the shadows of that

desolate bridge in the night time loom now from the corners of this gloomy room. Her son's isolation in his last moments was her own loneliness now.

Then she beat the shadows back with a stern little shake of her head. She was a stronger woman than I. "He said nothing about any trouble. Nothing. He talked about his future projects and the latest one which was a new little collaboration with a newspaperman who was proving a touch unreliable but nothing of any note. The police asked about shell shock, and at the time I didn't really know how to say for certain it wasn't, but I'm sure now he never gave me any sign." She paused and looked uncertainly at me; focussing on me, I think, for the first time. Her voice was suddenly a little firmer, a little harder. "He did mention you at one point, but I don't think it was anything important."

My heart began to beat.

There was another pause and I began to worry that I would have to decide whether to prompt her or to let it pass but then when she spoke I realised that her hesitation had only been because she was carefully editing his phrasing. I was sure Rhys would not have put it so politely. "He said you were going to try to take the gallery from him."

Sue Williams gave a brief pursing smile at my exclamation. "You're in Lancashire for now aren't you? Your sister told him – she's still in his neighbourhood isn't she? – that you'd started dabbling again. Perhaps Rhys thought you might want to come back. I don't know. He wasn't very clear about it. But I told him that you wouldn't; you couldn't. Not that you mightn't have the right but I was sure even you wouldn't be so cruel as to take the rug out from under his feet, not when he had such talent."

I was thinking; *dabbling?*

My voice was perfectly measured. "I don't want to go back there; I thought you knew that. I'm sure he knew that. Gregory certainly did. He wasn't remotely surprised when I refused after he called the other day. So I can't imagine what Rhys thought could possibly have changed my mind."

Her odd little pursing smile came and went again. I'd actually surprised her. Rightly or wrongly, she had expected me to be quietly bewildered by Rhys's doubts. Now I was decisive and clear. The funny thing was that Sue gave the distinct impression that she approved of the change. She even made me wonder if she might have liked me better had I been like this in the days of my marriage.

It made me think if this was a new me I must be getting things very wrong indeed.

Or perhaps this was just the old patterns repeating themselves. I hadn't broken them as much as I had thought. These people had always made me feel terribly guilty. They'd always made every desire of mine feel somehow like a selfish whim; even in the days when I'd been an optimistic young thing and the desire had been to love their son.

Now I was feeling the shame of coming here and burdening this woman with my questions when I ought to have been displaying the grief she was looking for in the ex-wife. I felt guilty for forcing her to acknowledge I was the survivor when Rhys had died. I felt guilty for thinking she was the sort of person that would think like that when she and her husband were probably perfectly decent and it was only my own petty resentments that made me so inadequate here.

I saw her glance at the clock. It made me realise I should leave before her husband came home. I shouldn't have come here, knowing what I was facing. I should never have imagined that I could withstand this encounter with the past.

Of course, if I hadn't been trying to deal with an appalling threat, I would never have been desperate enough to have come here at all.

Very carefully, I rose to my feet and stepped down the passage. The door opened. I would have to step outside but first I concentrated specifically on the selfish whim of wishing not to be persecuted in my ex-husband's name. I made her squint against the unaccustomed light. "Just one more thing, if I may? Have *you* had any unexpected visitors? Anyone else asking questions?" I knew the answer before she even spoke. There never were going to be any witnesses to confirm my story.

There was a pause, and then she added with a terrible blandness; "If they find his body, I'll let you know. For the funeral."

That was supposed to be her final word. It had every right to be her final word. But as she prepared to shut the door, I paused and turned back, asking entirely on an afterthought:

"Was there a film in his camera? The one they found in the riverbed, I mean?"

Her expression blanked and for a moment I thought she was going to close the door before she conceded, "Yes. I think so. We were shown some pictures at one point so I suppose there must have been; yes. The police still have it." Then her face wrinkled and I realised with a sudden pang that I thoroughly deserved to feel guilty this time because I'd made her cry. She added, "I can't bear the thought of his beloved things lying in a storeroom somewhere. I wish you hadn't reminded me. I suppose I could ask for them back but I just can't bear that either. I wish you hadn't reminded me."

I put out my hand to her then. I gave her fingers a little squeeze. I was sorry. I really was sorry. For all of it.

----

I'd been sustained until now by the belief that I was pursuing something that might yield my escape. Now I'd paid this visit and discovered nothing except guilt and the very bitter truth that after this I had absolutely no purpose at all. If I wasn't careful, I'd find myself forming a new plan, any plan, even to the extent of sneaking off into that impenetrable gorge and personally scouring beneath every rock within about four miles for Rhys's body; just for the sake of doing something, anything rather than giving up.

I was hurrying once more down that increasingly familiar street that led to the pier and the turn to the hotel. It was colder here. The buildings at the left hand side were extraordinary. They belonged to the university and were a long line of insanely tall towers and halls that had all the magic and style of a misplaced Arthurian castle. They cast a long shadow but it wasn't this that made me cold.

It was because there on the far side of the road, under the

calm gaze of the towering university buildings, stood a black Morris Eight.

I'm not even sure which was worse; the fact that the car was there at all, or the knowledge that I had been wandering about all morning with barely a thought for where its owners were. I glowered at it for a moment, disbelieving; trying to convince myself that it wasn't just a coincidence; this wasn't another needless panic about a perfectly common breed of car. I didn't need to debate with myself for long. Even with the risk of further embarrassment, the case for inaction wasn't one I was going to win.

I did at least pause long enough to take the precaution of scanning the street in case someone should be watching or even worse there was some sign of the owners, innocent or otherwise. About a dozen more swift cautious glances at the street, the buildings and behind me – always behind me – as I crossed the road told me that no one was around. No one was watching. There was no one in the car either. I made sure of that. The whole place was so still, the only sound of movement was of the distant wash of the tide on shingle.

The black car stood there trying to look innocent. I glared at it. It felt like an extension of the meeting with Rhys's mother. Faintly unreal, like it was manipulating my emotions purely for the purpose of challenging my resolve. The difficulty began with the fact that I had no memory of the licence plate, not even of one digit. Somehow I'd thought the image of it would pop up in my mind as clear as day the moment I needed it. The letters on this vehicle's plate proved that it had not been registered in Gloucestershire, but this taught me nothing when

I realised any old car might well have moved home many times since its original registration. I cupped my hand to the glass and peered inside, trying to see if there was any sign of the owner's identity. I believe I was expecting to find a photograph of me or something else profoundly obvious but there was nothing of the sort, of course.

A newspaper lay curling on the back seat but bar it being a tattered edition of yesterday's local newspaper, it wasn't conclusive evidence of anything. A tin of sweets had fallen to the floor but I wasn't remotely confident that the memory had been accompanied by a particularly strong scent of liquorice. I moved round to the other side and cupped my hand again.

I could just make out a few scraps of paper on the shelf under the dashboard but salt and grime had crusted the glass and it was hard to distinguish more. With another quick glance along the deserted street and paying particular attention to my unguarded back, I ducked against the wing to peer inside. Hoping vehemently that no one would spot me in this position I wiped the glass, squinted against the gloom, and finally saw what the papers were.

The first was a till receipt for drinks and bore nothing but a few numbers and a code for the items bought. The second was a garage receipt but I couldn't make out much from the scrawl of handwriting; the final scrap was just the remnant of an empty matchbook with no branding whatsoever. Frustrated, I wiped a little harder and squinted again at the handwritten note.

It was, it transpired, a receipt for fuel and a top-up of oil.

I couldn't make out the name of the garage. I rested my eyes for a moment before looking again.

There was, predictably enough, the word 'Garage'. Something Garage, Garstang Road, Ca— I concentrated fiercely on the untidy lettering. Of course. *Catterall*. I enjoyed a moment of triumph at identifying this small garage in a small town on the road south from Lancaster; before crashing back down to earth with a very sudden bump indeed.

My first thought, after all that watching and waiting, was not 'they're here; they've found me', but with a kind of desolate relief: *It's true.*

# Chapter 7

There was in my mind a certain terrifying wish for them to take hold of me again because then it would all be over and I could stop this ridiculous pretence that I could do anything about it. The other part of my brain, the sensible part, was already propelling my body sternly back up the hill towards shops and shelter from the stiff breeze, and down again towards the police station. I wasn't intending to beg for sanctuary. I'd learned that lesson before and I wasn't that desperate. Yet.

I had a small, very fragile germ of an idea and I suppose it was growing from the sudden shock of finding the car. Nothing else would have had the power to cut through the fog of helplessness that had followed me from that house. It was just a shade unfortunate that the relief of finding a new strategy – or indeed any strategy at all – subsequently led me to veer off course into the telling of downright lies.

The police station stood on the main shopping street opposite the post office. The street was called Great Darkgate Street and fittingly the police station was constructed in fearsome black stone and had crenulations. It squatted menacingly between dwellings and innocent shop fronts like a miniature fortress. Or perhaps that description was just indicative of what I wished it to be that day.

A woolly-haired sergeant looked up from her post behind the desk as I entered, clearly very busy and clearly very worn out by the world. She was not at all pleased by the interruption. She gave me a brief look up and down and I think she could scent fear, but mistook it for guilt.

"Yes?"

At her resigned bark, I withdrew my hands sharply from where they had been defensively thrust into my deep coat pockets and approached the desk. "I'd like to talk to someone about viewing Rhys Williams' possessions, if that is possible. Are they available?"

"I don't know. Do you have a case number?"

"No, I'm sorry, I don't. He died. At Devil's Bridge. The investigation has concluded, I believe. That's why I'm here." I counted breaths in an effort to calm my sense of urgency as she fussed with some documents, and stumbled blindly into telling my first lie. "His mother was told the possessions they found were ready to be collected. I believe someone is expecting me?"

"I don't know."

"Oh dear – perhaps I can speak to the policeman in charge? Is he available?"

"No."

Failure stung. "Is there anyone else I can speak to?"

"No."

Perhaps lying really did reap its own rewards. I was about

to add a little truth when she abruptly deigned to expand a little. "You have to see Detective Inspector Griffiths. It's his case."

I waited. I don't think I was being brave. I think the truth is I was numb. I don't think I was really thinking anything except that I didn't want to have to go back out onto those streets like this. So I waited, face moulded into something bordering on polite encouragement and at long last she mustered the energy to concede, "He's back in tomorrow. Would you like to make an appointment?"

"On a Saturday?"

She peered up at me beneath lowered brows. Meaning, I think, to imply that a policeperson's work didn't stop for the weekend.

I said contritely, "Yes, please."

"Eleven o'clock suit you?"

"Yes."

"Name?"

This was where I made my second mistruth. Some wildness within me made me say after only the tiniest of hesitations: "Mrs Williams."

The foolish thing about it was that technically I was still entitled to use that name. It was on my passport and on various other documents such as my account with the bank. However my latest ration book was most definitely in my maiden name and it was the one I had very recently taken to using on a daily basis so really the truth here was a touch blurred. I suppose if I'd been truly honest I'd have dictated Mrs *Kate* Williams (indicating divorcee) rather than Mrs *Rhys*

Williams (indicating that a husband still had ownership of me).

I watched as her hand carefully entered the name in the large diary on her desk. Then the hand recorded the name of the case I'd mentioned in my enquiry. The pen paused hovering over the paper. After a moment she looked up and suddenly seemed considerably more human. "I'm terribly sorry, Mrs Williams, I'm sure Inspector Griffiths will be glad to help you. I'm sorry he isn't in today. It's his mother's birthday. Is there anything else I can do for you?"

Lies really are an ugly thing, and they definitely do bring their own punishment. I walked out with my head wavering between the unexpected return of hope and the rather grimmer calculation of waiting another day and whether or not it mightn't be wiser to abandon everything and make for the nearest train, and I only came to when I caught myself glaring fiercely at every man I met as I hurried along. My heartbeat kept intensifying until they were past and I was safe again. Which was ridiculous because if they were that close it was already far too late. And as it was, I ought to have been watching more closely for someone else because Jim Bristol was following me.

Or rather, remembering my terrible mistake yesterday with another man from the hotel, it would be more accurate to state that he was sauntering along at his ease some way behind me.

It was hard to be sure. He seemed to have his head thoroughly buried in his guidebook so he might have just been completing his much discussed tour of the town. As I hurried along another shopping street towards the promenade with half a plan of going from there to the hotel to retrieve my bags and pay my bill, I kept throwing little glances over my shoulder and at first I thought I had lost him. But the second time I looked, a carefully staged examination of a pair of gloves in the window of a gentleman's outfitters, I saw him more clearly. He seemed to vanish just as I turned but I was confident now that I was not mistaken; he was following me.

It was exhausting work guarding myself from this specific threat at my back at the same time as remaining ever watchful for the uncertain threat of the two men who might approach from any side they chose. It was exhausting to the point that it made my brain ache. Part of the difficulty lay in the fact that with each passing day since the accident, I was growing less confident about my memory of those men from Lancaster. I knew I would recognise them if I saw them. I also knew they weren't Jim Bristol and I'd managed to eliminate the other faces I'd met so far from my endless watch. But these days when I tried to fix my mind upon a definitive description, their eyes and noses slid away into nonsense. Sometimes the faces in my memory were the doctors at the hospital. Sometimes they had the faces of old friends like Gregory or even my husband. And the more I fought it, the more I found it hard to tell if any of it was real. As was happening now, in fact, with the uncertainty of being followed.

In the end, I opted for ambush. I turned a full circle and doubled back up the main shopping street. I crossed again as I neared the junction onto the street that led down to the pier. There was a tearoom there, just on the corner. Jim Bristol was still behind as I followed an old lady step for step around a man selling newspapers and finally slipped inside. I waited by the door for a few thrilling moments; nerves and eyes fixed on the street outside and eventually he obliged me by walking past. His coat today was a well-cut pre-war sports jacket. It was burgundy and unmistakeable. I shrank back in case he saw me, but he only seemed interested in the antics of a group of young soldiers on the opposite side of the road who were clearly on leave. They still wore their uniforms even for a day at the seaside.

I waited a while longer before finally acknowledging the waitress's ushering and I allowed myself to be shown to a table in the heart of the room for a rest and a sandwich. It was an expensive bolthole. After the outlay of funds for the train journey and the hotel it was perilously close to being above my means but it was the perfect position. I was screened from the street outside by the line of crowded booths that were arranged along the high glass windows and yet I could see the car. It was still entirely deserted and ordinary.

The tearoom was reassuringly ordinary too. It was the sort that appealed to wealthy older couples and thankfully none had the fearsomely brutish form that my two would-be kidnappers must take. The patrons did unfortunately put me through the usual rigmarole of making my heart jolt every time one of them spoke in a tone that was reminiscent of Rhys's voice or turned their head in just such a way to cause a momentary spark of recognition before it evaporated again, but I was getting used to that by now.

Then my solitude was disturbed by a loud call of 'Katie'

and it was clear that someone had managed to surprise me here.

Mary James bore down on me like a whirlwind through a rose garden and to be honest it was a relief to find that it was only her. I'd been surveying the shadows around that parked car. I hadn't imagined I could have been so inattentive to the traffic through the door.

Mary draped her coat over the back of the chair opposite, dropped like a bomb into its seat and stole a sip of my water while the bright whirlwind slowly settled into the standard garish print of her day dress. Modern frocks were frequently rather garish. The cynic in me suspected that it was a deliberate tactic – probably engineered by a committee somewhere – founded on the principle that we women might not notice the shortages and hardships of our daily lives if we were sheathed in bright things.

If that was their aim, it hadn't worked for this woman. I had thought before that she was testing the peace for its tedium and now I saw she was actively working to break it at any cost. She was made up again today with rather too much drama about the eyes that outdid the customary flash of crimson upon her lips. Her frock was narrow-waisted but whereas the extreme restrictions of a girdle made her sister look angular and severe, Mary only looked impressively fashionable. I didn't think the cost of my lunch would have meant much to her. She observed cheerfully, "It smells of cabbage in here. Are you having a nice day?"

She must have noticed my rather blank expression because she gave me an astonishingly genuine smile. She leaned in to rest her chin upon a hand and said in a confidential whisper that was anything but discreet, "I've been abandoned by my sister. Dear Aged Albert has decided he feels unwell. Oh no, nothing serious, don't worry." There was a waft of her hand in response to my automatic shift from bewilderment towards polite concern. "Being a doctor he is well versed in a variety of complaints that aren't awful enough to mean he shouldn't take his usual luncheon but still absolutely require his wife to tend him lovingly. It just means that our planned adventure has had to be postponed yet again so I'm at a loose end – and sulking like a five year old."

I began to feel a stuffy prude. There was something truly disarming in this assault – there is no better word for it – by her determined good humour. I'd seen it at work on the men at the hotel and scorned their weakness then. But now I couldn't help asking amiably, "Does your loose end happen to extend to having lunch? I'm just having mine. There's some tea left in the pot if you can get a fresh cup."

In many ways she was a very clever woman.

Mary shook her head. "I've already eaten, thank you. I couldn't face waiting any longer. What are you going to do now? Do you fancy being my chaperone for the day? I fully intend to drop you as soon as my sister is free but if you don't mind I'd love to borrow you for a while. We could catch the bus to Ynyslas."

I thawed and only then did it occur to me to wonder if she was somehow a rogue sent to winkle me out of my hiding place. But she didn't leave much room for scepticism because she was already hurrying me into finishing my tea and in truth, I wasn't particularly hard to persuade. That fatalistic part of my brain that wanted to end this hadn't faded away with the brief rest in this tearoom. The defiance had revived a touch but that was all. If they had found me, this was it. If Jim really was part of this, I had no hope of evading anyone if they chose to come and get me. And if he wasn't, I didn't want to pin my hopes on being able to hide away in my room till the next day, attempting to turn the hotel into a garrison with the other guests cast as my guards; achieving nothing and doing nothing until the time came to face the race across town to my meeting with the inspector at the police station tomorrow. That was the kind of waiting game that felt it must leave scars on the mind.

So I paid my bill and climbed to my feet with absolutely no expectation other than that I would soon know precisely what part she meant to play if I followed her.

That being said, the first step outside was taken a little less recklessly. Regardless of my decision I couldn't help glancing behind as we stepped out on to the pavement but if Jim Bristol was there, I didn't see him. I didn't see those two men either. Their car was still waiting serenely beneath the university building. I was just checking the darkened telephone booth and deciding that it was likewise definitely empty when the woman beside me suddenly let out a wild shriek and leapt into the road. Quite understandably, it was a moment or two before I realised the rapidly approaching car was a red Rover 10 and her scream was a cry of delight.

It was delight though, and now Mary was laughing like a maniac. She was standing there in the middle of the road, striking a pose of careless elegance as she turned back to me, eyes bright and absolutely determined to defy the box-like nose of the car that squealed to a stop, quivering, barely inches from her knees.

"Are you insane?" Adam didn't sound remotely amused. I suppose it was Mary's way of proving the cost of following her sister's orders to ensnare her man; it was just unfortunate for her that her sister wasn't watching to learn the lesson and we were. I watched Mary sashay around to the driver's door and found myself alternating between fascination that anyone could really act like that and make it seem such a natural part of herself, and watching the road for any of the men who might be after me. There was also a part of me – the wiser part – that was adding Adam to the list and contemplating scuttling off while he and Mary were distracted. In the road, Mary had come to a rest with her hand laid artlessly along the top of the driver's door. Her coat was trailing from her other hand onto the grimy tarmacadam.

"Yes, I've gone mad," she admitted firmly. She'd noticed the coat's plight and draped it carelessly about her shoulders with about the same elegance as a millionaire with a fox fur. "As I've been telling everyone who'll listen, I'm at a loose end and acting like a five year old."

"Most five year olds that I've met have learned a little road sense."

Mary was unsquashable. But she did at least moderate her voice so that it was a glimpse of her real self. It had the bizarre effect of making her whole appearance – clothes, make-up and all – seem like borrowed plumage applied under the strict supervision of another. "Where are you going? You promised to take me with you."

I saw him suppress a smile as he shifted the car out of gear. "A castle."

"I *love* castles." The idea that her charm was a front was gone again. She chose to be this way too. A finger ran along the top of the doorframe and I swear she actually simpered.

Adam only raised an eyebrow. Mary laughed. "All right, I don't like castles; they're boring. I was going to catch a bus to the beach but it's hardly the time of year for it and perhaps you'd let me come with you instead? It'd be so nice to actually go somewhere, even if it is a castle. Please? We'll be quiet, I promise; won't we Katie?"

I baulked at this sudden inclusion. Now I really did wish I'd taken the opportunity to slip away. She jerked her head and beckoned me closer to add weight to her plea but I gave a quick silent negative and remained where she had left me, hovering foolishly on the edge of the pavement. His gaze followed hers to fix on me for the first time and as a respite from the usual terrors, the embarrassment was excruciating.

I made it worse by saying; "If he's got things to do, I'm sure he'd much rather be on his own."

Mary rolled her eyes. "Oh, ignore her; she just doesn't want to admit that she'd much prefer your castle to my beach. And she's got to come. She's playing the part of the maiden aunt to my youthful heroine. Please?"

Adam's resigned sigh was carried on the light breeze. With a triumphant smirk at me, Mary darted round to the passenger door and slid in. She fixed me with an expectant stare but

Adam was already climbing out and dragging open the rear passenger door for me. He gave a brief jerk of his head. "Come on," he said with that slight smile of his that might have been teasing, or it might not.

I moved towards the open door. He wasn't looking at me any more but that may well have been because he too was noticing the approaching bus. It was squeaking huffily to a halt behind the stationary car instead of running me down. All the same I flinched aside instinctively. And then I gave a self-conscious laugh that couldn't help turning into a lift of my eyes to Adam's face when I realised he'd been sharing the thought too. But he'd already suppressed his own reaction and was chivvying me into the back seat so that he could press the door shut on me and release the impatiently idling bus. Then, with an apologetic lift of his hand, he climbed in and prepared to send the car cruising away down to the promenade.

He didn't even get as far as releasing the handbrake. Mary exclaimed *'Jim!'* and a hand met the door handle to my left as a different male voice said cheerfully, "Room for one more?" Then Jim Bristol was sliding in beside me to share the cramped confines of the ridiculously small back seat and smiling at me while I was fumbling with the door catch on the other side with every intention of getting straight out again. Unfortunately Adam had already sent the car on its way and Jim was distracting me with an idle pleasantry on the delight of meeting friends until I got confused between the impulse to escape and the impulse not to be rude. And then it was too late.

# Chapter 8

Our escape from the town was a lurch into a different kind of tension. The wide curve of the Victorian seafront promenade vanished at the turn beneath the vast art deco King's Hall with its amusements and tea dances, and it seemed only a moment later that we were emerging from the crowded crush of shopping streets to trace a course inland. With these two men in the car it felt like I was a captive but I couldn't be. I couldn't be. Not really.

If I told myself that enough times perhaps I would believe it.

Beside me, Jim was leaning slightly forwards so that he could join Mary's animated conversation in the front. I think he'd guessed pretty quickly that all he was going to get from me was a thin-lipped smile. We were literally inches apart – the car was so narrow that his knee kept knocking mine. I had felt trapped by him at Devil's Bridge but the muscular presence I'd experienced there had been nothing compared to the inescapable closeness to him here. He seemed insufferably strong in this tiny space. It wasn't hard to see that this was a man who had taken a firm grip upon the trials of army life during the war and found he was more than capable of meeting them. He was also truly very handsome. He was, as I have said, leaning forwards slightly and it cast his profile into elegant relief so that his jaw was perfectly defined with just the barest grain of a fair shadow beginning to show. His mouth was mobile and the brief gleam of teeth as he smiled in response to something Adam said was very engaging. None of this really fitted the part of sinister collaborator to those two men. I also wouldn't have expected their only weapon to be the well-thumbed tourist guide now held in his right hand. I permitted myself a glance at the reflection of Adam's face in his wing mirror. Where Jim shone with amusement, Adam's expression was calm and concentrated, and I couldn't tell what either man was thinking.

I did at least recognise the road we took. We crossed the river at Machynlleth and traced the winding road northwards into deep craggy valleys that had long since settled down for the coming winter. I began to feel a vague nervous excitement about where we might be going. My trips with Rhys had only rarely taken me inland. Rain-soaked mountains oppressed him he had said and our filial visits to the area had only really reached as far as busy towns and fishing ports where he might be able to steal some shots of the locals.

Wherever Adam was taking us today, it was safe to say populated areas were not his target. The car swung left off the main road and rolled gingerly down an uneven lane as Adam navigated his way without needing to refer to a map. I briefly toyed with the idea of panicking but I didn't do it and eventually, with a wide valley below us and the distinctive sweep of the lower range of Cadair Idris above, the car drew into a wide gravel lay-by and the engine was silenced.

It wasn't a popular destination. There was no house, and no prison to match my imagination either. Only two other drivers had managed to conserve enough fuel for the trip to this remote spot; a blue Morris and what looked like a farmer's run-about. Nothing moved. The hush was sudden and very intense, and I sat there in a questioning stillness, listening for any sound at all, until Mary tugged on her door handle with such a clunk that I believe Jim and I both jumped.

Jim laughed. She climbed out, shaking the creases out of her skirt. She gave a little turn. "Well."

"Well indeed." Adam was out and dragging open my door. I think Jim had expected me to slither meekly out after him at his side but I didn't. I climbed out through the door Adam opened for me and stood there while he locked up the car feeling absurdly like I was expecting him to shield me.

I don't know what from because there was nothing here except a crude lay-by and a footpath into the short scrubby woodland on the far side.

Adam spoke over my head across the roof to the other two. "Ready for a cultural delight?"

"If this cultural delight involves any more sheep droppings, I'm staying in the car." Mary was examining the gravel beneath her flimsy shoes. "Why are we here again?"

Adam pocketed his keys and set off towards the dense little woodland. "I'm here to do research. Jim's here because it saves trying to sidestep the petrol shortage by paying for a hired car if he uses my fuel instead, Kate's here because she didn't know how to refuse and *you're* here, I believe, because you threw yourself into the road and begged to come, but forgive me if I'm wrong."

The footpath was wider than I'd thought. It was obviously well used. I trailed along in their wake beneath supple limbs of overgrown hazel that swiftly closed in overhead. I couldn't hear a thing beyond the whisper of old leaves in the branches and the distant questioning mew from somewhere up above that was a buzzard. It was very hard to judge whether we were still near the valley floor or rising as I thought. Then the tangled thicket opened to clear rocky grassland and I had to forget everything, even every little doubt, for a moment.

Adam had stepped aside to let us pass. To our left, the land fell dramatically away to a vast glacial valley that curved gently away towards the distant sea. To my right stood Adam and beyond him were the shattered remains of a castle. The landscape ached with the memory of the lives that had sheltered within those walls.

Mary took control of the scene. She cast a look around with wide eyes, dismissed it all with a shrug – because that was what she was expected to do – and then turned back and pouted. "Go on, Mr Adam Hitchen: explain. What's so special about a mouldy old ruin?"

It transpired that this was Castell y Bere, a Llewellyn stronghold and an 800-year-old monument to a defiant people and the vital trade routes they had guarded. What made it particularly special to me was that this was the first place in days that allowed me the peace in which to absolutely set aside my fears and even my scrutiny of my companions' motives.

Even Jim left me alone here. He seemed content to watch the artist from afar as she settled comfortably on top of the cool stones of the curtain wall, pencil in hand and the faithful sketch-book lying open across her lap. Mary had long ago vanished to seek excitement elsewhere and Adam was out of sight on the other side of the structure, doubtless writing notes and staring intently at the tumbled stones by his feet. That left only me and Jim and, as I have said, he was content to leave me alone now. He was sitting on a broken flight of stairs about fifteen yards away, hands about his knees and idly contemplating the view.

I sketched in the turn of the river as it snaked across the floodplain to disappear behind Jim's shoulder. That done, I was lucky enough to discover that I still had some water in the very stale flask that lurked in the bottom of my bag. Tipping a few drops into its metal cap, I began to add the little hints of watercolour here and there which would bring my painting to life. No one would notice that this whole piece was composed just so that I could make a sly portrait of the man in the foreground.

"Are you painting?" Mary suddenly reappeared and threw herself down beside me. "May I see?"

She took the sketchbook with her customary self-assurance and leafed interestedly through the pages. She paused here and there to ask a question about the subject or scene and it was very sweet how she took care not to smudge the drying paint.

"Who's he?" She wasn't looking at my cunningly signed and dated record of Jim's presence. I saw with a jolt that she had discovered the sheaves of paper that I kept as little treasures inside the cover.

"Rhys," I said, carefully scrutinising her face for her reaction. "My husband."

"Your *husband?*"

"Ex," I clarified. Her reaction was reassuring. He meant nothing to her, except more idle intrigue.

"Oh," she said softly, examining the vivid green eyes as they stared insolently back at her. It had been a good likeness; in those days my figure work had emulated the flowing energy of those portraits by El Greco whose subjects seem to be perpetually in motion. This quick study of my husband's face had captured his expressive good looks with the dramatic lighting that had been my specialism. Rhys had always claimed that the intense shadows made him look sulky. *If the cap fits*, I had later thought, but not dared say it.

Mary asked, "When was that? Your divorce, I mean."

"We divorced last year. That portrait is from ten years before that – the year we were married."

"Oh," she said again, reading the pathetically soppy inscription that recorded the date: 12 June '36. "Is that how you met? Through painting?"

"It was," I confirmed. This at least was a relatively painless piece of my past. I had been a freshly arrived young student working under my uncle. There was no embarrassment in remembering the crucial first exhibition I'd helped the old man hang and how it had also been my first introduction to his fearsomely precise photographer friend. I'd thought Rhys was the most inspiring man I'd ever met. He'd liked me too. He'd liked my youthful enthusiasm for his old friend's small Cirencester gallery and my optimism allied with the fact that, as a student of art, I was almost as passionate about the scope of Rhys's work as he was.

Mary was examining his face a little more closely, perhaps reading the traces of the rise and fall of my marriage in the uneven brush strokes. Then she returned the wad to its home and handed the sketchbook back. "We thought you were a spinster. You're so self-contained."

That made me smile. "No."

We sat for a while in a companionable silence, her contemplating the view, me finishing my painting, before, with a sigh, Mary abruptly twisted in her seat to draw her feet up onto the broad stonework and began fiddling with a bracelet. I painted for a while longer but then she sighed again, more loudly, and I realised what she wanted.

"Is something the matter?" I finally asked, just as I was supposed to do. She was staring at the metal band that encircled her wrist and her face had set into an unusually serious frown that was somehow very endearing.

She said abruptly, "It's irresponsible, don't you think?"

"What is?"

"The fuss they've been making about the Royal Wedding. They're deliberately bombarding us with the fairytale of being a princess and being swept off one's feet by a beau and it's unachievable."

I couldn't help smiling. "But the bride in question *is* a princess."

"Don't laugh; it's true. It sets an unobtainable standard and gives rise to all sorts of pressures and expectations. And they keep making such a big statement out of the fact the poor woman has had to hoard her clothing coupons like the rest of us as if that's a good thing. I'm so heartily sick of having to make-do-and-mend."

I caught a brief fluttering glance beneath those elegant lashes. It made me say blandly, "Well at least if you wanted to escape all the fuss, I suppose you've come to the right place."

I saw her blink at me incredulously and then blink again. "Are you being serious? You *are* being serious." She laughed. "Haven't you noticed that the town is overflowing with people and events and tea dances? It's November: the town should be battened down for the closed season and instead all the usual summer entertainments are out in force. It's like that tale of the swallow that stayed for winter or something. They've got the funicular running up and down the hill for heaven's sake and I should know because it was the only activity remotely pertaining to a holiday that I managed to do yesterday."

I stared at her blankly. I really hadn't noticed.

She continued, "It all makes a bit more sense now that I know you were married. Your independence, I mean. We had wondered if you were a real oddity; you know, one of those aggressively intellectual women who purse their lips and forge their own path come what may and are destined ultimately to decay into irritating habits and dressing in frills for dinner like the Miss Bartlemans."

Something unguarded in me made me say rather dryly, "I'm flattered that you think I'm an intellectual."

I'd surprised her. Obviously she didn't expect me to react at all. She blinked at me and drew her coat more closely around her waist. There was a chill in the light breeze here. Having secured her coat with its belt, she then returned her attention to the heavy bracelet around her wrist. I saw the corners of her lips curve. "I suppose it's natural that you wouldn't feel the burden of being in a nation obsessed by a wedding. You've done your stint in acting the part of a romantic. You're free to be alone now and no one can judge you for it."

I had to raise my eyebrows at that. She cast a sly sideways glance at me and grinned.

"All right, everyone gets judged. All the time. But it's not the same, you know it's not. A few years ago I drove ambulances – at least I did when the old drivers let me which wasn't all that often – and looked glamorous while I did it and everyone said it was a jolly good thing because we were keeping the image of the merry English Rose alive so that the troops had something to dream of while they were laying down their lives to defend us. Now the men have come home again and it's important we still keep hauling out our tired old glamour even if it is all getting rather worn and thin, because now our job is to be swept away by marriage like the blushing females they dreamed of."

I asked gently, "Marriage is your new job?"

"Oh yes," she said with an arrogant toss of her head. And then laughed at herself. And then said rather precisely, "But I don't quite think it is an equal trade. Not when it turns out men aren't the fascinating species we were led to believe. They're just like us and patronising and ordinary, or never speak, which is even worse. And," she added in a confidential whisper, "don't you find that they're so terribly easy to control?"

I must have looked doubtful. She screwed up her face. Then she said in husky note of scolding, "Now, Katie. You know full well you'd have all the men eating out of your hand if you'd only try. Alice noticed that you really are quite beautiful in your own way. And then *I* noticed that you refuse to use it. You talk to men in exactly the same way as you talk to the rest of us; which is about as little as possible, isn't it?"

She was sitting there on her piece of broken wall, dramatic, energetic and utterly bemused. By contrast I gaped. I felt incredulous and utterly dreary with my handmade clothes and my props in the form of my sketchbook and the loneliness that seeped through my past like ink through blotting paper. I felt like retorting that *of course* I preferred to talk to men rather than teasing them into servile stupidity. But then she made me wonder how much easier this past week of isolation might have been if only I'd begun by fluttering a few eyelashes and drooping attractively at a suitable male. I wasn't sure which was more disturbing: the laughable failure that would have ensued if I'd attempted to pull it off or the idea that a few well-placed maidenly looks might have made all the difference.

She said boldly, "What are you so afraid of?"

She didn't mean that she had noticed my current predicament. I knew she didn't mean that. She couldn't, but all the same she shook me.

"Look," I said reasonably after a time. "Haven't we got this the wrong way round? I'm supposed to be the jaded cynic and you're supposed to be brimming with youthful optimism so that I can sneer at you and tell you that you'll understand the futility of it all once you've wasted the best years of your life on an undeserving wretch."

"*Did you?*"

"Mary ..." I protested helplessly. I'd meant to lighten the mood but now the trap was looming of having to talk about Rhys and it was impossible to convey just how desperately I didn't want to. Eventually I fixed my gaze upon a buzzard that was soaring out across the valley below us – we were so far above it that I could see the darker brown of its back – and said a shade mischievously, "Anyway if marriage is a job that doesn't suit you, hasn't it occurred to you that there is a perfectly simple alternative before you?" I caught her glance. "You could take up real employment."

Mary gave a theatrical shudder. Her eyes widened as if I'd said something disgusting. Then she smiled and shook off the feeling to say instead on a note of mocking resignation, "Oh no, there is no escaping my fate. I'll exert my powers, I'll catch my man and it'll turn out that he's as much of a fraud as I am and the only winner will be all the younger girls who have succeeded in driving another rival out of their race to snare the good ones."

"Romance isn't a competition, Mary." Suddenly I was laughing. "It's not a case of beating off all the opposition to win some man's affection, as if any chap would do. Can you honestly say that you've missed out on that one remarkable man yet? In my experience either you like a person enough to make them special and they reciprocate, or they don't. If you like each other the other people don't matter at all."

There was an undertone of irony in that but Mary didn't notice. She was looking out over the valley. She wasn't seeing it though. She said, "So says the divorcee. What went wrong with yours anyway? I suppose he came back from the war a changed man?" She flicked me a little daring glance before dropping her attention back to her bracelet. She'd pulled it off and was twisting it round and round through her fingers. It was the same silvery grey as the sky.

"Actually," I remarked wryly, "the war didn't change him at all. He came back with another woman."

"Oh–*Oh!*" Mary's response was a drawn-out expression passing from realisation to disgusted amusement and onwards into sympathetic understanding and a not inconsiderable amount of 'I told you so'. Which promptly made her laugh. She said incredulously, "You really do have a policy of keeping out of the competition, don't you? Don't you have any pride? Didn't you fight for him at all?"

"I—"

She interrupted me hastily. "I'm sorry," she said, suddenly, fiercely sincere, and after a moment her eyelashes dropped to shield her gaze from me. The bracelet glittered as it twirled within her fingers.

Mary was not the first woman of my acquaintance to question my lack of fight. I didn't know how to explain to her that it wasn't enough to blame me for choosing to endure three years of unfaithfulness until the war took him out of my sphere and then several months more once he came back again. She needed to first understand the complexities of the hurt behind discovering sometime in the midst of my seventh month of marriage that while my husband and I did indeed both share the same deep abiding passion for his art, his own passion tended to get a little diverted along the way, into his subject's bedchamber.

There was no way to ever make a bold young confident woman like Mary comprehend why it had happened in the first place or how his affairs hadn't seemed to stem from a lack of the appropriate feelings for me. Or how the nature of my reaction to that first instance set the pattern for the next time and the next and the next until I felt that pursuing the obvious option of setting my wedding ring down upon the kitchen table and storming out would be the greatest betrayal of them all.

It was one of the reasons why I never tried to compete with those women. With any woman. We weren't children. I knew that when blame came to be apportioned for the failure of my marriage, a good deal of it must come my way. Mary was right to say I didn't want to enter into a battleground where the weapon was my femininity. But she was wrong when she called it a lack of pride. It wasn't all weakness. And I didn't need to be told now that I should have been tougher; I should have handled Rhys differently; that I should, in fact, have been anything other than myself. I've always thought it must be a very strange relationship that depended on the threat of wrath to keep it from straying.

And besides, in my own way I fought very hard indeed during that time and all the months since. After all, however belittling the experience was and regardless of how frequently I failed to rise up and give body to the anger that did indeed lurk within, I think I must still have always retained at least some sense of my value. I never stopped believing that surely, if I had just one job to do in our marriage and that was to make him happy and I failed, it was because of things I couldn't change; things that were always out of my scope. It wasn't because I simply didn't fight hard enough.

I didn't say any of this to Mary. As well as being very hard to articulate, the recent advent of Rhys's death had rather clouded my memory of that history so that it was very hard to remember now precisely what he'd done and how I had felt about it all. And besides, me being me, there was always the distinct possibility that I'd misunderstood something vital somewhere along the way and I'd been making a stand all this time on a completely pointless battle line.

Mary wasn't really worrying about me anyway. The bracelet span and clattered on the ruined wall and she cursed as she snatched it back. There was a pause while she forced it back over her hand onto her wrist. Then she said as if it were the end of the world, "I like Adam, you know."

I twisted to follow her gaze and we both looked over to where he had appeared beside a tower, now staring up at its broken flight of steps with notebook still in hand.

She added glumly, "He's very clever, don't you think? And far too famous for his own good. But at least he's *nice*. Not that being nice counts for anything. Take Jim Bristol for example. He's nice too, and he actually speaks and he's never been married either—"

I interrupted her very abruptly. "Adam's *married?*"

"Widowed."

And yet I knew this. How did I know this? I didn't really need her to explain that he had been widowed just before the war. Then it came to me how I must have learned this. He must have told me very simply and plainly over tea at Devil's

Bridge. It was just a shame that it must have been lost in that confusion about seeing Jim and admitting the bus accident because I couldn't for the life of me remember what he'd said.

I interrupted Mary again in the midst of her puzzlement over whether she could bear to be the second love of a man's life and asked, "Mary, when did Adam come to the hotel? When did his visit begin, I mean?"

Her eyebrows lifted. "A little over a week ago I think. He's been before. He was here when we arrived, busily receiving a lecture from the man who guards the door at night about old mining waste coming down the river into the harbour."

"But why *here?* I mean, why choose Aberystwyth and just *now?*"

She smirked. "Ask that question of the author and he'll probably reluctantly tell you something utterly brief but tedious about the local industry. And yet, why not here, anyway? It's got roads, trains, good hotels, Welsh mountains. You might just as easily ask the same question of me or the Miss Bartlemans, or Jim or that woman with the small boy. And he really *is* an author. Does it matter?"

She didn't wait to see my swift shake of my head. She reverted to the topic that interested her. "I'm glad to say Jim isn't nursing a broken heart for his long-dead wife but he's never going to be the subject of a lecture on what constitutes a great catch."

She grimaced. I took this as a hint of the disagreement that had occurred between her and her sister that morning. Proving it, Mary leaned in with mock secrecy to confide tartly, "Alice has very fixed criteria for the concept and she's very good at explaining it. Which is ironic because I know full well that she raced towards the first eligible male who came well laden with funds and she's been fighting boredom ever since."

"I—see," I said, understanding her feelings at last. "Oh dear."

I could guess now who was coaching Mary into her weary cynicism and it wasn't the legion of boring admirers that waited in the wings. I could also perceive why I thought Mary *dressed-up* in her elegant finery like a doll put out on display. I suppose Mrs Alderton expected reasonable repayment for her investment when presumably it was Dr Alderton who was funding Mary's adventure in wealthier circles in the first place.

Beside me, Mary's hands had found themselves a new occupation scoring a scrap of stone upon the stonework by her right hip and it was at that moment that I realised of all things, what she probably needed most was a thoroughly motherly hug.

Instead we sat in silent contemplation of the subject of her upset for a while before she spoke again, and when she did her voice was very quiet. "Do you know anything about him?"

"Adam? No, not really. In fact, it would seem considerably less than you ..."

"And Jim?"

It was said very carelessly. The solid stones of the castle wall were cool beneath my hand. I said, "He told me he does something in local government, but I don't know what. General dogsbody he said, but I doubt that. He doesn't look much like anybody's dogsbody to me." Then, in an unguarded moment, I added, "I don't quite trust him somehow."

Having finished scoring marks upon the broken wall, Mary

had turned away, instantly distracted by something beyond one of the towers that I couldn't see. "You don't? Well that's easily remedied. I'll sit in the back with you on the return trip and then you won't have to talk to him." Then she looked back at me, reverting in an instant to the lively extrovert that I recognised. She stood up and brushed off her skirt, suddenly impatient to be off. "I can't *believe* I'm discussing their comparative merits like ..."

"Like they're a pair of new socks?" I suggested.

She grinned. "Precisely. And you already know my opinion of clothing shortages and the principle of make-do-and-mend. So on that note I think I'm going to explore over ... there. See you in a little while. And Katie?"

"Yes?"

"Don't let the rotten stinkers make you sad." And she jumped down off the low curtain wall to vanish into the trees. It seemed the obvious moment to abandon my pretence that today's painting was anything other than a screen I was trying to hide behind and instead I packed away my things and climbed carefully to my feet.

I found Adam peering down into the deep square well that yawned black and wide in the heart of the castle. Jim had drifted away a while ago; sometime in the midst of Mary's rant about men returning from war I believe. There was nothing to frighten me here. Except the suspicion that having just been thinking empowering thoughts about fighting the right battles and not the ones that people set for me, it was high time that I proved I really was as brave as I claimed to be. I should make my peace with the next person on the list.

Adam was absorbed in making a rough sketch of the well, adding a little note here and there on the construction, and didn't look up when I appeared beside him. I stood there for a few minutes, waiting while his hand moved confidently across the page and noticing the worn engraving on the neat little mechanical pencil that bore the initials JH.

It was probably his wife's. Janet? Jane? Jennifer? I couldn't remember.

His hands were strong looking but with pleasant fingers that were indicative of a lifetime of writing. The warm jumper had been rolled back to reveal neatly muscled forearms and a battered old Rolex on a brown leather strap which was fraying a little at the edges.

Still he didn't look up. I began to suspect I really wasn't wanted here. Perhaps I should have sashayed up to him with eyelashes bristling – or whatever they did – Mary would never have stood for this. Then I wondered if I should just keep to my own character and slip discreetly away again and leave him to it. Just as I was about to move, an eye rolled sideways towards me.

"Thank you," he said while turning a page, "for waiting. You know how it is when you're pursuing the faintest thread of an idea. One small hesitation and it's gone. Are you having a nice time?"

"I am," I replied equally softly. "Thank you for letting me come."

He wrote a few rapid lines, indecipherable handwriting filling most of the page. Then he added, "I wasn't sure that you wanted to."

*Ah.*

There was a wealth of meaning in his statement. I knew then that I had not been forgiven; yesterday would not be forgotten. I took a breath.

And was beaten to it by his unexpected confession.

He paused over his notebook and said in a forceful rush, "I think you must have been already on your way out of the lounge last night and didn't hear but I told them in no uncertain terms that as far as I was concerned it had been a pleasure to have your company yesterday on the drive back to the hotel and if you ever needed to go anywhere else, I was sure you knew you only had to ask." A pause, then more gently, "And you do, you know."

"What?"

Suddenly he had turned his gaze upon me. "Only have to ask."

"Oh," I said, very meekly indeed. "Thank you."

Those startlingly grave eyes were fixed on me, pinning me there. It was deeply disconcerting and he knew it. A muscle plucked at the corner of his mouth. I was finally realising that he had tried to say this in the passage outside our rooms this morning. Only I'd been too busy being offended and then Mary and her sister had appeared.

He said, "It was very wrong of me to make you lie about how you got back yesterday. I only asked you to do it at all because I've had some absolutely awful research trips where every move has been dissected by strangers. It gets absolutely maddening sometimes. Particularly when I know at some point someone'll start hinting about having a walk-on part in the next book. It's far better if I avoid giving them any additional ammunition. But you do understand that I didn't mean to make things awkward for you, don't you?"

I did understand him. Something else struck me when his attention returned to the well before his feet. I said on a slightly accusatory note, "It was you who left *Jane Eyre* for me outside my bedroom door, wasn't it?"

I saw his eyelashes flicker. After a momentary hesitation, he acknowledged the truth with the briefest tilt of his head.

I was peculiarly shaken. He wouldn't have told me if I hadn't asked. And yet with him it was the discovery of one misinterpreted gesture of kindness after another. I suppose I should have anticipated this. After all what was it that had particularly coloured my greeting to him this morning? It was the idea that last night I'd done something that had so disrupted his peace that he'd felt it necessary to give me a firm set-down before our fellow guests.

Unfortunately, now I was having to learn just how insulting it was to him that I was requiring him to explain that his remarks had been nothing of the sort.

It made me say rather humbly, "Thank you so much. The book was a life-saver."

"It was? How so?"

I felt a fool as I conceded, "I don't sleep very well at the moment. Your gift of the book saved me from having to spend several hours of last night staring at the ceiling."

"Oh," he said, fiddling thoughtfully with an earlobe. "Is that a normal thing for you, or is it from your, um, brush with the bus?"

I gave him a faintly sheepish smile. "That bus has a lot to answer for."

"Concussion and insomnia as well? You must be absolutely shattered."

I laughed. "That," I said, "is something of an understatement."

It was more than insomnia; it was nightmares too. In the dreams that stalked my nights I was weaker than I was in daylight. Those men found me and their voices were darker, rougher than Adam's; and harsher even than they were in my waking memory of that scene in Lancaster. By night they might have come straight from a film script with every gesture a kaleidoscope of every silver-screen villain ever played. Their words were a blur of confusion. Perhaps a reference to the gallery, or Cirencester; and then the one absolute certainty of the reoccurring phrase: *Where is it?*

Each night for the past week I had woken to darkness, sweating and fighting the panic while every sluggish blink of my eyes plunged me back into that last horrible scene from the nightmare. Water, the constant roar of falling water. And last night it had been worse than ever because now I had a memory of the real landscape to add to the stage-set as I dreamed I was watching Rhys fall...

There was another confession I needed to make here. I said quickly, "That bus *does* have a lot to answer for. I'm sorry, Adam. About yesterday I mean, when I glared at you in the middle of saying goodbye outside the telephone box. I can't imagine what you must have thought." His pencil was hovering over the page once more but his attention was only vaguely fixed upon the great void dug into the ground beneath us and I knew he was waiting for me to continue. "No, correct that; I can imagine. And if you *had* meant to make things awkward for me last night I'd have deserved every moment of it. You didn't do anything wrong; you know that, don't you? And I really *am* sorry."

I heard him draw breath to respond but suddenly I was gabbling an explanation, straying into telling him precisely what I'd promised myself never to say. The silly thing was I was almost grateful to do it.

Before I'd even identified that this must be another miscalculation I was admitting grimly, "It's because of the concussion you see. I've been getting these impossible ideas ever since – suspicions I suppose you'd call them – which only require a person to say one little thing for me to plunge headlong into embarrassing myself in some new excruciating fashion. Then I wake up and realise that it's just my imagination again and it's awful. I truly am sorry. I hope you'll believe me when I say I'm trying very hard to contain it and I never meant to let it level any accusations at you—"

"Of course."

"—of all people."

He had turned to face me. He'd interrupted before I'd finished. Why had I said that last part? It made it seem – I don't know what it made him think – but in my head was the horrible, absurd idea that I really had betrayed something I shouldn't this time. I think in the midst of the past few minutes a very genuine appreciation of his core decency had crept in and I didn't think it would ever quite leave again. But I certainly hadn't intended him to know that.

There was also a fear that this sudden warmth of feeling was only part of that damned tendency to lurch from one extreme of feeling to the other. Yesterday my heart had performed at least five swoops in the course of one afternoon at Devil's Bridge. Today it was trying to climb to the giddy heights of pretending that I was growing to know him just that little bit better, before presumably making an even bigger plunge into an abyss.

The thought made me stare at him rather intently and ask, "Why *did* you intervene in the lounge last night? I mean thank you very much and so on for saving me from further embarrassment but it didn't seem to me that Mary was particularly worrying about me."

There was a brief formless silence while he seemed to be turning over his answer in his mind.

When he didn't rush to answer, I carefully directed this at the surrounding landscape, "In fact, I should have thought that by speaking, you were sacrificing rather more of your peace than your ongoing silence would have claimed of mine. You must have known that."

I couldn't help thinking of the way his interruption had blundered into the midst of all that mess of the waterfall. I was thinking that his interjection hadn't saved me from Mary, it had saved me from going up to bed with a head full of Rhys's death. I don't know what I would have done if his answer had confirmed it.

Only it didn't. Finally his silence was broken gruffly by, "It wasn't right to ask you to lie and then leave you stranded while our lively little friend and her sister entertained themselves at your expense. That was all. I'm very sorry for it."

He was very stern. Unexpectedly so. It drew my head round only to find myself being gifted a faltering but thoroughly heart-felt smile. It seemed designed to quash any impulse from me to embarrass us both by pursuing his motives further. I felt my breath go out in one long silent easing of tension. My answering grin was shy. Now he turned his attention back to his notebook. He seemed perfectly relaxed. That pencil was now occupied with blocking in a quick plan that showed the relationship between the well and the boundary walls and the gatehouse.

After some time of standing there watching him work, it made me ask instinctively but entirely inappropriately, "What did she die of?"

Unsurprisingly, it took him a moment to realise how I might have seized upon this as a suitable topic of conversation given what he'd lately said about the prying ways of strangers. I allowed my gaze to lead his to the engraving on the metal barrel of his pencil. He turned his hand slightly to see the marks better. Then, as surprise passed and he told me – an entirely ordinary, unimaginably cruel car accident – it occurred to me that he'd told me this part too once before. I really should have listened properly at Devil's Bridge.

"I'm so sorry," I said quickly.

He misunderstood, but it was probably for the best. "Thank you," he said. "But these things pass." A quick smile. A light dismissal. Then, in a tone that bordered on a rather hard kind of impatience, he said, "Actually, they don't pass, do they? That's such a conventional line we give and yet it falls so short of the truth it's almost offensive. And it's all because it feels somehow socially embarrassing to answer the question truthfully."

He told me curtly, "June died a little under nine years ago. I'll admit that the almost clinical process of bereavement followed its natural course in the months afterwards but that doesn't mean the sense of loss has diminished, does it? You understand don't you? *You* must have similar feelings yourself."

"I—"

For a brief, dangerous moment there, I thought his decisive tone was being directed from one widower to another; appealing to the understanding of a woman who had also lately had to grieve for a spouse, even the one she'd divorced. There was a faintly intimidating blaze behind his eyes. It was for a moment an utterly exhilarating glimpse of the deeper mind within. It was like he was daring himself to risk a little of himself and all he seemed to be seeking in return was a genuine piece of understanding.

He must have seen the debate running behind my own eyes. I saw impatience suppress something; I sensed withdrawal as though he was remembering a harsh lesson temporarily forgotten, presumably where he'd imagined I was the sort of person who would meet the awkward topic with equal honesty. Then he clarified, "I mean you must have grieved for the end of your marriage, naturally?"

It was a very close escape. Now I agreed hastily and slightly untruthfully while my heart performed one of its acrobatic leaps. "I did, but it passed quickly enough. Compared to your experience my divorce was just a nice simple legal process and a sense of time squandered. I can't imagine what you must have felt; or must still be feeling."

I wasn't surprised he found this a thoroughly unsatisfactory answer. I was disappointed myself. It was an answer that bore the air of understanding but was really just a means of ensuring that I didn't actually say anything at all.

It was the sense of ugliness about it which goaded me into formulating the clearer effort that followed. We weren't unalike, him and I. We both prized honesty.

I was looking across the vacant ruins of the castle without really seeing them as I confessed in a firmer voice, "Actually I *do* understand, Adam. When I divorced my husband, it was a shock and a challenge and it hurt terribly. It took no little time to adjust to the new life and find it better. But it *is* better. I don't have to lie when people ask me how I am ... Or at least in the main I don't." This was a wry concession. He too remembered how I'd brushed off his concern at Devil's Bridge.

"But you," I added. "I imagine you're in that awful place of still passionately caring for your wife and yet at the same time life has followed its own path in the years since and it is liveable and even pleasant and joyous. But you can't tell anyone that because either you're committing the terrible faux-pas of baring your feelings to the world, which is very much not the done thing; or you're in danger of casting yourself as cold and unfeeling because you're falling well short of that old romantic ideal of the tragic figure wasting away for the loss of a dear dead love."

My summary made him laugh. The almost defiant blaze in his eyes had faded abruptly. And with it my sense of this man's identity – looks, nature and physical presence – rearranged itself with a fierce little unexpected pang.

It almost felt like I had never really shared anything of

myself with him before. He must have noticed that I had still evaded giving any real glimpse of my own experiences and turned my answer to focus on my appreciation of what his must have been, but he didn't mind now.

He added easily, "And there's a third option too. There's the one where my widowhood is a point of fascination for people who have about as much tact as a bludgeon."

I smiled at him. "Meaning, I suppose, that this is yet another part of your life that is considered public property by people determined to forge a connection with the author in the hope of winning a walk-on part in your next book."

"Amongst other things, yes." It was said blandly.

Abruptly I knew that 'tact' really was the word. It was purely tact that made him pretend that these well wishers were only interested in his work. I'd witnessed Mary's – or perhaps it was fairer to say Mrs Alderton's – onslaught. I knew what they wanted from him. I knew how they might want to fix the memory of this very real tragedy as a signpost on the imaginary pathway to his heart. And all of a sudden I was very conscious of how I too had just spoken of the memory.

It made me wonder how on earth I could justify myself for prying like this, when I knew I'd probably only asked at all because those deep unyielding layers of distrust within me had told me I must probe a little deeper for my own safety's sake.

I made amends in the only way I could. I told him rather too urgently, "You can't control how people think of you, Adam, and you shouldn't try. In the end you'll find that the only solution left will be to change yourself to suit them. But you mustn't. In fact I firmly believe that just so long as your actions are generally harmless—"

"Harmless." Now an eyebrow was raised in a different kind of doubt. I think I was mistaking his experiences for my own. He was being lightly teasing.

I had to work to suppress the answering glimmer as I persevered, "Yes, harmless. You can laugh if you like since it is a pretty meek sort of ambition and it isn't glorious or noble. But when you know you aren't doing anything that could harm anyone, you also know that no one has a right to ask you to go against your nature purely to suit them. I can give you an example. There does seem to be an awful lot of expectation these days that as a divorcee I should rant and rage about my marriage just to ensure everyone knows how wronged I was. It's as if by being too lacklustre to hate that man now, it's tantamount to confessing that I must have been too wet, too feeble, too insipid to keep my husband entertained back then. Only I won't do it. I refuse to even when the price is my dignity. I can't tell you why, but believe me when I say this is a level I've set for myself and it matters that I keep it."

And here at last I admitted the darker depths of my divorce only I think he missed it because he was remarking gently, "Well in that case I should say you can safely relax. Those aren't the words of someone who sounds even remotely insipid, just so you know."

Reassurance was sudden and disorienting. Then he took a uneven little breath, rather like a sigh in reverse, and said in an altogether harder voice that showed, excruciatingly, that he hadn't missed a thing, "Look, this is going to sound a little odd after what you've just said about forging your own path but I've got to say it. Take it as a little piece of well-intended concern by way of tit-for-tat if you will. You gave me honest advice just now and now I'm going to give you mine: Don't you think you would make things a little easier on yourself if you just took things a little more quietly for a while? I mean, if you only said—"

"Oh I don't know, I—"

I didn't add the rest. The response was cheery enough but he must have read something of the change within in my face because he cut across me to say swiftly, "I'm sorry. You've got enough to deal with without adding the weighty opinions of another overbearing male to the mixture. Forget it. Shall we move on?"

And he folded away his notebook and then we were turning together to make our way towards the crumbling gatehouse.

For me, the sudden impulse to rebuild the defences came so sharply it was like a headache. I caught my mind trying to decipher if I'd been mistaken for thinking my own curiosity had been leading this conversation, when I had in fact been deliberately steered into betraying myself and my emotion. He couldn't have known this but it would be a novel kind of manipulation for me, being drawn into sharing my thoughts. Now I had to distract myself from re-running those few endlessly revealing lines about my husband, worrying about whether I'd slipped into calling Rhys by name instead of his usual innocuous title of 'husband'. I hadn't. I was sure I hadn't. And what had Adam learned after all? That I had experienced an unhappy marriage and an equally unhappy divorce? It was hardly dangerous.

The part of my mind that wasn't tainted with the memory of that Lancaster shop doorway searched desperately for something, anything to say that was vaguely normal. We were walking side by side across the grassy heart of the keep. I asked, "Are you always fascinated by creepy dark holes in the ground or is it just for this book?"

"Excuse me?" He looked a little startled for a moment. But then he emerged from the depths of wherever his own thoughts had taken him and said, "Sorry, you mean first the tin mine and now here? No, it's just for this book. Why do you ask?"

"It makes me worry for your hero, that's all." I negotiated the crumbling step from one level to the next. "It's going to be tough if he's got to brave an abandoned tin mine and now a bottomless well, poor man."

"Poor man indeed. Believe it or not, he's afraid of the dark."

I laughed. "How very heartless."

"Very."

He had stopped and turned towards me a little. I blinked and looked up at him, feeling a rush of self-consciousness as it struck me with a little pang that there was in his posture a faint stoop of the sort a person does when they like being near you. For a moment I floundered in that old panic of asking myself *why*. But then I pulled myself together.

I said briskly, "What about Nanteos Mansion?"

"Nanteos?"

"The Georgian Mansion. Do you know it?"

I saw him frown a little, considering, as he waited for me

to lead the way out of the keep. "I don't think so. Would you like to go there?"

"No, well yes, but ..." I tackled the ancient planks that spanned the moat. Nanteos Mansion was on the road to Cardigan, about four miles out of Aberystwyth. It was a grand old place with huge columns and a fabulously ostentatious stable yard. I'd visited it when they'd put on an exhibition featuring the famous Nanteos Cup. It was supposed to be the Holy Grail but to me it had just looked like a tatty wooden bowl. I'd had to peer through a crush of invalids wanting to touch it so it must have been the most unhygienic thing in the world, now that I came to think about it, with all those ill people hoping for a cure.

"Anyway," I said, having told him all that. "The cup isn't the only myth about the place ..."

I trailed off. Adam had only made some noise that implied polite interest. As a complete reversal of the moment before, the space between us felt like yards and his posture now indicated complete distraction. I paused, wavering between doubt and scolding myself for always being so blasted ready to discover I was unwanted.

"Sorry," said my companion. We were outside the boundary wall now and lingering on the limit of the scrubby woodland. "I am listening. I was just wondering where Jim and Mary have got to. The light's going and I don't want to turn this into a protracted night-time adventure." Adam glanced down and gave me a quick smile. "Let's wander towards the car in the hope that they're there. So go on, what other myths are there?"

Friendship triumphed smugly over dejection. Which typically gave me room to remember that I really had intended to remain aloof from my fellow guests. Ignoring my own wisdom, I walked beside him and told him, "Well there is another myth, one which is probably more relevant to what we were talking about before."

"Really?"

There was something in his tone. It made me cover my mouth with my hand and forget everything else. I laughed. "Heavens, I'm doing it too, aren't I? Interfering with your ideas. Next thing you know I'll be suggesting very seriously that I know a good character name beginning with the letter 'K'."

The last of the daylight was casting a rust-coloured gleam across his skin. "Go on," he prompted. I couldn't quite tell what he was feeling. Perhaps he thought I was committed now. Perhaps he thought he might as well get it over and done with and let me finish.

"The present house," I persevered doggedly, "only dates from the 1700s I think, but there was an earlier, much older building there originally. I heard a story once of a tunnel in the cellars – it was supposed to pass between the house and the coast in fact, so that the resident lord could make his escape in times of strife, or smuggle in his wine or whatever. I don't think I've ever heard of anyone actually using it, or even finding it. It would have to pass beneath at least one river after all. But that needn't mean that it doesn't exist. Or at least that there isn't proof enough for the purposes of your novel. The myth is pretty robust at any rate."

"Oh," said Adam in a rather more respectful tone. "I see.

And knowing my love of dark creepy holes, you thought I might be interested. Well, well."

Thinking of dark places, we were deep in the shadows of the overgrown path and his last remark was because we had a view of the cars and quite clearly neither Mary nor Jim were there.

Adam turned back to look up the path into the trees before dropping his gaze to me. He turned to face me fully. Those grey eyes were vivid in the shadows. His right hand lifted to rest warmly upon my arm. To him I think it was a natural culmination of the past minutes. To me it brought a conflict of nerves, both exquisite and bleak. "Look," he said seriously, "why don't you stay here while I go and retrieve them? There's no point wearing yourself out; and if any of them come you can stop them from wandering off again." His hold on me was an easy grip that hardened for a moment and then he let me go. It was a friendly gesture. Bracing. Designed to convey sympathy and nothing more. My never ceasing tiredness must have been showing on my face and in my limbs all the time, which was rather a depressing thought.

What he did next couldn't be so easily dismissed as ordinary understanding though. He lifted his other hand; and very briefly, very tenderly laid his palm against my cheek.

---

It was, needless to say, a shock. It was designed to be a deliberate and decisive conclusion to the disagreement that had driven me from the lounge last night. It was a warming assertion that he perceived the way my mind naturally shied towards reserve and it mattered that I had at least tried to overcome it. My skin burned.

I wasn't worrying any more that this man might frighten me with allusions to Rhys's death. Adam was clearly determined to confront the deeper emotional defences created by my husband during his life.

I came out of my shocked daze to find myself making a slow amble, alone, towards the car. It was sheltered here and very peaceful in the dimming daylight, and my cheek was still burning with the evidence of that single, powerfully disorientating touch. It was terrifyingly, exhilaratingly, beautifully near to being wanted. It was fully a minute later that I registered the danger.

There were no more cars now than there had been before but beyond the Rover, parked neatly between it and the rough farmer's run-about and looking just as innocent as it had in the hotel car park, was a black Morris Eight.

I stared at it. A moth, lured out of hibernation by the mild autumn, inspected my hand unnoticed before dancing away again. I could swear the Morris parked here before had been blue.

A noise behind made me whip round. This place was suddenly not very peaceful at all. There was no sign of anyone, not even a sheep. I made another slow turn, eyes scanning the road ahead and behind, and the path towards the castle, but there was still absolutely no one there.

Another rustle. This time it came from behind the low hedge that bounded the road and my nerve broke. Emphatically. Without so much as a pause to consider, I turned and bolted back into the dark woodland. There was Adam, walking quickly ahead of me. He was nearly at the limit of the trees. I called his name. I think he heard; he certainly paused, turning to look back along the path in surprise. I think for a brief unnerving moment he thought I was running to him. It certainly would have been a dramatic reaction to the peacefulness of his one simple gesture of some degree of care.

But distrust was like a sickness in me at the moment. To me he was a man I didn't know once again, who mustn't reach out to touch me because then the idea would rush back to the fore that I had to test it against my memory of the force of those two men at that Lancaster bus stop; and then I wouldn't be able to be near him at all.

So I stumbled to an unattractive stop in the gloom before him and hugged myself tightly, defensively, signifying my alienation even as I craved the comfort of being near him. I twisted anxiously to look back at the unmoving cars and the empty corridor of leafless trees and gasped out, "The car ... Adam, that car—"

I'd thought my panicked race along the path had been near the tipping point into frantic overflowing but it turned out it hadn't quite conveyed itself like that to him. And he wasn't as much of a mind reader as I'd thought because now he was covering his own reaction – which was rather cool – by saying firmly but very kindly, "The car is locked isn't it? I'm sorry; I should have given you the keys before. Here, take them and go and sit down. No, please don't let's argue about the car again – Mary won't be far, I won't be long and then we can get on our way."

He was already ushering me back down the path again. It was done in a way, it must be said, which certainly didn't include any kind of move to take hold of me. It was a relief of course but I think it was then that it struck me that to any normal man the transformation in my posture must be taken as rejection and this was a man whose past had been in many ways more isolating than mine. I ought to have said something, attempted to restore something of the impression I'd given before of my heartfelt willingness to try despite my apparent eccentricities, but I was already saying with a frightened note of stupidity, "But what if Jim comes?"

"What's wrong with Jim?" It was the mild enquiry of a man who had finally realised he was handling another strange outburst from a woman who had already given him one too many.

I whispered, "I don't like him."

"Well," said Adam reasonably, "I won't be long."

Those few words restored his worth to me with a jolt. They acknowledged it too. Helplessly, I found myself being piloted back into the open by the silent cluster of gleaming cars and felt the distance between us collapse when he pressed the warm metal of the keys into my hand.

"Adam—" I finally began in a surer voice but he'd gone. Long gone and I hadn't the grit to race after him again. Common sense told me how impossible it would be to explain myself convincingly enough to not seem insane. Suspicion nudged in at the corners and I began to wonder if he'd intended to leave me stranded like this all along...

I glared at the Morris again. There was a relentless pounding in my veins as I wavered by the red wing of Adam's car, undecided and uselessly defiant.

There was still, of course, no sign of anyone. After cautiously stalking down the length of the Rover as if it would mask my approach, I crept up to the small back window of the black Morris and peered in. It was empty. A fresh newspaper lay on the back seat and the receipts and the sweet tin had gone. The car was worse than it had been before: this time it was unidentifiable.

I stood back for a moment, thinking and casting yet another searching glance around, wondering where they might be. They couldn't be watching, surely? If they wanted me, this was their chance. A little calmer, I stepped round to the bonnet and put my hand on the dirt-spattered metal. It was cool. Now the shelf under the dashboard was occupied by a touring map of the area and a pebble decorated with a painted seaside scene of Aberystwyth.

Before I knew it, I was dropping between the two cars and forcing the nearside front tyre to surrender its cap. I jammed my fingernail into the air valve and was rewarded with a satisfying hiss as the tyre started to deflate. I let out about half the air before restoring the cap to its place. Then I quickly slipped to the back wheel and did the same.

To this day I don't know why I didn't let out all the air and leave them marooned. Perhaps my own natural sense of responsibility would only degrade so far, or perhaps I wasn't as ready for the fight as I'd thought. I suspect it was that I still couldn't remember that crucial licence plate and I couldn't bear to think of this turning out to be a family car and that there was a junior owner of that gaudy seaside souvenir. This time I drew out my sketchbook and made a note of the registration number in the back.

Defiance faded abruptly then and left me stranded in the silence. I couldn't leave and I barely dared wait. I had to climb into the back seat of Adam's car through the gap between the front seats because somehow I couldn't find the lock for the rear doors and it didn't occur to me to reach inside to work the handle. I can't describe how relieved I was when I heard a familiar female laugh coming down through the woodland.

Adam had found Mary but not Jim. He was teasing her, reminding her really without needing to scold, that she still had to keep his literary identity secret. She was clinging to his arm and saying hotly, "Who have I told so far? Who? You're just trying to pretend that you don't love the attention when the truth is you'd hate it if no one knew who you were because then you'd have nothing to complain about."

I saw his smile as I climbed out to meet them – now I used the interior handle for the back door. Adam's smile wasn't his fully warm one but it wasn't his reserved one either. He said, "Your sister knows. As does Jim ... and Kate ... Let's try to keep it to that, shall we?"

I joined their banter brightly. "Listen to him as he coaches you, Mary. Today has just been a very pleasant and impromptu sight-seeing trip." And then I had to suppress a grimace. My voice had that awfully giddy pitch of joviality that belongs to a person trying to make the pretence of friendliness when she knows she's already decided to be permanently a stranger to these people after today. I saw Adam conclude the same when I held out the keys. Intimacy was an experiment that had failed for me. That black Morris Eight by our side was a footnote to the day, bringing my attention sharply back to the real task. This afternoon had only been a dream, a fantasy of escape. I wouldn't be seeking distraction again.

In some ways it was reassuring to retreat once again into cold calculating reason. The eyes that waited to meet mine as Adam lifted the keys from my open hand were gravely enquiring but they slid away swiftly enough once I mustered the nerve to satisfy him that the last outburst was under control once more. Then he walked round and opened the other rear door for Mary, unlocked the passenger door in anticipation of Jim's return and dropped himself into the driver's seat. We waited for five minutes or more before finally Jim sauntered into view. He'd been walking in the lane somewhere. There was dirt on his trouser hems.

There was still no sign of the owners of the black Morris as at last we reversed out of our space. We turned in a gentle arc and then we were running, trundling in a happy chatter about the view, the setting and the adventure of visiting a real castle back towards the gated lane, and no one followed us on the main road south to Aberystwyth.

# Chapter 9

I learned that I had slept for the last part of the journey when I stirred to find myself crushed in the corner where the seat met the doorframe. It was intensely disorientating. Particularly when I surfaced into the darkness of early night with the disturbing fantasy that we were descending a hill into an entirely different town. Such as Cirencester.

We weren't. A blink or two later and I knew this was Aberystwyth and my neighbour, instead of scowling sinisterly at me through the gloom of the back seat, was only smiling a cheery greeting. I had a horrible feeling that I'd made a squeak as I'd jerked from dream into alarm and from there into wakefulness. In the seat in front of me, Adam's attention was naturally fixed upon the road ahead but my rousing drew Jim's attention. By the glare of amber street light I saw the gleam of that man's face – admittedly moulded into friendliness – as he turned in his seat to peer back at me. My handbag had slipped away from me towards the floor and I distracted myself by reaching to reclaim it.

As before, Adam left us as we neared the hotel for the sake of that telephone box. And true to form, Mary's joviality was forceful enough that it carried the rest of us along with her. Even me. I had her hand linked under my elbow. Her other hand was linked under Jim's arm. It was like walking in a cocoon of girlishness. Those men with that car would never dare to invade it. And then we were safely past the turn by the gaudily lit pier and climbing the steps into the hotel and Mary was being true to her word and dropping us all in favour of her sister.

I didn't sit with Jim of course. I found myself a spare seat beside young Samuel, who had apparently decided I was his friend after our brief interaction in the lounge last night. His rather significantly less noisy mother was now able to speak to me too, owing to the fact that I'd proved my value during that previous encounter by giving her son a small supply of blank pieces of card with the instruction to decorate them for suitable relatives. I always kept cards to hand in my sketch-book, ready for the inevitable crisis when I remembered at the last possible moment that I'd forgotten a valued friend's birthday. Samuel had, I was told in some detail, spent a very serious hour or two before lunch adorning these cards with incomprehensible illustrations of the many daredevil adventures he'd encountered on the seafront and then this afternoon he'd spent another serious hour buying sufficient stamps to send them.

The boy followed me into the lounge for drinks too. There I was allowed to discover that today's other excitement had featured the near-capture of a seagull on the rocks under the pier. His stalking skills, he conceded with due humility, were second to none.

"Here. You'd like one of these I should think." A full-grown man's voice took advantage of the boy's belated pause for breath. I looked up to discover Jim offering me a cup of coffee. He settled with his own on the low sofa that stood against the wall and then amiably set about wondering whether Samuel's hunting skills had yet extended to catching anything edible.

"Aren't children just darling!"

Mrs Alderton's exclamation was so abrupt that it was very nearly a shout. She was sitting with Mary on their customary spot near the wireless. She was dressed in something very expensive and black and very, very tight around the middle. It made her look brittle and all sharp edges. Rather like her voice. It effectively silenced the man and boy's debate on the techniques of crab hunting and, satisfied, Mrs Alderton announced grandly, "Mary here is fabulous with children. She's naturally very loving."

Beside me, Samuel's mother was nodding with that anxious agreement people adopt when they receive the slightly bewildering benevolence of a person of higher social class. Then it seemed to dawn on Mrs Alderton that the usual object of her exuberance had still not returned from his telephone call and there was something very odd about the turn of her expression. I didn't know what she thought she had learned from Mary about our day but it was making her faintly manic, like ambition had tasted a tantalising morsel of success. I could only hope Samuel's mother, who was just beginning to herd her unwilling boy towards the stairs and bed, was out of earshot before Mrs Alderton's shifting mood led her to muse instead upon the absence of the boy's father and how the noisy habits of a child might perhaps give one the smallest, tiniest hint about the condition of his parents' marriage. I presume she was wondering whether the lady was a divorcee but since none of us had thought to enquire, we couldn't really supply the answer.

I was just concluding that it was high time I retreated to my own bed when one of the Miss Bartlemans abruptly launched her own shout across the assembled room, "Excuse me, Miss Ward; I hope you won't mind my asking?"

It was the elder Miss Bartleman and this was all she said.

Her hands met nervously across her bosom. She blinked at me, wide-eyed and beaming and I wondered if she had been building up to this for a while. Her lipstick was a little lopsided and her attire was the exact opposite of Mrs Alderton's. It was blue with heavy lace collars and cuffs, and had absolutely no corners at all. I smiled encouragingly and after a while she added in that same carrying muddle, "I gathered from something Miss James – Eh? Very well dear, we'll make it Mary if you insist – said that you paint beautifully and I wondered ... Well, if perhaps you might ...? If it isn't too much trouble, that is."

It took me a while longer to extract the request from her but eventually I managed by degrees to decipher that she wanted me to make a card for some family friend whose birthday she had forgotten. She had seen me give the card blanks to Samuel and hoped that if I had any left, I might save her the embarrassment of being late. Her manner of asking made it all seem very complicated but I just about understood that some friends would be leaving on the early train in the morning, before any shops were open, and those good people would be able to post the card when they changed at Birmingham for it to arrive on time the next day. "... Because it could take more than a day for something to go by post out of Aberystwyth and her birthday is the day after tomorrow. I'm frightened we'll miss it ... Do you really think that you might be able to help?"

"What's that? A birthday?" Mrs Alderton's odd hysteria burst out of her again. "Mary, you remember the one I—?"

"Of course I can help." This was one of those silly moments when two people speak together; it was just unfortunate that it had to be her. I reached under my seat for my bag while the Miss Bartlemans launched into a seamless string of self-congratulatory compliments to one another on the success of their plan.

They were still going strong when I reached in and fumbled absently through the collection of purse, diary and other bits and pieces that were collected there. I was already thinking through my usual designs and trying to decide which their friend might like, so it took a while to register the fact that so far my probing fingers had not closed upon the sturdy cover of my sketchbook. Then impatience made my mind actually concentrate on the job at hand and I set the bag down on the neighbouring seat to carefully run my hand over the assorted rubble within. Pencils, brushes, diary, small flask, scraps of paper, my purse, revolting lipstick that I never used, nice lipstick that I did use and a hat pin all mingled chaotically within but it was no use. The sketchbook was not among them.

With a sick feeling that would have seemed a gross over-reaction to any non-artist, I cast my mind back to the castle and pictured myself packing my brushes away. I could clearly recall testing that the paint was dry before putting the book in my bag and moving to join Adam. I know I of all people couldn't claim perfect recall but surely even I couldn't be mistaken about *that*. I wondered then if it could have fallen out in the car while I slept but given that the bag's fastening was a heavy clasp and this had been securely closed, it seemed highly unlikely. And thankfully so, because I had no desire to bother Adam yet again.

My heart began to beat.

I didn't even quite understand why yet but that heavy pulse grew to a crescendo as I slowly reclosed the fastening. And then, suddenly and with a swiftness that surprised even me, I was on my feet and standing in the heart of the room.

"Good gracious!" The younger Miss Bartleman gave an exaggerated start. Her dining wear was a deep brown silk that looked like it had been reworked from an Edwardian gown. "Whatever is the matter, dear?"

I stood there at the heart of the fading carpet, eyes scouring one glowing face after another as they in turn examined me. My lips moved to tell the nearest old woman, "My sketchbook's been stolen."

She didn't actually hear me properly the first time. She said, "Pardon?"

Her older sister repeated my words. The younger said again, "Pardon?" and finally the elder Miss Bartleman snapped crossly, "Her *book*, you silly woman. It's gone."

144

"It's gone?" The youngest Miss Bartleman echoed at last. "Oh dear. That *is* a shame." She reached out to pat my hand where it gripped my bag, found it cold and unresponsive and decided not to bother. "Well, never mind dear, I'm sure you can get a new one. And don't worry about the card, we'll just have to be a day or two late that's all." She beamed complacently before casting a sweeping nod around the room and absorbing the presumed general approval for a practical response.

I couldn't tell her that I didn't give a fig for her card. I was clutching the bag to my chest as if it were a shield and with an effort I reclaimed my seat to perch on the very edge. I felt utterly claustrophobic. The room was full of people. The void of the archway into the dining room was dark and empty. The places were set in there ready for tomorrow and just discernible in the gloom. My eyes were running blankly over every corner and as ever finding no tangible proof, while my mind searched for any other possible explanation and discovered only fear.

They were in the hotel.

Memory was flooding my mind with those old sinister, searching, grasping words: *Where is it?*

But this wasn't the stuff of my dreams now; this was real. And yet, when precisely were they supposed to have slipped in to make their spot of thievery? While I was dining and the bag was on my chair? Or just now while I had been talking to Samuel and the bag was nestling behind my feet? And was I now to believe that all along they'd simply wanted my *sketchbook?* It didn't make any sense.

"Are you sure? *Quite* sure it's gone? Perhaps you left it somewhere?" Jim was staring at me with an odd expression on his face, which may have been a peculiar reflection of mine.

"No ... No, I couldn't have," I assured him breathlessly, only to find that my racing blood turned cold.

All of a sudden I was standing in the centre of the floor again. I knew exactly why Jim might be keen to suggest I'd left it somewhere. I had been right about his involvement after all – he had been asking to see my sketchbook for days and at long last my careless slumber in the car had offered him the perfect chance.

I was standing there, icy, raging with hands as fists by my sides and looking rather absurd. My handbag was hanging hard from its strap against my thigh. "You took it," I hissed. I could see for myself that he hadn't got the sketchbook beside him now. That smart jacket wouldn't hide that sort of bulk in its pockets. But I could recall his absence after dinner and I was perfectly capable of calculating all the opportunities he must have had for secreting it away for perusal later.

Jim Bristol was absolutely dumbfounded and he told me so.

I jerked my head. "You heard what I said," I snapped, reaching and failing for any kind of calm. "Give it back."

He stirred uncomfortably, sitting straighter on his chair and eyes working right and left. An excellent display of embarrassed discomfort, it seemed to me. A disbelieving smile came and went on that supple mouth and finally he settled on giving a little nervous laugh. "Excuse me?"

"I want it back. Now."

That perfect bewilderment faltered. Now I saw the grit beneath. "I haven't taken your sketchbook. I haven't seen it; in fact I don't even know what it looks like. The closest I've come to it was today when you were sitting painting on that wall. You *know* that." He sounded both injured and increasingly exasperated, and it was brilliantly done. What was worse was that what he said was perfectly true.

A shocked hush possessed the room and, standing there on the dismal island of the lounge carpet, I felt the ludicrousness of my stance. My conviction didn't slip but my sense of fight did. I knew that somewhere beyond the row that housed the Miss Bartlemans, Mrs Alderton was smirking. Low on his settee against the wall, Jim added sternly, "What on earth should I want with your notebook anyway?"

"It's a sketchbook."

My retort amused him for a fleeting second. "Very well, Miss Ward. What should I want with this sketchbook?"

"Perhaps you left it somewhere," suggested Mrs Alderton helpfully. "Perhaps it's in the car; or on the side of a mountain? You *did* go on this trip to the castle today, didn't you?"

She had the most extraordinary way of putting it so that she sounded like she was scoring a point off my participation in Adam and Mary's day. I shook my head, not in denial but in order to retain my grip upon the one fact I could prove.

"I didn't leave it anywhere," I repeated weakly. I had to put my bag down before I dropped it. There was a low coffee table somewhere nearby. It stood at the end of the row that housed the Miss Bartlemans. I put out my hand in its general direction. A very small part of my mind noticed that Mary was kind enough to reach past the old ladies to intercept the bag before it fell with a clatter. I was already saying with weakening force, "I had it earlier, I know I did. Jim, *please* – I don't know why they think they want it but that doesn't matter; it really doesn't. Just give it back to me. Please."

I saw a deeper kind of assessment strike his face. Colder, somehow more real. "But I—" Then it was swept away and his gaze flicked with relief over my shoulder. "Ah, here he is."

My heart changed rhythm so abruptly it hurt. Someone had stepped into the room from the bright stairwell behind me. I jerked round. Then the information penetrated that it was Adam and Adam alone and the release made my brain ache with a different kind of tension. Suddenly I knew this was not going to work. I'd made a mistake. I don't know in what deluded world I had expected any good to come from confrontation. It never had in the past. And now it was too late to stop it.

Jim's voice was already adding patiently from behind, "Perhaps *he* can tell you if you left it in the car."

Adam stopped dead about a stride away from me. He'd been about to pass me on the way to quietly claiming his usual chair. I saw the tension in the room hit him as he realised he'd walked into something unpleasant. His brows lifted as his gaze ran from me to Jim and back again to my pale and agitated face. "If she left what in my car?" His look was a question for me. I could feel the stain of my recent fury marking my face, only it was fading now to something like a sense of impending doom. On his face was surprise, discomfort and a slow dawning of faintly irritated resignation.

I said in a hushed undertone just for him, "I wish you hadn't come—"

"Her sketchbook." This was Mrs Alderton. "She's accusing poor Mr Bristol here of stealing it, but if you'll just tell us that she's left it in the car, we can all go back to enjoying what remains of our evening. Have you eaten, by the way?"

Adam's eyes didn't leave my face as he answered to say that he'd eaten fish and chips by the harbour. There was no warmth in his manner and I knew why. For the second time in two days he was about to find himself being required to abandon his hopes of a peaceful evening for the sake of saving mine, and in front of people who were delighted to scrutinise his every step.

Sudden revulsion that had nothing to do with the loss of my sketchbook made me sharply take a step away. The coffee table met the backs of my calves and I abruptly sat down. It hurt but at least we didn't need to stand united before this crowd.

He hadn't noticed my retreat. For him nothing had changed. Everyone was still staring at him, expecting him to somehow wade in and resolve this as if he were my keeper. I rivalled him for irritation. This shamed me too. Propping myself up with one hand fiercely gripping the edge of the table I twisted awkwardly about to snap angrily at the room, "Don't involve him. He hasn't got a part in this."

Nobody listened. They were still waiting for Adam. I

thought he spoke with remarkable self-possession. "No, I didn't see anything in my car?"

It was meant as a question for me. I looked up at him. I had to calm my growing outrage and tell him in a stiff little voice, "Jim's taken it. I know he has. But that doesn't mean that you should—"

He didn't listen, or rather he did listen but not to the right bit. I don't think my hints that he should distance himself from me were being taken in quite the right way. I think it was with a certain degree of resentment – and perhaps decency since technically Adam was at least going through the motions of defending me – that he turned his attention to the low settee beyond me. He asked Jim, "Is this true? Have you?"

I don't think Jim realised this battle was already won. Jim hadn't seen as I had, painfully, the moment that comprehension worked to its natural conclusion in the mind behind Adam's eyes. I'd known this was how it would end from the very moment that Adam stepped into the room but still defeat hit hard. This was the consequence of daring to admit my tendency towards paranoia. I'd told him that I was suffering from imaginary alarms and in the next breath murmured something about distrusting Jim; and promptly gifted Adam the perfect reason to disbelieve everything I said.

But Jim didn't know any of that and the question made Jim finally lose his temper. He gave an exasperated cry. "*Of course* I haven't got her book! What kind of ludicrous idea is that?"

I too lost my temper then. The impotence of it all – powerless to bully him into a confession, powerless to take back the accusation now, powerless to make them all leave Adam alone – it all made me abandon what good sense I might have once had. I twisted upon the tabletop and rounded on Jim and my voice cracked sharply as I snarled, "You know full well how I got that idea, Mr Jim Bristol. Even if you have convinced everyone else that your story is true, you'll never get *me*. I'll give you some advice if I may – if you're going to follow someone, I'd suggest that you don't wear such a conspic-uous coat!"

Jim gaped. In fact the whole room gaped. He paled a little before blinking mutely and developing a very unattractive hint of red. His hands worked across the panels of that expen-sive burgundy jacket for a moment and my accusation seemed to have robbed him of all his poise. I was breathing hard. I shouldn't have said it. I knew I shouldn't have said it. Then a woman's voice rose gently from the floor beyond my little table.

"Um, Katie?"

It took my body a few seconds to trace an awkward twist round further to find my bag opened on the floor and my possessions spread around for all to see. Mary was kneeling there, barely inches away from my table, perhaps a yard more from her sister's seat and no more than two yards from Jim's. A stack of receipts stood neatly to one side and a pile of brushes and pencils lay in her lap. And reaching over Mary's shoulder was Mrs Alderton's hand. Clasped within those fingers and looking perfectly innocent as she lifted it from the pile, was a very tatty leather-bound notebook. My sketch-book.

Disbelief hit me in a punch to the body. The triumph in Mrs Alderton's face was palpably different from the one that had gone before but it was nothing to the sudden rush of doubt within.

The cruelty of it robbed me of my breath. It was harsh to go from drawing rapid gasps to absolute stillness. I sat like a statue. A rigid, beaten statue, fingers gripping the edge of the tabletop.

Mary was carefully packing my things away. Then, without meeting my eyes, she handed me both the book and the bag.

"There," said Mrs Alderton, settling back in her chair and dusting off her hands with very evident satisfaction. "Mystery solved. Case closed. It was never missing at all. Perhaps now the lady can put aside her unnecessary histrionics and leave perfectly innocent guests to enjoy their coffee in peace?"

I sagged. But every muscle bolted when a hand suddenly met and gripped my elbow and drew me to my feet.

There was a laden hush as all eyes stared at me. Now I think I was expected to say something. I wet my lips. I might have given way to the maniacal laughter that waited in the wings but that, with an odd little sigh, Adam confirmed his responsibility for me in the eyes of everyone in that room, and steered me by the arm to the door and out into the foyer. He piloted me like I was a feeble wreck on the verge of collapse.

I wasn't on the verge of collapse. I revived when we reached the foot of the stairs. I snatched my elbow from his grip and snapped icily, "I can escort myself to my room, thank you very much."

He was still with me when we reached my bedroom door.

I think he meant to take my key from me when I fumbled for the lock but I shook his hand away that time too and snarled, "And I can manage to unlock my own door."

He didn't leave. Instead he leaned a shoulder against the wall by the doorframe and quietly picked up my handbag and held it for me when my clumsy fingers dropped it. I resisted the urge to ask him whether he too wished to raid its depths for my sketchbook.

There was a creak of hinges as my hand pushed open the bedroom door. I glanced at him then. He was leaning there, watching my face and trying not to smile at my childishness. It came as a shock because I had been bracing to meet some sort of reprimand for ruining his trip in pretty much every way I could. Admittedly, he'd been trying to look severe I think. Only instead here was a little slip into the kind of understanding that had formed between us before. I'd been about to concede a sheepish little smile myself but the thought stopped it dead. I couldn't cope with this.

He saw the emotional hatches batten down. The price of my decision was that it made him suddenly consider whether the incident had been more serious than he had thought. That faint curve of his lips hardened. His chin lifted defiantly and he spoke curtly as he told me, "You've had quite a time, haven't you? First me, and now Jim. Are you going to accuse all the guests in turn do you think?"

"My sketchbook *was* missing."

"So does that make it Mary's turn next?"

With a little flinch because it was probably the truth, I snatched my bag from his hand and stepped quickly into my room. I turned, meaning to swiftly shut the door but something curbed my flight. I couldn't quite bring myself to look at him so I fixed my gaze resolutely on the faded burgundy carpet by his feet. Long use had very nearly turned it green. "No," I said stiffly. "I think I've embarrassed myself quite enough in front of strangers, thank you."

"Kate …"

He didn't like to be numbered amongst the strangers. The murmur of my name was a barrage of reasonableness when it would have been easier if he had been sharp. It jerked my head up but I still couldn't look at him. The edge of the open door was cool against the palm of my hand. I touched my forehead to it, briefly, for a matter of seconds and no more.

Finally I drew enough strength from it to say uselessly, "I still don't trust Jim."

"Nor me, by all accounts," remarked Adam lightly, straightening from his lean against the doorframe. "And yet, when have you ever been right?"

This, then, was the real reproof. He stood there in the corridor before me. He wasn't barring the door but he was certainly willing me to meet his gaze. I did and I felt my heart lurch again as I fully realised my loneliness. Amusement and anger had both gone from his eyes to be replaced by something altogether more gentle.

I had been fearing this. A different kind of agony nudged its way into the scene. There was that impulse to tell him everything. There was more than a hint here that he thought I should. Again I had to wrestle with the knowledge that any concession on my part would soon be followed by layer upon layer of blame for not saying the sort of truths he wanted to hear.

I couldn't bear it, this constant working upon my self-belief; not by him. The only hope was to sever this connection with all of them. With a very great effort, survival triumphed over every other normal civilised feeling and I succeeded in keeping my voice steady as I managed a very conservative, "I'm sorry."

It wasn't remotely what he wanted from me. For the first time I sensed the steel in him. "Kate, please. I have to say—"

I had to interrupt him. I said exhaustedly, with finality, "Goodnight, Adam."

It checked him. He saw my desolation, my decision. He bit off whatever fresh claim he had been about to make upon either my conscience or my self-respect and with an effort limited himself to giving an understanding nod. "Goodnight," he said. I saw him step backwards from my door, giving me leave to close it. Then he said, "Sweet dreams." And he meant it.

I shut the door gently. I shut out the day and him, and permanently ended my association with both, I thought. But I should have known that this latest disaster hadn't finished its work on me yet.

# Chapter 10

What sleep I got that night was disturbed and even more fitful than normal to the point that at about one o'clock in the morning I actually developed the fevered conviction that my coffee had been drugged. I was not drugged, of course, it was just the effects of a stimulant on an already overwrought mind but all the same, the much revisited flight across tumbling rivers was wild and terrifying and long before sunrise I woke with a kick, convinced that he had been in my room. Not Rhys or Jim or Adam or those two unnamed ever-present dangers, but someone whose appearance in my dreams drew on far older stresses, from the days of my marriage. The man was Gregory; Rhys's old friend and patron.

Sweating, sickened, I slipped out of bed towards the window and the salvation of fresher air. Once there, my breath began to come a little easier, my stomach churned a little less. Someone was snoring next door. There was a creak of bedsprings as they turned over and then peace once more while I watched pigeons roosting on the bizarrely truncated ladder that was bolted to the wall beside me.

Breakfast, when at long last it came, was about as near to

tranquil isolation as I could have wished. I was early – it was before eight o'clock – and I only had to share the room with the serving girl and the Miss Bartlemans who were racing to make their meeting with their friends. I was calm, collected, detached. Today the two sisters occupied themselves by discussing the sea fret that had rolled in with the tide and it was only as I was contemplating the dregs of my last cup of tea that I noticed the other discussion unfolding in the distance.

Mrs Alderton was delivering a fresh lecture. The door into the foyer was wide open so it was easy to catch her tone even if not all the words. From her pitch it was possible to discern the moment that a male guest joined them at the foot of the stairs and from the lack of enthusiasm establish that he wasn't the particular male Mrs Alderton wanted.

It was my cue to make my exit. I began gathering my things but just as I was finishing that last sip of tea in readiness, I was startled into full consciousness by a cross whisper from one elderly Miss Bartleman to the other:

"Well I don't care one jot whether she's married or divorced or whatever. Even after that upset last night, she still painted us the most exquisite little card."

"It had heather on it," remarked her sister.

"And mountains. And a dear little sheep."

That was the moment that I realised Mrs Alderton was now talking about me. Or, to be specific, her discovery of my status as a divorcee.

It must be said that I didn't really mind. If I had cared to keep my marital status secret, I would hardly have told Mary. And after all, even discounting last night's scene, I had given

Mrs Alderton plenty of legitimate reasons to dislike me in the long two days of my stay and this discovery probably sealed it. I even managed to not mind that Mrs Alderton was now treating this news as her own private discovery. She was not the first woman of my acquaintance to distrust divorcees in general. In men, the lapse was deemed barely forgivable. In women, predictably, our uncertain social standing was a signpost for moral corruption.

I rose to my feet as Jim enquired after the arrival of the day's papers. His light question to the lady at reception was drowned out by Mrs Alderton's idea of a brittle whisper: "I do think, Mary, after all the turmoil of our recent war it has become all the more vital that we rebuild stronger family values. One's vows are made to be held, not just abandoned at the drop of a hat. And divorcees always lie about it too, and try to cover it up." Then she added a shade regally, "Mr Bristol, the gentlemen's newspapers are waiting in the dining room. They always are."

There they were; a stack of them lying beside the serving dish that contained the kedgeree.

Outside the door, Mrs Alderton was adding on a little note of outrage, "That woman has been masquerading as a nobody when all the time she's been a Mrs Somebody, divorcee. Why *should* she get away with it?"

Oddly enough I felt for her. I could see now that this discovery had been the cause of her triumphant agitation last night. Previously she must have only idly considered me a rival in the supposed race for the gentleman's affections. Mary must have told her over dinner and for a moment Mrs Alderton had probably thought my handicap was enough to count the race won before it had even begun. Then I'd begun flinging accusations about and for the second night running Adam had come to my aid. I wondered if my fitness as a rival had festered overnight, so that she now had visions of a greater plot; one where I used my agitated state and the feminine wiles of an experienced schemer to seduce the great author as he left me at my bedroom door.

As I say: poor woman. I suppose she saw it as her duty to expose me now.

I'd left my book on the table and had to go back for it. The Miss Bartlemans said something to me but I was too busy noticing the way Mrs Alderton's voice altered as she spoke again. I didn't need to hear mention of his name to know who she was speaking to now. She had after all been waiting for him. Mrs Alderton said rather more loudly, "It's a disturbing way to carry on, don't you think, Mr Hitchen?"

His footsteps stopped as she snared him. He'd been nearly at the dining room door. After the tightest of silences, I heard him say what I'd been forcing myself to keep from doing. I believe I'd even engineered the delays such as finishing my tea, forgetting my book and a hundred and one other little things just so that I absolutely could not go out there and make the obvious retort. I didn't need to be responsible for any more scenes.

Adam wasn't making a scene. He was saying calmly, "Actually, she told me as much on the first day. So to be honest she's not really the best example to support your cause."

I really wished he hadn't said that. It was kind of him, of course, and honest but he ought to have politely agreed and kept walking. Instead he provoked Mrs Alderton into saying shrilly, "How interesting that she told you, Mr Hitchen. What else did she tell you?"

Someone moved out there. There was a scuff of shoes upon polished marble; perhaps as Adam turned to face her. More distantly, a child's voice prompted an answering greeting from a startlingly large number of adults. It made me dive across the gap into the unlit lounge. I didn't think the group loitering in the foyer saw me but the Miss Bartlemans watched me go, wide eyed and goggling. Then there seemed to be a general rush for the dining room door. I waited for Adam to prove that he was moving with the crowd and conveniently leave the way clear for me to make my discreet exit through the door of the lounge into the space beneath the stairs but he didn't.

He stayed to listen while Mrs Alderton confided forcibly, "I notice she has no children. I shouldn't like to wonder if that was why he left her. Perhaps that's why she's been clucking over the little boy here. Perhaps she feels that fawning over other people's children is her last chance of motherhood, poor dear. What do you say to that, Mr Hitchen?" The demand was an echo of her mania last night. Presumably it betrayed rather more about her preoccupations than it did mine. I'd only been pleasant to Samuel because it was easy to be. For her, this point about parenthood mattered.

"Alice," remarked Mary quietly, "they got divorced because he wasn't very nice. The idea of having children probably didn't suit him."

Mary was right; the idea hadn't suited Rhys. By rights there ought to have been a string of illegitimate children scattered up and down the country in his wake, but there wasn't a single one. I don't mean to imply he was the sort of beast that pushed women into having abortions or anything horrific like that. It was just that Rhys would have found a child a tedious distraction and I think nature must have believed it too.

Mrs Alderton didn't even falter. She retorted, "Well Mary, since you know so much; did she happen to tell you why she's here? Because it can't be for a holiday. No self-respecting single woman would choose to travel alone as she has, without a friend or organised tour group or anything. And as if her behaviour last night to poor Mr Bristol wasn't odd enough—" I heard the catch in her voice. It was followed by the soft click-click of heels across the marble floor as she closed the space between herself and her target. Her next words took on a confidential hush that made the room around me infinitely darker. "Seeing how quickly she attached herself to you, Mr Hitchen, *did* ring a few alarm bells. After all, the rest of us manage to retain a certain degree of dignity in the company of a celebrated author, particularly when that person is the wonderful A. E. Woolfe ..."

*Oh no.*

No.

I saw the stillness that consumed the dining room. I saw the way the Miss Bartlemans exchanged raised eyebrows. Suddenly I was out of the clutter of dark furniture in a dark lounge and in that space under the stairs. I believe I intended to make a scene after all. I knew what this would mean to him. And it was being done in my name. But it was too late to salvage this. They had already moved. Mary, Mrs Alderton and Adam had already passed into the dining room and Mary's shocked reproof was all that met me out there. "*Alice!* It was supposed to be a *secret*."

There were still a few people lingering in the foyer but I didn't acknowledge them as I slid along the length of the stairwell. I barely even saw them. In the dining room, Mrs Alderton was already gabbling out her excuses, "It was? Oh yes, oh dear; I forgot we were in the special position of being guardians of your identity, Mr Hitchen." Her voice dropped to a strategically carrying whisper, "But I'm quite sure that you can depend on everyone here to be discreet ..." And then she sought to distract him from her error by lurching deeper into her attack on me.

She confided desperately, "*That* woman ... Not only has she failed to make clear her real position amongst us but I have to tell you I believe she has actually gone to some lengths to conceal it."

I heard the creak as someone, presumably Adam, sat down, then the scrape as two further chairs were drawn out.

Mrs Alderton lectured breathlessly, "In fact, don't you think – Mary, you said something like this last night—"

Mary wouldn't help her. "No, I didn't."

"Yes, you did. You said it wouldn't be a stretch to believe she's here, travelling in this odd way, because this is his town and she intends to attempt a *reconciliation*."

If at any moment I had truly been tempted to find something in this insane attack funny, I might have laughed at that – if she had only known my husband.

"I doubt that." This was from Adam. At last he spoke. It was dry and deliberate and seemingly not at all angry.

I must have put my hand onto the heavy newel post at the foot of the stairs. I stared, fascinated, at the way my fingers were trembling. They felt like something removed from me. In fact they had absolutely no feeling at all. Or rather, too much. I could feel the warmth and the peculiar contradiction of the cold as painted wood met bloodless fingers.

"Why?" Curiosity piqued Mrs Alderton's voice. I couldn't see much of the dining room. The open door obscured most of the tables. But I could tell she didn't like being corrected. She also had an air of puzzlement at finding herself lurching into open scandal mongering when she had only ever meant to indulge in a thoroughly enjoyable moan. It was almost as if she had anticipated that her attack would goad Adam into running away, leaving her with nothing but the delicious agony of further reasons to worry about my hold on him. Only here he still was, calmly contradicting her. She covered her surprise by asking silkily, "Did she tell you that too? It certainly would explain her unusual behaviour if he's rejected her, don't you think? Jealousy can take a woman like that."

"No."

"Oh, but ..."

There was a clatter of plates behind. The serving girl bustled out of the kitchen door that stood at the furthest point of the stairwell and then abruptly turned about and banged back in again. She hadn't cared who I was. By contrast, the dining room seemed oddly stiff as if the Miss Bartlemans were frantically trying to indicate that I might still be listening. They needn't have bothered though. No one spoke my name but I was absolutely certain that Adam knew I was out here.

And it was in spite of that knowledge, or possibly because of it, that I then heard him say:

"Mrs Alderton. *If* she's been a touch emotional, I believe it has been with very good reason."

I'd been mistaken when I'd thought his calm voice matched his mood. He was very angry indeed. The lady saw it too. Her reply was faintly tremulous. "It has?"

"Yes. It has."

A pause.

Then he added, "Because Rhys Williams killed himself two weeks ago, almost to the day."

I stepped out of the lee of the stairs in a daze. There were people out there, Jim amongst them, I think, but I moved through them swiftly as I made for the street outside.

If I had thought the public revelation of Adam's identity was cruel, I don't believe anything could have prepared me for the revelation that this man had known the secret of my visit here all along. It wasn't the fact he had known; that at least was an eventuality I had prepared for. But now I had to realise that all the time he had been talking cheerful nothings at Devil's Bridge and pointing out harmless distractions like sleeping owls, he had known the grim purpose of my visit there. And he had done nothing with it except act with quiet kindness in the face of my endless distrust and buy my lunch.

Now I had to learn that he was the sort of man who would do all that – spend two days proving the harmlessness of his friendship – only to deliberately betray it suddenly and crudely like this; and I had to wonder what it should mean.

# Chapter 11

There was his name in bold type, or rather A. E. Woolfe's, on the shelves of the town's most established bookshop. I'd spent the last three hours in a tearoom frittering away a little more of my precious reserves. At long last and several cups of tea later, eleven o'clock had drawn near and I couldn't put off the dash through the dirty streets to the police station any longer. Only I didn't entirely dash. I cursed the fact that in my haste to exit the hotel I'd stepped out into the cold damp blind of a Saturday morning sea fret without stopping to collect my coat. And then I took a little detour into this shop.

The latest of Adam's books was here, as anyone might have guessed. It was in its second edition already and by virtue of the way these paperbacks always list the author's other works, it proved that the copy that Mary had been tossing around the downstairs rooms at the hotel was his first. This book and the middle one which was promoted on the last page showed that Mr A. E. Woolfe had thoroughly immersed himself in the genre of gritty crime fiction. They also proved he had been telling the truth when he'd told me that he'd been unable to think of anywhere else but home all the time he'd been away at war. The plots of both his second and third books unfolded in his native high Cotswolds.

It was hard to have the evidence before my eyes, robust and indisputable, that Adam knew Cirencester and knew me. It put a different texture on his attempts to befriend me over the past few days. Rougher and more calculated to confuse.

In some ways, though, it was liberating because it reminded me that this was not a repetition of the days of my marriage. Back then, there had been an endless feeling that I should at least attempt to understand what my husband wanted from me and an ever increasing wretchedness for never quite getting it right. But I was married then. It really had mattered to me that I tried.

Now, I reminded myself, I was not that same woman and this was not a petty crisis of confidence in an unhappy life. This was something hard and complicated and I didn't have to try for these people or play that endlessly futile guessing game of trying to buy peace by moulding myself into whatever they wanted me to be. After all, my marriage had also taught me how that game ended.

Continuing the theme of rough people connected to a place I desperately wanted to avoid, there was neither sight nor sound of those two men or their car on the last dripping stretch of shopping street before I reached the dark fortress of the police station. I was shown into an interview room, one of those dank badly lit holes with a table bolted to the floor and a set of thoroughly battered chairs that looked as though they doubled as leverage when a suspect was holding back the last grudging speck of evidence.

"Sit down. Wait here." The desk-sergeant's dismal weariness hadn't improved with the arrival of the weekend.

I sat. I waited. I had to suppress the urge to fiddle with my handbag. It was impossible not to recall that my recent experiences involving policemen had not exactly been positive. It didn't help either that the interview room was a blank and inhospitable box with a stain on the floor in the corner. Imagination cheerfully decided it was blood.

The door opened and a light switched on, rendering the room merely yellow and tatty in the manner of a converted storeroom. I could see holes on the wall where shelves might have hung. The chairs, I could now tell, were just grammar school rejects bought by a hardworking service run on a limited budget.

Further defying expectations, my policeman was not built like the caricature of a Welsh hill-man; short and all shoulders with a curly mop on top. Instead, Inspector Griffiths was so English as to be almost embarrassing. He was wiry with a sallow complexion beneath fair hair just beginning to turn grey, and eyes slightly creased around the edges as if he'd spent a lifetime squinting after cricket balls. The only thing more fearsome about him than his manner was his moustache, which was thick and well combed, and covered his upper lip completely. It was suddenly easier to comprehend the depression that afflicted the desk sergeant.

The inspector slid into the seat opposite. "Well, Mrs Williams." His voice was clipped and his eyes were set deeply beneath fine eyebrows that went up and down when he spoke. He set an evidence box down on the table before me. It had the name Rhys Williams written on it, above the name Dafydd Evans which was crossed out, and the names Alun and Kyffin Morgan below that. Inside were a few ragged and moss-smeared clothes, one sock and a broken Olympus camera.

Inspector Griffiths lifted out the latter and placed it on the table so that he could rummage deeper in the box. The camera was old, good in its day but battered now and dirtied, with a nasty looking split in the casing at the back. The neat lettering that indicated its maker – Olympus – gave me a jolt because I had been bracing myself to encounter a Leica. That camera had been a gift in honour of our wedding, a beloved Rangefinder and his faithful servant, and it had travelled with him everywhere. But not, obviously, on this last journey.

Perhaps the Leica's importance had faded in the two years since I'd left. Perhaps it had finally broken.

"Well it's certainly broken now."

"Hmmm?" I looked up, startled. I must have spoken that last thought out loud. I drew my hand back to my lap. I had been reaching out a finger to very quietly, very cautiously touch this contraption which had been so much a part of Rhys's life that it was practically an extension of his soul. "Oh, er, yes," I said hastily. "I suppose it is."

"Which is why, I'm afraid, that a good portion of Mr Williams' film was damaged. Light was getting in through the cracks, you see."

"Yes," I said. "I do see."

The inspector extracted a contact sheet and a few enlargements from their paper envelope and spread them before me. The contact sheet was a direct copy of the negatives on a piece of photographic paper and it illustrated his point about the damage. A good half of the set was scarred by a flare of bright white so only the earliest exposures, and therefore the innermost on the reel, had escaped unscathed.

The first of these were not by Rhys's hand and I would have been sure even if I hadn't been able to identify his figure amongst the group of people arranged within the miniature prints. They lacked his confidence. Even Rhys's throwaway shots had a certain penetrative quality about them. It was as though his unfortunate subject's most private thoughts were laid bare on a platter and with his customary self assurance, Rhys always captured them without question.

The rest, however, were unquestionably by his hand. Even at that tiny scale I was able to recognise the symmetry of landscape and model, and there too I was left a little surprised. She had the same grace and the same extraordinary figure as all the rest of his models who had in turn each been the one, his *muse* and so on and so on until the faces and figures had merged into one in my memory. But this woman was different. She seemed to have lasted the course.

"You know her?" The inspector passed me an enlargement and I took it gingerly. After years and years of having it drilled into me, it was very hard not to snap at him for leaving fingerprints on the fragile surface.

There she was, in full bold black and white; confident and beautiful and alluring, and the living embodiment of Rhys's experience of war. "Yes," I said. "Christi Bollini; he met her during the Allied push into Italy. She worked as his model when they came back to England, although out there she was rather more impressively a Classical scholar's daughter who stayed throughout the war to record whatever she could. You must have heard of the Four Days of Naples when the desperate inhabitants initiated a liberation of their own just before our troops got there?"

"Unimaginable bravery." I could tell from his ponderous way of speaking that his was the mind that had pushed Rhys's grieving mother into conceding that her son had shown signs of shell shock. For the policeman, my own reference to the awful war-torn scenes only mattered in the way that I was reinforcing the idea he was nurturing of Rhys's general fragility since his return home.

Reluctantly now, I added, "This woman was there. I think her father's training must have been an influence because she made an archive of the survivors' stories. She's a very talented woman, actually."

Inspector Griffiths nodded very sagely over the elegant pose. "Yes," he agreed. "I can see that she is."

Then the smile was abruptly twitched away beneath his moustache and he handed me the next enlargement. It was one of the group photographs – presumably taken by Christi – and since I'd already experienced a jolt when I'd encountered the physical proof of Rhys's life, and death, in the form of the old shattered camera, I really should have anticipated the impact it would have on me to see these photographs of my dead husband's face.

It was a recent image. It was from an exhibition party at the gallery and I could tell it was recent because there was a poster pinned to the door of the office declaring that the next event would be the opening night of a special exhibition celebrating the lives of the Royal Couple. Rhys was standing dead centre in the frame, lazily consuming the limelight and surrounded by a beaming cluster of his most prized patrons. He looked well and happy; at least, I should say there was that pinched look about his mouth that he always wore during the build-up to the opening night and his hair was more flecked than it had been before. But the confidence was there and intact. There was no trace of the kind of desperation that might carry a man to the head of a waterfall only a few weeks later.

It prompted me to say with no small degree of difficulty, "Forgive me, Inspector, but I haven't had the opportunity to ask this until now. How do you know what happened to him? How do you know he jumped? Since no remains were found, I mean."

"No forgiveness necessary, Mrs Williams. It's a perfectly natural question. I can tell you that several witnesses saw him do it. A woman, a poor spinster at the hotel, was practically hysterical. We lose people with alarming regularity to the rivers in those valleys and most don't conveniently leave proof of their identity as Mr Williams did. In some ways we are fortunate he left these things."

Then he coughed a little as he realised that the word fortunate was perhaps not the most appropriate term to be using in these circumstances.

I didn't care. I was saying earnestly, "No, you misunderstand me. I mean to say that I do accept that he fell, but all the same you should know I truly believe it's impossible the war

171

did this. I have to ask; are you sure, *absolutely* sure he was alone? Was no one else involved?"

I already knew that no one else had been seen there at that time. Of course they hadn't. They wouldn't have been so careless. But this was the inspector's chance to ask me the same question. He could ask if *I* thought someone else was involved. If he had, I might have observed that it was rapidly becoming for me the only reasonable explanation for the dramatic transformation in Rhys's state of mind. I would have used it as the cue to risk it all by telling the policeman the truth of my own experiences. But he didn't.

He only said, "The witnesses all gave the same description of events leading to his fall."

"And you have his note."

"We have a note that usually goes with such things, yes." The inspector was surveying me carefully. He remarked, "You know, Mrs Williams, it is very natural at times like these for a grieving spouse to seek someone to blame, to seek some other explanation. But I'm afraid I can't give you that kind of consolation. I'm very sorry."

His attention strayed back to the enlargement that lay on the table before me.

Gregory was there as well of course. He was sporting his customary blazer and a debonair smile, and beside him were art historian Clifford Davis and Lord Alfred Warren, local magistrate and writer for an arts magazine. Rhys always did collect the very best. Behind them was a mêlée of assorted guests, all of whom had at one time or other either bought an artwork or been gifted the delight of an exclusive interview with Rhys. Since there was only one male amongst the group that I didn't know, presumably he was the latest lucky journalist to be gifted that gem. On the wall behind him was one of the exhibition pieces, a painfully beautiful reworking of that famous painting of *An Experiment on a Bird in the Air Pump*. In the original painting, a dramatically lit family alternately gasp and shudder at the wonder of science managing to suffocate a bird. Rhys's version was an enormous photograph in black and white and the assembled figures were watching with varying degrees of hope, trepidation and disbelief as a dying loved one received penicillin.

"Forgive me," I began carefully after the inspector had led me through the list of everyone's names. Presumably he'd had this information from Rhys's parents and perhaps been encouraged to apply to Gregory for the names they wouldn't know. "But I had been given to understand ... I mean I had hoped that I would be able to collect his things today. Are you in fact still investigating? Do you need to keep them?"

Inspector Griffiths smiled, his mouth disappearing completely behind its fringe. "The desk sergeant mentioned you'd said as much. I don't quite know where you got the idea we were ready for the family to collect his belongings. It's a touch premature. But we have concluded our investigation. There really is little we *can* do in cases like these, where no remains have been found; are unlikely to ever be found."

As he said this, his deep-set eyes gleamed black above angular cheekbones as though he were exceptionally shrewd and alert and ready to deal with the most gruesome of discoveries should the need arise. Then I realised that he was just very bored by it all and very well-practiced at hiding it. Rhys would have found him a captivating subject.

After a suitable period of scrutiny while Inspector Griffiths decided just how much more he wanted to prove his authority by releasing Rhys's possessions today, the policeman announced that I could take the prints, the broken camera and the clothes for the basis of some form of family memorial. The negatives and a copy of the most important prints were being retained, "Just in case the coroner wants them."

Quite unselfconsciously, he stuffed the images that were deemed important back into the box and left me to pack away the rest in a string bag that I dragged from its crumpled knot in the bottom of my handbag. The chosen few he retained were of the scantily clad woman.

"May I just say, Mrs Williams ..." Inspector Griffiths paused as he opened the door for me. "Your dignity has been impressive throughout. We weren't expecting you to come all this way to see us but I'm very glad you have."

"Oh," I said, more than a little taken aback. "Thank you."

"Yes. You might not wish to consider yourself a war widow, but the war certainly stole your husband and I'm sorry for it."

There didn't seem much I could say to that, not when he must have thought he was being sympathetic and I couldn't help imagining he was alluding to the woman in the photographs he'd kept. So I mustered a quick impression of a smile. Then I took the bag of a dead man's possessions and walked back through the narrow corridor of the police station to sign away my conscience on innumerable forms for the release of his things.

# Chapter 12

This time when I took my place in the tearooms on that street that led down to the pier there was no black Morris parked by the gothic university college buildings and there was no Mary to disturb my solitude either. I pulled out the envelope of photographs again while I waited for my tea and soup. Here, away from the oppressive room at the police station, the sight of his face on the glossy enlargements was only a variation of that endless habit of shocking myself into imagining Rhys was the man in the corner with his head bent over a stew, or perhaps the man outside on the pavement peering in to see if there was a vacant table, or even the very aged, very wizened old man who had waggled his hand in the air about two minutes ago for his bill. By that I mean to say that the experience of examining his photographs was unnerving but not unmanageable.

The fourth or fifth print in the pile proved to be by his hand rather than by that other person. It was a portrait of the woman, fully clothed this time with unforgiving ironwork just behind and a leaf pattern from an unseen canopy casting pensive shadows across her face. She was about ten years older than me – more equal to Rhys's age – and had the sort of confidence that makes a woman beautiful regardless of how her features have been arranged. I wondered if she mourned him.

A pot of tea arrived. I smiled my thanks and reached for the next image, one of the group shots with its sea of once-familiar faces. The warmth of Gregory's smile gave me almost the same peculiar twist that my husband's face had given me.

This was because Gregory was, in a slightly roundabout way, the man who could claim almost absolute responsibility for causing my divorce.

It seems odd to put it like that. It seems very odd to admit at all, particularly after the inspector's parting comments about war widows, that in actual fact it really wasn't the insult of Rhys's return with a fresh woman in tow that had made me leave. Admittedly, the crisis had stemmed from my husband's infidelity, but not in the way that might commonly be presumed. The difficulty for me began long before the war with the fact that Gregory saw the hurt and sympathised, and where he sympathised he grew to imagine that I wished to seek comfort on another man's shoulder. His own.

Gregory Scott was Rhys's oldest and most valuable friend – so much so that he introduced Rhys to another great friend, my uncle, and through him the artistic avant garde. But Gregory wasn't just an enthusiastic supporter of other people's talent. He was himself a much-decorated rowing champion with the grit to still dominate the sport now that he was off the water and in his early fifties. He was kind, loyal and incredibly generous to us all yet somehow remained the image of the perpetual bachelor; too hard for the women he wanted, and too critical of the women who wanted him.

His pursuit of me grew so slowly that I was two years into marriage before I was sure of it. It was the insubstantial kind of infatuation that was never explicit, absolutely uninvited and astoundingly impossible to suppress given the fact that in the main he was his usual friendly self and he held a very special status as my husband's most valued patron. The best example I have of Gregory's behaviour at that time is that he suddenly took to doing that awful shying away thing that men sometimes do when I confided even the smallest difference of opinion – such as cringing if I said it was drizzling when he said it was fine; and we could both see the mist of rain upon the window glass. It was infuriatingly impossible to curb this mannerism since any word of mine was treated like the banter between young loves; and just to be clear why such playful teasing should have been so offensive, I don't believe that affection has any part to play in a strategy that begins with ridiculing a person's capacity for independent choice.

As it was, he didn't get very far. It never escalated to a row because I wouldn't let it and when my husband went away to war, life became easier simply because without Rhys there, Gregory couldn't visit much either. Then Rhys returned home and Gregory, without so much as renewing his pursuit of me, destroyed what was left of my marriage.

To those who have never experienced the infidelity of a spouse it must seem strange that it took a row about Gregory to give me the impetus to leave. Rhys came back in 1945 with yet another muse but the real betrayal lay deeper within his artistic needs. He brought with him one other commitment: an unshakeable, unflinching determination to offer his old friend a temporary place in our office for a period of six months or so while they undertook a career-defining collaboration.

When I told Rhys that I didn't particularly like Gregory and I didn't want him working in this place that was also my home, my husband's reaction was to remind me that he couldn't be expected to sacrifice a vital creative project for the sake of an imaginary infatuation, and a historic one at that. I'd never issued an ultimatum about the models. I quite genuinely had never dreamt that this would rank as one.

But it did. Rhys made it very clear that it wasn't so much that his creative impulses led him to stray but that he saw absolutely no reason to concern himself with his wife's welfare whatsoever. It hurt. After all those years of believing myself valued if not entirely loved, this hurt.

But silly as it sounds I still won't blame him for it. I'd said to Adam that it mattered to me that I didn't give way to resentment and it's for a good reason. I can't deny that I feel angry and I think if I had ever wanted an excuse to be bitter, this would be it. But it's the kind of anger that belongs to me; to being humbled and having to learn that I was less than Rhys needed me to be after all those years of pretending that he hadn't blatantly lost interest. It was one of those last inviolable standpoints in my marriage, that I retained the power to make my own decisions. Rhys challenged my feelings but he never controlled what I was, or what I did. To blame him for the life I led would mean consigning myself to the status of powerless victim and for me that would be a far, far more dangerous choice.

---

My first glimpse of what true powerlessness really meant had come to me two weeks ago when rough hands snatched for physical control of what my mind would not do. And now I was sitting in this tearoom in Aberystwyth and instead of carefully examining that first tiny idea of what I should do next to ensure it never happened again – identify the one man in all the photographs who was a stranger to me – I was worrying about a different kind of snare. I was worrying about Adam.

I think it was because every idea I had of what powerlessness might feel like was dependent on a man trying to bully, trick or, in the case of the psychological uncertainty of Jim Bristol's interest in me, generally bewilder me into doing what he wished. Adam simply asked. I just wished I knew what he might ask for next.

There was a clatter in the doorway as an old lady knocked over the umbrella stand. I looked up with that familiar jerk of tension only to subside again almost instantly. It didn't really matter what Adam wanted. It didn't matter in the slightest that his manner of steering me felt fundamentally different from the way it had unfolded with Rhys or Gregory all those times before. It didn't matter that the incidents that had led Adam to show his disappointment were rather more about what I refused to take from him rather than what I refused to give. Those two men and their car didn't matter either. Or Jim. I had a plan and it was one that began with paying my bill, signing out of my room at the hotel and then catching a train to anywhere that might be obscure enough to hide me for a day or two while I made a few subtle telephone enquiries about that man in the photograph.

I decided all that and then I blinked, doubting.

Slowly I raised my eyes to the doorway once more. The tearoom was filled with the lunchtime rush and a second girl was already hurrying through busy tables with a fist full of rags towards the spillage of umbrellas and dirty rainwater. But beyond her, sitting at a neat table against the far wall, was a familiar face and if I hadn't been thinking about him at almost the very same moment that I had previously glanced up to survey the chaos, I would never have noticed him at all.

Today, Jim Bristol didn't look like himself but the jolt didn't come from that usual mistake of imagining his half-familiar form was Rhys. Jim was idly sipping his tea while watching a youth with a young dog on the street outside and clearly my angry accusation over the missing sketchbook had made an impression. Because today, instead of the distinctive burgundy jacket, he was wearing a faintly shabby navy suit and the loosened tie and unshaven jaw of an overweight salesman.

Jim Bristol was following me again and I didn't know what to do.

I focused on my tabletop. Very quietly I began to repack the photographs into their envelope. The soup arrived and I ate it quickly, ignoring the scalding of my mouth. I didn't look at him again; I didn't need to. Then the stew came and I did the same with that. Swallowing the dregs of my meal, I drew out my sketchbook and, opening it at the back page, carefully wrote his name beneath the untidy scrawl of the vehicle registration plate. After a moment's hesitation, I added Adam Hitchen below that. Then I scrubbed it out again.

The waitress took away my dish. She also took the empty teapot and with it the last of my excuses so that I had no choice but to make my exit. It was either that or tackle him. I looked up after all. He was still there, uncharacteristically downtrodden now like a salesman who was losing his touch and presently entirely absorbed in the task of consoling himself with his dessert.

The packet of photographs was swept with my sketchbook into my handbag which in turn was gathered together with the unfortunate shopping bag that bore the collection of clothes and the camera. I let the whirlwind waitress slip past and then swiftly followed her. Conveniently her duties took her almost to the door and her wake carried me until I had only to make two strides past the small table by the wall with its seedy patron. There was a blur in the corner of my eye as someone moved and climbed to their feet but I didn't betray my awareness of him by turning to see whether it was the salesman or the very genteel couple behind. Then an excess of politeness very nearly ruined everything. I found myself stepping back again through the open door and facing the incoming mother's belief that everyone had time to wait for her child's prompted murmur of thanks. Eventually, however, I squeezed past and out, and hurried downhill along the tiled frontage towards the seafront.

Permitting myself one brief second to turn and check, I only saw that ugly navy suit still sitting harmlessly at its table as if its owner hadn't a care in the world.

# Chapter 13

The descent to the seafront slid by in a euphoric state of adrenalin until it dawned on me that I was going to have to be absolutely sure now that neither he nor the other men nor any guest from the hotel saw me leave for the train station. With that in mind I crossed the road in the midst of a chattering Women's Group on an outing and found myself a position from which to do a spot of surveillance.

The entrance to the pier was daubed a worthy shade of brown as if someone had made a desperate bid to restore mislaid gentility over the garish orange beneath. I dithered a little on the threshold. The door swung shut on me, abruptly screening me from the street outside and I had to be very glad it did. Because while I fussed and wavered and decided I was being a fool for standing here cold in a damp frock when my coat was only half a minute away in that hotel, my salesman emerged like a black pillar out of the sea fret and reached the street corner.

He stopped. Instinct made me press back against the faintly sticky wall of the foyer. He wore a long raincoat over the cheap suit and a hat tipped low over his brow so that the pale brim very nearly covered his face but it couldn't conceal the fact that he was scanning the street while trying very hard to look as though he was only waiting for a gap in the thin traffic. The whole seafront was a monotone blur. The buildings blended with the screen of the rolling mist and the only movement came from the black shapes of cars and people, looming into view and gaining colour before diminishing again to grey. I watched, waiting in my turn with every muscle and every breath stilled while he made his decision. But then he plugged for the promenade to his left and passed beneath the turrets of the college buildings towards the castle.

It was, significantly, the route away from our hotel. I could see that building to my left, two neat pillars forming a classical porch and white paint only a little shabby despite the difficulties of sourcing materials through the war. I peeped out of the pavilion doorway. It was tempting to make a dash for it. It was too tempting.

I couldn't see Jim any more but that wasn't reassuring. His decision to walk towards the castle felt too much like an invitation. I nearly took it anyway. But then Mrs Alderton peered out of the hotel foyer to assess the condition of the sky – low and settling – and ducked back in again.

Fifteen minutes later found me still dithering in the mouth of the pier. Twelve cars of indeterminate varieties had come, disgorged their occupants and gone again. None were the Morris and I couldn't see Jim. No one else had shown themselves on the steps to the hotel but I wasn't now brave enough to imagine I could get in and out unseen. The obvious thing to do would be to abandon my possessions and leave without paying my bill but aside from the questionable legality of sending payment later, it meant that I would also be unable to reclaim my ration book. Without it I wouldn't be able to take a room anywhere else. And that meant that instead of running to ground somewhere obscure, I was left with my sister in Cirencester or the mad dash back to the trap of my parents' deserted home in Lancaster. Neither of which were remotely tempting prospects.

But I had to go somewhere and I couldn't stay here. Certainly not when I crept forwards enough to run my gaze across the front of the pier pavilion towards the metal railings of the promenade and stared straight into Jim's eyes.

He was leaning patiently against a lamp post and watching me beneath the brim of his hat with a very genuine expression of amusement on his face. He had clearly been waiting there all along. As soon as he caught my eye, the face transformed itself into the blank indifference of that shabby salesman again and I had to suppress a sudden chill. Until now, I'd been confronted by an infuriatingly persistent fellow guest by the name of Jim Bristol. This man was a stranger. Now I was afraid of him.

Suddenly I didn't want to strike out across the town, even for the hope of a train and real escape. There were too many streets between me and the station and too many chances for that black Morris to loom out of the damp air. There was too great a sense that Jim was waiting to be the man who placed me in its back seat.

So instead, when a large family of people bustled through the small eatery next door on their way to the end of the short pier, I went with them. If I was lucky they would find the view disappointing since it was only varying degrees of deepening grey – smooth grey above and rippling grey below. When they finally conceded defeat and attempted to seek better entertainment in the town, I'd go with them then too. There was security in moving as a herd, even if I knew that it would do nothing to shake off Jim.

Unfortunately, this family was not easily bored. The youngest child had a bucket and piece of string with bait attached and an ambition to collect crabs. There was space for me at the farthermost point where the metal railings met in a corner. I rested my forearms on the barrier and stared down at the water for a moment, eyes following the silver thread of a more serious fishing line to the distant spot where a float bobbed in the void. Drawing a deep breath, I braced myself and turned.

Jim hadn't followed us. Of course he hadn't. The pier was small so it was easy enough to discount his face from the few. This seaward end was just a narrow rectangle floored with wooden boards and fringed with sturdy metal barriers on all sides. The pavilion and its untidy tearoom stood between me and the formless void where the promenade would be if only the waterlogged air hadn't been so thick. I could just make out the amber orbs of street lamps and passing traffic. The effect was very much like a severe smog in London except that I didn't recall the city ever smelling of anything so pleasant as rotting seaweed and ozone.

There was a terrible sense of having walked myself into a trap. There was a very good reason, I supposed, why Jim hadn't followed me here. He didn't need to. I might well have succeeded in taking myself to the one place inaccessible by car, but I had also cleverly left myself only one exit. He only had to wait for me to walk back out again into whatever the real trap was.

The tide was out. Behind me the very faint swell ran shushing over angular black granite. The sound drew my thoughts unshakably to that other watery place, the waterfall. There the water roared; here it was a benign silken film rippling across lines of rock. Its call made me turn again until my eyes found the glassy sea.

Unwillingly, ludicrously, my mind revisited that other growing theory. The probability that someone else was there that day that Rhys took his life. Time and time again I was being presented with the single reoccurring judgement of Rhys's character: it was not in his nature to succumb to desperation quietly. Here the pier was perhaps twenty or thirty feet high at low tide. It wasn't the towering height of Devil's Bridge but still it was perhaps just tall enough to make the attempt worthwhile for them. Particularly when my own recent past indicated there was every likelihood that the incident would ultimately be chalked up as self-determined regardless of whether or not I lived to tell the tale...

With a jolt, my mind swerved violently away from that particular line of thought. Instead I cursed, inwardly muttering to myself. If this was the great secret; if their single ambition was to push me into joining Rhys in his watery grave or an incarceration of a different sort, they could keep it. It was almost a relief when I saw Jim again and not nearly close enough to tip me over the barrier.

He was now guarding the exit into that dirty tearoom but not with any appearance of immediate violent intent. He too was leaning back against the metal barrier like any normal visitor to this seaside town and as well as taking the time to smile at a child who was pedalling past his feet on a tricycle, he had also apparently taken the time to draw out his old prop of the Aberystwyth guide book.

It was the sight of that guide book that did it. Being hunted and wet and cold was one thing, but it was asking too much to be laughed at. It was a pointed reminder of my failure to confront him last night. With one angry slap of my palm against the metal rail I propelled myself away from the end of the pier and across the wooden boards towards him.

I'm not entirely sure I didn't mean to tip him over the barrier myself. If I did, my fury never found its release. The interval between my arrival on the pier and his had obviously been put to good use. He must have taken the time to make contact with his friends. The doubts that had for days been clouding my faith in my instincts vanished just as predicted when the first of those two men stepped out of my memory and into reality through the pavilion bar onto the decking.

# Chapter 14

The man was tall and narrow, and much younger than I remembered. His businesslike suit was a little smart for a damp day by the sea and the dark pinstriped jacket was well cut and not the lumpy sack my mind had fitted to the muscle-bound thug of imagination. He wasn't muscle-bound anyway. He had dark auburn hair and it was swept back from his narrow face in a long curling style that belonged very much to the civilian world and showed he had either dodged his national service or was just old enough that it had finished with the war. I spied the other man as he stepped around the telescope stand on the end of the pier in a perfectly executed flanking manoeuvre.

I had always presumed that when I saw them I would have the opportunity to make a fight of it – forewarned as I was that capture meant a car ride – but disbelief ruled the day first. A giddy laughing disbelief. Because by now I was reasonably certain that a car ride wasn't what they intended for me.

The ginger-haired man was creeping closer and reaching out cautiously towards my arm and I retreated swiftly until my back met the hard metal of the barrier. My shoulder brushed the arm of a holidaymaker. For one brief second I saw surprise and their recoil. And then the red-haired man's hand snatched, reaching. It groped. It traced my movement as I twisted aside, sinking, clinging; anything to make that precious barrier between me and the drop higher. I was probably screaming. My body carved a line between my startled neighbours and the railing, and they gave way, jabbering, only to tut and scold instead. Everyone could see this was a joke amongst holidaymakers. They just didn't think it was very appropriate for a grown woman to play a variation of that game the children had enjoyed on the steps by Devil's Bridge. That inescapable reach swooped, adjusted and then abruptly the hand made contact with my elbow. It dragged me back easier than a fisherman reeling in his fly. Once the hand was sure of me, there was nothing I could do. Smiling like a good sport, his fingers locked on my arm in a grip that shut off my flight just as surely as if it were a switch and then we were moving wherever he wanted me.

Relief learned it was not over the barrier, but smoothly, calmly into silence and towards dry land.

Relief was more debilitating than their touch. The shorter fellow's hand met my other arm. He was wearing a cheaper suit and his face was rounder beneath his grey felt hat. He was nearer my age. His grip closed more gently; perhaps he didn't see the need to be cruel now they had me. I felt his free hand settle low upon my back just to be sure that I couldn't duck away as I had that time at the bus stop. Everyone else relaxed. They had known all along that it was a joke. For me the days of strain and the dreaming terrors of my nights were nothing. That instant of dread and then the release of knowing it was a mistake made the advance towards the promenade a swooping plunge into the unknown.

My salesman, Jim, was passed without so much as a whisper of recognition from either party and it barely even registered as a surprise. I turned my head, looking back at him, but the gaze that met mine beneath the brim of his hat only seemed blankly ignorant before it was quickly withdrawn.

"You won't get much help from him." At my side, my captor broke his silence. His eyes had followed mine and that supple mouth formed a confident smile. I couldn't tell whether he was being scathing of a poverty-stricken stranger, or respectful of his secret contact.

They took me along the seafront past my hotel and onwards along the promenade towards the cheaper hotels where the funicular railway rattled and many cars were parked. Disorientation faded. I was alive. My hair was damp enough to stick to my face. Streetlamps beamed yellow in the gloom. It was only shortly after lunch and it might well have been dusk. I was resisting every step and barking out variations of the same idiotic question; "Where are you taking me?" followed by "I haven't got what you want." They gave me no reply except the rasp of their breath and the heavy tramp of their feet.

Actually, someone replied. Someone's voice answered mine. There was a squeak of my name and a sudden cold flood of seawater across my feet and then a childish exclamation of surprise as if running with a full bucket had never ended in disaster before. By my left ear, a spluttering of sharp curses clarified abruptly into a low "Why, you little ..." only for the ginger-haired man to be silenced in turn by his shorter fellow with a swift caution of, "*Clarke!*"

All of a sudden the tall brute had a name. It made a world of difference to me. It sharpened my state of mind somehow. So did the fact that my arm was free. Clarke was in the process of giving the boy a nasty shake. To me he was considerably less formidable now that he had a child-shaped gritty imprint on his side and saltwater weaving a dark stain across his well-polished leather shoes. It took me a moment to realise what the boy must have done. With that absolute single-mindedness of the child, he had seen me and decided that I must be delighted to see the fruits of today's hunt under the pier. Now poor Samuel looked like he was going to cry. I was instantly awake in the grip of the other man's hands, no longer a hostage but a normal human being resenting this outrageous bullying of an amiable little boy.

The bucket, now rolling across the promenade in a graceful arc, had blessedly only housed rocks and seaweed and a small crab which was now rapidly calculating the possibility of escape. I picked up the bucket as it neared my toe and prepared to beat Clarke over the head with it.

"Clarke!" The second man relieved me of the bucket with a snatch and a scowl. He at least was looking rather more the stereotyped brute of my imagination now that his temper had been unleashed.

Clarke snarled, "What?"

His answer came from another male who was no one I had ever met. "What is going on here? Sam? What have you done?" His voice wreaked a transformation upon Clarke. By the time Samuel's father arrived bringing salvation and a resounding contradiction of another of Mrs Alderton's sweeping judgements – the claim that noisy children came from broken homes – Clarke's long fingers were nonchalantly smoothing down the creases of his suit.

No one was holding me.

Clarke's head turned towards me. He moved. He snatched. He stopped. Only his eyes followed me while I began to back away. He didn't dare do anything else in case I made a scene. He didn't know that I didn't want one either; I just wanted to get away. Samuel's father, looking very much the part of the irate father on holiday – newly arrived from his office and resplendent in warm clothes but rolled trousers and bare feet – was only too pleased to have the opportunity to vent all his stresses on a man who was scaring his son.

His glare turned Clarke's growl to a simper and the small audience who were treating this as a stage spectacle shielded me as I turned away and began to run.

Clarke left it just a few seconds too late to hiss beneath his ingratiating smile to his fellow. "Leave this. Get after her, you fool."

----

At the moment that Clarke snapped out his instruction to his companion I think I had a lead of about ten yards. The crowd was thicker on the street heading inland. The press of people reduced my lead to eight yards. Then, suddenly, a swarm of Liverpudlians made it fifteen, then twenty. By the time I went to ground in the first safe place I could find, I'd lost sight of the man just as surely as he must have lost me. It seemed a miracle.

The great art-deco entertainment hall loomed ghoulishly and I dodged through the hordes seeking cheap amusements in the basement and the better-dressed clientele destined for festivities on a Royal Wedding theme on the floors above. I had a wild ambition of sustaining my lead all the way to the train station but beyond the dance hall, a small stampede of people turned my ideas and my path towards the rather more achievable aim of a picture house. And besides, I couldn't have escaped their pull if I had tried. I ducked left and followed them inside. The air on the crowded stairs was musty and the electric lighting yellow.

"One, please. Balcony." My hoarse murmur was enough to get me a ticket and then I was pushing through the double doors marked Coliseum and casting wide-eyed glances at my fellows as I crossed the auditorium to the winding metal staircase on the other side. It seemed incredible that this little swarm of damp people had been sufficient to conceal me. The curtain was still down but the cramped rows of seats in the popular stalls were already filling in anticipation of the next showing. My ticket bought me access to the first floor and I tucked myself neatly into a seat on the tip of the arc and furthest from the screen. Instinct told me to find a shady corner in which to hide but both arms of the balcony had doors that permitted access to the stairs and I didn't relish the idea of anyone sneaking up behind. So instead I settled into my vantage point at the heart of the balcony with a wall at my back, two possible means of escape and an unimpeded view of the stalls. It must be said that I didn't much enjoy this latest view over a steep drop after those intense few seconds at the tip of the pier.

My clothes dried as the seats filled around me. My hair was beyond salvation. Luckily none of my neighbours were interested in this little wide-eyed figure of a woman. These were the cheaper seats so my companions were the older locals; a cheery bunch and many showed signs of a day spent in the nearby bars.

The curtain lifted. It took perhaps another half hour for my breathing to ease and another beyond that to remember that the bag I was clutching tenderly contained a dead man's clothes. The cartoon reels flicked through their never-ending variations of the same teasing antics and in the pause between one scene and the next, I drew out my sketchbook again and made a note in the back. Clarke.

The main showing began and the audience settled; a few hundred faces staring at the hypnotic screen. Sadly, instead of picking a day when the feature was something useful like Hitchcock's *The 39 Steps* or *The Count of Monte Cristo* or any one of the other man-on-the-run type films that might have given helpful tips to a woman like me, I had the detailed report on the marriage between Her Royal Highness the Princess Elizabeth and her tall man of choice, Lieutenant Mountbatten. To this day I cannot endure the footage of that happy event without recalling the stifling restlessness of hiding away in that place. To me her carriage was a prison cell and the ranks of royal dignitaries in the congregation were spies and jailors. And the bells, always the ringing of Westminster Abbey bells mixing with the sweet shrill tones of the boy choir. They were the unceasing rhythm of the shallow waves passing over rock beneath the pier.

It was dark when the showing ended. I fully expected them – whichever them it was, whether Jim or the brutes – to be waiting outside when my ruby-cheeked neighbour and I were finally ushered towards making our orderly way down the nearest stairs. According to my watch and the stiffness in my limbs, it was well beyond half-past nine, I had missed dinner and I had certainly missed the last train. Even if I hadn't, I wasn't sure I had the nerve to run for it. I barely had the nerve to step outside at all.

They were not outside however, and even if they were, it was perfectly possible that they had chosen to mark the wrong one of the three available exits. At least no hand met my arm as I hurried along in the midst of a family of raucous cousins and no low voice disturbed my peace as I left them to run up the last few steps into the hotel. The door was locked but the night porter appeared almost immediately in answer to my anxious rap and then I was calming myself and smiling a greeting as I passed through the door, and waiting while he firmly bolted it behind. He told me confidently that no new guests had taken rooms today. We hadn't been joined by Clarke or his friend.

An afterthought made me accost the man and insist on settling my bill. He was reluctant because the manageress had locked up the safe for the night but my eagerness to assure him that I would be leaving very early indeed was matched by my willingness to give him the change for my payment as a tip.

Finally I was free to slink across the foyer towards the stairs. The door into the lounge was open, casting a warm beam of light across the tiles and up onto the fifth step. I stopped in it as I caught Mary's bright laugh. I stooped to peer through the railings. Out of sight, Mrs Alderton's dry tinkle followed but then I heard a deeper tone make its reply and I knew precisely why no one had been waiting for me outside the cinema. There had been no need. Not when all Jim Bristol had to do was presume on my stupidity and wait in the hotel for my return.

It had occurred to me when I first encountered the various male guests at the hotel that the mysterious threat who awaited me in Cirencester might well have decided to save me the trouble of travelling. I realised now I had been fearing all day that Adam was the man. If he were, he must have shown extraordinary foresight since he'd arrived days before I'd even dreamt of pursuing Rhys's last steps. But Jim hadn't. Jim had arrived only a few minutes after I'd signed my name on the register.

I heard Mary laugh again, a happy friendly sparring, and I wondered what I should do. Then I remembered I could do absolutely nothing at all. He had, I realised, been extraordinarily lucky last night in finding himself the victim of one of my outbursts. He could be certain that no one would believe me now.

A flutter of white drew my eye. It was Adam, watching me silently over the brim of his newspaper from his usual place in the corner. I sketched him a quick meaningless smile, and hurried away to my room.

# Chapter 15

Isuppose I must have known it was another dream. The combination of the dark space between pillars like a scene from the Royal Wedding at Westminster Abbey and the ever-present waterfall was probably enough of a clue. I climbed out, dripping, onto a sunlit platform, much the same as one for a derelict factory with rusted ironwork and invading greenery. The other spectators were leaving. They didn't notice me; they were translucent like ghosts and their speech was as garbled as scraping nails. They didn't notice the car either. It was standing in the midst of them, sunlight running dappled from its open door and making a strange rapping as its engine cooled. Rhys was waiting there beside it. I was supposed to ask him something. He wasn't quite listening.

As I said, I must have known it was a dream; I was already beginning the slow fight upwards to lie blinking in the familiar dark. But then the light exploded.

The room was small and suffocating and suddenly I was sitting bolt upright in my bed. I was caught like a hare in a lamp-beam. The yellow blade spread from the door. Its glare was agony. At its source wasn't Rhys, but two shadows belonging to my living nightmare. They had found me. They had been let in. They had searched out my room and forced the door. Even a locked door within a locked hotel was not defence enough. Their shadows loomed as the door made its rattling rebound off the wall to be steadied by an outstretched hand. I heard my voice scramble into a cry. It was instinct that made my body fling itself over the far edge of my single bed. As I went, the leaner of the two separated himself from the doorway and lunged across the room.

Something snatched me back. Not him; it was a cruel stranglehold about my neck like rope. It was a third assailant and one I couldn't see. I fought him – *it*. It didn't have limbs. I was choking, panicking, raging to find the edge of the bed and succeeded only in colliding agonisingly with the head-board. But he was on me too and I was fighting him as well. Still my hands were caught and held and my desperate fury firmly hushed, and the bed sheet worked free from where it had inexplicably coiled itself around my neck. And then I was sitting in a tangle and panting violently, staring up at the heavily shadowed face and finding nothing there but a calming sort of manly kindliness.

I shuddered back out of the waking nightmare as Adam was saying with disorientating firmness, "It was just a dream. A bad dream. Don't be afraid. And you don't need to fight me."

I gasped for breath. I opened my mouth to ask him just what the hell he thought he was doing.

And broke instead. It was almost a relief to do it.

He didn't comfort me of course. This wasn't one of those

moments and I'm not sure how violently instinct would have made me react if he had. So I turned my head away and wept desolately and wetly into the palm of my hand while trying to ignore my heartbeat pounding to the point of oblivion and listening only to the fuss of guests outside my door. They were commenting on my capacity for waking the whole hotel. None of the voices belonged to Clarke. It took me a while to believe that.

The minutes that followed were odd. I had always imagined it romantic to be confronted in the middle of the night by the very definitely bare chest of an attractive man. But romance depends on believing it was an act of heroism. It doesn't admit the ugliness of crying or the desperate desire for solitude even while absolutely dreading that moment of being flung back into isolation. And it certainly doesn't appreciate the inconvenience of belatedly realising that the embarrassingly elegant nightdress bought by a well-meaning mother had also ridden up to show an appalling amount of thigh. I tried to remedy it and it was only then that I realised my left hand had been enclosed thoroughly within his all along.

He was half-sitting, half-kneeling on the side of the bed before me so that as I twisted to one side to screen my face, my hair was actually brushing against his bare shoulder. It shook me. I could feel the heat from his bare skin radiating against my cheek. My left hand was pressed by the weight of his grip against the mattress beside my exposed knee and when I stirred and impulsively began to try to get myself into some kind of order it tightened and urged me to remain still. Then I felt his mouth dip towards my ear.

"Hang on," that familiar voice said quietly, and he meant it.

Then in the next moment I really was alone because he'd let me go. It was a jolt to suddenly desperately feel his loss in the midst of this claustrophobic crowd when before I'd been wishing him far from here. He moved across the room to meet Mary as she arrived with the night porter in tow and Adam used him as the excuse to push the door closed. Adam must have been shielding me from the curious stares of the disturbed residents. The people outside were talking to Mary, alternately being sympathetic and dissecting my wilfully neurotic tendencies – it was easy enough to guess who was taking which side – and it was then that I learned the explanation behind this intrusion. It really was a rescue. The general theory was that I'd had a bad dream and cried out and brought them all running.

Only I hadn't cried out. It had barely been a nightmare at all until my door had been broken in. I swear it hadn't.

I sought Adam in the gloom to beg a little clarity and found myself blinking as the ceiling light clicked on instead. Harsh light brutally exposed the tangle of my sheets, the smallness of the room and the way my body flinched as it craved the obscurity of darkness, like a hunted animal in its hole. There was a bustle in the corner as the unlucky porter was put to work wrestling with my shattered lock. Adam was crouching over the toolbox beside him, helping. And the other man? The second shadow from the doorway who could only have been Jim?

He was still in my room. All along he'd been standing

quietly in the corner by the little table that held my things, doing nothing while those people out there peered in at me and answered Miss Bartleman's anxious questions for the umpteenth time. He'd left it to Adam to shut the door. Only Jim Bristol hadn't been idle all this time. He had my handbag in his hands. He was no better dressed than I. He was wearing rough-looking trousers and his chest was bare revealing a torso marked with enough old injuries to do justice to the impression he gave of a pretty fearsome war service. His left arm had a raw-looking weal in the defined muscle below the shoulder from a younger wound that had only just healed – it made me wonder if bullets tended to stalk him in peacetime too. The muscle moved as his hand turned something over. A rectangular piece of card; a photograph. He had pulled out the envelope from my handbag and was leafing through its contents.

The sudden glare of electric light from the ceiling had disturbed him too. As I watched he paused over one, examining it, and then swiftly folded it in two and slid it into the pocket of his trousers. I might refute the claim that I'd screamed before but I certainly squeaked then. The shock of it had me half out of bed and reaching for my long housecoat. He was already moving with the sort of purpose that turned his face harsh. He must have seen me move but apparently he'd already dismissed the threat as negligible. He returned the envelope to my bag. No apology, no guilt. Not even an acknowledgement. It was an uncompromising reminder of that business over my sketchbook; and of that moment of passing him on the pier and looking back.

I began to declare, loudly, that I knew now this hadn't been a dream, I hadn't cried out and brought them rushing to my rescue. I wanted him to explain why he'd broken in like this just to steal a photograph. Only, just as I was beginning to lurch across the room and Adam and the night porter were beginning to register my movement amidst all the fuss outside, Jim had already slipped through the door and gone. In his place, Mary was bustling in with a heavily laden tray in her hands.

"Tea, Katie dear?"

She sent me back a step. I barely looked at her. The same blind panic that had sent me flying to the edge of my bed a moment before sent me raging after him now. My breathing was short. My icy hands spared a few hasty seconds to draw the long housecoat closed about my waist. I moved, only now I found the door shut firmly before me. Mary and her tray drifted aside but Adam was in my path. He had his back to me, helping the other man to reattach the battered keeper to the doorframe. The porter was having to raise the lock to avoid the splintered wood. From his crouch Adam had his arm outstretched, holding the door firmly shut so that the porter had a firm surface upon which to work. His skin had none of the scars that marked Jim Bristol. Now his head was turning to catch the moment as I tried to dodge past. His feet were bare. So were mine. The hard electric light at this time of night cast strange shadows across his face. It probably did the same to my face too. I felt like I'd aged about a hundred years.

I must have spoken my alarm about the stolen photograph.

Adam didn't speak but Mary looked and sounded like her usual cheerful self and her disbelieving smile followed me merrily when she remarked boldly, "Nobody's taken anything, Katie. Don't be silly. You've had a bad dream, that's all. We all heard you scream. At least ... that's how it was, isn't it, Adam?"

The porter worked some screws into place and permitted Adam to drop his hand. Now he rose to his feet beside me. His roughened hair made it clear that he really had been dragged out of bed. It seemed to take an eternity for him to give me the faintest tilt of his head in confirmation.

The acknowledgement that it was my cry that had first disturbed the hotel was reluctant. He knew how it would make me feel to be told I was guilty of making a scene again. And all the while, in my head was the unavoidably vivid memory of Jim's recent exit from my room. His jaunty farewell and the pat on Adam's shoulder as he left had almost been one of thanks.

I was breathing like I was in the middle of a marathon race. Here again I was being confronted with a maddening choice between what was possible and what was probable, and what I dared do about it. It all hinged upon whether I believed what Adam had to say.

Earlier, I had been utterly paralysed by the belief that I'd been destined for a watery grave beneath that mist-shrouded pier. The illusion had robbed me of those few vital seconds when I might have acted more wisely as Clarke approached. I might well have managed a better escape then. Or perhaps not. Now I was trying to decipher whether the illusion lay in Mary's claim that I'd drawn this invasion into my room by calling out, or in my determination to cling to the belief that I hadn't. And whether Adam was part of the lie or even more duped by it than I was.

The common thread here was Jim. He set up these situations and watched as I worked myself yet again into the position of having no one to debate with except my remaining self-belief. Given the stiff lesson I'd learned with the sketchbook, there was every chance that if I made a scene now I would find the photograph had never been missing at all.

Adam's serious grey eyes were fixed upon my face. His voice was carefully expressionless as he asked, "Do you want to go and knock on Jim's door?"

Suddenly, I found myself smiling. Warmly, unexpectedly. I don't think anyone but me would have found those dry words worthy of mirth. But after all my thoughts on powerlessness earlier and the principle differences between this man's methods and all the other threats, the very fact he was asking this was an almost implausibly perfect illustration of his character. Only it wasn't too perfect. He remembered our words last night on this very same threshold. He really was trying very hard to show that he knew I had the right to make my own choice. He was trying very hard to do the right thing.

It was a little piece of beauty in the midst of all that bitter isolation. Distress suddenly retreated, quivering, to a shady corner. Not gone completely, but farther off. I laughed, though perhaps that too was a symptom of shock. I shook my head. "No," I said. "I think we both know what the general fuss would be, don't we? Particularly when I've just done it again to you now."

I saw his eyebrows lift. "Done what?"

I said, "Turned your trip into a public drama. This wasn't a last-ditch attempt to lure the famous author into my room. It really wasn't."

Adam's mouth gave me the beginnings of a smile. He'd caught the reference to Mrs Alderton's remarks overheard during the last public scene that had involved my name; the one that had proved irrefutably that he knew Rhys. He knew it was a forerunner to daring to demand that same degree of openness that he'd been urging me to share all week. I saw his attention quicken.

Mary, on the other hand, read it all wrong. She made us both jump by throwing open my bedroom window to let in a welcome gust of damp night air and then claimed my bed and followed the act with a very scolding tut. She said, "He's clearly not going to admit it so I shall do it for him. We don't know whether it was all in that pretty little head of his or quite simply everyone is too afraid of my sister. But either way, it turns out that the famous author might not be quite as universally fascinating as he'd generally supposed. Barely anyone has dared speak to him today let alone give him a critique of everything he's ever written. In fact my poor brother-in-law deserves your sympathy more than Adam here. Everyone knows he's a doctor and this evening he got to hear all about Miss Bartleman's friend's idea of a cure for hysteria. Which apparently involves laxatives. So be warned, Katie, dear. But don't let Adam bully you."

She meant it as a joke. She was arranging herself artfully upon the tossed pillows, looking of course as supremely elegant as ever. Behind Adam, there was a blur as the long-forgotten night porter finished repairing the damage to my door and bolted into the now deserted corridor with toolbox rattling. I think he'd been dragged from his bed too.

I was suddenly conscious that by remaining standing, I was making rather too much of a thing about being near Adam. I abruptly claimed the point midway between him and Mary by perching rather less impressively on the edge of the bed on the pretext of passing her a cup of tea. This of course made it worse for Adam because now I think he began to feel his awkwardness standing in well-worn slacks and bare feet before two seated and significantly better-dressed women. Oblivious, Mary sipped her tea and said kindly, "No one really blames you, you know, for being a bit ... um ... prone to nervousness. Not now we know he died recently."

I turned my head. I said stupidly, "Who?"

Of course I was stupid. Mary said, "Rhys. You said his name just now."

Had I? It came as a deeply uncomfortable shock to learn that I really was capable of uttering speech without being remotely conscious of it. Those thoughts had been private. And it raised rather ugly questions all over again about the belief that no cry of mine had justified Jim's invasion into my room.

Mary's eyes were even larger in this harsh electric light. She saw my clouded face. She said seriously, "You must miss him."

I uttered a hasty correction and made her raise an eyebrow. And then I realised what I'd implied. I gabbled, "I mean, I—" and followed it with a complicated ramble about the difficulties of knowing what to say to a question like that. Of knowing whether I should declare roundly that I had lived a calmer life without Rhys, or act like the normal civilised human being who must naturally feel the loss of a man's life irrespective of how infuriating he'd been as a spouse.

I made her smile. I felt like a fraud. It made me abruptly reach for my own cup of tea from the waiting tray. Somehow, miracle of miracles in this time of rationing, she'd even managed to purloin a couple of biscuits. I nibbled one tentatively. It was a mistake. It awoke my stomach to the concept of dinner. But at least it was a way of ignoring the fact that Adam seemed to have forgotten that we were supposed to be discussing the mention he'd made of Rhys's name in the breakfast room many hours ago. Instead he seemed to be closely scrutinising my behaviour now. His examination was intense.

Bravely I lifted my head. For my part, this wasn't the kind of openness I'd hoped for; I hadn't intended it to be me who was baring yet more secrets. I'd expected him to make the confession. I'd been wishing that he would make the obvious declaration that he wasn't a criminal; and that he wasn't part of this game being played with my mind. And above it all, I really wanted him to tell me that he was definitely not a grief-ridden former friend to Rhys.

I didn't get a chance to ask him any of it. Mary told me brightly, "We went to your house, you know."

"My *house?*" I blinked, confused. Now I had to calculate what else might have spilt out of my mouth unnoticed. "Which house?"

"The one with the mysterious tunnel. That Nanteos place."

Mary pouted. "Only there was no gaping tunnel-mouth ready to welcome us. Just tales of ghosts in the attics where the nuns lived during the war." She gazed thoughtfully at Adam as he gave in and reached for his cup. Then she turned her attention back to me. She remarked dryly, "Though apparently for some people that counts as atmosphere."

Adam had relaxed again. He was examining the state of his cooling cup of tea. And it was a good job too because it meant he didn't notice the way Mary was examining him and measuring him against the impossible muscle of Jim Bristol. I think she was interested to note that he didn't exactly suffer for the comparison.

Then Adam's head suddenly lifted and she was looking at me innocently with a smirk behind her eyes and saying, "You know, you had us worried when you missed dinner today. We thought you'd left."

"Oh?" I said lamely. "No."

She wasn't satisfied. She continued, "And thinking of unexplained absences; where did Jim get to? I brought him a cup and everything. He's your real hero, Katie. He was the one that heard the fracas and raised the alarm. Though perhaps it's a good job he didn't stay otherwise we'd get terribly muddled. He's a James, I'm a James; imagine how confusing it would be if we were married. I'd be Mrs James Bristol or perhaps even Mrs James Bristol-James ... By the way, you do look truly very tired. Shall we go? We'll go. No, don't get up."

She reached across and gave me a motherly kiss upon the cheek. "You do brighten up life around here, Katie."

She got up and fussed over the effort of rearranging her

hair – which was immaculate – and swept the shadows from under her eyes, which, continuing the theme of the day, were entirely imaginary. And then while she adjusted the opening of my window and Adam moved to return his cup to the tray, I said urgently, foolishly, *"Adam."*

At a distance of only a yard or so from me, his eyes were very dark. He knew what had alarmed me, even if Mary was wilfully blind to it. It was the proof that Jim alone had heard the supposed cry that had necessitated their break-in. It was Mary's admission of her warmth of feeling for that man.

My heart was beating fiercely as he told me, "We'll talk about this in the morning."

He stepped closer and reached for my empty cup. His eyes were his own again. As I nodded, I knew all my stern lectures to myself this afternoon were for naught. If the game for these men was to find yet another way to gently erode my sense of control, so be it. Adam had what he wanted. Every speck of my willingness to believe in him lay burnt upon my heart.

He etched it all a little deeper when he told me quietly, "We terrified you just now and I'm sorry. At the time it seemed necessary but now I can see it wasn't entirely ... wise. You look exhausted. Sleep well, Kate. And if you need me, you know where I am."

Then he took my cup and the tray and they left, gently clicking the door shut with the air of those who were leaving me quietly tucked up in bed. Only I wasn't a child and of course I had to get up after them because I had to lock the door. This time I put a chair under the handle too.

# Chapter 16

I slipped along the corridor to take a bath just as soon as the first kitchen lights shone out onto the courtyard beneath my window and I couldn't be accused all over again of disturbing the perfect peace of my fellow guests. I hadn't slept. It was impossible when there was too much to think about.

There was the hope that Adam's words in the dead of night had implied that he was already beginning to suspect the truth about Jim and his interest in me here. There was the fear too that I was mistaken. At least today I had a strategy for my escape. It was not a particularly good strategy, consisting for the most part of simply leaving this place by the earliest train possible, but it would do and I had a timeframe too, dictated as it was by the decision I had made while brushing my teeth. I would stay just long enough to recount the whole mess to Adam. And Mary too, if her sister would let her listen.

I slipped back to my room again and locked the door and dressed, selecting at last an off-the-peg skirt in a sensible shade of beige. The brightly coloured frocks of the past two days had been creations from my recent past, a sort of crimson-hued experiment I'd made for myself in recognition of my re-emerging status as a practicing artist. Today's choice was an older and more faithful servant and inconspicuous enough under the matching jacket and my coat.

After that there was little to do except pack. The case was only small – part of a larger set of luggage that before the war would have been used to transport a lady's make-up and smalls rather than my entire wardrobe of clothes. It had a shoulder strap and a dent in one corner where the cardboard lining had been bashed. The borrowed copy of *Jane Eyre* was left out on the bed to remind me to return it to the lounge library. The shopping bag containing the ruins of Rhys's clothes and his battered camera was rejected, I am afraid, to save room. On that thought, I reached into my handbag and drew out the packet of photographs. Only one was missing, as expected.

It was one of the group shots, the one where Rhys had been grinning happily in the foreground with his admirers and his new work gleaming just behind. Stuffing them back into the envelope, I had to pause over another image. It caught my eye because it was that portrait of the model – Christi – and behind her was the same twisted metalwork that had featured in my dream. I knew now where I had seen it in real life as well. It was the line of sagging railings that fringed the edge of the road at Devil's Bridge.

I opened the door. The holes that showed where the lock keeper had parted from the doorframe were ragged but not as ragged as they might have been had the metal plate been attached more securely in the first place. Then I stopped thinking about hotel maintenance very quickly indeed.

Clarke must have been standing at the bottom of the stairs because I couldn't see him but still his applied charm carried along the corridor with all its accompanying terror. I hesitated, door only slightly ajar, and listened.

He was saying smoothly, "First floor, you say? And what number?" Then less patiently, "Yes, yes of course. It's just like I said yesterday. She's been a touch unwell."

Then another short stutter of speech, and one that sent my heart plummeting. It was Adam. Very gingerly I pushed the door closed and locked it. I set my bag and my case down blindly upon the bed. I moved the chair back to its place against the door as a second line of defence. There was no telephone in my room or, of course, any other exit. There was only the space beneath the bed, a small slatted wardrobe and the window.

The window.

In a flash I had the lower sash up and was hanging out, examining the rusting metal of that favourite roost of pigeons: the crumbling fire escape. It wasn't designed for me, perhaps after all it was only intended to facilitate access for the chimney sweep to the roof, but I judged that if I leaned from a perch on the windowsill, the nearest rungs could just about be reached, and that was chance enough. I slipped back across the room and listened at the door. I didn't need to listen hard because there was a rap right beside my ear. I jumped back.

The next part sounds mad, even to me. Slinging my handbag and suitcase over my back, I slipped to the window, straddled the sill and then slid my feet outside. The gap was much farther than I thought, and so was the drop to the slimy green stone flags in the small courtyard at the bottom. Then I realised that my coat was likely to get in my way. I slipped back inside, took it off and bundled it into a knot on the strap of my handbag and then tried again. This time the view from the window was far worse now that I'd had time to think about it. But then I heard someone try the door. There was a faint whisper of something entering the lock. It is amazing how quickly I made that twisting slide across the gap.

Somewhere in the distant past I was sane. Sometime ago I would have found a practical solution to being cornered like that; such as screaming the place down, or letting them take me down the stairs first and then screaming the place down when the odds increased of someone actually seeing them and believing me. But today I had no faith in reality ever working how I expected it to. And I certainly didn't intend to leave it to someone else to ensure my salvation.

So I hitched up my skirt over my knees so that I could freely move my legs, adjusted my grip on the ladder and began to descend.

It was easy after all. My hand was in its place, my foot met its rung smoothly and took my weight, and then found the next and the next. Unlike the rickety wooden things of my childhood that a neighbour had used to clean his upper windows, this ladder was blessedly secure. But unfortunately it was also a difficult descent in a flapping skirt and flimsy shoes. All the same it seemed to progress quite well. Until, that is, I reached the bottom rung.

The gap between this and the grimy yard was not, I realised

after braving the swift glance down, the full three yards I had thought. It was at worst only two but even so that was quite far enough. The trembling began in earnest and my hands were sweaty now so that the grip on the rusted metal was tighter than it needed to be, and painful. I looked down again and winced. My only hope was to lower myself as far as I could and then trust that the remaining drop would not be too much. Very carefully and with a fair few anxious searches of the empty window above, I moved my hands down a few rungs. This didn't help much because with my feet firmly fixed on the lowest bar I only achieved a position that was inconveniently like an upside down version of a child preparing to play leap-frog.

I intended then to lower my feet from the ladder. I had planned to hang by my arms to brace myself for the drop. What I hadn't anticipated was my total lack of upper body strength, the pain of increased weight on my hands or the drag of those bags on my back. I fell about six feet.

In fact it was probably the presence of those bags that saved my life, or at least saved me from serious harm. I landed in a heap and that was bad enough but thanks to the case I had a buffer between my back and the ground. It was a nasty jolt, all the breath was knocked out of me and my suitcase was now seriously crushed. There was a great deal of unpleasant green staining to my skirt. It blended nicely with the oxide streaks from the rusted ladder.

After a few numb seconds while my brain ran through a check on all the usual body parts, I managed to stagger to my feet. I don't think it had occurred to me that a fall could hurt quite so much. There was a smear of blood on my ear. I think it was then and only then that the other options crossed through my mind. I was suddenly aware of the very grave danger I had been running of giving my head another serious bashing. The doctors had been very severe on the likely consequences if I should risk sustaining a second concussion so soon after the first, and at the time of mentioning it they had only been scolding me for wishing to walk out of hospital rather than allowing myself to be wheeled out to the taxi in a chair.

A shoe had disappeared beneath some crates but I found it and replaced it. I pulled my coat over my dirtied clothes and then I was weaving an unsteady path through the kitchen, through the exclamations of the cook and serving staff and out through the door into the void between the stairs and the lounge door. The serving girl followed me, talking anxiously, and there were people in the doorway to the dining room but I didn't acknowledge any of them except to give something that resembled a drunken smile as I darted past into the foyer. I was already passing the reception desk when I heard Adam call my name.

I should have known he would be the obstacle that delayed me.

I whipped round. I saw him step out from the dining room. In two seconds he had crossed the floor. In the next he had laid a hand upon my arm. It startled me. I don't think he even knew he'd done it. He was saying hastily, "Are you coming for breakfast? I hope you slept well." Then his eyes settled on the battered case slung from my shoulder to hang behind my left hip. Those lovely grey eyes widened. "You're leaving? Without even saying *goodbye?*"

I didn't really have time to register that he was absolutely dumbfounded. He was saying, "If you're worried about what the other guests will say after last night ..."

I snapped, "Of course I'm not." I couldn't even begin to tell him how little I was worrying. I was glancing past him to the stairs. There was no sign of my two men. Then a sudden prickling on the back of my neck made me throw a desperate look behind. The doorway was safely clear and beyond was only the dull grey of the promenade and the equally bland sky above and then sea; beautiful, featureless sea.

He still had a hand on my arm. It was on the point just above the elbow where Clarke had gripped and hurt me yesterday. It was obviously the ideal spot for taking hold. Adam's head was briefly drawn towards the agitated serving girl. She was creating quite a fuss. Guests were not allowed to walk through the kitchen.

His attention returned to me. His brows were puckering into dawning suspicion as he realised that he hadn't met me coming down the stairs. I saw the deepening disbelief as the only alternative suggested itself; and then the release as logic dismissed it as impossible.

His mouth was already framing a lighter tone as he said, "Oddly enough, I'm leaving today too. Do you have to go right away? Can you come and have breakfast with me first? You said we'd talk this morning. Come on." There was something painfully different in the way Adam was speaking. Today he was not the man who had helped me last night. Or perhaps

I wasn't the same woman. All along I'd had a sense that regard-less of whatever else had been left a secret between us, it was important to him that everything that was spoken was at least safely grounded in basic honesty. But now, whatever this speech was, it wasn't honest.

He was rushing on amiably, "My sister is having a family crisis so I've got to get back to collect May. The perils, you might say, of——"

His eyes had alighted upon the rust marks on my skirt and the scuff upon my stocking. Those grey eyes returned to mine. I suppose it didn't suit him to acknowledge my distress. I could read all the options passing behind his eyes, all the possible ways of handling this latest inconvenient disagree-ment; of handling me. Alternately confrontation and kindness. I despised them all.

The stairway was still empty. Presumably my little barricade was holding Clarke.

Adam was saying slowly, thoughtfully, "You know, you're looking at me like you hate me again."

"No, no I don't. It's——" My denial failed pathetically, dismally, frantically when I ran out of words to explain that it wasn't him I hated, but his present actions. He had been steering me step by step back across the foyer. I pulled back while some-thing else worked its way across his mouth. I wasn't afraid of him but when he drew breath to speak, I broke in desperately, "Why did you tell them about me? Don't you even know why they——?"

But he didn't hear because he was interrupting me.

"Look," he said. He'd released my arm to unconsciously

put up his hand to his hair. He found his room key already in his palm and impatiently thrust it into a pocket. No wonder his grip had hurt. "This is going to sound strange, but I've got something to ask you. Don't rush off like this. Come and sit down for a few minutes. You can do that, can't you? Please?"

He had hold of my hand now. Somehow he'd moved to place himself between me and the front door. My breath was coming in short jerks. Adam was saying persuasively, "Don't you think you've drawn this out for long enough? Surely you can see it's the best way to resolve this? Even you must know this is the only way to bring the whole thing to a natural ... conclusion. All this running away, it's not helping. Trust me. Come with me."

I said disbelievingly, *"Resolve* this?" It was hard to keep my eyes fixed on any single point. Then, more sharply, "Go with you where?" Now my eyes were fixed firmly on him.

He said, "Where do you think?"

He was looking down at me as though I were stupid, or mad; which I suppose I was. I knew where. He wasn't talking about breakfast now. He meant Cirencester. The draw of his hand upon mine did what he thought it would. The memory coursed through my mind that I could trust him. I could depend on him. I just had to make him understand. It was a very cunning ruse. The stairs rumbled with the distant sound of footsteps, coming at a run.

When a figure stepped out on this lower floor from the dining room it didn't surprise me to learn it was Jim. Today he was clean-shaven once more. He'd decided that today he would make his play in the open without disguises.

"Have you asked her?" Jim was as relaxed as ever.

Somehow I'd put out my other hand to cling to Adam's. He said, without ever lifting his attention from my face, "I just have."

"And?"

I knew now these actions were Jim's, not his own. Adam was behaving like a man who'd been given an uncomfortable job to do and was almost as displeased about it as I. I saw his mouth compress into a line and it was because of the predictability of my reaction now as soon as Jim's part in this was revealed. Adam must have warned them that this was how I'd take it.

I hated this. I've mentioned before the incessant pattern of Gregory's attentions and the sense of being steered by the implication my dissent meant I was in the wrong; a disappointment and a fool. This was like that except that I never let Gregory get this close. I snapped out wildly, repulsed, "Did you even *ask* him about the photograph?"

I read the answer in Adam's eyes. I said more reasonably, "Of course you did." Then, raw as the truth sank in, "And naturally you believed him?"

Meaning, I think, why couldn't you choose to believe me instead?

He didn't have an answer. At least not one that didn't invoke my gender; because the male sounded calm and reasonable so the female was therefore wrong. There was movement high above on the stairs. It made me flinch and Adam's hand tighten in turn. I supposed Jim wanted this finished before Clarke arrived and it degenerated into yet another chaotic attempt to force me into that car.

"Adam, please don't make me ..." I faltered and with an effort pulled myself back together. He wasn't making me do anything. I chose to stand here debating the issue with him when I should be making the scene that would end this. First I said more surely, "Why did you have to betray me to them?"

"You call this *betrayal?* I—" Adam checked himself. Then with a considerable effort he enquired calmly, "You heard our discussion just now?"

"I heard."

He felt the change in me. The switch into decisiveness. A fleeting sharpness passed across his face. There was the briefest turn of his head towards Jim, though his attention never left me. Guilt. Doubt. There was something rather too much like defiance. His mouth hardened as he said persuasively, "It's not what you think. They're trying to help you."

Then his expression changed. It was like he'd abruptly abandoned the pretence of being what they thought he should be and did what he probably ought to have done all along. He became only himself instead. He added more swiftly, privately, "I'll be there. I'll help you."

He completed the transformation by cautiously easing his right hand from my grip and lifting it towards my cheek.

It all happened in a heartbeat. One minute I was standing there, numb except for the torture of clinging to him even though I wanted to break away, in the next there were footsteps on the stairs; two sets coming down the last flight at a run. The drift of his hand towards my cheek was given uncertainly, like a man playing an unfamiliar part. The gesture was real enough but it was done falteringly, doubtingly as though he was still half caught in the script Jim had given him. It made the world tilt. Every nerve thrilled like static on a wireless while absolutely nothing else in me moved. This wasn't the same as his former efforts to get me to go with him quietly. This was something else. This was about him. And need and trust. The worst of it was that when the lightest whisper of Adam's touch finally connected, it very nearly worked.

Then I slapped him.

I'm not sure who was more shocked. His hold on my other hand was dropped sharply and beyond his shoulder I saw Jim Bristol start forwards as if to intervene. Then there really was a glimpse of movement on the stairs and I was wrenching myself away from that darkened gaze stripped to the raw emotion underneath. This, suddenly, was the real man. He was exactly as I had thought. He wasn't weak. He wasn't a fool. Reserve was a thin veneer worn to protect the mind that blazed within. He terrified me.

I turned for the bright freedom of that blessedly open door. Behind I heard Jim swear, violently, and utter a rough, "Leave it, Adam. I'll go."

I was already running.

---

I ran, bags flapping, all the way to the station. The streets in between were a blur. The white smear of the station clock tower seemed more lonely today without the bustle of coal carts about its feet. It was Sunday but the first train was set to depart from the nearest platform and a steady stream of travellers was pouring in from the street. There was also a queue outside the ticket window.

There were in fact three windows, one for each of the classes of traveller. The First Class line was empty, the Third Class line went around the concourse past the public conveniences and behind the newspaper stand so for the sake of my nerves and my pocket, I picked Second.

I only had to wait thirty seconds; thirty very long agonising seconds. But then I was ducking my head towards the little square hole, murmuring my order and then turning and hurrying down the length of the tatty old carriages of the eastbound train. On the neighbouring track another train had just drawn in and the noise and mess flooded the station like a blessed screen. I stowed myself in the first vacant seat I found. It overlooked the empty tracks and was furthest from the platform, and my first act was to open the high window. My second was to turn up my coat collar as high as it would go. Then I had nothing left to do but wait.

About a minute later, Jim Bristol walked past. He didn't see me; I had picked my seat for a reason and I turned to watch through the long screen of disorderly passengers and dirtied windows as he marched down the platform. He didn't return. I heard the whistle and the bangs as the guards began to shut the doors so I knew he must be on the train. My knuckles turned white where they were gripping the strap of my handbag.

The guard walked past on the platform edge, moving to fasten us in. Behind, I heard the rattle of the connecting door between carriages as it opened and was firmly shut. I didn't turn round; I didn't want to. With my face to the window and the stiff high collar screening at least some of my features, this had to be enough to disguise me. The hairs on the back of my neck told a different story. I could sense him moving closer down the carriage, examining each of the travellers in turn, just as he had done in the previous carriage and the one before that. I caught sight of my eyes reflected in the grimy glass. They were wide and scared, and undeniably mine.

In a flash I was out of my seat and dragging my bags behind me. My case caught on the knees of my neighbour but his protest was lost as the guard climbed into the carriage and gave his whistle its final blast. He reached to pull the door closed as the train gave a shudder and began to creep into motion. Behind was a blur. Someone was barging his way through the remaining passengers and, without even a pause for thought, I thrust the guard's arm aside, ignored the man's startled cry and the other's shout of my name and stepped out onto the rapidly retreating platform.

For the second time that morning I very nearly lost a shoe. But then I heard the carriage door slam shut conclusively, and my balance recovered and I was scurrying down the platform as the train and its reluctant passenger were borne away inland without me.

A few seconds more and the concept of escape changed again. A distinctive pair of pinstriped trousers thundered past only to stop barely yards away and curse furiously at the lately departed train. Then for good measure Clarke cursed my name too and ran past again to the ticket office. He didn't see me there, beige coat merging seamlessly with the stonework. He was too busy interrogating the occupants of the little windows. It hadn't been for nothing that I had only bought a single ticket to Birmingham. I had meant to change trains at that vast city station, safe in the knowledge that my onwards route would have been very nearly untraceable from there.

Unfortunately, since I'd failed to keep my place on the train, I should have been immediately searching the platform behind me. There the second man was, stalking me from the far side of a porter's trolley.

# Chapter 17

Clarke's fellow was a man named Reed judging by the sharp invective that followed me as I dashed for the exit. Reed had made a snatch for my arm and it missed by a cat's whisker.

I went across the road outside without so much as a glance for traffic. I felt the smack of air as a car rushed past. It must have held them for a good few seconds and it was long enough for me to turn the corner and make use of the scattering of Sunday people. I turned left up the main street past a number of securely shuttered shop fronts and then I was darting from one pavement to the other to hammer on the door of the first place I could think of. I knocked again. Desperately. Clarke and Reed must have read the sign above me because they had faltered. Behind the heavy wooden door there was a tramp of feet, a rattle of many keys and finally someone sluggishly turned the lock. I stumbled in over the threshold into the police station.

Detective Inspector Griffiths really did sleep there. His moustache was uncombed and his shirt looked greasy about the collar. I'm not entirely sure he thought much of my appearance either, particularly as it brought with it a highly undesirable sense of urgency. Under his arm was a newspaper and a sandwich.

"Miss Ward," he said and smiled. Someone was shouting about breakfast in the cells at the back of the building – either the fellow hadn't had any yet or what he'd had wasn't good enough. I sympathised. That single biscuit I'd had in the dead of night hadn't gone very far. Whereas the detective's infuriatingly, tantalisingly well-filled sandwich accompanied us into the interview room.

"Sit down, sit down," Inspector Griffiths said pleasantly and ushered me towards a chair. "What can we do for you?"

I stared at him uselessly. I hadn't really intended to throw myself into this sanctuary. I gathered myself to haltingly tell the policeman everything I would have told Adam and Mary, only it sounded even stranger without the gloss of friendship. I told him about the accident and the journey here and the tireless perseverance with which these people had pursued me in the past few days. I gave the inspector their names, Clarke and Reed, and also Jim's. That long, forlorn face watched me sagely. He was so good at the act, it was hard to be sure that he was really listening.

Perhaps I'd done him an injustice. The moustache twitched as I finished; his long fingers remained entwined on the tabletop. Then he asked me to confirm that these men were outside now.

"Clarke and Reed are, yes."

I was suddenly hopeful in spite of everything. I watched as he climbed to his feet. He stood there, hand jiggling the coins in his trouser pocket, like he was steeling himself for the confrontation. Then he gave me a last long assessing look and left the room. I suppose he didn't necessarily get much practice at making arrests. I had an overwhelming urge to give him an encouraging word, but I didn't of course.

He returned after about twenty minutes, looking pretty much the same as before but this time clutching a document under one arm.

"Well?" I demanded eagerly. "Did you find them?" It was almost too much to hope that the paper in his hands contained a confession. By way of reply, one long-fingered hand slid the document across the tabletop towards me.

It was a folder and it was titled 'Mrs K C Williams'.

It was then that I'd noticed what had been out of kilter all this time. As he'd welcomed me he'd said *Miss Ward*.

"I must say," he remarked, taking his seat, "we were quite surprised when we put two and two together. You really did have us convinced with this whole charade. Did it amuse you to pretend to be his wife?" He took an enormous bite from his sandwich. I could hear him chewing and the gulp as he swallowed the mass.

"But ..." I was staring at him. "But I was his wife."

"Yes, Mrs Williams. *Was*." His moustache quirked to one side. This little emphasis on specifics amused him. The inspector carefully wrapped up the remaining half of his sandwich and set it to one side. He leaned forwards, hands clasped before him on the table. "It was quite a clever act. You actually had me fooled." He gave a conspiratorial wink. "Your one mistake, you know, was switching back to your maiden name while you were staying here. Miss Ward one minute and then Mrs Williams the next. You really shouldn't be disappointed that we found you out."

It couldn't be possible. Surely, it couldn't be possible. I said desperately, "But I really am Mrs Williams. You must know I am. It's written there, before you. That wasn't the mistake. I didn't lie to *you*. Mrs Williams is still my legal name. My little disguise was in using the name Miss Ward at the hotel and that doesn't affect you at all. That was just so that I could feel a little safer during my stay."

Inspector Griffiths gazed at me steadily. He managed to communicate a whole wealth of feeling in that stare. Disbelief, condescension and a particularly patronising touch of enduring patience.

It prompted me to add haplessly, "And it's not really a lie to use that name either. I do have a legal right to *both* names after all. I've been experimenting with using Miss Ward a little lately, for a couple or months or so before this trip to Aberystwyth. It's a very new idea I had. Miss Ward is on my ration book. I changed it in a tentative attempt to really come to terms with the divorce, you know?"

It was the wrong thing to say. If his habit of sleeping at his desk had come about because his wife had thrown him out, he was going to be the last man to be reasonable now. Instead, he waited for me to reveal what further lies I wished to peddle on this visit. I hadn't got any so instead he tipped his head towards the document before me.

Helplessly, I flattened out the card folder. Within it were three sheets of paper and the first was dated two days ago;

Friday. It bore a handwritten note forwarding the contents with all due respects from the Lancaster constabulary for his attention. The next page was a typescript report from the officers who had performed the interview at my hospital bed. It summarised my encounter with the bus and the hospital's decision to defer psychiatric testing, and it concluded with the judgement that the policemen saw no reason to dispute the doctors' findings. The doctors believed that I had suffered what was dubbed a brief *'delusional state'* as a result of the acute emotional distress brought on by Mr R Williams' sudden demise. There was, however, the caution that a pre-existing undiagnosed mental disorder might subsequently prove to have been a contributory factor.

According to the final sheet, headed paper from the hospital itself, any recurrence of the delusion must necessitate immediate admission to a specialist ward. In which case there was, it suggested, indication for treatment with the electric shock.

I set the report down with an unsteady hand and lifted my head. It was then that I knew I would never escape this. One way or another I was really going to have to learn that some-where along the line a man would always have the will to make me become whatever he thought I should be. Mad, cowed, stupid or weak. In some ways it didn't matter a jot if it was Clarke or Reed or Jim or the doctors, or even Rhys. I'd told Mary that I didn't believe every encounter with the other sex must always come down to a play for power. But there was almost no point in fighting it any more. Almost.

Inspector Griffiths had gathered the pages back together

and now he smiled at me through his moustache. "Well?" he encouraged. "Anything to add?"

I said nothing.

He told me, "This information came in the post yesterday, just after you and I spoke." He leant forwards and rested his elbows on the table, jabbing a long finger for emphasis at the folder before him. "I have my own theory about you. Would you like to hear it? Is that a nod? Yes?"

I gave him the appropriate glimmer of agreement.

"Well," he said, "I have an idea that the lonely and impressionable Miss Ward—"

"Mrs Williams," I corrected numbly.

"—*Mrs* Williams, had a bit of a shock when her ex-husband suddenly died, and it went to her head. She came to this town to say her farewells and instead got a bit scared and a bit panicked and although she didn't mean to cause any trouble when she began talking about the war and claiming the sympathy due to a grieving spouse, the story got out of hand and now she's sitting in my interview room wondering if she's about to be arrested for fraud, theft and wasting police time."

His tone was suddenly very severe indeed. I had my head down, but I could feel his gaze on me across the table. "Well?" he demanded.

"Sorry," I finally mumbled. I managed to lift my eyes. He was watching me very coldly. I gave up; I gave up on all of it and seized this small thread of a lifeline with all the feminine simplicity I could muster. "I'm so sorry, Inspector, I truly am. I was upset and I have been very scared; and I suppose it made me come over a bit silly just now. I didn't mean to cause you any trouble, I really didn't. I know I shouldn't have said all that about those two men and disturbed your meal and ... everything. I know you have better things to do with your time than worry about this sort of thing." I reached into my various bags and drew out the envelope and placed it on the table before him. "You'd better have the photographs back. I'm afraid I left the camera in the hotel. Am I in a lot of trouble?"

He was silent for a long time, considering. Then he climbed to his feet. "Yes, Mrs Williams, you are. A divorced wife is not his widow. But luckily for you I am very busy and there's no need to make a fuss about the ... um ... *loan* of Mr Williams' effects to the wrong person. After all, what harm has it done really?" He retrieved the sandwich, the folder and the evidence of his own mistake in the form of the photographs, and walked to the door. He held it open for me and I needed no second invitation. "So let's say no more about it, eh? But don't let me see you here again, otherwise ..." He gave an informative waggle of that moustache.

"I can promise that you won't," I said with perfect conviction, and hurried away from him down the corridor to the street door and the glorious freedom of the space outside where two men waited to take me to their car.

# Chapter 18

In an accident of usefulness Inspector Griffiths must have stepped outside to look, just in case. They didn't snatch me when I emerged into the quiet disorientation of a November Sunday. They didn't close in either when I turned downhill and hurried, not back to the station where their car was waiting, but left to the seafront and the darker end of town where the beach met the cliff edge. It was the only route of escape I could think of. I couldn't hire a car because I had never learned to drive, and besides it was Sunday and the garages were shut. I wouldn't catch a bus because what with my past history with long waits at bus stops, I wasn't exactly keen on the idea of standing in line for half an hour while one came. A cab would have been a possibility if one had happened to come by but it didn't and the rank was, needless to say, outside the station. But there was a path along the cliff top that led to a different station on the Birmingham line and I knew a train was set to call there in roughly two hours.

They let me take the funicular railway to the summit of the hill where this path began. I had long since give up the pretence that I had any control over this. If I had, I might have convinced myself that the inspector had made them wary or that perhaps they didn't know about this path to Borth and I might really have this chance to get away. But I didn't believe that. They were playing out a plan of their own while I occupied myself with mine.

All along the seafront the Royal Wedding celebrations were still running. The bandstand was open and this was where the crowds were. The clifftop was quieter. After the neatly ordered streets, the landscape up here was shockingly wild and open until it came to an abrupt end a dizzying hundred yards or so above the sea. There was a stiff breeze that cut through my flapping coat. Suddenly this bleak granite coastline teetered on the brink of winter. The hilltop path stretched from left to right, south to north, with the distant grey of the next town just discernible through the smudged sea air. The alternative train station was there; only about six tantalising miles of deserted landscape stood between me and it.

The green surf moved and sucked at the foot of the cliffs. I could see now why they might have been willing to let me stray up here. It was the incident on the pier all over again and this time the distant sea didn't need Jim to plant the thought of falling in my head. The hiss of rolling surf was mesmerising, crawling, alluring and it whispered of lonely visits to high waterfalls and dead husbands. I kept moving and I kept well back from the edge. It was the only way to cope.

Luckily, I had no intention of making a madcap dash along the clifftop today. I stepped into the tearoom beside the busy Camera Obscura and had a hasty discussion with the serving boy about directions for the route to Borth. Then, trail safely laid, I found the crude, narrow track that ran left – in precisely the wrong direction for Borth – and followed it cautiously downhill back to the town between thorn bushes that snatched at the case in my hands.

My watch must have stopped while I was up there. I noticed it when the next clattering funicular carriage rose, suddenly very close, and I found myself a few seconds later lying in the grit with my hand by my face. Then I was safely down and hurrying alone and unseen up the short rise onto the back street that ran behind the high seafront hotels towards the town.

There was a brief flash of red ahead. An old car with a canvas hood was crossing the junction at the end of this street, ready to make the long run inland. I won't describe what I felt when I saw Adam go.

---

I hadn't lost Clarke. There is a method of hunting that is practiced, I am told, by people with a taste for big game. It is the sort that picks up a scent and trails it, sometimes for days, herding its quarry away from food, away from rest, away from all hope, until the desperate prey is so bewildered that it simply forgets it is a wild free thing and goes patiently to its death.

Clarke was doing it now.

He was alone so he must have believed my decoy enough to send his companion up to the hilltop and tracing the cliff path to Borth. But he had not gone up there himself. From the moment my feet had regained level ground at the foot of the cliff, he'd been there, about ten yards behind me, and he must have decided there were more subtle ways of avoiding another fuss. Now he was driving me, goading me, letting me exhaust myself amongst all these people until I had no intelligence left to even beg for help. And he was enjoying it.

He was amused when I rebelled and attempted to defy him by drawing attention from a passerby. I did it twice, once to a strong-looking man and once to a woman with her family. The man was middle-aged and he turned his head just in that perfect way that tricked my mind into thinking he was Jim. I was used to the apparition that was my husband – Rhys's presence was so familiar now that it was almost a game to see when my mind would make him pop up – but it was considerably less pleasant to imagine I'd plucked at the sleeve of Jim Bristol in yet another disguise. The man didn't understand my incoherent request for help anyway. The woman only made a protective snatch for her gawping child. It fleetingly occurred to me that Mary might believe me but I lost my nerve when finding her meant braving the trap of the hotel. I didn't waste the effort on anyone else.

Clarke smiled when I tried instead to become invisible. I walked everywhere; anywhere where there was a chance I might be lost within a mass of people. I took Clarke on a tour of the town's sights, even to the oppressive ruins of the castle, and finally followed the rush as the tourists returned to modern shopping streets with their minds fixed on the prospect of an afternoon pot of tea. Clarke stayed with me, an unshakeable extension of my own footsteps, but my attempt at invisibility must have been more successful than I'd realised because the postcard seller with his small trolley of gaudy souvenirs didn't notice me at all when he stole my path with me still in it.

The blow to my ankle was agony and we both tangled in a heap, the trolley and I, and painted seashells and pebbles spilled everywhere. I barely waited to see the carnage. It was enough that the blow had reawakened my senses. I was a person, alive and ready for flight.

There was an instant rush of people eager to look, to help the man pick himself up and no doubt help themselves to some of his fallen cargo. No one helped me to my feet, not even Clarke. He was somewhere at the back, jostled aside by merry elbows.

I shook off the last of the seaside debris, snatched up my poor battered bags and dived into the first place I found.

# Chapter 19

Clarke lost me for about three hours. For three long hours, I had nothing to do except calculate my options and then dismiss them all in turn. My space was dank and musty and the hymnals that made up my perch smelt faintly of mildew. I was hiding in the cupboard of a Methodist chapel and the wide wooden floor in the centre led the eye to the demure altar in its recess ringed with elegant lettering. I stayed there until the tinted light that shone through tall graceful windows across the vacant gallery had faded to match the heavy black of the town outside.

I sat there while Clarke came in and searched and I stayed there when he left again. I found the dregs of the water flask I used for painting in the bottom of my handbag. It was stale but I drank it all the same.

Night had fallen by the time I slipped out through a side door that led through a silently sleeping schoolroom. It was probably only about five o'clock but my weary body thought it was midnight. My muscles were hollow in that way they have when you're down to your reserve energy but I didn't have the strength to brave a meal somewhere. It would be tantamount to consigning myself to another night in this town.

So instead I set myself a new target and it wasn't one I had tried before. I think I might have thought of running to Devil's Bridge in passing once, but I'd never intended it to be a serious plan. Now it was the only route that seemed to make any sense. I'd take the little train that was timed to ferry the workers back home to their hillside homes and I would spend the night in the hotel there. In the morning I wouldn't run. I might not have the choice anyway. But if I did, I would do what I would never have been brave enough to attempt before. I would see how far I could climb down the river gorge and try to be the one to find Rhys's body.

This wasn't about escape any more. Or logic. This was about knowing. And defying with every ounce left of my existence this impulse they had to hound me to despair.

It was driven by exhaustion and hunger and the improbable dream that tomorrow I would have the strength to attempt such a rough descent of that valley. It was made possible by deliberately deluding myself into believing that if only I managed to get onto the little narrow gauge train and escaped Aberystwyth at last, everything else would be just that little bit better. It didn't matter that I knew it was a lie. It was enough that it kept my body moving.

The Rheidol railway line hugged close to the towering bulk of the mainline station. The last Birmingham train was long gone but all the same, when I finally neared the wide street that held the big station building, I was careful to keep myself out of its line of sight.

Some people passed me, shop girls and visiting hillmen walking purposefully towards their homeward bound train.

Clinging to the deep recess of a dirty doorway, I examined each of their faces in turn. They each gave me the shock of seeming to be Clarke or Reed or Jim or Rhys, but they weren't.

After a while I followed a group towards the turn onto the little road beside the station. Everything was dark except the railway station. The few streetlights made the station clock tower shine white. My little group of serving girls were hurrying. The train must be nearing its time. I scurried with them, trying to look youthful and businesslike. Then there was a shrill whistle.

It wasn't from the station master; it was closer by and it dragged my head round like a shot. They were there. One was in a shabby hotel doorway as lookout, the other breaking cover from the space behind their car where it lurked against a distant kerb.

I abandoned the little train. I abandoned Rhys. I ran again.

---

My flight this time took me steeply uphill and it finished me. Reed's whistle had been badly timed. They must have been as tired as I. I heard them shouting abuse at each other and making a general agreement to get the job done this time and play no more games. Then suddenly I had nothing but the pounding of my heart and rasping breath because they must have lost me in the dark stretches between streetlights.

I wouldn't have got away otherwise. I doubt my pace even equalled a walk and perhaps I might have got along quicker if I had treated it like a stroll rather than a run. But a sharp turn and then another and suddenly here was sanctuary that had not occurred to me. The tall buildings of the area around the station had given way to the long terraces of the ship- wright's quarter and their neat regular frontages were a little breath of hope. No doubt I would be as unwelcome here as I was unexpected, but I defied my ex-mother-in-law to actu- ally turn me from the door.

I slackened my pace and sought out the right one; it was blue. I always remembered the woodwork was blue. I found the knocker and gave it a rap.

The street was silent for a moment. Then the lights of a car went slowly past the top junction. I heard the pitch of the engine throb change as the pressure was taken off the accel- erator. This was why they'd drawn back from following me on foot. They had a tool that could outpace me. The muted squeak of brakes being applied brought a sharp internal grind of despair that sent me staggering into the house wall. No one moved behind the barred front door. There were no lights on inside. No one had heard my second urgent rap. I was already peeling myself away from the comforting solidity of the cold stone wall and plunging blindly on.

I ran into a man who was walking up. He made my heart lurch and I'd have cried out if I'd been able to muster the breath. I must have terrified him too. He wasn't Reed, if Clarke was the man driving the car. I rebounded off a solitary parked car and shied past him, both of us angling our bodies away to give each other room. I suppose the gleam of streetlight on a blood- less face probably made my features singularly fearsome. For me the dirty yellow light did that awful thing of making me think he was my husband. I couldn't bear it. I span away. Blind. Numb. I couldn't look a second time. And then I did and found he'd gone with a sharp bang like a cannon going off that was probably the sudden slam of a house door shutting me out.

It was very odd but I was finding it suddenly hard to see my way. It was very dark, that was why; and there wasn't even a hint of starlight up above. The steps down onto the harbour were black and strangely musical. The yards of the boats in the dry dock were jangling like tiny bells against their masts in the chill air. I picked a clumsy path above them along the high dock wall and skirted the drying lobster pots with half my mind on the fearsome drop that was only discernible by the subtle variations between textures of gloom. My lungs ached. My footsteps echoed as the single robust reminder that I was still on solid ground.

Then that sound changed. Wide wooden planks met my feet. I followed their course purely because the weathered wood shone very dull silver. I think I must have been growing a little disorientated. I didn't realise immediately that I'd stumbled onto a jetty. Somewhere I must have lost my suitcase and then my handbag but I'd barely noticed. I didn't realise that I'd walked myself into a dead end either until it was too late. I was lucky there was a robust rail at the end.

The sea was beautiful in the night time. The river ended its run here where ghostly boats rocked and jet black swells with turquoise crests lapped against the distant sea wall. The breeze that had been building all day was ice against my skin and a light was blinking out to sea. A fishing boat or perhaps just a trick of the eye.

The steady inrush of the tide was hypnotic. It distracted me from paying too much attention to the brief flare of car headlights before they were extinguished in the dark void beyond the harbour buildings. My hands clutched the barrier. It was wooden and it met me securely across the middle. The rolling mass of water below was mesmerising; an inky lure that sucked and sighed beneath the salt-encrusted boards. I caught myself in the midst of seriously contemplating the practicalities of trying to swim my way to freedom. The sheer madness of the idea made me laugh.

The water whispered death. This was the voice that had called to Rhys when he had looked down at the gaping void of the gorge. No human hand had done the work for him. No mortal speech had goaded him to his end that day. He'd been driven to that place by desperation and found every sense shrouded by the incessant calling of the waterfall. I knew now how he had answered.

*Oh Rhys.*

If only he'd left me a note, a sign, an explanation for what was to come. Clarke would have what he wanted now. Distantly I heard the thud and creak behind of weight on wood and braced myself to meet him. I had nowhere else to hide. And it hurt most of all that this was it, and I still didn't know why.

Only instead of the impatient tramp of eager footsteps, there was just one step and then another and a rough voice that I recognised, that I had thought never to hear again.

"You little fool." And a curse and a hasty approach when I whipped round and cried out as the small of my back came up hard against the barrier.

It was hard to see him. Hard to see anything in this meagre light. He loomed. My hands met the wood behind me. Gripped bloodlessly. I don't think I could have contained the impulse to shrink screaming to the floor otherwise. He wasn't taking any chances anyway. He didn't take hold of me but the force of his presence was such that he might just as well have done.

"I've used half a tank of fuel looking for you." His voice was angry. Everything about him was angry. I shrank against my barrier. My heart was pounding. I hadn't prepared for this ... hadn't the reserves left to stave off the sheer uncomprehending panic. I wasn't afraid of him. I was afraid that this was a mistake and Clarke had come and tipped me in, and the water was already claiming me, leaving me with only the dream that this man was here in their place. The savagery in his voice was real. It told me flatly, "You're coming with me. I'm not letting you go again. You can't run away from this any more."

Despite the intense darkness I saw his hands move restlessly by his sides as if he were wrestling with the impulse to take hold of me and give me a bit of a shake. But he contained it. Just. After that sharp unexpected introduction to the real Adam Hitchen this morning, I didn't know who this man was. He stood there, shadows marking his face and scowled me into speech.

I dug up my last bit of faith in life. I couldn't look at him. I clung to the secure anchorage of that wooden rail and kept my head down as I said it.

"All right, Adam," I told him finally. "Yes."

# Chapter 20

I was right to fear a method of hunting that depended on running the prey until it had no fight left. I think at that moment of admitting his mastery of my mind, my body must have strayed into the dangerous wilderness somewhere between defeat and unconsciousness. He'd had to steer me into the passenger seat of his car. Now I was awake but I think even my eyes forgot how to blink. I had never really believed before that I could be driven to the kind of physical breakdown that robs a person of their wits, regardless of what various people had been saying about my general state of mind, but in hindsight I think this came very close.

Then we stopped briefly somewhere on a blank stretch of road in the mountains behind Aberystwyth, and it probably saved my life.

Adam had stopped to empty the last drips of his last can of fuel into the tank. My salvation came from the little nudge he gave to my wrist after he climbed back in with a glass bottle of water that he must have retrieved from the rear seat. The bottle jarred against my arm so that the contents swirled and then settled.

My body could remember how to move after all. I clumsily took it. My hands fumbled to open the stopper. The water was warm and stale from a day in the car but it allowed me to think again. And once I was able to think, I was able to sleep. I let my head fall back against the low seat and shut my aching eyes. I opened them again. My driver was tense. The winding roads between the Welsh coast and England were being taken so quickly that trees and hedges smacked past with a violence that made the roof shudder. But the road behind was entirely vacant. They were probably ahead of us.

I slept. When I rose to consciousness, it was to the sound of an urban scene. Somewhere there was music and the sharp tang of tobacco smoke. It was hours later. I was cold even with my coat wrapped tightly about me. The car swung left and right in a maze of turns. We had arrived. It was insane to realise that all these people had expended all this energy over a course of days for the single purpose of carrying me back to Cirencester. Into my head popped that one question dimly remembered from my first encounter with Clarke and Reed. *Where is it?*

I must have said it out loud. The instant snap of Adam's voice was sharp. "What did you say?"

*Beg him.* My mind broke loudly into the silence that followed. *Beg him now.* I opened my eyes.

Whatever pleas had formed on my lips died unspoken when I saw the town houses by the kerbside. They were very tall, very impressive Georgian town houses and they were typical of the grand white terraces of Cheltenham, not Cirencester. The car drew to a halt at the foot of a short run of steps and the engine died. The sudden silence made me flinch. My eyes dragged themselves jerkily round to Adam's face. He was staring at me through the inky haze of a street lamp, considering. Then he moved.

I flinched again, violently, but he was only reaching to open his door. The sounds of the busy spa town rushed in with the cool night air and I could hear the distant rhythm of a dancehall.

"Stay here." His order was curt and didn't anticipate contradiction. Then he climbed out, shut the door and stepped behind the car to knock briefly at a black polished door set within a tall pillared porch. I could see him if I turned my head.

After a few moments the big black door opened a crack and then wider once the person inside identified their late visitor. I watched as Adam glanced back at me briefly before stepping over the threshold. His return was accompanied by something awkward and cosseted by the woman who had opened the door. She followed them both, talking ceaselessly as Adam descended the few steps to the roadside before reaching in through the driver's door to unlock the door behind.

The dog. I had completely forgotten about the dog.

Then the rear door swung open and the creature climbed into the back, and my surprise came out as a pathetic jerk of the heart. There had been a whimper as he moved to press the door shut, a small plaintive whine of protest, and it was the sulky complaint of a tired human, not a dog. I twisted in my seat, mind and body in sudden agreement, and saw a child's face. Then Adam moved between her and the street lamp and cast her into shade.

"Is she ill?" The woman's voice was distant now, disembodied concern passing unseen outside the car after a brief duck of the head to peer in at me. All I could see were the backs of Adam's legs where he had moved to conceal me.

"She's fine." The reply was terse, dismissive, but then I heard him add in a voice more like his own, "I'm sorry. I'm sorry David's mother is unwell; I hope she's feeling better when you see her tomorrow. I'm sorry that I was away just when you were having a family crisis. And I'm truly sorry for this too by the way – for being so late and that she's been so fractious tonight – I promised her I would be home long before."

"David's mother will be fine, I'm sure, old dragon that she is. As will your little one when she gets into her own bed. Having her daddy back again will be enough to set all the world to rights, I should think."

*Daddy*. I barely noticed when he made his farewells and slipped in beside me. There was a momentary silence while we watched the woman disappear into her house and then he said, "Here, hold this." And started the car.

There was no sign this time of the angry corners that had followed us from Wales as our vehicle rolled away from the kerb. There was no aggression either as it picked its way through turns and junctions towards the road that ran up the steep heights of the escarpment. Something soft and warm stirred in my lap and I looked down; and had to wonder if I were lost in some drowning fantasy after all. The fuzzy object moved again, pushing keenly at my hands, and I stared with unbelieving eyes at the living thing nestling against me that was, of all things, a kitten.

I found that somehow the discovery made my throat burn.

A road sign flashed past; Cirencester, and a smaller flaking sign below, *Roman Capital of the Cotswolds* before being enclosed by buildings. Everything was burning, eyes, limbs, throat and soul when the car drew to a halt against a kerb in a quiet domestic street and Adam silenced the engine.

When he had finished extracting his daughter from the back seat and came round to open my door, I climbed out automatically. It was only then that I remembered that he had given me the blanket sometime after the petrol stop. It tangled briefly about my knees. I'd had the water bottle in my lap too and it fell with a crash. It made a terrible mess. I bent with the kitten cradled in one hand and reached to collect the shattered pieces with the other. My hand was shaking. Somehow it seemed vital that I scrabbled to tidy up. I was sure it was wrong to leave this trace of myself. I heard Adam's voice behind me, sharply authoritative. "Leave it, Kate." Then when I didn't stop, couldn't stop, I felt his hand reach down to touch mine, briefly arresting. That ordinary fraying leather watch strap was there on his wrist. "Kate," he said more patiently. He waited until I turned my head. "Leave it. Come along."

He stepped up the short path to the middle of three matching Cotswold gables set in a terrace. Each was three storeys high and built in dark stone cast by a distant streetlight to dirty grey. The row was set slightly further back from the pavement than the lighter limestone buildings to either side.

A sudden burst of light hit me hard in the face and the uneasy peace was shattered by the opening of the front door to be followed seconds later by the noisy bustling of an ageing woman who went past me with a glare.

She hauled my bags out of the boot. He must have collected them as we left the jetty and I hadn't even noticed. I was still staring when she barged past me again and into the house. Adam was standing in the doorway with his daughter clinging to his hand. He jerked his head at me. He meant me to follow. His expectant look grew impatient when he saw that I hadn't moved.

"But ..." I said weakly. None of this was remotely how I had expected it to be. "I don't understand."

His reply was equally flat. "Just as you say." Then he gave another jerk of his head. "Come on."

# Chapter 21

Inside was the gloom of a long hallway, a quick glimpse of firmly closed doors and then the sudden heat and friendliness of a family kitchen.

"Sit," he ordered, extending a hand to point out a chair by the heavy wooden table. I obeyed.

I perched there, small in a quiet hunch while he moved about his kitchen, apparently occupied by the hunt for nothing more deadly than a pan in which to warm some milk. The child had her arms about his middle, hampering every step he made. She was probably about eight or nine – I was hardly in the best condition for making guesses about age – she was just tall enough that her arms could wrap about his hips and every once in a while I caught the swift gleam as she glanced at me before burying her head again. Further away, I heard the rough creak as the woman moved up and down the stairs and bashed about in the rooms overhead. Then she appeared again, glowering and middle-aged in the doorway and clearly not very happy at all at having a hostage of sorts in her house. Presumably he would never have brought me here if the lateness of our return and the importance of collecting his daughter hadn't necessitated it.

"Do you think you could find her something to eat?" The slight tilt of his head was all that indicated he was talking about me.

Having to feed that hostage as well seemed very nearly the last straw but in the end the woman settled on giving a grudging nod as he took himself and the girl up the stairs. I only sat there cowed and quiet, cradling the warmly sleeping kitten on my lap, and waited for someone to show me what they had in store for me. The woman didn't speak to me; she was fixed upon clattering about her kitchen as she found first a pan for the stove, then a jar containing soup and lastly a loaf and a bread knife. She was careful to keep the latter very far from me. I wondered what she had been told.

"Give me that." Her snatch for the tiny creature jerked me out of an unnatural haze and I blinked at her as she shoved the kitten carelessly into a fabric-lined cardboard box and then set a bowl down before me. Then a spoon appeared with a similar crash that jangled the nerves at the back of my mind. After a moment of stupidity, I mustered the intelligence to begin eating.

I couldn't have actually said that I was hungry, or even that the thick soup tasted of very much but something tenuous began to assemble at the tips of my toes and work its way northwards that can only have been good for me. I looked up. Something of my condition must have penetrated the woman's displeasure because when I discovered her standing there, supervising me, she almost forgot to scowl. Then she took herself off to crash about bringing the rest of Adam's bags in from his car.

The house grew quiet. I suspect she wasn't supposed to leave me unsupervised but she did. The now deserted front door waited only a few yards from where I sat alone in a strange room, blinking while the minutes passed, frozen to the bone even though the stove was well stoked. Waiting was excruciating torture. Between one sluggish blink and the next, I jerked awake to find my face pressed into the corner of my elbow upon the table, the emptied bowl by my hand and a hot cup of tea steaming gently beyond that. It was the sharp bang of the latter as it landed that had woken me.

Uneasily, I pushed myself upright from my childlike sprawl, already aware of who must have come into the room at last and feeling even more off balance than ever. Adam was there, claiming a seat opposite and very deliberately absorbed in the task of consuming his own portion of soup. There was something about the quality of his silence that told me he was relieved to find me still there. His features had returned to how they had looked when I had first met him, if a little worn from his journey, and his eyes were fixed upon the bowl in his hands so that it was possible to believe it was all a simple misunderstanding.

His gaze lifted. It wasn't a misunderstanding. I blanched and hastily turned my head away as if that was any kind of defence while he pushed back his chair and stood up. I felt the pause when he stared for a moment at my averted face before turning away to carry his empty bowl to the sink.

I saw him stand there, hands resting on the edge of the

washbasin and breathing deeply before his lungs suddenly took in a sharp little burst and he turned back to catch me watching and demanded, "So you think I'm going to *hurt* you now?" Then I heard the clatter as he dropped the spoon into the sink after the bowl. "No, don't answer that. I don't want to know."

I kept my head turned away now, feverishly avoiding any fresh contact with that angry grey gaze. I continued avoiding looking at him while the kettle was snatched from the stove, refilled and then set to boil again. I stared fixedly at the floor by my feet as he moved about his kitchen, tidying washed crockery away, and I managed to escape acknowledging him right up to the moment he placed a fresh cup on the table before me.

Then I couldn't help but turn my head and follow the hand upwards to the fine-drawn face with its hardened jaw to ask my most stupid question of all, "*Who are you?*"

For a moment, surprise washed his features clear. Then he ignored it. He moved to set his hands upon the tabletop; he was leaning over me, practically forcing the confrontation so that now he was in the position to fire a question of his own. "Do you really miss him that much?"

"I beg your pardon?"

"Why didn't you just *say* something? Why have you been hiding it, ignoring it, *nurturing* it all this time when you could have just told me the truth from the start? It needn't have come to this, you know." I only stared while he added grimly, "Why did you let me think—?"

He broke off. There was hurt here. Something far more raw

than anger; something he was accusing me of that was more personal than anything Clarke or Reed wanted from me. Bewilderment made me say on a disbelieving laugh, "You think I wanted to follow in Rhys's wake?"

"My dear, don't even try to take that tone with me." Adam had himself in hand again and had withdrawn to a calmer distance. Now he bent to rest his forearms on the further corner of the table. Its surface was scuffed and hollowed by years of use. His head turned; an eyebrow lifted. He sounded like he was gearing up to scolding his child, although I couldn't imagine he would have ever used this tone with her. It was too hard.

He said, "You were attempting to throw yourself into the sea – there's not much mistaking that, I believe, even if in the event the tide would have probably just washed you straight back in. Are you aware of what might have happened if somebody else had found you first; some person from the town?"

"But—"

"You *do* know where they would have sent you, surely?" Then he added the answer just in case his meaning wasn't painfully clear. "You would go to prison."

"But that's the whole point," I said slowly, watching his face for a reaction. He'd straightened his arms again so that he was propped on his hands. It was a posture that implied wearied patience. I told him, "I wasn't trying to kill myself. I was trying to get away. This whole week I've been trying to do that. I've been trying to disappear."

"Oh?" His expression of polite interest was insulting. And

it brought with it the first germs of doubt. They were like a wash of cold water. He was already saying, "And that's why you've been crashing about the place like a wild thing all week, is it? I knew you'd been shaken up by his death but I had no idea things had got that bad. Why on earth didn't you just talk to me? I mean, I know things have been pretty turbulent these past few days but I should have thought you knew by now you could rely on me enough for that. Why on earth didn't you just tell me ...?" The tirade faltered. Then I saw him lift his chin defiantly and add very deliberately, "Why did you have to let me think I mattered if you were only going to fling it all away for *him?*"

A harder silence. He was angry with me, I could see that well enough, and hurt I think by my refusal to gift him the innermost workings of my mind, but it was all wrong. It was all so absurdly personal. I suddenly grew impatient. "*What is it* that you want me to say? You've got me here now. You can ask me anything you like. Why don't you just get it over with and ask me where it is?"

Then it hit me with a sudden shudder of realisation. "Unless ... unless you're only waiting for Clarke to arrive so that he can ask me himself?"

It took Adam some time to reply. Then he only repeated in an oddly cautious voice, "Clarke?"

"Oh, didn't you expect me to discover his name?" I said nastily. I was sitting hunched on my chair by his table, an exhausted wreck of a woman who was bracing herself to meet a final assault that would never quite come. His expression belonged to a man for whom things had just taken a turn for the worse. "I heard you speaking to him on the stairs this morning, showing your two new friends which room I had taken."

"What two friends? There were none of mine on the stairs, or at least no one that I spoke to."

"Please, Adam!" I couldn't imagine what cruelty was driving him to still conceal his plans for me. The sudden energy in my voice startled him. I saw his gaze run up to the ceiling above his head as though warning me to avoid disturbing his daughter. I put a hand up to my eyes. I said in a desperate whisper, "You know I heard you! You spoke to them. You admitted it!"

"I most definitely did not." He had straightened up again. He was standing there, absolutely, convincingly dismissive as he told me, "I don't recall seeing anyone on the stairs, unless you count passing that little boy's father at the bottom. You're delusional."

I jumped in my chair like he'd struck me.

Nothing, no one had the power to reduce my self-belief to shreds as that single accusation could. It went through me like an icy arrow. This was the point of this interview. This was why the mention of Clarke had disturbed him. He had no questions to pose here other than these few to test my sanity. "No," I whispered. Grief made my voice catch as I added, "You admitted it. When I told you I'd overheard this morning, *you admitted it* … and when they failed to catch me, you seized your advantage and brought me here yourself."

He stared at me. Then he said very clearly and precisely, "I'm not sure we're talking about the same thing … I spoke to Jim and Dr Alderton in the *lounge*, not on the stairs and they would hardly need to ask which room was yours. You publicised that for yourself with the drama last night." He stepped closer to lean over me again. His fingers showed white where they gripped the edge of the table. "That was, in fact, the thing that decided me. You were clearly exhausted and getting worse, and I thought it wise to consult someone who knew about these sorts of things and might know what should be done. I'd just learned I was going to have to cut short my stay and both the doctor and Jim agreed that it could be foolish to leave you friendless. The doctor even went so far as to suggest that it might be helpful to you to come back here; to face your fears head on so to speak. Not," he finished grimly, starkly innocent at last, "that any of us had any idea of it coming to this."

"Oh my God." It was minutes later and it took a moment for me to realise that these words had been forced from my mouth. "Oh God. Face my fears? Do you know what you've done?"

My hands were trembling in my lap, in fact my whole body was shivering with an energy that I didn't know I still had. It was shaking as my voice fought to formulate sound and I made him start in surprise as I hissed, "Jim's one of them. He's tricked you, and now you've brought me back here – just where they've wanted me all along."

There was silence. I sat there, reduced now and shrunken in my chair while he leaned over me, frozen and not even breathing. But then, instead of looking surprised, or alarmed or any of the other expressions in the spectrum of emotions that I might have wished for, he laughed.

He said, "Come on, my dear. *One of them?* Which 'them' do you mean exactly?" He paused long enough to sweep some crumbs from the tabletop, though he didn't move away. "You told me yourself that your imagination runs wild. Don't you think that you're carrying it a bit far? If you must know, Dr Alderton joined Jim in suspecting that the combination of Rhys's death and your recent concussion was affecting your sense of proportion. They both were keen that I should invite you to come back here. The idea was to give you some time to adjust and recover. It certainly wasn't a trick. And our decision to interfere was quite possibly just in the nick of time too, judging by the scene I found on the end of that jetty."

As he said it, the truth seemed to hit home to him just how serious all this was. A person suffering from the sort of desperation he was describing couldn't exactly be cured by one hard lecture over his dining table. It was, I think, a shock to his feelings. It was a shock to mine too. I had to admit that all this time he really had been angry and hurt because my actions had implied that compared to the loss of Rhys, the man before me could never be that important. Now I saw that it had dawned on him that for his own sake and his child's peace *I* mustn't be allowed to matter to *him*.

He added in an altogether more subdued voice, "I really had no idea. I honestly thought you'd just been over-doing things and needed a little time to rest and come to terms with the shock of his death, that's all. I fully intended to leave you to it today after our latest nasty little disagreement, only I saw you wavering on the street behind the promenade when you were supposed to be on a train and had a fit of conscience just as I neared Devil's Bridge so I turned back. If I hadn't ... well, it just doesn't bear thinking about."

I think he was hoping for thanks here, or at least some words of apology that might show things weren't quite as bad as he feared. But I just sat there and stared at the raised grain of the wooden tabletop in numbed disbelief. My regained faith in his innocence was nothing to the discovery that just like all the other people I had mixed with recently, nothing I did now would stop him from ultimately concluding that I belonged in a specialist hospital. Even if he didn't want to be the one to put me there.

He was speaking again, earnestly and warmly. "We'll get you some help. You might not believe it now, but you will get better." He was suddenly speaking very gently indeed. He gave me a brief flash of a reassuring smile before adding in a bright, jovial tone, "And the first step is probably a good night's sleep."

He straightened and took my cup to set it in the sink. Then he turned back with that same carefully constructed mask that told me he had finally understood that he was facing a woman on the brink and should avoid aggravating her further. Tomorrow he would be calling the nearest doctor. I felt the sickness rise up at the horror of it.

"I'm not mad," I said, possibly more to reassure myself than to inform him.

He gave another appeasing smile that was utterly repulsive. "Of course not. Just a little overwrought, that's all. Come on, let's get you to bed."

He put out his hand but I just stared at it as if it were

something alien and horrible and fixed mine tightly in my lap. The cheery smile slowly faded as his hand dropped to his side and I realised he was wondering what he could do to coax me from the room. It was that old mistake of the charitable person. He'd picked up a needy vagrant from the street and now this wild, dirty mad thing had taken anchorage in his kitchen and he had absolutely no idea how to shift her.

It was a moment before I noticed I was speaking.

# Chapter 22

This frail stranger's voice began by going over the same story that had been told to other men countless times before and just the same I knew exactly what he would be thinking. So I didn't look at him. Instead I kept my attention on my hands and recounted with bitter honesty the memory of the bus and the hospital and my agonisingly unsteady flight from that place via a different ward because I knew they would be watching for me. I told him about packing my things and leaving a note for my holidaying mother, just in case, and that terrible journey south on the train for the grim purpose of retracing a dead man's last steps. I even told Adam of the fear that had coloured my encounter with him on the lonely hilltop that first morning. I told him about Jim and his disguises and the incident on the pier and the one in my bedroom where Jim had stolen the photograph, and all the time he listened in silence from his station by the sideboard.

It grew harder when I had to tell him about this morning. "I heard them on the stairs when I came out of my room; talking to you, I thought." Here I looked up and wished that

I hadn't. His expression was truly awful. I dropped my gaze to the hands in my lap again. "I understand now I was wrong about that. But I wasn't wrong to be afraid that Jim had broken my hiding place and to know it wouldn't be long before they were bundling me into their car again."

Here he made some involuntary noise and I lifted my head once more and felt my mouth form a sympathetic smile. "Oh, I know what you're thinking – you're thinking that I could have done a better job of disappearing these past few days. But tell me just how many times you actually saw me begin a conversation with the other guests? How many times did I find myself at the centre of things voluntarily?"

His stony stare made me drop my eyes but still I said bravely, "You of all people know what it is like when you're craving a little anonymity. It just seems to galvanise everyone into pointing at you more."

He conceded that with a dry little inclination of his head.

Then he said coolly, "Actually, it just so happens I wasn't thinking about your social habits. I was thinking about Jim and that perhaps it would be helpful if you showed me this packet of photographs, since they're apparently considered so vital that he would steal one."

I said limply, "I can't. I had to give them back."

His silence said everything.

I told him of my flight from the hotel and my leap from the train to leave Jim trapped as it sped away inland. I spoke of the endless hunt around the streets, the funicular on Constitution Hill, the cupboard, and my eventual exhaustion as I struggled away from the station for the final time and knew at last that my efforts to get away were at an end. And all the while he just stood there staring, without moving.

Finally he spoke. "Why haven't you been to the police?"

I lifted my gaze. "I have. Twice. First at the hospital and again today. But they don't believe me."

He only stared back at me, eyes devoid of expression, and I sat in silence for a minute longer, gathering my own thoughts before finally adding, "I knew I was finished when I reached the harbour. It was a dead end and I hadn't got the strength left to turn back. I was just watching the waves and waiting there for them to do whatever they intended to do. It wasn't about Rhys or missing him at all."

"You said his name." Adam's voice was very quiet. "You were staring at the water and you said his name."

I kept my gaze fixed on the spread fingers in my lap. "It is true, I was thinking of him. But not in the way you mean." My hands were icy and I slowly rubbed one against the other as if it would make any difference. "I was thinking about what he had done – ending it like that – and was wondering how he had managed it. I couldn't do it, even when it meant surrendering to those two men. I wanted to live too much. When I heard footsteps I thought they'd come."

I looked up at him then, unavoidably, and added with a kind of fearful disbelief, "But you were there. You'd come."

There was a peculiar silence and I went back to massaging the life back into my hands. Adam stood like a statue and didn't move for a full five minutes. Finally he pushed himself away from the sideboard and set about putting some cutlery away. When at last I heard him speak it was directed to the open drawer. "That's quite a story."

I closed my eyes and felt the roughness of a graze beneath a finger. "You don't believe me." I spoke perfectly calmly. It was more a confirmation than a levelling of any kind of blame.

He turned back. "You've spent all week accusing me, accusing Jim, in fact accusing any man you've met of some heinous crime. You told me yourself that ever since your accident you've become paranoid, why should I believe this is any different?" A hand lifted to silence my protest. "No. I can see that something has frightened you terribly. And somehow I think it must matter to you that I do believe you when you say this wasn't all for the memory of Rhys."

A quick hesitation that seemed designed to convey something deeper before it was swept aside and he went on to add almost reluctantly, "But I never saw those men on the stairs, or heard Jim say anything about you that was anything other than friendly interest. The very idea of two men no one else has seen, who want something you've never heard of, and want to bring you to the one place that holds painful memories for you ... It just seems unlikely, that's all. I do think that after you've had a rest for a few days, you'll feel quite differently about it."

I looked up at him, feeling sad and lonely again. His eyes were a very kind and gentle shade, and this time the expression seemed genuine. He moved to the doorway and turned there, waiting for me. He must have read my sadness. He said, "You do know, don't you, that at the very least I have to look into these people. And you know too, that although neither of us remotely expects me to find anything, the fact I'd try has to count for something, doesn't it?"

He gave me room to absorb his words, then he added, "With that in mind I'd like you to give me just one more piece of honesty, and it happens that for now it is the most important piece of all."

He indicated that it was time I followed him. Feeling wrung utterly dry of all emotion, I climbed stiffly to my feet and joined him on the threshold. He looked down at me and his mouth formed a very small lopsided smile. "Will you promise that you won't try to disappear again? At least not without telling me first?"

I looked up at him, feeling suddenly very emotional indeed. I don't quite know what I'd been fearing he would ask of me but whatever it was, this wasn't it. This was something softer that spoke, unexpectedly, of comfort.

Finally, I managed a nod. The expression in his eyes flickered for an instant but then he simply turned and quietly led the way out of the room. I followed him into his darkened house.

# Chapter 23

It was the first time in weeks that I slept without fear of waking.

The ascent of the stairs last night had been a slow climb past more closed doors. There must have been something of a tour because I knew that the first floor contained the blackened thresholds of the bathroom and tiny modern toilet, his bedroom and the faintly lighter shade of his daughter's. But all I can really remember is that first glimpse of the room which was to be mine, nestling into the eaves of the high street-front gable. Adam had whispered an apology for its cluttered state, then I was suddenly alone with nothing but the warming prospect of a thick eiderdown and an inviting bed.

That had been many hours ago. Now the instant of opening my eyes once more was like a continuation of the dream. Not *that* dream, but a new one. Instead of the sickening lurch of dread, I was only met by a comforting blur of greens and blues which, when I next blinked a few hours or more later, solidified into the fading pattern of a much used floral curtain.

Sometime during the afternoon, the mottled light cast from

the window ran from the sloping ceiling by my feet onto the floor towards the door. At its limit stood a girl. The change in the quality of the stillness in this room must have been what had woken me. I'm not sure if I recognised her at that point or if I just accepted her presence as naturally as I took in the sight of my abandoned clothes strewn carelessly over a chair. Whichever way it was, I only watched mutely as she first examined me from behind the shield of the newly opened door and then abruptly came to a decision and approached the bed.

She set a glass of water down on the table that was by my head. Then she whirled away and crashed out of the open door and down the stairs. I heard the distant clump and the burst of lively chattering as she jumped off the last step.

I stared at the water, wondering if I could muster the energy to drink it, and as I did so slumber must have stolen up on me again because when I next woke, the door had been closed and the glass replaced with a teacup and another steaming bowl of that nourishing soup. This time I was quick enough to consume some of it before sinking once more.

It was well into evening when I next climbed sluggishly out of the dark into the dim gleam of a distant street light. It drew me back to full consciousness for long enough to scrabble at the switch for the nearby lamp and peer at my watch. It said two o'clock but when I looked again a few minutes later it was still showing the same time. It was more than a little odd to have this silent reminder of its damage on the hillside. Adam's words had been so reasonable and so convincing that I half expected to find that with this awakening

I really would be ready to believe it had all just been a terrible delusion.

It wasn't. Blearily, I propped myself up against the pillows. By the laden chair were my two bags, the mess of my roughly discarded shoes and stockings; and the unpleasant debris of a quantity of foliage, grit and a few unlucky insects. It was a disgusting sight. On the back of the door, however, was the altogether more appealing vision of a large yellow bath towel.

Getting to it proved a little bit more of a challenge. My limbs had been turned to stiffened wood and yesterday's blow to my ankle – was it only yesterday? – from the hand-cart had resulted in quite an impressive bruise. I made it, however, and clutching the towel, my folded nightdress and that faithful housecoat to cover my current unfortunate choice of brassiere and under things, I quietly eased open the door.

Opposite was another door. It was shut and I presumed it belonged to the woman. She wasn't a second wife because she was too old and too cross. She didn't really act like his mother...

The stairwell was well lit and deserted, and no one stepped out to accost me as I slunk gingerly step by aching step downwards to the bathroom. As I slipped inside the door and locked it, I heard the quiet murmur of a man's voice from the child's room. They were reading a bedtime story.

Safe inside the little sanctuary of his modern and immaculate bathroom, I occupied myself with the hunt for something nice to add to the torrent of steam that issued from the tap. It felt a little criminal to be going through their private things and it felt all the more so when my search was interrupted by a light rap at the door. I tiptoed a little closer.

"Hello? Kate, is that you?"

Adam. I tried my voice and it worked. "I was going to have a bath," I whispered to the door, and then added quickly, "Is that all right? I'm not disturbing you, am I?"

"No." His hushed return was calm. "But if you're looking for fragrant whatnots I'm afraid Nanny keeps hers locked away in her room upstairs. I can go and ask her for something? Or I think there might be an ancient pot of bath salts in the cupboard above the sink ..."

I padded silently back across the cold linoleum. Inside the cupboard was an assortment of shaving brushes, razor and spare toothpaste safely stored out of reach of a child's wandering fingers, and also an unopened jar of faded lavender-scented bath salts. "Perfect," I told them as I lifted them out.

"Got it?" Adam's whisper recalled me to the door.

"Yes," I said softly to its bare white panels, "thank you. And Adam?"

"Yes?"

"Thank you. And sorry ... For everything."

I didn't hear his reply. I had just found the bruise above my elbow where Clarke had gripped me. And was wondering if I had left a similar mark on Adam's cheek.

---

My next awakening was harder. It was harder to ignore reality. The soft aroma of a hot oven was wafting up the stairs. It was a confusing sort of rousing; it felt safe, secure like being part of a family and it reminded me of the truth of my visit here. Somewhere below there was the distant ringing of a telephone.

It took a little longer to get out of bed this time. The stiffness that had marked my climb downstairs yesterday had only been a little forerunner to today's. It took me about half an hour to dress, with several sit downs in order to catch my breath. Also, someone – Nanny presumably – had whisked away my worn clothes; dirtied frocks, housecoat and all. That left me with a choice between something quiet and something subdued. I opted for the plain grey frock on account of it being warmer. The old tastes and habits of Mrs Kate Williams were back in force. Only she'd never looked this drawn.

I managed to descend the stairs without doing anything stupid. I even managed to make myself release my fierce grip on the banister rail and take that last step down into the hallway. I did it by taking hold of the doorframe into the noisy kitchen instead. Unfortunately, having got here, it became clear that whatever nervous introductions had been running rehearsals in my mind, they were entirely unnecessary.

"Adam's not here," I said lamely, as if it wasn't obvious.

The girl was staring owlishly at me from her place at the table while the older woman turned away to clatter impatiently with the stove. It was, I realised now, giving off enough heat to warm the whole house.

Nanny had a smart brown housecoat over her clothes and her short grey hair was set into impressively tight curls. There was also a kitten clinging to the back of her skirt. I wondered if she knew.

"Good morning." It was a touchingly formal greeting from

Adam's daughter. She was indeed about nine years old. She was in fact old enough that she probably should have been at school. Perhaps she'd been for the morning and was home for lunch.

"Good morning," I replied kindly. "May, isn't it?"

She nodded madly, returned my smile shyly and then hid her mouth behind her hand and turned wide eyes towards the older woman. I asked carefully, "And you are? I'm terribly sorry, I don't know your name." I was hardly going to dare to call the lady 'Nanny'.

"Mrs Francis." The reply held a trace of Cheltenham elocution which covered an even fainter undertone of the Gloucestershire burr and it was accompanied by a sharp shove from her hip at the open oven door. It swung shut with a snap. "And *Mister* Hitchen is in his study. Working."

Oh. The tone of the reprimand ought to have been rendered considerably less humbling by the fact that she had a kitten somewhere about her person, but it wasn't.

"But you never call him that. You know he doesn't like it."

The small-voiced confusion stopped Mrs Francis' violent stirring of the gravy in its tracks. Mrs Francis shot her a wild look. It looked for a moment like the old woman might weaken and I swear a corner of her mouth twitched. But then the impulse to establish my status here had its way and, with a waggle of the spoon in her hand, Mrs Francis simply directed me to stop lingering stupidly in her doorway and take a seat.

Oblivious to adult assertions of territory, May decided that this was the appropriate moment to slip from her chair to rescue the kitten from within the heavy folds of the skirt.

Remarkably, Mrs Francis still managed to maintain her fearsomeness even when she realised that all this time the creature had been using her as a climbing frame. She resorted to doing something aggressive with roasting vegetables.

"This is Timmy." The small and slightly resistant kitten was manipulated into gravely offering me his paw. "He's mine. Do you like cats?"

I shook Timmy's paw, just as I was supposed to. "I do like cats. I like all sorts of animals."

"Horses?"

"Yes."

"Dogs?"

I surveyed her suspiciously. "Is this a trick question given your liking for cats?"

May smirked. "Snails, hedgehogs and birds?"

I didn't expect my agreement to cause such excitement. I found myself mistress of the kitten all over again and then I was dragged from my seat while the girl's other hand snatched a pot from the sideboard with one hand and her mouth formally asked Mrs Francis to excuse us. May set off down the hallway at a tearing pace that made no concessions for the state of my limbs. I followed her more sedately. The hallway floor was prettily tiled and it led beyond the stairs towards a door that opened into a garden.

This was a wild place. It ought to have been given over to food production but the only sign of order was the dry brown tangle of neglected beans within a mass of red stems from a dogwood that defiantly contradicted the drab shades of winter. The space was really just a long corridor between high walls and sheds belonging to the neighbouring houses but it all felt incredibly remote. The end of the garden looked out onto the silvery smear of a shallow river. It came as a bit of a surprise when a person walked past on the other side with their dog.

May was rummaging about beneath a dormant plum tree that had kindly decided to drape itself over the wall from next door. The kitten and I followed her rather more gingerly since it required the cooperation of various joints to duck under the mossy boughs. The contents of her little pot were kitchen scraps and she deposited the lot upon the top of a neighbouring bird table. She was, I could see now, small for her age and quite slight, even for a child from the era of rationing. I wondered if she was like her mother.

Adopting a pose of stealthy concealment by my side, May announced grandly, "I'm making a study." A robin obliged her by fluttering in to land on the bird table. It had such assurance that I was sure it was used to its little audience. There was also a mouse hole by our feet and May shook her head over it. "That's what the cat is for. I'm allowed to study them in the garden, but Nanny won't have them in her kitchen; she just won't have it. *Daddy!*"

My attempt to find an appropriate response to what were clearly the parroted words of a much older person was rendered unnecessary by her sudden dive from cover.

She was caught as she charged from our hiding place and turned upside down and tucked carelessly under an arm. She was all at once a small child again and laughing hysterically. I heard his voice with a lurch of nerves. Somehow I'd imagined that I'd managed to put off this moment. He said, "What are you doing out here anyway, young lady? Don't you know it's dinnertime, hmmm?"

She giggled in a strangled sort of way as he turned about. "We had to feed the birds – it's their dinnertime too."

"*We?*" Adam stopped in mid spin and suddenly saw me, still crouching like an idiot beneath the foliage. "Oh."

My smile was given awkwardly. As was my murmur of, "Hello."

I straightened and picked my way out, clutching a kitten and no doubt yet again trailing a certain quantity of filth and matter from my hem.

"Hi," he said. It was impossible not to notice how mobile his mouth was when he was laughing with his daughter. And how it was now settling towards that familiar calm once more. Although not entirely. This man who had formerly been forced to judge my levels of madness said pleasantly, "Sorry to scare the birds away. Do you like our wildlife haven?"

"Very much. It was clever of you to let it grow so tall and tangled." Then I realised that he was probably being serious and stammered hastily, "But it is, um, very pretty."

He replied levelly, "You know, you're not too big to be tucked under my arm too if you're going to insult my garden." He was eyeing me strangely; that is to say he was staring at me as though he was meeting me properly for the very first time and he wasn't entirely sure he understood what he saw. And why should he when, regardless of who he thought he had brought back from Aberystwyth, now he was meeting only odd Mrs Williams.

Mrs Kate Williams. She felt like a stranger to me too, but she was me all the same.

"You can't do anything to me," I said very quickly indeed. "Kitten." And held it out to prove the excuse.

After a moment's consideration he only said, "Hungry?" and then set his captive down and ushered us ahead of him into the house to meet Mrs Francis's wrath and eat her lunch.

Mrs Francis turned out, in actual fact, to be most particularly angry with him. She scowled at Adam as she took her seat beside him and, judging by the faint lift to that man's eyebrows as he received his plate, I think even he noticed that she had served him the smallest cut of pie. But at least May remained oblivious and incapable of doing anything but chatter continuously to anyone who would listen and thankfully that someone mainly seemed to be me.

She told me about all sorts of things; her plans for the kitten, a plan to cultivate earthworms that might have been about to happen, or had happened, and also her aunt's allergy to horses. It was wonderful in many different ways, but mainly because her chatter meant I didn't have to look at Adam. He was alert to everything I said. He was trying to assess just how much I had been improved by rest and I thought I could guess why. I would have been doing that too if I were a parent and I had introduced someone into my house who might just happen to expose his daughter to some deeply unsettling outbursts.

It was as we stacked our plates for May to deposit on the washboard that he finally joined our discussion to say,

"Speaking of grubby pastimes, little one, would you like to take a walk in the park later?"

His daughter beamed and then stopped to glower at him suspiciously. "You're going to send me back to lessons this afternoon, aren't you?"

Breaking my rule, I saw his smile. "Sorry."

Reverting back to her usual cheerfulness again, May turned to me. "You'll like it. There are conker trees, though that's not now." A brief calculation of the seasons before she shrugged the complication off and continued brightly, "And birds and lots of paths that go for miles." She considered me for a moment and then looked doubtful. "It *is* a very big park."

"I know," I said gently. "I've walked there many times myself."

It was about twenty minutes later that I found myself alone and finding respite outside the back door, listening to the run of the stream at the end of the garden. It was a boundary of sorts, but not one I couldn't escape. I knew my tiredness wasn't really the tie that kept me here. Nor was it was my promise to tell Adam before I left, and the fact I would have to brave his disbelief a second time in order to do it, and worse, face the probability that his first reaction would be relief. I knew I would have to confront what lay ahead and soon. The simple truth was that it made my soul ache to think of having to leave his peaceful home.

Back inside the kitchen, I knew May was making a determined effort to draw a map of the park, just so I would appreciate how far she was talking about. I heard the distant clatter as she dropped another crayon.

There was a different sound behind and a rustle; an adult's footsteps on stone flags this time and I felt an excruciatingly thrilling rush of alarm at the thought that Adam might have decided to follow me. The sound of a heavy breath betrayed it to only be Mrs Francis with washing for the mangle. She went past me with barely a glance.

After a moment, I went to help her. I wasn't sure that she wanted it, and she certainly conceded me the task of sorting the tangled wet clothes very grudgingly, but she didn't actually go so far as to ignore the garments as I passed them to her so I presume the assistance didn't go entirely unappreciated.

I bent to tug something from the tangle of laundered clothes. When I straightened she was crushing the water out of a child's skirt with mathematical accuracy and something in the act prompted me to say, "You've looked after him for a long time, haven't you, Mrs Francis?"

"I've known him since he was a boy." She said it as though I had accused her of being a liar. "I watched him grow up and become a man and marry June. And kept house for him ever since Mr Francis passed. No, the yellow one next."

I meekly returned the man's trousers to the pile and picked up the girl's blouse.

"By the way, since we're being civil; whatever you're up to here it won't work." She paused in her vigorous turning of the handle long enough to give me an extraordinary glare. "He's no fool, no matter what fantasy you're trying to cast him in. And you needn't look like that either. I know how you single girls and scheming damsels think. You think: Here's money and fame – reluctant fame, naturally – and he's a parent to a darling motherless girl and it couldn't get any closer to the romantic ideal, could it? Only it doesn't work like that. He's living flesh. He's moody and infuriating and driven; and all the more difficult because he's been away for so many years and been allowed to get away with not speaking for so long. But perhaps you think that means you should save him?"

I could have pointed out that she couldn't have guessed even half of the roles I had cast him in during the past week. But I didn't. Instead I picked up the last of his shirts, smoothed the collar and reached for the handle of the heavy mangle.

Mrs Francis straightened. "You look tired. Give me that and go and sit down." It was an order. I obeyed.

----

There must be, I knew, a sitting room somewhere off the long passage of the hallway. Habit suggested that it would be the room at the front of the house and, putting my hand to the broad wooden panels of the door, I turned the handle and went in. I was wrong, of course.

Instead of comfortable settees, I found Adam at his writing desk in the midst of a chaos of notes and typewriters and piles of books on chairs. He'd lifted his head when the door had opened and now he was looking at me with that blank stare of one who was definitely not used to being interrupted when he was working. It took a while for any kind of smile to reach his eyes.

I was utterly ashamed. "So sorry," I said and bolted from

the room. I did at least think to shut the door behind me. It smothered the call of my name.

The next door was more successful. It opened onto a small room at the back, tucked in the lea of the stairs, and it was perfect. The walls formed a friendly kind of library with shelves from floor to ceiling bearing books and pictures and family photographs, and on one of the nearest shelves, I even found another battered copy of *Jane Eyre*. It felt very appropriate to read the part about discovering the madwoman living in the attic.

I carefully transplanted some abandoned toys onto a table, tucked myself into a corner of the settee and began to read. It was easier to be calm here in the little oasis of the back room, with no interruptions but the occasional blur outside the delicately latticed window as Mrs Francis huffed by to set to with the grinding again on her mangle. In fact it was very calming because when I woke a little while later, it was to the sensation of the book slipping from my hand and the soft clunk as it hit the floor. I bent to retrieve it, and only then did I notice the weight clamped against my side.

Turning my head, I found the fair hair and curled-up form of the child nestling against my hip with one hand hanging out over the floor. She hadn't gone to her afternoon lessons after all. She must have crept in to find me and grown tired of waiting for me to wake so she could show me her map and fallen asleep instead. The kitten must have come with her because he in his turn was sprawled across her in a similar pose of slumbering abandonment.

Trapped, I let my head fall back and resigned myself to

meet the next wave of sleep. It was an easy slide into oblivion and warm and only seemed to last a moment before it was interrupted again by another soft whisper of paper against my hand. Blearily, I opened one eye against the glare of the window to find Adam standing only a yard from us. He had bent to rescue his fallen book. With a rush I jerked fully awake and with heart beating I hastily tried to sit up but the dead weight of the child was an effective restraint and I had to settle for adjusting my position so that I didn't feel quite so much like an ungainly lump.

With a disjointed attempt at a greeting I began to make some kind of explanation, only to realise belatedly that I didn't even know what it was that I was trying to explain. "Sorry, I er ..."

Adam only gave an uncomfortable sort of twisted grimace and set the book down beside me on the arm of my chair. Where its cover had been bent a little I could see the initials JH, his wife's.

"Sorry," I said again, uselessly.

He stepped away to the window. "You're saying that a lot at the moment."

I wasn't sure whether to apologise for that too.

He turned back then and suddenly shrugged off all the tension. "It's not required, you know," he said with a smile. The first warm smile I had been gifted for days. "We're going to go to the park at half-past three. Which should be," – he glanced at his watch – "*will* be in about ten minutes. Do you want to come? Or would you prefer to stay at home?"

I blinked at him, trying to gauge what he was thinking. It

was an impossible task. "I think," I said, matching his light tone, "I should let you enjoy your walk with your daughter in peace." Then I realised that this sounded like I was fishing for a contradiction or worse that I was trying to reopen the discussion on my fears of what awaited me outside and with half my mind conscious of the proximity of his sleeping child, I hastily added, "And I'm really very tired so I think I'd better stay here. If you don't mind?"

"I don't mind," he confirmed, mouth contracting to a line once more. After a moment he turned back to the window but not before he had gazed at me with that new assessing expression that made me feel like I was a mistake he didn't quite know how to undo.

His hand hung loose beside a small table adorned with a line of metal picture frames. There were a pair that were presumably his parents; people from a bygone era. The first image of him was a photograph from some years ago of him and his wife on a seaside holiday taken by one of those opportunist professionals. He was younger, less angular perhaps but perfectly recognisable; she was pretty and lively and they were both to be left forever on the brink of laughing. The next was a photograph of a man on leave after Dunkirk. I could tell it was then because he looked exhausted and he'd told me that it was the only time he'd been allowed home. The frontage of his sister's Cheltenham house was behind him and his daughter was in his arms, a shy little baby of about eighteen months at most. She was tiny. When he'd come home at long last four and a half years later she must have barely known him. It was so very sad.

A few moments later, May came noisily back to life. Guilt had just begun to jerk a fresh attempt to say sorry out of me, only this time I was making the one apology that I really owed him, for invading the precious peace of his family home. I was saved by her sleepy mumble and the disarray as she kicked a cushion to the floor. Then she turned over and very nearly crushed the kitten.

In the ensuing flood of tears and necessary fatherly comfort, I slipped silently to the door. Then, like the coward I was, I dived up the stairs to the relief of his quiet little attic bedroom.

# Chapter 24

I wasn't sure what had woken me this time. It was dark, and the house and the street below were quiet so I hadn't missed someone bringing me another meal. I didn't think it had been a dream either, though I couldn't be sure. At any rate, I couldn't actually remember revisiting the waterfall and I could only hope to goodness that this wasn't a version of the incident at the hotel and I hadn't woken myself – and therefore the whole house – by making some frightened sound.

I lay there for a moment, caught in that familiar trap of blinking at the blackened ceiling, worrying. Then I reached out and switched on the lamp.

The room was its usual harmless, homely self. There were my bags, his piles of unsorted clutter and my coat hanging from a hook beside the towel on the back of the closed door. Beside me was a fresh glass of water that I hadn't carried up the stairs myself and I propped myself up on one elbow to drink it. Someone must have thought to try winding my watch and had set it too because it now ticked and said a different two o'clock. No wonder the house was silent.

Then I saw the note.

For a nauseatingly terrifying moment I thought they had been in my room and the click of the door closing was what had woken me. My mind instantly turned the fear into truth by tracing the perfectly simple route they might take across that shallow stream and into the garden and from there easily into the house. Their climb would take them past his room, past her room and onwards up to mine. But then I noticed the untidy initials in the corner where the stamp should be.

The letter had been delivered today, by hand and by some harmless errand boy who, when traced, would doubtless be unable to remember their faces. It was addressed to me, or to be precise Mrs Williams, and somebody had quietly placed it on my bedside table to be there when I woke.

With less than steady fingers, I opened it and drew out the single sheet of paper. It was written by hand, so they hadn't yet reached the extremes of using newspaper cuttings to form the words. The style was simple and every word crafted to strike the right undertone:

'*Dear Mrs Williams,*

*Your host was kind enough to take the trouble of telling us exactly where you're staying now, seeing as we missed you the other day. The next meeting is arranged for 2 o'clock tomorrow afternoon at the gallery. Any later and it'll risk ruining the little girl's next family outing.*'

And that was it. And I had just one thought in my mind. Adam.

Without so much as a pause to allow for the inevitable

discomfort from moving so swiftly from horizontal to upright, I slipped across the room, opened the door and tiptoed silently down the stairs. The light in the bathroom had been left on, as a night-light for May I supposed, so the unfamiliar house was not as eerie as it might have been. But it was still very daunting when I found myself on the short landing between the open door of the child's room and the partially closed door of his. It was another touching little indication of parent-hood and a good deal of me wanted to find any means necessary to maintain the pretence that this latest assault on their lives had never happened. But the alternative was too hard. It was bitterly selfish, I knew, but I didn't want to try blind flight again.

I reached out and touched the cold painted wood of his bedroom door. It swung a little wider, wide enough to admit me and I took a breath and stepped in. There he was, lying diagonally in a tangle of limbs and sheets on his front with his head to the wall. He was not, I noticed, wearing a shirt but at least he had on what appeared to be a respectable pair of pyjama trousers.

Dodging the noisy pitfalls of abandoned slippers, a small stuffed puppy which had to be May's and a very well camou-flaged chest of drawers, I moved a little closer. He didn't stir. He also didn't notice when I passed between him and the pale light cast from the street outside, and then I was standing by the side of his bed and finding myself left with no option but to cautiously reach out to lightly tap him on the shoulder.

For a moment I thought that hadn't woken him either. But then with a funny little snoring breath he lifted his head and touched his face as if he did not know why he had stirred. He must have caught my wavering form out of the corner of his eye because he mumbled something about children waking people up at the oddest times and twisted round. And then stopped abruptly when he saw it was me.

I thought for a few humiliating seconds he was going to turn away again but then with a sigh – the sort of sigh someone makes when they're still half asleep – he rolled completely onto his back and rubbed his face a second time. "What is it? Another nightmare?" His voice was blurred.

I shook my head and, after a few more seconds of stupidity, thrust the letter at him. He blinked at me and it, but then at last he took the paper from my hand and, half propped up on one elbow, tried to tilt it to catch the meagre light.

"What is it?" he asked again, peering at the brief lines with brows lowered from the effort. I saw his eye flick from the letter to me, still standing dumbly before him.

I fiddled mindlessly with my fingers before finally managing in a voice that squeaked with the strain of being quiet, "It's … I … you need to read it." Then I sat down abruptly on the edge of his wide bed.

I was, typically, wearing that ridiculous nightdress again. It was at least long enough to cover me nearly to my ankles but what it made up in length, it lost by having flimsy straps and a very deep 'V' at the back. He had moved his legs a little hastily to accommodate me and I suddenly realised he was probably afraid that this, the latest in a long line of social disasters, was a bizarrely excruciating attempt at a late-night seduction. I wrapped my arms about myself and turned my head away so that he wouldn't think I was staring at his chest.

I felt the mattress dip as he climbed off the end and padded lightly to the door. He listened for a moment until he was satisfied his daughter was sleeping soundly, then he eased it shut. The bed tilted again as he moved past me to reclaim his place. He reached for his lamp and suddenly the room was filled with strong yellow light. I hugged myself a little tighter.

"Right then." He sounded more bemused than anything. "Let's see what all this is about."

Then there was silence, a darkening silence. He had been on the verge of smiling but all that faded before he reached the end of the note. I saw the flutter of white as he turned it over to check the reverse and then he reached out a hand and took the envelope from me too.

"I didn't write it," I said hastily, seeing him examine the courier's marks.

"No," he agreed, reading the note through again. "And this arrived today?"

"Yes, well that is to say, I think so."

"You think so?"

"It wasn't there when I went to bed. But I woke up and saw it. I had a funny dream, or at least I think I did and I had to switch on my light. I probably wouldn't have noticed it otherwise." I was gabbling stupidly.

"Yes, yes," was all he said. He was staring at the paper, not reading it any more, just staring and staring and his voice when he next spoke was tinged with disbelief. "They were watching us in the park. They were close enough to hear May's questions about you as she collected hazelnuts for the squirrels."

"Yes, I know. I'm sorry."

He looked up at that. Then he reached out a hand and put it over mine where it had dropped to my lap.

His eyes narrowed to glare fiercely at my hand. "You're freezing."

I shook my head. "No, no. I'm fine."

"No, you're not. You're practically shivering."

"Honestly, I'm fine." For a brief terrifying second I saw his gaze drop to the rumpled blankets by his side and consider offering their warmth but then, I think to our joint relief, he spied his dressing gown hanging over the back of a nearby chair.

I didn't contradict him again. The long robe was warm, made of flannel and it covered my hated nightdress perfectly. After a while, when all we had done was stare blankly at that sheet of paper some more, I said carefully, "Well, at least I'm keeping part of my promise."

"Your promise?"

"To tell you. You'll hardly hold me to the other half now they're trying to intimidate May."

"Kate?"

"Yes?"

"Be quiet."

"Oh," I breathed.

"Just let me think for a minute, would you?"

I did let him think for a minute, and then I let him think

for a few minutes more. I think it was a relief to finally let someone else do it. I was still loitering quietly on the edge of his bed when I woke some three hours later to the sudden tilt as he climbed out and padded softly to the door. Victim yet again of that overpowering urge to sleep, I was curled up in the comfortable warmth of his dressing gown and at some point he must have folded the corner of his blankets over my feet. I heard the creak as he opened the door.

"Good morning, little one." The whisper had a smile in it.

"Your door was shut." A pause, then, "Why is she on your bed? Did she have monsters in her room?"

"More like a bad dream."

Ah, was that what it was?

"Did you get her some hot milk? That's what you always get for me."

The warmth of another smile. "No, I didn't. But I will next time. Anyway, what do you want at this godforsaken hour? Is it time for school already?"

I heard May's giggle. "It's still dark, silly! It's only six o'clock. I just thought you might like to play a game with me."

"Right." One simple word conveyed amusement and fatherly disapproval in equal measures.

"I thought Snap." Then May added hopefully, "Will she want to play too?"

"No. I think we'll let her sleep, she's had a rough night. So shush."

Another giggle. Then the happy clump of her feet skipping down the stairs followed by the soft whisper of the door being eased closed.

My face was concealed within the curve of my elbow. The warm fleece was soft where it pressed across my eyes and it smelt clean and crisp which meant disconcertingly that it presumably smelt of him. It also covered the fact that I was awake when he stepped quietly back across the room again to switch on the lamp. At some point while I'd been slumbering on the edge of his bed he must have reached across to switch it off and settled down beside me to wait for the morning.

He was standing there. I concentrated hard on keeping my breathing steady and regular, and it must have worked because after a few long seconds I heard him turn away and begin pulling at some drawers. I was still practicing my breathing when he left a few seconds later.

A few minutes after that, the door opened and he came back in again. There was a sharp pattern of footfalls, different now because every movement had the added texture of daytime clothing, and then silence. Then an impatient sigh very close to my head. "You know, there really is very little point in pretending to be asleep. We both know why you're in here, regardless of what I choose to tell my nine-year-old daughter."

I guiltily lifted my head. I saw him give a short nod of satisfaction and step away. He said, "You should get dressed. I've given my sister a call and she's got a cab coming to collect May. I can't deliver May to Cheltenham because if you recall the car was running on fumes by the time we got home the other night. My sister should be here in about fifteen minutes. Can you hold tight until then?"

I sat up and folded the dressing gown demurely across my

knees. He was wearing his usual uniform of warm woollen jumper rolled back past his wrists and good trousers which had seen far too much walking, or mangling at the hands of Mrs Francis. I asked, "Will she be safe there?"

In the past a question like that would have been his cue to start telling me all the reasons why I was imagining things. It was disorientating when he only said mildly, "I think so." Then, "Go on; get dressed. I'll be the one in the kitchen waiting for the kettle to boil. I really don't think the world is going to come to an end before we've even had breakfast." And on that unanswerable note of domestic calm, he left me alone in his room.

---

Adam's sister was a little older and her light eyes were cautious, and very serious like his, though I suspected her face was generally more used to laughing. I descended the stairs just as she and her little charge were leaving. May was bounding about in the midst of the protective cluster of her father, her aunt and another man who was presumably the lady's husband. May was, thank heavens, still completely oblivious of the reason why she should be being suddenly gifted another day off school. No one noticed me blending with the pale brown carpet of the stairs while they sorted their young charge into coats and accompanying bits and pieces including the kitten; that is no one noticed until Adam's sister happened to look up and catch me there.

She greeted me carefully. I wished I'd been more of a coward and stayed hidden in my room until they'd gone. It wasn't bravery that had made me do what was right but a sense of what I owed her brother.

Adam's head snapped round as I made my reply; he had been rummaging in a cupboard for shoes but now he moved towards me. "Can you hang on a minute?" He was speaking to his sister.

"Adam, I really think ..."

He cut across her as he climbed a few steps with that easy authority of a sibling. "Just give me a minute. This won't take long." Then he approached and lightly took my arm to lead me back up into the doorway of the bathroom. We both heard May's laugh. Guilt made me shiver.

His hand dropped from my arm. We were back in the tense distance of yesterday as he searched for the right way to put this. His voice was stern. "Listen, Kate, I'm just going out to the car to see them safely on their way and then—"

I interrupted him. I'd been mistaken. It wasn't a relief to let someone else do the thinking. There was no thrill in finding myself not so wholly on my own. I mumbled incoherently and yet firmly about something to do with May and him going with her, and responsibility.

He actually gave an exasperated jerk of his head. "Look, I gathered long before this that certain parts of your past have tended to make you feel perpetually at fault – though I doubt you'd admit it if I asked you – but will you please *stop* apologising? You didn't cause this, did you? You didn't make them hound you. You didn't create this ... this fantasy. They did. They're here, they've threatened May, and you definitely cannot control it by saying sorry or pretending you should tackle this alone again. Hell, you didn't even ask to be brought *here*, did you?"

His manner was reserved, hard, and not at all like the gentleness I had grown to depend on in Aberystwyth. The bathroom was tiny with him in it too but there might as well have been miles between us. He was running a hand through his hair as he said, "Now listen, you interrupted me just now but this is important. I don't want you to panic, but someone's here to see you. I think he can help." He caught my questioning look. "Jim."

He didn't need to feel my flinch, he saw it. I found the cold edge of the doorjamb hard at my back. But his voice followed me. He wasn't using his blunt delivery to increase the distance between us. He wanted to curb it. His voice checked me as he said urgently, "Please don't look like that any more. It's the expression you were wearing on your first night in this house and I couldn't decipher it at first, but then you began speaking to me and suddenly I could. It's the look you have when you're thinking the only thing left for you is to try harder to disappear. The hopelessness of it makes me afraid that one of these times you might succeed." Then, while I stopped trying to make sense of things I could never understand and stared up at him, frozen except for heart and lungs which were pounding, he added in a lighter tone, "And besides, in this instance, it truly isn't necessary. He's a policeman."

I suppose I really should have known.

Everything slowed down. And I mean everything. In the clean white space of the bathroom, the space between us contracted. By Adam's side, his hand made a movement to touch me, then hesitated. No doubt his jaw was remembering what had happened the last time I'd been distressed and he'd taken hold of me. Then he deliberately defied the memory. Suddenly his hands were upon my shoulders. Then roughly, unexpectedly, that wasn't enough and I was wrapped in his arms. It was a decisive sort of hug. Fierce. I was crushed into his chest. I was clinging to him too. My face was turned against the curve of his neck. His jumper was warm against my cheek, against my eyes where they were pressed tightly shut and beneath my hands where they knotted in the loose folds of woollen fabric behind his back. I felt his chin move against my hair. He was saying very softly, "You know, that's the second time you've trusted my word without argument. Last night and now; I believe we have progress."

He meant when I hadn't taken the message in Clarke's note as it was written and accused Adam of deliberately informing them that he had me.

After a moment more of intense stillness while humour faded to something far more complicated, he added, "And I'm sorry. This is the real apology that is owing. I've known for certain about Jim since he called me yesterday morning and I've have told you if you'd stayed in any room with me long enough to let me speak. Or if you hadn't looked like one more mention of that business might break you. I decided I shouldn't force you to listen. I think I've done quite enough in the line of making assumptions about you one way or another, and I judged it better to let you rest and enjoy some peace and approach the subject in your own time. I'm sorry. It was wrong of me. But it ... it has been a very difficult conversation to know how to begin, weighed down as it is by the knowledge I was unforgivably hard on you the other night and I could see it had made you shy of me."

It felt safe, hidden away there in the warmth of his shoulder. The sort of place where nothing more could find me, not even emotion except for something very simple and under-stated. And the slowly dawning realisation that the reserve that had coloured his manner and the mistake he'd spent the past day trying to undo hadn't been the fact he'd brought me into his home. The mistake had been in his manner of doing it.

Below, May was calling impatiently. Rather more briskly, he added, "I'd better go. Will you manage for a few minutes?"

I nodded into his jumper. After a moment more when I was supposed to let him go – but somehow didn't and he didn't either – I took a very deep breath. My voice surprised me by being remarkably normal as I finally confessed what I had known for some time, "I don't know how to face this."

It took him a few long seconds to formulate his answer. His hands adjusted their grip and then a second time. Then, with his mouth near my ear he said soothingly, "Of course you do. You've been doing brilliantly all this time. You're just worn out, that's all. And you're forgetting that I really did mean what I said. I am here now. I'll help you."

His grip tightened further while my mind ran through everything he'd ever said to me and realised with a little bolt of shock that he was referring to a promise delivered in the hotel foyer which at the time I'd discarded as a lie.

The realisation made my lips form the sound of his name. "Adam ..."

After a brief steadying intake of breath, he supplied the rest. "You're sorry. I know."

That mocking note was back.

It made me laugh a little. His arms tightened painfully, as if to crush this feeling into me. Then he let me go.

He hurried down the stairs, took his daughter firmly by the hand despite her protests and moved in a throng of people down the hall and out onto the street.

In my turn, I squared my shoulders, took myself at a rather more sedate pace down the stairs into the now vacant hallway, and turned left to meet Jim in the kitchen.

# Chapter 25

"Why, hullo, Kate. You look well."

Jim Bristol's greeting was warm, friendly and I think he would have risen to embrace me had my decidedly uninviting stance not stopped him in his tracks. Instead he settled on climbing to his feet like a well-mannered boy and reaching into a trouser pocket. He pulled out a police warrant card and dropped it onto the kitchen table.

That ever present cheerfulness didn't falter as he watched me slowly reach out a hand to pick up the folded leather. The greying pasteboard inside indicated that it belonged to the Gloucestershire Constabulary, that the bearer held the rank of Detective Sergeant and I examined it thoroughly before deciding it was authentic and setting it carefully down again. I remarked pleasantly, "Well at least you were honest about your first name."

He looked sheepish, but only for a moment. His surname was Fleece. Then he put out a hand and pocketed the warrant like it was a trophy. "Don't be too hard on me, Kate Williams. Or is it Miss Ward?"

I only glared. He smiled back at me as he reclaimed his seat; handsome and as ever unabashed.

Then abruptly he conceded a little truth. "You gave me the worst day of my life, Kate."

It made me take my place at the table. He watched me draw out the chair opposite him and then he added, "When you abandoned me on the Birmingham train, and I couldn't find you when I finally got back into town, I got into a bit of a panic and thought they'd got you. Forgive me if I say that whatever you suspect them of, you don't know the half of it. I left messages for you anywhere that I could think of. One of them was here. After a comedy act of mis-timed calls, Adam and I finally spoke yesterday just before lunch. I gather you'd already filled him in on the more grisly details. He called me very early this morning and told me about *this*."

I saw then that the letter lay open on the table by his hand. He picked it up and read it again. "'*Any later and we risk ruining the little girl's next family outing.*' Nice, isn't it, how they've carefully avoided actually putting their threat down in plain black and white. Makes it all so much harder to build a case. Not," he added with a sudden hush in case May should have accidentally reappeared, "that I intend to let that stand in my way. Not now that I've got you."

"Oh?" I enquired with a polite lift of my eyebrows.

There was a rustle of feet in the passage behind and Mrs Francis bustled in, making a big show of squeezing past in the space between my chair and the sideboard. I was sitting in the chair Adam had used on that first night. For once the older lady didn't scowl at me. Instead she took herself to the heavily cosied teapot by the stove and poured a fresh cup. Then, to my increasing surprise, she set it down on the table before me. She very pointedly didn't offer more tea to Jim.

Jim was watching me. He remarked thoughtfully, "I don't think I'm only wearing the disguise of a policeman today but I guess you never can be too sure."

I gave in and stopped glowering. In the hallway outside, the front door rattled as it was opened and then shut.

Mrs Francis waggled a tea towel at me. "You're lucky. When the boy delivered a letter for a Mrs Williams yesterday, I was all set to turn you out of the house with a flea in your ear. I thought Adam finally had run mad and had taken it upon himself to make off with somebody's wife." Her lips pursed as that man stepped into view and paused there to lean a shoulder against the doorframe. She scolded, "You introduced her as a Miss! You said she was a stray. When that letter arrived I thought you must both be in hiding from an irate husband."

Adam's smile was a little worn. "Sorry," he said. "I didn't exactly understand it myself that first night."

Jim spoke from the other end of the table. "You've done the right thing, Hitchen. That man is one of the best in the force. He'll keep them all perfectly safe."

"That was another policeman?"

Jim smirked in response to my question. "You're not very good at spotting us, are you, Kate?"

There was something faintly unnerving in his bold gaze that was rather too reminiscent of the deliberately applied charm I had encountered at the foot of the waterfalls at Devil's Bridge. It made me flush.

Adam left his doorway and stepped into the room. For all his earlier confidence, he was clearly not very happy. He caught my glance, shrugged off my concern and took a cup and saucer from Mrs Francis. "Thank you," he said.

He took up position behind the chair next to mine. He took a mouthful of his tea, scalded his lips and then said across its brim to Jim, "So, are you going to finally explain why to all intents and purposes you had me commit kidnap three days ago?"

Jim's smile faded. Abruptly businesslike again, the policeman fixed his attention on Adam. Adam met his gaze squarely. Even seated, the policeman's bearing and unceasing self-assurance made Adam seem very much the minor guest at this meeting, even though this was his kitchen and the hands that cradled the teacup were by no means weak. The cup was lifted for another tentative sip and I wondered if Adam was aware of the comparison being forced between them. I also wondered if, like me, he too was being toyed with.

"So, Adam," Jim began. "You had no idea there was more to Kate's behaviour beyond the natural grief for Mr Williams' demise until you arrived back here on Sunday night?"

"You know I didn't. We've been through this already."

Jim's mouth twitched. "Humour me."

Adam sighed and dropped a hand to lean his weight upon the stout wood of the chairback. He set his cup down upon the tabletop and flicked a quick glance downwards at me. He didn't like to revisit what had been said lately about my grief both to me and to others. And while for me the fact he had known of Rhys's death was somehow less vital now – eased as it was by the relatively plausible connection of living in the same town – he was aware we had yet to discuss how he had known me well enough to recognise me as the man's former wife. The detective, I could perceive, had already probed this detail and been satisfied. At this moment all Adam could do was reiterate what he'd made plain before; that all along the most he had understood about me and my behaviour until the moment of our arrival here was that I was utterly worn out by Rhys's death, and showing it.

"I didn't," he added very carefully indeed, "even understand her when she told me about it that night. It was only when I picked up the note Nanny had left about an hour or so later, telling me you'd called and giving the number of your station in Gloucester that I really began to grasp the full story. You're lucky I went with my hunch and decided you weren't quite the brute I'd had described."

"I'm a brute, Kate?"

Jim's expression was that of one who was just after the facts. I didn't believe it for a moment.

Gripping the back of his chair with both hands, Adam said for me, "Well, Jim, you did bully her, pursue her, hand her over to Clarke and Reed and capitalise on a dead-of-night invasion into her hotel room to increase my belief she was cracking up so yes, you are a brute. Why exactly were you pursuing her anyway? Why didn't you just say something? Why didn't you tell us who you were?"

Jim was unmoved. He retorted idly, "Concealment is rather the general idea of being undercover, wouldn't you say? You can't go dealing out your real identity to anyone, not to friend and not to foe."

It suddenly struck me then. The policeman was not here to play the part of tame detective. He wanted to use us, not make us like him. Somehow the discovery was liberating.

He told me, "For your information, Kate, it is your own fault I didn't realise early on that you fell firmly on the side of friend. You popped up into the middle of a very complex operation and instantly took to trampling all over it in a manner that made it look suspiciously like you were in cahoots with those two men, Clarke and Reed. Every act of yours might have been perfectly geared towards setting up a clandestine meeting with them. So you weren't the only one who got frightened out of their wits when Clarke collared you on the pier. You were supposed to be helpfully implicating yourself so that I could make the first in a long line of arrests and instead you gave me the second-worst day of my life. You looked back as they led you past."

Jim spoke quickly across the other man's sudden sharp movement. It was accompanied by a hissed intake of breath. Jim was saying, "Luckily you gave them the slip, although unluckily that meant you gave me the slip too. I was existing in such a high state of nerves by the time you reappeared, that I spent most of the night drifting back and forth past your door on some pretext or other, just in case. When you then said something, or whimpered or whatever it was in your sleep I'm afraid I completely overreacted. I thought they'd somehow got in there with you."

Adam's hands moved restlessly on the back of his chair.

"So that was how I ended up being called on to rescue a woman from her own bed covers? She didn't cry out at all? At least not until two men burst in through her door in the dead of night barely hours after two other men had given her the fright of her life?" Adam's question was delivered with flat disbelief. I think he was remembering how he'd been privately blaming me for not being strong enough in the wake of my ex-husband's death. I was remembering the way he'd held my hand that night.

Jim was unrepentant. "In my defence, Kate, your name had been brought to my attention long before you pitched up in Aberystwyth. I first wondered about the innocence of Mrs Kate Williams about eight or nine days before, when the reports of your husband's apparent suicide first reached me." He leaned in to rest his elbows upon the tabletop. "Did you happen to notice that when the policemen called at your house to inform you of your husband's death, they took particular care to establish the date of your last visit to the gallery?"

I shook my head.

Jim's eyebrows lifted. "And you didn't think that it was a touch odd that the police came in person to tell you, when under such circumstances it might have been rather more normal for the ex-wife to learn of her husband's demise through the family?"

"No," I said. I don't think it would have ever occurred to me. It had seemed perfectly natural at the time. A little gesture of humanity from the authorities at a time of loss. Which showed how ludicrously naïve I was. It was a miracle I'd survived this thing at all.

There was a smell of burning toast. Mrs Francis began crashing about rescuing it. Over the clatter of drawers as she hunted for a new tea towel, Jim said easily, "Amongst other things, your visiting constables were able to confirm that you'd left your husband in ..." Here he reached into an inner pocket on his jacket and drew out a notebook. He flicked laboriously through a few pages until he found the one he wanted. "Let me see ... late December 1945 and you only saw him again in late 1946 when your divorce was finalised. You haven't been back to Cirencester since."

My remark was dry. "You're very well informed."

A quick twitch of a smile. "As I say, the police constables who visited you were given a very specific set of questions. They were tasked with eliminating you from our investigation."

"The investigation into Rhys's death."

He didn't reply because he was already adding, "Crucially, we were able to confirm that you weren't here in Cirencester between autumn last year and March this year."

Rhys had died about two weeks ago in Aberystwyth. This wasn't an investigation into his death. Whatever Jim thought he was looking for, Rhys's death had ranked as nothing more than a postscript. I couldn't help wondering what mine would have been.

Perfectly calmly, Jim slipped his hand into that inside pocket again and drew out a brown envelope. Within it was another envelope, an ordinary white letter envelope this time, and this one contained a small portrait of the sort that had smoky edges and belonged in a silver frame. It was accompanied by a single fold of paper that was covered in handwriting. He opened the latter and laid it flat on the table before me. "Read it if you please."

Adam and I dutifully leaned in.

It bore the date 12 September 1946 – it was a little over a year old. It was a note in a clear, steady hand and written by a man by the name of Richard Langton who was a war invalid – judging from the fact his address was a London military hospital – and most of it was personal in the extreme. It relayed to the reader the news of a second injury, this time to the heart. I wondered how this Richard felt about having his private affairs carried about the country to be pored over by strangers.

The remainder wasn't quite so raw, however, and it said:

*'Anyway, to answer the real point of your note: Rather belatedly, here is the name as promised of the family contact at that gallery in Cirencester. He helped source some of Mother's choice artworks. Presuming he's still active and hasn't packed up or died, Benjamin Dillon is probably just the person to help.'*

As soon as Jim saw that we had reached the end, he asked me, "Do you know the name Langton?"

Suddenly there was eagerness in the policeman's manner, though his style of speaking didn't change. The gallery this Richard Langton described was my gallery. Benjamin Dillon was my uncle. This was that same uncle who had gifted me training, experience and a home before retiring to his daughter's house in West Bromwich many years before this letter was written.

I lifted my head and caught Jim in the act of quietly examining my face. He said, "You ask why it was important we established you weren't at the gallery a year ago? This letter is why."

"Is this him?" I reached out a tentative hand towards the photograph.

With a wave of his hand Jim indicated I could take it. The person contained within the oval edges of the sepia print was young, younger than me, and utterly charismatic. I'd never seen him before in my life. I lifted my hand to show the portrait to Adam and he reached out a hand and took it from me. He examined the photograph for a moment and then he too shook his head.

Across the table Jim watched as Adam reset the portrait upon the tabletop. The policeman said slowly, "In March this year we recovered a collection of artworks that had been looted locally during the Blitz. The man who had them had been tasked with finding a buyer but he was no thief. And no expert on the value of artworks either. Someone else had that dubious honour and until this letter came to light we hadn't the faintest clue who that might be."

Jim paused for emphasis. I looked up at him sharply. I was almost laughing at the ludicrousness of it. "You think Uncle Ben is a *thief?*"

Jim didn't smile. "During the war, several grand townhouses in this area were hit by looters. The collection we unearthed in March represented the spoils from just one of the houses but I believe the same man was behind all of them. I think our thief is the sort of man who would know some pretty high-class people and I think he used the chaos gifted by the Blitz to send in a little team to create a little bit of 'bomb damage' of their own and relieve these people of a number of cultural gems. I think our thief lacked the means of disposing of his stolen hoard and so he recruited a series of middlemen to do it for him. And if this letter is a clue, your gallery is where he did it."

"Sure he did," I remarked hotly. Before me the man in his photograph was beaming lazily. "And now you think that since Benjamin Dillon is a notable art dealer with the right sort of experience of handling fine paintings, he'd have known precisely what to take. And he has an open invitation to some of the grandest houses in the country. But you're also over-looking the fact he's got all that because he's one of the best dealers there is. He wouldn't need the petty contacts of an ignorant middleman to get his artworks out of the country. And besides all that, he retired in 1939 ... He hasn't been here." A sudden realisation made my voice become very cold. "But then you already knew this, didn't you? You didn't say that the name in that letter is the clue, but the gallery he owns."

Jim's manner was just as hard as mine. If there had ever been any doubts about the authenticity of his latest persona of a policeman, they were swept away now. He replied coolly, "You're quite right. Benjamin Dillon hasn't lived in Cirencester since he handed over the reins of the gallery to a young and enthusiastic woman who happened to be his niece ... And her husband, of course. Isn't that the case, Kate Williams?"

I sat back so that my chair creaked, shaking my head. Not because it wasn't true but because of the lunacy of it. I said vaguely, "It just gets worse ..."

From her corner by the stove Mrs Francis startled all of us by proving that she'd been listening very attentively indeed. She had the letter in her hands. "Why can't you just ask this Richard fellow? Surely he can tell you who he met?"

Unexpectedly, Jim smiled. "Richard Langton is just another person whose life was very nearly robbed of everything he holds dear by his proximity to what is, not to put too fine a point on it, a toweringly murderous greed. The person who was caught with all the contents of a Cheltenham grandee's art collection was Richard Langton's brother. This brother's message is penned on the reverse of that letter."

There was a crinkle of paper as Mrs Francis hastily turned it over and then a short while later she slipped the paper down onto the tabletop before us. On the reverse of the neatly penned letter, a bold confident scrawl declared: *'At long last I am in a position to help you, now that Richard has finally recovered his wits enough after that ruinous conquest to remember to send the name ... I would, by the way, be very happy to lend a more personal style of assistance should you wish to have support during the negotiations. If this Dillon fellow haggles excessively over that particularly foul and yet valuable muddy painting of yours, you know I'll help.'*

My eyes strayed to the portrait of that young man. I understood now that Jim had allowed us to presume these features belonged to the other brother as a test. Now I saw this face with new eyes. He looked too cheerful to have been the author of the unforgiving reference to his brother's curtailed romance. Jim's voice was hard as he asked me very specifically, "Do you know him?"

I was actually disappointed to be unable to help, though Lord knows what it would have meant for me if I had known who the man was. I said regretfully, "I'm sorry, no. I've never even heard the family name."

"Why don't you ask *him* then?" This was gruff, from Adam. He knew we were being tested with this man's identity and he didn't like it.

Jim was singularly unrelenting when he replied bluntly, "He's dead."

He caught my look. "Oh, this art thief didn't kill him. But he might as well have done. It's the way this thing seems to go."

"Oh." It was hard to know what to say to that. Jim had after all dubbed this a crime governed by a toweringly murderous greed. Then something struck me. My gaze sharpened to meet Jim's. I said accusingly, "So when precisely did you decide I was the orchestrator of all this?"

Somewhere in the background Mrs Francis was clattering discreetly with pans. She was doing it in that peculiarly hushed way people have when they are doing something noisy so they do it very slowly as if that will make it quieter. It barely registered with me but I think Jim had to wait some time for the volume to decrease again before conceding, "I never did think you were our thief."

He said it almost apologetically as if I should be affronted by the oversight. He explained, "If your uncle is exonerated by virtue of the fact he wasn't in Cirencester at the time this letter was directing John Langton towards the crucial meeting at your gallery, the same rule applies to you. You weren't here. You left the marital home in late 1945, long before this letter was written. You didn't see Rhys Williams again until your divorce a year later. You weren't here at the crucial time."

"But Rhys was?"

Jim's posture was suddenly impatient. The memory irritated him. "You should be aware that when this note came to light we immediately got our warrant and undertook a thorough investigation into the business of that gallery. We've been inside that place. We've turned everything over; every record, every sale logged in the accounts, every detail of every delivery company you've ever used, every transaction in cash and through the bank, and found nothing."

I was surprised. "Not even a record of this particularly 'valuable muddy painting'? Because if it was entered into the general selling exhibition for that year, it'd be listed in the exhibition catalogue at the very least, even if it never sold."

Jim shook his head. "Apparently this man's prospects improved so abruptly around that time that he felt able to promise the vendor a loan and the painting was saved."

I persisted, "So you've got nothing that proves this Langton fellow ever went there?"

"Put in those terms, no," Jim conceded. "And there's nothing we needed to learn about Rhys Williams except that he is utterly convinced he is the great maestro in that place. Sorry." This last was an apology to me. I didn't mind. "We had to discount him, we discounted Benjamin Dillon; and we discounted the downtrodden ex-wife in less time than it took to cross your name off a list. For months that's all we had. Everything was absolutely still and calm, just as it had been before this note came to light. As you've quite rightly observed, I had to finally consider that the lead was absolutely irrelevant. Then two weeks ago something changed. Two weeks ago, it all started up again. The chain of brutality surrounding those looted artworks lifted its head above the parapet and finally stretched out its hand to decisively include your gallery. A man disappeared. And still I don't know why."

"Rhys Williams." My voice was hoarse.

"No!" Jim's slap of his hand upon the tabletop was so emphatic that he made me jump. "*Not* Rhys. He came next. A missing policeman is the man that matters to me. And a record of him turned up entirely unexpectedly in your hands."

For the third time he reached into a pocket, this time on the other flap of his jacket, and drew out a folded card. He flattened it out. It wasn't card; it was a photograph. In fact, it was the photograph he had stolen from me that night in my hotel room. Jim was watching me carefully, for all that he had already declared I wasn't under suspicion any more. He was examining every nuance of my facial expressions, every manner, every action for even the slightest trace of guilt.

He asked me, "Is *this* man familiar?"

He meant the only man in the photograph that I couldn't identify. The man standing in the gallery on an opening night within the little cluster of hopeful journalists beyond the glowing artist with his close-knit group of friends and patrons. The man that had been the fundamental part of all my plans on that last day in Aberystwyth, only it had all gone wrong. I shook my head. My heart was beating.

"Do you know the name Steven Leicester? What about Philip Black?"

He fired the names at me. Again I shook my head. Beside me, Adam's hands moved restlessly upon the chair back. Protectively. I think Jim noticed it too.

Jim said, "Well, he's perfectly familiar to me. I told you just now that after our failed search we went back to the station to formulate other plans and this was it. This dishevelled gentleman who looks like he must have stumbled in from the nearest bar to unexpectedly land at a launch party is none other than Detective Constable Philip Black, a colleague of mine. Three months ago we put him in the gallery as a newspaper hack by the name of Steven Leicester who cunningly persuaded your egotist of a husband that it would be delightfully prestigious to collaborate on a spot of reportage. That gallery was concealing something, something so subtle it required a subtle man to winkle it out. My friend and colleague was the man tasked with doing just that."

Across the table, Jim sat back in his seat with a sigh. He didn't need to tell us that it hadn't worked. The detective conceded grimly, "It was a fine waste of everybody's time. He was there for weeks and months and had nothing to report except that Rhys Williams had taken some truly extraordinary photographs. It was a damned expensive way for the force to fund an artistic project and not quite the glittering demonstration of talent that Philip Black had been looking for. Phil was a uniformed constable in the spring just as I was. Phil caught the attention of our Chief Inspector in March, as I did, and was moved into CID in the summer with me. We both shed our uniform for plain clothes at the same time and Phil's been with me every step of the way since. This was supposed to be his big case. We put him in that gallery to have a little look about and he found absolutely nothing. Until Rhys Williams unexpectedly killed himself by launching from the top of that waterfall ... and we learned that Philip Black had disappeared a few days before."

There was deeply strange little silence that was broken by Mrs Francis abandoning her stove to reach across the table for the photograph. Its stiffened corner scraped noisily across the wooden tabletop.

Jim was watching her as she examined his friend's face. His voice was suddenly sober. "I wasn't following you at all, Kate, at first. Phil's disappearance meant that he must have found something. I don't believe he vanished voluntarily and the probable suicide of Rhys Williams only a few days later indicated we were wrong to discount that man after all. It even went so far as to suggest that Rhys might have been our thief and the shame of discovery had finally tipped him over the edge. I went to Aberystwyth to see if anything had turned up in his effects that might make a hunch become fact. Only that drew a blank too, mainly thanks to the inspector in charge demonstrating a complete lack of interest in, well, anything. I was about to head home with my tail between my legs when *you* arrived."

"You saw her get off the train." The break of Adam's voice above me was expressionless.

A short nod from Jim. He said, "I'd just bought my ticket. Then a certain woman walked boldly past." He told me, "I recognised you from a photograph we'd picked up from the gallery during that fruitless search. It was an old one so Rhys Williams didn't mind it being mauled over by the police. Your hair was long in the photograph so it required a second glance to be sure, but your kind of features don't alter much and then it was easy enough to tail you and take a room at the same hotel. You didn't suspect me then, did you?"

I shook my head mutely.

Jim said musingly, "There I was, thinking that Phil had uncovered something, something so awful that the thief's only escape was to kill himself, and you turned up and proved me wrong all over again."

"How did I do that?"

"Because, Kate, you proved that your husband's death was just another number to add to the tally. If he'd been the man we're after, the tally would have ended with him. Your arrival proved it hadn't. I realised you could claim to have a perfectly innocent explanation for your visit but it was pretty clear from the start that you weren't simply planning to lay flowers at the head of the falls, console his parents and so on. You were definitely skulking about in the shadows and you made it very clear that you were alert to being followed. It looked more like a fact-finding mission than any kind of homage to the dearly departed and even at the spot where he ... at Devil's Bridge I mean, you were nothing but perfectly self-contained. Unconcerned, even. I watched as you messed about in the car park during our trip to that ruined castle. You looked like you might be leaving a note or sign for the owners of that car and then the very next day you attempted to ditch me by the pier. I saw you make what I thought was a prearranged meeting with those men, who by the way I'd never seen before, and I thought I'd struck the jackpot. Only then you happened to look back as they led you past."

I tried not to fidget uneasily. I could feel the tension emanating from Adam in waves. His hands were gripping the chairback to the point that his veins were proud about his wrists. I was counting out the deaths – Langton, Black and Rhys – and realising that I, by the barest bewildering mercy of the man beside me, really had escaped being the next.

I remarked incredulously to Jim, "But you must have known about my accident?" Mrs Francis set a plate of cold and badly buttered toast down before me. "Thank you. You must have known what I'd told the police there? It was in their report."

Jim shook his head ruefully. "Actually, I didn't. You keep forgetting that we'd eliminated you. Until you arrived at the hotel, I had absolutely no reason to wish to know more about you. The local force had your accident pegged as just that – an accident. They certainly weren't going to think to pass the information on. It only came to light when I leaned heavily on our mutual friend Inspector Griffiths and he got the Lancaster Constabulary to send everything they had on you by first-class post. It wasn't easy given the fact he holds the senior rank. But the file arrived on Saturday. I read it that evening – after I'd given myself a nice fine shock by standing idly to one side while Clarke tried to snatch you right beneath my nose."

He leaned in. "Do you know, I spent a lot of time running around after you that day. First I had to deal with the realisation that you weren't Clarke's accomplice and then play my part to ensure you got away. I was frantically wracking my brains for some sort of distraction that would leave my cover intact when young Samuel and his bucket of crabs appeared on the scene. His father conveniently delayed one fellow and my shady salesman character neatly stumbled into the path of the other, and then once every man there had lost all trace of you and we'd all wasted several hours staring at the railway station in case you attempted to take a train, I took myself down to the police station once more and threw my weight around. Eventually even our moustachioed inspector got interested enough to show me the file that had come in the post, which included a report of the accident."

"So that was your fault, was it?" I remarked accusingly as light dawned. "You told him I was in hiding at the hotel. You got me into a lot of trouble. He was very angry that I'd used my maiden name at the hotel but given him my married one."

Jim wasn't remotely apologetic. "And so he should be. I'd have given you a pretty stiff telling-off too if I'd known you were attempting to dodge the likes of Clarke and Reed with only a switch from your married name to your maiden name. Didn't it occur to you to assume a completely different identity?"

"It's all right for you," I retorted. "I presume you can get a plethora of ration books and licences and everything in any name you like. When you're a normal person like me and there are rules about taking rooms in hotels, you're stuck with the name on your real documents. My ration book just happens to be in my maiden name so I used it there, that's all."

Another cup of tea appeared by my side. It arrived without Mrs Francis ever leaving her station by the window so I presumed she could just conjure them at will.

"Why didn't you tell me all this during our chat that last morning at the hotel, Jim?" Adam's voice was even cooler than ever and it drew my eye. He gave me a tight-lipped smile. "Surely once you'd established she was vulnerable, getting her safely out of harm's way must have been your first obligation? Or were you too busy nudging me towards deciding to bring her back here?"

For the first time in what was possibly his life, I saw Jim look briefly guilty. "I did want to get her back here, you're right. They seemed dead set on achieving it, Rhys Williams lived here and Philip Black disappeared from here. There had to be more than just chance symmetry behind that. But I thought I could control this if I just kept my cover for a little longer. I thought I'd got a route that kept Kate nicely protected, and with *you* back here," Jim levelled his gaze at me, "it was a dead cert *they'd* come back here. At long last I might have a chance of seeing the real players at work in this game. And I had to use Adam. I couldn't very well ask you to come back here myself, could I? You wouldn't listen to me but you did listen to *him*. I knew I'd never get you to come back otherwise. You hate it here. Since your divorce, you haven't even paid a visit to the town to see your sister." He acknowledged my startled glance. "Yes, we sent men round to interview her too when you pitched up at the hotel. Everyone's a suspect now."

He gave Adam a conciliatory smile. "And I did get someone to probe into your background too before forming this plan." He said it as if that made everything all right.

Adam's voice was as cold as the breakfast congealing on my plate. Without lifting his gaze from the chair beneath his hands, he said, "This plan of yours nearly scared her off completely. It left her covered in scuffs and bruises and bearing a particularly interesting cut behind her left ear – which, judging by Kate's reaction just now, she didn't think we knew was there. It very nearly ended with your entire case being lost to the sea." Then he looked up and his eyes were as hard as slate. "Did you give that careful consideration beforehand too?"

I stopped trying to reassure myself that my hair covered the mark that had been made by my fall from the ladder and dropped my hand to my lap. I couldn't help watching his face, and the stubbornness that tugged at his mouth which told me – even if not the others – that he'd noticed it when I had been curled up asleep on the edge of his bed.

That unforgiving voice continued. "And I wouldn't, by the way, use the term 'unconcerned' to describe the way she looked that day at Devil's Bridge."

The silence was so complete I could hear a clock ticking in the hall.

About a minute later, Mrs Francis drifted towards the stove. With the art of one experienced at smoothing over any dispute, she asked the kettle, "More tea?"

"Yes, please, Mrs Francis," replied Jim. Then he added smoothly, "Then I can tell you what I want Kate to do now."

# Chapter 26

In the brief lull while the housekeeper fussed with the pot, I forced down some toast and Adam quietly collected our cups. Jim took the opportunity to say, "Do you know, Kate, you really injured my pride that night when you confronted me over your lost sketchbook and gave me a thorough dressing down for following you. I thought I'd been so sly. Though as it happens, with regards to your sketchbook, I really wasn't ever particularly interested in it. As I recall, I was just making polite conversation. Whereas Mary was so interested she stole it. And slipped it back into your bag while you were building up a good head of steam by berating me ..."

"*Mary* took it?" Adam was leaning against the sideboard behind me, midway through eating a piece of toast. His expression was odd; confused now rather than tense. I suppose it was hard for him being confronted with all the ways he'd been misled these past few days. "*Why?*"

I expect I looked a little doubtful myself until it finally made sense. I said on a little note of realisation, "She wanted to show her sister the portrait of my ex-husband."

There was a nod from Jim across the table. "Mary told me

what she'd done while I was packing my bags for my return here."

I stared at him. He must have confided to her who and what he was. I was suddenly thinking, poor Mary. She always did seem to think men were set to be a disappointment. I wondered how she'd felt when she'd learnt that her playful fantasy of becoming wife to the muscle-bound Mr Bristol was in fact a dream of being Mary Fleece. And what if the fantasy ran to having children? The temptation amongst the witty public to call them her little lambs would be tortuous.

From his position just behind my left shoulder, Adam was looking at me strangely. I think I must have gone from my usual wearied pallor to trying not to laugh. All the same he was saying bluntly, "So what is it that you want from her, Jim?"

It had the effect of sobering me up very rapidly.

Jim was surveying Adam thoughtfully. It occurred to me then that Jim really was toying with him. Jim had been goading me into declaring my innocence just to see what effect it had. And while Adam's general instinct to protect me was on some level mildly thrilling, it also made me wonder why Jim thought it should even need testing. I was rapidly coming to understand that Jim said and did nothing without measuring each act for its value to a deeper purpose. He was a handsome man, yes, but beneath the good looks he was as hard as granite. Now he was saying calmly, "I think the real question you should be asking, Adam, is what do *they* want from her. Wouldn't you say, Kate?"

Taking my cue very carefully and keeping my gaze fixed

firmly on the hands that were now clasped nervously on the tabletop, I said, "I really don't know what it is I'm supposed to give them. They seemed to think Rhys had given me something before he ... died. I swear they made some mention of the gallery that day in Lancaster but I can't remember their precise words now. I don't believe they've said anything about it to me since. When I last saw them, they seemed simply determined to get me into their car. And of course now they've made absolutely no mention of surrendering anything but myself at the meeting today. And yet—"

I dared to lift my gaze. This was Jim's cue to say something very specific and reassuring about nobody being required to surrender themselves to anyone but he didn't. Instead he simply raised his eyebrows and prompted, "Yes?"

"Surely they know by now I haven't got it. They know I'd have given it to Adam at the very least and now they've seen you arrive. They *must* know I haven't got this thing."

Jim reached across the table and lifted the photograph of that busy opening night at the gallery. He examined it for a moment. Then he said crisply, "They do. Three weeks ago at about this time of day, Philip Black was beginning another day on a tedious sleuthing job that at some point was going to have to be drawn to a close. Three weeks ago we were still no closer to proving that this gallery was the hidden connection between a thief and his dead middleman. Then all hell broke loose and a policeman disappeared without a trace, a notable photographer supposedly committed suicide and two previously invisible men lurched out into the open to undertake a reckless pursuit of a lone woman across England into

Wales. Philip Black found his evidence. They thought Kate had it. And now suddenly they're issuing invitations to a lunchtime rendezvous with the full benefit of public scrutiny. What does that tell us?"

"That the thief is desperate?" This was warmly from Mrs Francis. She was looking excited, like she might singlehandedly solve this thing herself.

Jim shook his head. "Not quite. Let me put it this way. About a year ago, the thief decided to use a middleman to handle the sale of a collection of respectably valuable artworks because this man had skills he needed, namely the capacity to run any gauntlet for a bit of ready cash. Three years before that, he'd hired a team of professionals to undertake the original theft, because naturally he needed people with subtle talents. Now he's using Clarke and Reed as a sort of hostage delivery service and who are they? Murderers? Brainless heavies? No. Now I have their names," a brief nod to me, "I can tell you that they're a pair of quite ordinary scoundrels who have been using their military service to develop a nice little sideline in security now the war is over. They're hired sleuths. This thief always uses people who have just the right skills for the job. He's been paying them to retrieve this missing fragment of evidence."

"No," said Adam, emphatically. The sideboard clattered as he adjusted his position. I twisted to look up at him in surprise. He wasn't looking at me, he was staring fixedly over my head at Jim. "No," he said again.

Jim repeated stoically, "Clarke and Reed are being paid to retrieve whatever it was that Philip Black uncovered. Clearly in the midst of making him disappear, they failed to get him to divulge where he'd put this treasure. They had reason to believe he might have passed it to you, Kate. They promptly took to hounding you. Then, equally abruptly, this thief abandons that plan and decides he wants you. In person. And why? Because he believes now that it's still lodged somewhere in that gallery and you're the woman to find it for him. You have a skill he needs. And it doesn't matter to him in the slightest that by inviting you there he's risking exposure himself."

"Perhaps he's just trying to silence her." Adam's retort was curt.

"Well he needn't, because as this investigation currently stands, they could still get clean away. If I collared Clarke and Reed now, I might get them on a charge of using black market fuel perhaps, with all this driving about the country they've been doing ... Or at a pinch we might manage to build a case for attempted kidnap in Lancaster if someone could be persuaded to remember that they saw the pair of them by the bus stop after all. But I've got nothing on the man who's giving them their orders. Everything changed for all of us the minute they sent the invitation to go to that gallery. They know you wouldn't be unguarded now. That tells me that there's something so vital that this thief wants from you that he is prepared to risk our presence to get it."

"That's absurd reasoning. It doesn't make any sense."

"Would you find it more digestible if I confided that I suspect the truth is that it doesn't *matter* to him that she might bring me along?"

"Not remotely. You might as well pretend that he actually wants you there. Either way it means that somehow this thief has planned to get what he wants without any fear that in the process he'll give you even the smallest glimpse of what *you* want. And that all points to the same thing. I say again: No."

Jim seemed to understand his meaning rather better than I did. He said, "Listen to this, Adam." Then he proceeded to read from his notebook, though I suspect he knew the contents by heart. "Philip Black disappeared approximately three days before Rhys Williams died. The day Black vanished, witnesses placed him at a sporting event in the company of Mr Williams. They were working on their collaboration; something to do with the psychology of gambling. It was Phil's idea and, if you recall, purely a front. We picked horse racing as Phil's journalistic niche because Rhys Williams had undertaken a collaborative project once before on a sporting theme and the results had sold well, and also because Phil was a man obsessed by steeple chasing. They say the best lies are built upon a germ of truth after all. We only know the rough time of Phil's disappearance by virtue of the last known sighting that placed him on his motorbike travelling towards Cirencester on the Saturday evening, three days before Rhys died."

"He was on his way to the gallery?"

"Presumably so, Adam, yes."

"And is your witness reliable?" Adam was blunt.

"Yes." Jim was equally matter-of-fact and for good reason. "He's me."

After a pause Jim added, "I shadowed him to this race

324

meeting and I can tell you the only characters there were Phil and Rhys Williams and a lot of people screaming at horses. Phil was his usual self. He hadn't found anything yet. The next day, Sunday, he failed to make his weekly catch-up with me. We thought nothing of it. He often ducked out of sight for a while. But two days after *that* Rhys was apparently motivated to dramatically end his own life. We called in Philip to explain what had happened and that was when we learned he'd disappeared. Three days later I went to Aberystwyth and four days after that you appeared, Kate. And with you came Clarke and Reed."

"You keep saying that apparently Rhys killed himself." Behind me Adam was speaking through gritted teeth.

"I beg your pardon?"

"You keep saying *apparent* suicide, or *supposedly* he killed himself. Aren't you certain?"

Jim gazed at Adam steadily across the expanse of his kitchen table. "Not absolutely. The evidence says he did. Inspector Griffiths did get something right at least; he found a good witness. A Londoner by the name of Miss Diamond or something or other – I'll find the name in my notes somewhere. Here. It was Christel. A Miss Anthea Christel saw him fall and others can corroborate her story. But am *I* convinced? No."

"And you're using the term 'was' when talking about your friend Philip Black, not 'is'. He *was* obsessed by horse racing."

"Yes."

Adam summarised, "He was at the gallery and after months of inactivity, something happened and now he's disappeared. Presumably he died."

"Yes."

Adam continued, "Rhys lived and worked at the gallery and something was uncovered that either drove him into a wild panic where death seemed the only way out, or someone did it for him. Either way he died."

"Yes." Jim's agreement was bland.

"The middleman who handled the looted artworks made a hash of his job and then he died."

"That's a loose interpretation of those events but for the purposes of your argument, yes. He died."

"And still you want Kate to give this man the help he's looking for."

Now I understood his intense opposition. My cheeks were burning. Which was odd because I was utterly cold.

"Let me make something abundantly clear to you both." Jim's voice was suddenly pure steel. "I've been inside that gallery. I've searched it from top to bottom, both when we first came across that crucial letter and again a fortnight ago when Rhys Williams died. I've found nothing. There has never been any trace of anything that shouldn't be there. Then Kate Ward appeared on the scene and suddenly the façade they've been hiding behind has slowly started crumbling. In one week you've exposed more about their activities than the whole of the Gloucester police force has achieved in nearly a year of investigation. You've drawn them into the open to the point that I have the names of two men I formerly didn't even know existed. Now they've categorically proved that we have the power to expose the person behind all this – that single person who knows how to recognise a valuable painting, who is sitting on a priceless hoard and who will willingly swat aside the life of a policeman in order to keep it. I am not proposing that Kate helps this thief recover the thread he lost when Philip Black disappeared. I'm proposing that she goes to this gallery with the benefit of a full escort and searches it from top to bottom with us until we have that blasted piece of evidence that will hang this man."

"Unless it's a woman." I don't know what made me say that. It was nerves I think.

"Yes," agreed Jim tersely, "unless it's a woman."

His harsh eyes moved beyond me as he remarked, "I know how you feel, Adam."

Adam was making that telltale gesture of running his hand through his hair. His gaze dropped to mine and his mouth twisted into a little humourless smile. "Of course you do."

"There isn't any other way. This man is moving on this now. We have to take him. Certainly, Kate could run again and go into hiding and hope he forgets her in the end. And while she's doing that I could put guards on that gallery and get a warrant and wait until a team has pulled it apart brick by brick and still I'd find nothing. And if we stop her from playing along with this man's little plan, how long do you think it would be before it occurs to him to instruct Clarke to simply burn it all down? Adam, I need your support."

"No."

"No, I don't have your support?"

"Just no. Absolutely no. No, no and no. It's immoral."

"Kate?"

"Oh sure," remarked Adam with a hard, bitter laugh. "Now

you ask her. As an afterthought. You said it yourself; you knew she wouldn't come back here under her own volition so you decided to cast me as her keeper. Only she was too independent for you then and this time I'm not quite toeing the line, am I? *Of course* I'm not going to join you in steering her. She's barely recovered from the last time you and I, along with this thief of yours, set about systematically eroding her sense of control. You and I both know that Kate is brave enough for almost anything, but do you actually *want* her to go to this place feeling alone again?"

We gaped at him.

Then we went to the gallery.

# Chapter 27

I didn't feel remotely alone when I stepped out through Adam's front door amongst a swarm of five or so policemen and into the back of a car. But I wasn't feeling quite the courageous woman Adam had described either, and it wasn't just the dread of returning to my old marital home that concerned me. It was the fact that now that the decision had been made, Adam was abruptly back on side. His simple act of climbing before me into the back of the police car was disconcerting proof that while Detective Sergeant James Fleece had been getting on with the awkward business of preparing us to help with his case, Adam had been quietly cast as the mainstay that would keep me afloat.

It was proof that while Jim had never really intended to leave me feeling isolated, he also clearly still had considerable doubts about my strength of mind.

I didn't get long to decide whether this was offensive or he was just being really, really practical. Gloucester Street, where Adam and his daughter lived, was one of the main routes into town. This was no Georgian spectacle like nearby Cheltenham. Cirencester was a place where the old and the not-so-old jostled together in cramped rows, all uneven charm, before bursting into the busy marketplace beneath the gaze of the grey church tower. Then we were weaving our way between busses and a horse-drawn delivery wagon onto Cricklade Street and drawing to a halt outside my old home.

The narrow three-storey structure that housed the gallery had steeply pointed gables and narrow stone mullioned windows. Its beautiful, characterful frontage was much as I remembered it from the day I had packed up my belongings and left, and it was hard to say when I had liked the sight of it less; then or now. The gallery was closed, unsurprisingly, since there was no one left to run it.

"Ready?" This came from Jim, twisting in the seat in front of mine. The car had stopped. Adam was sitting beside me behind the driver. A second police car was squeaking to a halt behind us too. Then the policemen, both uniformed and plain-clothed, were out and doing their routine again of clearing a path for us between the car and the front door and checking the crowd for danger. I wished they wouldn't. It made it all seem so real.

Adam's door was opened for him. He stepped out. He turned to wait for me. I was there, standing beside him beneath lines of bunting and flags and realising that like Aberystwyth, this town too was in the midst of its Royal Wedding celebrations. There should have been an exhibition in the gallery to support it – I could see one peeling poster between the glass and the internal shutters. The shabbiness of the window display made it seem like its last resident had been dead for years.

Then the shopkeeper from the watchmakers next door sneezed loudly and gracelessly, and abruptly reduced the funereal mood that weighted our first steps towards the door into something rather more commonplace. Someone behind me sniggered. Then Jim tipped his mouth slightly closer to my ear so that his words were for me alone as he cheerfully said, "It's a bit behindhand of me to suddenly ask you this now, but are you sure you're ready for this? You look pretty beaten about, if I'm allowed to be honest. And," he added, "it's not helped by your sudden transition into demure clothing, Mrs Williams."

His remark made me jump like I'd been touched by a live wire. Then I covered the reaction by turning my attention to a search of the contents of my handbag. The hem of the grey frock was just visible between the flaps of my raincoat.

I observed, "I must have been in disguise in Aberystwyth after all, don't you think?"

I withdrew my hand from my bag and found that Adam's gaze had fixed on me. He'd been listening. Then his eyes ran down to what lay within my fingers. He looked even more surprised.

"You have a *key*?"

---

I did have a key. For the very simple reason that the gallery was mine; or rather, it was my uncle's and since he was aged and retired, mine to enjoy until the old man's death.

Of course, given this minor detail of ownership, it was perhaps doubly odd that I should have allowed Rhys to stay while I scurried home to my parents with my head held low. But after all, his was the artistic talent that could be measured against present greats and in some ways the loss of such a place felt like suitable reparation for my part in our marriage's failure. And besides all that, as I was frequently being reminded at the moment, I had been deeply unhappy here and I had never really intended to ever come back...

I needn't have bothered carrying the key with me all this time either. Because just as I stepped forwards with the view of putting my hand to the lock, the door opened and in its stead stood an extremely carelessly dressed, magnificently attractive woman: Christi.

We stared at each other. Then Rhys's model and muse smiled. "Katarina."

She still had the same humbling figure I remembered; age and elegant curves united with a fearsomely aggressive femininity. It was accompanied by the same tireless energy, wildly curling amber hair with its defiant strands of grey, dramatic eyebrows and a mouth that was very much used to saying what it liked. That mouth now formed a pout as she examined me in her turn and then moved on to consume the two men with me and the crowd of uniforms just behind. She seemed to hesitate at Adam's face; her eyes hardened a little as perhaps she tried to place him. Then she moved on to Jim. She had clearly met him during his last visit.

"James," she said, with a little staged flicker of long eyelashes.

"Detective Sergeant James Fleece," he replied with that perfect calm of one beautiful person to another.

"Got a better list of questions this time?"

"Got Kate."

His reply made her smile, a brief flash of genuine amusement before she returned her gaze to Adam. Her voice was deep – far deeper than mine. "You'd better come in." And somehow engineered it so that I was the one left to shut the door.

I waited until the uniformed men had all shuffled in and then pulled a face as I dropped the latch. It was ever thus. It was the same game I had played with the first of Rhys's models when I wasn't supposed know, wasn't supposed to let on that I knew.

The front door led into the main exhibition room and no one had moved to open the sturdy shutters. I flicked the light switch and found that Christi, Jim and two or three of the constables had disappeared upstairs. Presumably they were completing a survey of the building to ensure it was safely empty of Clarke and Reed. I joined the remainder in the centre of the floor. It was cold in here. It had that cold of the grates being left empty for some time. The walls were clean and white and adorned only by a few bright oil paintings and a cluster of someone else's photographs. Presumably this was as far as Rhys had got with hanging that aborted exhibition on the theme of the Royal Wedding before everything had gone wrong. In the middle of the floor was the evidence of recent packing and it appeared that Christi, with all her style, personality and the distant Italian heritage that she seemed to turn on and off at will, was preparing to jump ship.

It was a moment before I realised that nearer by, Adam was

staring intently at the bottom-right corner of one of the three paintings. It was a portrait, a vivid representation of a local grandee in modern blues and greens with a rare flash of crimson, and actually quite good. He spoke without turning his head. "K.W. Is this one of yours?"

"Shocking, isn't it." I moved a little nearer.

"Not really," he said mildly, examining it again. "Why did I think you only ever painted landscapes in interesting shades of—?"

"Brown?" I supplied. The answer was easy. Figure work had been my husband's niche and once my uncle retired and we began setting our own exhibitions it hadn't seemed wise to turn the gallery into a specialist venue for studies of the human form. So my commercial work had always been land-scapes and these portraits and others like them had been my sly secret, the equivalent of the smallest illicit affair of my own, painted whenever he went away.

It surprised me to see them hung like this. These three portraits were tenuously connected to the theme of the Royal Wedding so perhaps not out of place but as I've already said, Rhys had never liked my portrait work. The gallery had only ever exhibited my landscapes. Which had always been, as Adam rightly remarked, painted in rather drab colours.

"Adam?" I began tentatively.

"Mmmm?"

I didn't get to ask the burning question because a figure moved into view from the office at the back and it was Gregory.

Rhys's most reliable friend and patron was dressed in his customary pale trousers and blue blazer that bore the badge of his rowing club. He was a man whose legs seemed fractionally shorter than the length of his spine required but the imbalance was a discreet reminder that Gregory Scott had once been a famed rowing champion, still with the broad chest to match. Two years ago he'd used his presence and respectability in the sporting world to set the theme for Rhys's first great project since his return from war. I'd never seen the final results of their collaboration but I'd witnessed their discussions in the project's early stages. It had been destined to be a splendid celebration of human endeavour for an audience hungry for reassurance now that the war was really over.

Now Gregory's greeting was warm. He looked well. Two years had passed in a blink of an eye for him. He moved swiftly across the room and embraced me in that easy way that we always had during my life here; the same way Adam had on that first drive back to Aberystwyth after a day at Devil's Bridge. A swift pressure of his hand upon my arm and a touch of cheek to cheek. Then, because we were particularly old acquaintances, there was a brief touch of our other cheeks too.

I stepped back and found he was surveying me beneath lowered brows. I felt absurdly unmoved by our reunion and I think it was because I couldn't quite remember how we had parted last; whether it had been amicable or if this greeting was inappropriately warm. I think I've mentioned the little complication of a sort of bubbling undertone of interest from him. He'd always teased that had our ages been more similar he'd have made his proposal before Rhys.

I'd always thought that age wouldn't have made any difference.

Today he had clearly completely forgotten all that and those supple lips were simply saying warmly, "I didn't think you'd come after our telephone call. You were very firm. I'm so glad you've changed your mind."

That telephone conversation after Rhys's death seemed a very long time ago. I remembered now. I'd hurt him then by being determined to stay away.

Now he was adding more soberly, "But what's this? Why all the policemen? Is it Rhys? Surely, they haven't found him? I mean ... is he—?"

The poor man's bewildered grief was etched upon his face.

I felt ashamed. I felt ashamed because these past few minutes I'd been reliving all that past unease and bracing myself to meet the subtle sense of always being at odds with his wishes. I hadn't anticipated that his wish at this particular moment would simply be to inspire an expression of our shared sorrow in the passing of Rhys Williams.

I found myself stumbling into making apologetic negatives that made no sense and then had to pull myself together and finally clarified my answer by saying more calmly, "No, no. This is nothing to do with Rhys. That is, Detective Sergeant Fleece will have to explain what he wants, I'm afraid. What are you doing here?"

I hadn't offended him. Gregory knew me. He laughed and told me plainly, "I came to harass poor Christi about those prints Rhys promised me. No one has been back before today."

He said it louder for Christi's benefit as she skipped down

the stairs and sauntered back into the scene. She smiled at him. The difficulty for me was that she proved precisely why I was being so clumsy as I went through the awkward process of renewing my acquaintance with Gregory. It was the unpleasantness of realising just how well both these people knew me, when I'd imagined I would have the security of feeling like a stranger.

"So," said Christi, standing in the doorway to the back room as the physical embodiment of Rhys's creative genius. There was the tramp of many feet after her down the stairs. Jim drifted into view in the office behind her. I waited for the policeman to exert some kind of authority over the scene – and my part in it. It felt like I'd waited long enough. But he didn't. He occupied himself with the task of dispatching several of his team into the little enclosed courtyard that stood beyond the office. And then I noticed that Christi was watching Adam with a lazy kind of curiosity. His presence here seemed to fascinate her. It made me restless. I'd thought he would be by my side but he wasn't. He had resumed his examination of my pictures almost as soon as Jim had reappeared.

Christi cemented my sense of being stranded by abruptly remarking quite forcefully, "How nice to see you again, Mr Hitchen. You were at our little soirée for Rhys's comeback exhibition in October last year."

I couldn't help staring at Adam too then. I saw him tilt his head at her in silent acknowledgement before he turned away to the photographic prints on the far wall. They were not to Rhys's standard.

"What are you doing here, Detective Sergeant Fleece?" From her doorway, Christi cast the policeman a mildly challenging glance over her shoulder. He was by the desk now. I could just see one cluttered corner. "Well?" she demanded, striking a dramatic pose with one hand on a hip. "Still hunting for your greasy friend?"

"Detective Constable Philip Black is still missing," Jim confirmed amiably. "Have you thought of anything else that might help me find him?"

She gave a tinkling laugh as though he'd made a private joke. It was as she turned to give him the full dramatic impact of her looks that I noticed that something else about her was geared for impact too.

Christi was wearing impossibly elegant slacks with a waist to rival Mrs Alderton's but, unlike that lady's fearsome denial of comfort, Christi's idea of grace was given carelessly so that she was utterly, intimidatingly feminine. She didn't need age to give her character; she'd been born confident. Now she lifted her hand to brush a stray mass of thick curling hair back from her face. It glittered a little in the glare of the overhead light.

In fact, it shone gold.

Now I understood the fragment of news that Sue, my mother-in-law, had been able to only hint at; the undisclosed secret that might well lead me into a fit of rage where the only revenge strong enough was to evict the great artist from his home. Sue hadn't known this though.

By contrast, Christi knew precisely what she was doing. She followed my gaze and affected surprise as she realised what I was looking at. "Oh," she said, examining the ring as if she were seeing it for the first time herself. "I'm sorry, did no one tell you?"

I was thinking that the inspector in Aberystwyth had, in his way, when he'd imagined that my identity shared the grave status of a war widow, then realised his mistake and blamed me for the falsehood. It still remained though that someone should probably have seen fit to explain the whole story to her new mother-in-law.

Christi stared at the band of gold, turning it on her finger before suddenly rejecting it as nothing and impatiently thrusting the hand into a trouser pocket. "Yes," she confided. "It's been about three months now. We're in the throes of seeking a new studio in London. Or at least we were. It would have been heaven. And yes," this was tart, for Jim, "we would have informed the police of its address when we finally moved."

It struck me with a little shock that these boxes and piles were not the signs of a sudden house move after all. This wasn't the flight of a bereaved woman after Rhys's death. This had been planned long before. They hadn't intended to stay long enough to leave room for me to indulge in a little petty revenge when the news got out. Which proved just how much importance they gave to their situation that they thought I should even wish to try.

It was at that moment, equally abruptly, that it dawned on me that Gregory was still beside me and lending me his company. It had an awful ring of familiarity about it; the symmetry of Christi scoring a point on Rhys's name, the sense of being undervalued in this place and the idea that at least one man here might wish to reassure me that things could be weighted the other way. In this case I don't believe Gregory was actually doing anything except standing where there was space for him but still it sent me though the crowded doorway into the office like a bullet from a gun.

---

The office was very light because the back wall was nearly all glass. There was also a door that opened into the shared courtyard behind our gallery. Two of the three uniformed policemen who'd previously trudged upstairs with Jim were now out there, as ever making a very serious business out of glowering fiercely at the various entrances belonging to us, the watchmakers and the houses behind.

Christi was watching me. The force of her resentment turned my head to look back at her. Her jaw had hardened. She didn't mean to reveal the bitterness beneath the flare, I think, but the feeling was genuine. This was hard for her and I found myself doing my usual thing of working myself into a tangle worrying about the feelings of this person that I didn't like before stumbling through some apologies for this invasion that the bereaved widow didn't want and certainly didn't hear. She showed it by saying idly, "Did you know he only married you for this gallery?"

I remarked dryly, "His timing was uncanny." It wasn't actually. Other galleries had been available. This gallery had simply been the convenience that had kept him here later, after his experiment with a gentler kind of infatuation had proved unfulfilling. But I was hardly going to give her the satisfaction of arguing the point.

I turned aside to leaf through some old press cuttings on top of the cabinet in the corner by the door. The office was in a far worse state than the exhibition room. The shelves were empty and half-filled boxes stood about containing a disordered mess of old volumes of my painstakingly recorded accounts. Books logging historic client orders cluttered the desk alongside various dog-eared exhibition catalogues and alone in a locked cabinet was that familiar Leica camera. I turned the key and drew it out. My fingers automatically found the roughened surface where I had paid to have it engraved with his name. "Is this broken?"

Christi was watching me, one shoulder propped against the doorframe and her fine eyebrows faintly curious. "No, I don't think so. Why?"

"No reason." I put it down again. Then I picked up one of the ancient accounts books from the box against the wall. Line upon line of sums and notes in neat little columns written in those years when I had been alone here. I had liked this place then. In fact I had loved it. It had been my home. I returned the accounts book to its place and moved towards the stairs.

"Do you have to go sniffing about?" Christi was sweeping her hair aside again, this time with less precision than before. "I know this is your house, but it's also my home. It was his home and now there are policemen all over it. They're outside, they're in the gallery and whatever your

341

tame police sergeant thinks, I *have* happened to noticed that one slyly stayed up there while we trooped back downstairs just now."

I stopped and stared at her. The raw honesty in her voice floored me. From her I was used to distain, pity, coldness; never sadness. "I—"

She cut across me. "You could at least tell me what you want before you start nosing about the place. You've been gone for two years, it can't be right that you just walk in like this? Without so much as a pause to ask how I am?" Then Christi was adding quite brutally, "I've loved him for longer than you, you know."

There was a crowd in the doorway behind her. Adam was standing to one side, listening but with his gaze fixed on something he was juggling in his hands. A screwdriver that he'd picked up off the floor. A pair of idle policemen stood beyond him and on the other side of the open doorway were the watchful eyes of Gregory. The ageing athlete looked alert. I think for a moment he'd been deeply surprised – he hadn't known of Rhys's marriage either. Now I think he was concerned, perhaps rightly, for the welfare of his friend's widow. Who now most definitely wasn't me.

Jim was swift to answer for all of us. "Of course, Mrs Williams, you must have known him for a long time. You met him when his posting with the troops took him to Italy. Kate only had him for the few years before the war. Barely any time at all. And you were very courageous in your enclave above Naples during the occupation. It is nothing short of tragic that sorrow has found you here like this. We're very sorry for your loss. Where have you been staying for these past few weeks if it hasn't been here?"

"With friends," she said curtly. The weakness switched off. She'd wanted to earn my sympathy, not his.

It made me ask, "Why did you come back today?"

Christi didn't care to answer my questions. She wanted to control me, or at least my feelings. Her reply was terse. "Because life moves on. Look, what do you want here?"

Jim interceded again. "Mrs Williams, let me be frank with you." To my utter amazement, he went on to tell her the truth of his missing policeman's search for the connection between the gallery, a thief and a dead middleman; and his own decision to return today to find it once and for all. He made no mention of my letter or my rendezvous with Clarke and Reed or indeed my part in this search at all. In fact he implied I was only here at all because my presence did away with the need for a warrant to search the place. The idea that I could just bring who I liked into her home sounded rather uncertain legal ground to me. I glanced at Adam and caught Gregory's gaze instead. The space between us narrowed, particularly when this old friend stepped into the room as if he'd intercepted my silent plea to Adam to end my isolation in this place and thought I wished him to lend me his support. The mistake drove me backwards a pace and I found my hands firmly upon a banister rail.

Christi wasn't remotely interested in Jim's theory about the form his crucial clue took. She suddenly snapped out, "It must hurt to hear him call me Mrs Williams."

Her voice checked me on the first step. This wasn't a calculated effort to draw a certain response. This was pure, desperate, impulsive venom.

Adam was in the room too now. He'd stepped in to lay his screwdriver down on a shelf where it couldn't fall and trip anyone. He was almost as close to me as Gregory was but he wasn't watching me. His eyes had flicked unsmilingly back to Christi.

Some devil within me, driven by the hatefully incessant tug and draw of this place, made me answer her sweetly, "Not at all. Mrs Williams is far easier on the ears than any of the other names I have for you."

No one spoke. No one moved and the heavy silence in this room was punctuated only by the irregular chatter of a customer in the shop next door and the distant murmur of traffic on the marketplace. Then Gregory made an appalled reproof out of my name. I think he was used to pitying me. I think the alternative came as a bit of a shock.

At the same time Christi stepped forwards and reached out a hand with a view, I think, of ejecting me from the building. She said, suddenly very Mediterranean indeed:

"Bravo, Kate. Perhaps if you'd been a little more like that and a little less like an insipid lackey you might not have lost him to me, no?"

# Chapter 28

For a moment there was absolute silence. Then suddenly everyone was talking at once and Jim was shouting warnings and throwing himself between us. Someone thrust us or, to be precise, thrust me roughly backwards. Above it all, Gregory was talking in a loud clear voice and recollecting an important meeting elsewhere and Jim was instructing him to stay, please, and taking me by the arm and propelling me none too gently up the stairs.

"Up," he ordered none too pleasantly. "Wait for me up there. I'll be just a minute."

I went. I reached the head of the first flight of stairs just as he was making a great deal of fuss about clearing a chair of debris for poor Mrs Williams. I was stepping for the first time in two years into the wide room that had once been my bedroom and I barely noticed. The policeman who had been left up here was drifting forwards through the gloom to meet me, then there was a movement behind on the stairs and the creak of footsteps on bare floorboards as Adam rose into view.

For a moment I thought he had the look where he was

about to start lecturing me again only it wasn't quite. And then Jim was behind him and leaning in to whisper, "Bravo indeed, Kate."

He was very nearly laughing. I was standing there on the bare wooden boards, reeling with a sort of impotent emotion that might have been upset and might just as easily have been rage. Christi's voice followed him. She was making the most of her disgust and I heard the murmur as Gregory tried to mediate. I stood there in the hollow disarray of a bedroom that had lately been sorted into boxes, glaring at them all in turn and breathing hard as it dawned on me that yet again I had a very strong man dictating that I couldn't just walk out through the door.

Jim's voice was strong too. Beaming broadly, he said very clearly, "Forgive me, Madam, but I had to get you away before the two of you came to blows." If we could hear Christi's complaints up here, I had no doubt she could hear everything Jim said to me. His manner was immensely condescending as he added, "I think it would be better for you stay out of the way up here while she and I have a little chat, don't you? Since you can't manage to restrain yourself before Rhys Williams' new wife. My dear lady, you just threatened a *widow*."

That stopped me. I might not have come remotely close to dealing in blows, but I had at the least lost my temper with a woman who had just lost her husband. What precisely did that say about me?

Only Jim seemed to be finding it funny. There was an expectant little silence while he grinned at me. Then beside me Adam gave a sigh. "Jim," he remarked very quietly indeed,

"Kate hasn't guessed that the scene down there was part of a greater ploy."

I looked from the one to the other.

Adam added, "You might also like to explain precisely why you gave me the high sign over that woman's shoulder to leave Kate stranded just now."

"Oh, very nice," I hissed. "Was it wise do you think, given everything that was said in Adam's kitchen earlier about my general wellbeing and the precarious state of my mind, to deliberately set about reducing my dignity to the level of a naughty child before these people?" Trying not to give way to a general apoplexy, I demanded in a fierce whisper, *"What on earth* were you hoping to achieve?"

Jim was unrepentant. In fact his hushed reply was aggressive. He growled, *"This."* He tipped his head towards the room. "That woman has made it pretty clear she doesn't want you up here. Now in one fell swoop Christi Williams has convinced herself that your status here is negligible, she's gifted me the perfect premise for banishing you upstairs and also given me the excuse for letting you search without allowing her to scrutinise every step. Is that clear enough for you? You've done it again, Kate. You've achieved in five minutes what would have taken me weeks to arrange."

In the dingy light of the bedroom, Jim's whole body was blazing with a fierce kind of triumph. His expression made me say incredulously, "You can't suspect *Christi?*"

"Why not?"

I had to pause for a moment. I hadn't actually thought why not. "Because, for one thing, it's too convenient. The other woman? It'd suit me down to the ground, wouldn't it, if I managed to find the piece of evidence that would prove Rhys's new ladylove was a thief all along. Christi *wasn't here* during the war, Jim, to loot these houses. And neither was Rhys."

"I've got my job," Jim replied arrogantly, turning away. "And you've got yours. So do it." Then he added as a conciliatory afterthought, "Please?"

I stopped him with my hand. "Detective ... Sergeant ... Jim – whatever we call you now – can I just confirm that you aren't imagining there are secret niches in the gallery walls concealing coded messages that only I could find; hatches in the floorboards; that sort of thing, are you? Because if you are, you're set to be disappointed."

There was a fresh gleam of a grin. He was quite frightening when he was happy like this. It was like meeting the real man, and the real man was enjoying the hunt. He told me, "No. We've searched the fabric of this place twice now. We know the connection is within the gallery's business affairs. And you're the woman to find it. You have to be. Because the thief wanted you here too."

He stepped back. Then he added severely in a ringing tone that echoed down the stairs, "This is PC Downe. He's going to keep an eye on everything, and I mean *everything* you touch. So tread carefully, Mrs Williams."

He descended the stairs. I heard him begin again in that bold carrying voice, "Mrs Williams!" And this time he wasn't talking to me.

We all stood there for a moment, listening as Gregory grew impatient and demanded to know whether a mere sergeant had the authority to ruin a person's day like this. It hadn't even occurred to me to ask such a thing but Jim calmly explained that his senior, an inspector by the name of Woods, was delayed by another case but would be here before the morning was out. He didn't add it, but he meant before this supposed two o'clock deadline set by Clarke and Reed. I turned abruptly towards the shrouded window and put a hand to the heavy curtains.

"Is this allowed?" I asked. PC Downe only smiled. He was a small mildly portly man of about my age with an amiable face. The wooden rings shrieked along the rails.

I heard Adam say quietly, "Kate ..."

I turned back to the room and found I was suddenly angry with him. Or angry with myself for minding quite so much, or something. And ashamed of myself for feeling it. It was this place. I'd expected a ghostly mausoleum to an old and dusty tragedy and found living conflict instead. I'd also given myself a different kind of humiliation. It was humiliating that after all these years of maintaining a reasonably dignified silence before all the petty insults embodied by these other women, I had at last been reduced to the level of jealous rival in the face of Christi's taunts. I didn't know whether anyone had noticed that the key that had finally done it had not been her claim on Rhys...

---

This room that had been my bedroom smelled a little of damp. It was bare – bare of every little piece of furniture that had made this place my own. In my day this room had been a mixture of library, bedroom and my studio. Now it was just an empty shell with a collection of about four overflowing boxes, a line of bookcases fixed to the wall, a pair of men's shoes and somebody else's expansive bed.

Even that was bare too. It was just a mattress on a heavy wooden frame. Through the doorway opposite, beyond the spot where the smudged rectangle of sunlight from the grimy windows reached its limit and Adam stood quietly to one side, I knew the narrow landing bore two other doors. The nearest was a kitchen with its narrow walls bearing cupboards, drawers and a very dubious oven, and beyond that a bathroom was tucked in the damp corner beneath the rising stairs.

Downstairs, Jim was calmly listening to Gregory's politely expressed frustration that he wasn't allowed to leave. The man had an appointment with his doctor. He hadn't intended to spend his day mediating between the police and sparring wives. I presumed I should probably examine the contents of the boxes. I dropped my coat on the bed and tugged the first box towards me and sat down.

The box contained reams of old contact prints, those direct copies of negatives laid out as miniature black and white images on stiff photographic paper, and wallets containing the negatives themselves. It was then that it struck me that this was a truly infuriating way to search. I had absolutely no idea what form this missing connection took and all the while I had to wrestle with the crippling suspicion that Jim had set me up as a miracle-worker. I was doomed to fail. From his stillness, I knew Adam thought the same. I'd braced myself to tackle a swift march through the home I had known, where any little alteration would stand out like a sore thumb. This slow drift through untidily boxed possessions was nothing more than an invasion into a barren unfamiliar world while the man who had promised to make me feel secure stood there helplessly adding to the eyes that watched me. My memories were no more use in this hunt than his were.

I couldn't help asking Adam then: "Is that how you know me? Because of her?"

I thought I'd managed to conceal my feelings perfectly. But I can't have because when I dared to glance up his mouth was compressed into one of those smiles that made a line. "No, Kate," he said.

He made me grin suddenly, and shake my head over the bundle in my hands. It brought sudden easing of tension. A sudden appreciation of my own ridiculousness. The policeman moved. It was just a simple shift of his weight from one leg to the other but it made me conscious of the negatives in my hands. Examination identified them as a mixture of Rhys's dry record shots – the equivalent of an artist's preparatory sketch – and Christi's own efforts taken at a large gallery event. It wasn't the recent launch party that had been attended by Jim's missing policeman. It was probably the launch of Rhys's comeback exhibition because – the only detail discernible at that miniscule scale – one of the gallery walls bore a vast portrait of a football team. There were even a few photographs of older events that were mine where familiar faces seemed to loom from every angle. They were rubbish. They were probably packed like this to make them easier to throw away.

Beside me, the policeman had his notebook out and was making a list of everything I touched. I showed him what was in my hands and then I put them back.

Then I heard Adam defy our audience – he was far braver than I – to explain, "I met Rhys during the summer that saw the release of my first novel when the publisher demanded a formal photograph; something suitably meaningful of the author surrounded by his favourite books. Rhys Williams was local so I commissioned him and it was, in the event, really quite brilliant. Although he did make it embarrassingly clear that I didn't quite rank highly enough on the social scale at that stage to deserve anything more than a slightly bored courtesy as he took my money ..."

Adam cast me a wry glance. He had drifted towards the vacant bookshelves that lined the wall. His hand began to leaf through a small pile of papers that had been left there and I saw him jump as the constable moved to peer over his shoulder. There was a rustle as Adam hastily set down the sheets of paper. One slipped and fell and he caught it.

As he set it back on its pile, he told me, "You and I were introduced shortly afterwards at an exhibition launch; the last one you did before we were all sent our call-up papers, I believe. I wouldn't have gone to the thing at all but for the fact that it was about five months after June had died and I felt it was high time I did some talking to grown-ups."

That brought my pulse up. "Dear Lord," I said with feeling. "I'm not sure I would have picked one of our launch parties for that. Was I friendly?"

"Of course." He'd turned his back to the bookcase. "You

were very polite and asked me how I was, and we talked about the town and the park, and then you offered me a glass of champagne. I already had one in my hand." He smiled.

I was leafing through a fresh bundle of something without even looking at it. I turned my head and found the collection was a tattered cluster of small prints of Christi. I hastily put them back. I said ruefully, "I was probably worrying about the discussion I'd just had with Lord Whatsit and Sir Someone Else and whether I had said something utterly clichéd that set Rhys's talent alongside the artistic greats of our time only to get the details blatantly wrong. Such as talking about Picasso as if he were old and dead, for example. It's been done, believe me."

In truth, Rhys and I must have inevitably had one of our rows, or rather he would have been having a creative crisis and I would have been quietly pacifying only for his charm to turn on like a switch when the first guest arrived. I, on the other hand, would have been left a wreck. I said sheepishly, "And then you bumped into me years later on a deserted hilltop and I was rude to you all over again. I'm so sorry. You won't believe me, but I *did* think your voice was familiar. And you didn't tell me about your wife – June, I mean – at Devil's Bridge, did you? I remembered it from meeting you here all those years ago. I suppose you recognised me immediately?"

Adam had drifted nearer to me and my little collection of rubbish. His coat dropped onto the bare mattress beside mine. "Not immediately," he said, "no. But I was sure when I saw you sitting there at breakfast. To be honest, when we met at the party all those years ago ..." His voice slowed as he was distracted by a bundle lying on top of the next crate but then he recollected himself and turned back to me. "I didn't think you were rude. I thought you were astoundingly normal in a sea of pretension."

He came closer and took that cluster of tired prints out of my hands. I must have absently picked them up again to restart the process of examining them all over again. He glanced at them and then added, "You see, last autumn when I received a condescendingly generic invitation to Rhys's comeback exhibition I accepted, I believe, for pretty much the same reason as before. And then I got Christi instead of you and was treated to a tour of the room like a new trophy, and received some quite extraordinary proof that I must have risen after all in the years since that first awkward photographic commission. Now I was a noteworthy personage who must be added to the collection. And you know how much I enjoy that sort of thing. To be quite frank it was almost a relief that you didn't recognise me over breakfast." A hesitation. "Almost."

He caught my eye. I flushed and hid it by turning my head back to the box before me. Then I observed, "No wonder Christi felt she had to claim you as her own earlier. The idea that I'd pipped her to the post would have piqued terribly." And had to bite my lip at the implication that I too thought of him in terms of ownership.

"You think she was suffering from jealousy? Is that what it was?"

I looked up at him in surprise. It hadn't struck him to resent my words at all. Or perhaps even consider them. This was different. This wasn't about me; this was about her. I asked quickly in a strangely tight voice, "You don't think so?"

"Perhaps. Yes, of course it was. Exactly."

There was something in his tone. Something repressive. I remarked dryly, "And that was a very enigmatic reply."

"Was it? Sorry." He didn't care to explain. Instead he moved on so swiftly that he almost left me floundering to understand his meaning. He said, "Was this how you met Rhys too?"

I stared at him blankly, then Adam turned a photograph round to face me. His expression was so carefully arranged into polite interest that it made me laugh. It was one of Rhys's set-up shots. It was a rough, untidy record of a scene so that the model's pose could be re-enacted in the future. It must have been a work from his last completed exhibition where great paintings were parodied in modern form; the one that had been recorded on Christi's camera only to plunge with him into the void at that waterfall.

The piece recorded in this particular photograph used a scantily clad Christi. Angular and dramatic, she was striking the pose of an *Olympia* or an *Odalisque* across a bed. She was accompanied by what looked like an ARP warden where classical paintings would place a slave girl. It seemed to me rather unusually vulgar of him to reference our nation's recent war in this way; a cheap trick playing on our emotions so soon into peacetime. Or perhaps that had been his point.

Adam wasn't worrying about any of that. He was asking whether I too had been Rhys's model. I had not. I had never been called on to drape myself artfully across a scene for him. When we'd met I had been a fellow artist, albeit an inferior one. I'd been a student who had stumbled into his world through the kindness and invitation of my talented, generous, gruffly spoken old uncle. I was the woman who thought she understood the scope of Rhys's concepts; I was never the muse that inspired them. Which was not, now I came to think of it, remotely flattering since every other woman he met had been.

I told Adam this without rancour and reached to pull the next box closer. I wasn't really meaning anything by it. I was already leafing through images of yet more launch events. Some of them seemed to be enlargements of the negatives in the other box. I could make out that there was traffic on the road outside the gallery window meaning that they dated from the time before the fuel ration had been withdrawn.

"Kate," said Adam sharply to catch my attention.

I looked up. "What?"

"Come off it," he said simply.

Oh.

Flushing, finally I told him what he wanted to know.

"Sometimes I wonder," I remarked lightly, flicking blindly through yet more photographs, "how it might have worked out if a trivial little disagreement about sharing desk-space in the office hadn't driven me into a fit of self-awareness. I honestly don't know if Rhys would have ever mustered the energy to tell me the truth about his feelings for ... well, for me as his wife and for these other women, and then more specifically, Christi. I think he might have let us all go on together, driving each other insane, but too lazy to make the change. It never really struck me how absurd it was. At the time I think we felt that although Rhys was the artist, we all had a part to play and we were all contributing to something truly great. Something greater than ourselves. The sacrifice we made in our daily lives – we women that is – was a natural requirement of his art, not a part of him. It was just something that had happened all through history with the wives and muses of great artists and was happening again to us."

"You actually believed that?"

"At the time," I repeated with a smile.

He didn't return my smile. Either I'd misunderstood his comment or it wasn't enough of an answer. After a little while I added rather dryly, "It was only later that I understood the truth about my role here. His models *were* an essential part of his art. But I wasn't."

Adam's eyebrows lifted.

I explained, "Do you know what the most brutal discovery of all was for me? It was learning that through the years of my marriage my husband had found reason to form many derogatory judgements about me; and the overriding one was that I was actually rather silly."

"Silly?" Adam queried the term.

"Silly," I repeated firmly. "Silly for staying put when he plainly didn't wish me to, silly for still caring for him when he was increasingly careless of me and definitely silly for believing I might ever have anything to contribute to a serious artistic endeavour beyond the ordinary housekeeping that anyone might do. The worst part was that he wasn't doing it deliberately. He wasn't trying to be cruel. This was just his genuine heartfelt response and to be quite frank I think it puzzled him that I grew to be such a disappointment. He knew he was making me sad and he was sorry for it."

I took a breath. "He actually *pitied* me."

I stopped. That last statement went ringing on and on in the room around us in a little pathetic shadow of that old loss of value. Now I really did feel a fool. I'd been speaking about my marriage quite easily and then suddenly up had crept this sneaking burst of true bitterness to the point that I felt like I was snatching for breath. I knew that this one old injury had underpinned all my reactions to the threats and accusations I had faced over the past few weeks. It had kept me going too. I couldn't bear to revisit that old appreciation that I was judged worthy only of someone's pity. But still I was terribly afraid that by coming here, all I had done was give these people the opportunity to teach me I was inferior all over again.

For a moment Adam was motionless. I had a horrible suspicion that he was about to launch into one of those excruciating declarations that I wasn't an idiot really, with the earnestness one reserves for the truly fragile things of this world. But he didn't. Instead, the photographs were reset upon their box. I watched him do it and then I said with a very odd sense of relief, "I do at least understand now that it's not all my fault that I didn't ..." I searched for the word, "suit him."

And it struck me then that I really did understand that. It was a new discovery.

"Absolutely," Adam agreed easily with his attention already on the next thing. "But by that reckoning it's not his fault he didn't suit you either, and it'd be a shame to have to admit that."

His dry retort sent ripples through my mind. He meant to observe that while I had been despising myself for trying and failing to be the sort of woman who could make Rhys happy, how much should I have been asking myself whether Rhys had ever really been capable of making *me* happy?

"No," I agreed with the sort of hesitation that implied the thought was rolling about in my mouth and it was trying it on for size.

Then as soon as the growing warmth reached my lips it dawned on me with a little disorientating shock that I'd confided all this while the policeman had been looking at Christi's pictures too, since he was tasked with supervising anything that caught our interest. Embarrassment descended like a cloud. I shot across the room to the door onto the landing at the head of the first flight of stairs. I stopped there, dithering and intensely conscious of the noise downstairs when Adam confided without so much as raising his voice, "Do you realise that I tried to tell you I knew who you were in almost every conversation we had, until that little piece of confusion by my car when we arrived back in Aberystwyth on that first day?"

Adam was bending over the box that I'd been meaning to search before I'd fled for the stairs instead. He waited for me to give a slight answering shake of my head. He continued, "I thought you'd remembered me when you made your fare-well by that telephone box, it was so much a piece of the style of goodbyes that you and your set did at that event in this gallery. Only then I saw that you *hadn't* and given that I thought I knew full well the sort of grief you were bearing and how naturally you might wish to avoid discussing it, I couldn't very well force the truth upon you, could I? So then the secret became mine and grew into a falsehood that I was having to cultivate through no choice of my own and in a fit of exasperation I made the appalling decision to broadcast your name to the entire hotel. I don't quite know what happened. I *think*," he added sheepishly, "I must have had the bright idea of steering Mrs Alderton into asking the right question because you couldn't reasonably avoid talking to me if it became public knowledge that we knew one another. For about a minute it made perfect sense. Then reality hit and I realised what I'd done."

He spoke as if this was his fault. The old paint of the doorframe was brittle beneath my fingertips. A sizeable fragment flaked and joined its fellows on the floor. The carpet was an ugly threadbare red like the one in the rooms downstairs at the hotel. It made me realise with a jolt that Adam had been working to save me distress that first night in the lounge too. The night when Jim's idea of conversation with Mary had been to go on and on about the waterfall. Adam hadn't been shielding me from Mary's little barbs at all. For a man so firmly fixed on honesty, he'd told a small mistruth about his actions that night. He'd known Mary wouldn't bother me. Adam had been saving me from Jim's continual descriptions of that drop because he knew what effect the policeman's words would have on me and he'd done all that he could to stop it.

I opened my mouth to speak but I had no idea what I meant to say. There were no words powerful enough to break through the sheer dumbfounded appreciation of this man's capacity for care.

Downstairs, speechlessness definitely wasn't the problem. Jim was sharing a bold joke, Christi was laughing like a drain and then Gregory contributed something by way of a retort. I had to wonder if that policeman always had some broader aim in mind when he led a person into conversation.

Adam must have puzzling over the same. I found that my mind was blindly fixing upon my job and my gaze was already running up the next flight of stairs but Adam's voice called me back.

He asked, "Did Rhys mean to marry Christi do you think?"

I hesitated there, my hand upon the banister rail. "Yes," I replied. "Yes, I believe Rhys did love her."

"And did she love him?"

I tipped my head towards the office downstairs. "Don't be misled by her mirth. She's as capable of playing a part as Jim is. And anyway, how are we to know what she should be feeling after only a few weeks?" Then it hit me what I'd said. Of course he would know precisely how it felt. "Oh, dear," I said. "I'm so terribly sorry."

I was truly embarrassed now and trying to both stay and bolt upstairs, but there was also something about finding that it really was perfectly possible to talk about such things, so I asked, "Would you have worked through all the months do you think?"

For a moment Adam was lost in the grim pattern of his

own thoughts. He looked completely blank. Then realisation dawned in a faintly amused little lift of one corner of his mouth. "Oh, I see. You mean May and June. Perhaps."

All of a sudden I was calm. I knew after a morning when all I'd done was endlessly draw support from him that I had to give something back. "Adam," I began, "thank you for coming today. I couldn't bear this place without you. I'd have still done it; but I'd have hated it."

"Think nothing of it."

"And I couldn't talk about it either, without you. This is going to sound silly but I'm going to say it anyway while I've got the chance: I like talking to you. You really are a beautiful man."

His surprise came with me as a little talisman as I climbed the stairs into Rhys's darkroom.

# Chapter 29

The stairs rose in an 'L' shape with the short leg at the top. The first thing I noticed when I reached the attic floor was that the policeman had stayed with Adam rather than following me. The second thing I noticed was that here at last was the explanation why no ghosts from my past life waited for me in this place. There was nothing left for me up here at all. Like the rest of the house, everything here had been stripped, even Rhys's cumbersome film processing equipment and the chemical baths. Only the infrared light remained, which cast the room into hellish streaks when I depressed the switch.

I think Adam would have loved it up here, given his predilection for dark holes and lost tunnels. The darkroom consumed the entire length of the attic, from one steep gable to the other. There would have been an impressively historic window at the street end if it hadn't been shielded by heavy wooden shutters that had never been opened in all the time I'd lived here.

This was Rhys's sanctuary. His bolthole, as well as a functional part of his artistic processes. It was odd to see it stripped bare and it occurred to me that unless Christi had abruptly sold the lot after Rhys's death – which surely must have raised a comment from Jim given his statement that the place had remained materially unchanged since his last visit – they must have already moved his equipment to a new studio. Which meant that she'd lied about the smallest little detail of not yet having moved to a new home.

I descended the stairs in about three seconds.

Adam and PC Downe were standing over that box; one tall and one boyishly chubby despite his years. I came to a halt in the centre of the room and began, absurdly, by saying in a rush, "I know why the place suddenly smells of damp. It's always been masked by the vinegar stench of his chemicals before."

Then I gave a shake of my head as if to drive out the clutter of intruding thoughts and asked Adam urgently, "All those questions about Christi's feelings for Rhys … What is it you suspect her of?"

It was the policeman who answered me with another question. It felt like the continuation of a conversation that had been going on only moments before while I had been out of the room. PC Downe asked me, "Can you tell me what Christi is short for?"

"It's short for Christine, I should think. She didn't tell you when you took her statement before?"

"She gave us Christi Bollini." The policeman meant it as a question.

I tilted my head at him. "But she isn't really Italian, no matter what she tries to imply. Christi Bollini is her professional name."

Keeping his voice low in case the people in the office downstairs should suddenly take to listening rather than laughing, PC Downe abruptly proved why Jim might have entrusted us to his care. He leaned in. "Will you say that again?"

I told him, "Christi Bollini is an assumed name. Legally acquired I think, but it really is barely more than a pen name. I don't know her real surname – before she married Rhys I mean and became the next Mrs Williams. She never used it. I've always imagined it was something painfully ordinary, like Smith or something."

PC Downe was nodding in a vague sort of away and proceeded to flick through his notes. He suggested in a voice that made it seem like he was a long way away, "What about Christel?"

I stared. He and Adam really had been talking while I'd been upstairs. This bore the signature workings of the author's mind rather than the policeman's.

Adam proved it in the next moment by adding on a wondering note of realisation, "Christi would be a contraction of her surname, would it?"

In the next moment he and I were alone while the policeman scuttled down the stairs and brought the mirth to an abrupt halt. We all heard as he discreetly asked his superior for a private word. He managed to do it in such a way as to imply that I had been mildly troublesome.

I returned to staring at Adam. I was questioning if he had deliberately waited until I was out of the room just now before sharing his suspicions. Adam raised an eyebrow. Then he said,

"Who's guessing Jim's already worked out that she was this prize witness at Devil's Bridge and this whole event is a side-show to another scheme? You don't think he's going to want you to go to London next, do you? To search their new home?"

I said, "What do you—?"

Adam cut me off short. He said, "Ready for this?" Jim's voice was already calling our names up the stairs. Then, while I gave him a puzzled nod and said impatiently, *"Adam, what is it? You keep not telling me things!"* he made it all so much more confusing by repeating that old gesture of briefly touching his hand to my cheek.

After such a morning in such a house, this was bewilderingly unexpected. I'd been thinking that contact between us had been left on the threshold to the gallery from the street outside and set aside for a quieter discussion at some other time. This sudden claim on my heart made my mind still. There was a breathless moment of doubt when it felt like he was reminding me of my fragility. Like he was telling me that I wouldn't really have been fit to share in his discussions with the policeman. Only he wasn't. He didn't mean to humble me. And he wouldn't question my energy like this. Not here, in this place, snatched in a pause between all these people who waited to discover just how cruel the past weeks had been only to use the knowledge to achieve their ends.

It was when his hand dropped that I identified the real feeling behind the gesture and it was far more unnerving. The act seemed designed to communicate, not pity as I had always known it, but something more equal and profoundly more powerful. It meant to communicate compassion.

I think I knew now what for. I meant to follow closely on his heels but some sense of completing my search held me back. Perhaps I was simply finding a convenient excuse for prolonging the moment before I had to speak to her again, and it is only with the benefit of hindsight that I'm convinced I knew then what Adam suspected and had been so unwilling to voice.

Below I heard the brief scrape of a chair and then a quick murmur of familiar voices. There was a short reply to some sarcastic comment from Christi followed by a more generous mention of my name from Gregory but instead of answering either person's faint query, I drifted a little farther along the narrow passage at the top of the stairs.

The kitchen was worn out and rather dirty. The cupboards were bare. Probing deeper into the gloom behind the stairs, I found the door of the bathroom ajar and the room within lit by the dingy light of a small and crusted window. The bath was partially obscured by the open door. It was in the same shabby state as the kitchen. The mirror above the equally ancient sink on the far wall reflected the corner behind the door with its ranks of yellow tiles and these, in a rare contradiction of the changes that had been wrought upon the rest of the house, were just as ugly as they had always been. And here, at long last, was the ghost I had been fearing.

Just like the last visitation in Aberystwyth, he seemed pale and distant and unnatural. I hadn't been confronted by this particular delusion for days and I had to brace myself for that old nauseating twist of my heart as reality righted itself. It never came. There was no sign either of the shameful outburst that usually wrenched itself from me in the moments after a surprise. I was utterly mute. In the mirror I saw the reflected green of his eyes. Then the eyes blinked.

For a moment I thought it had been my blink. It should have been mine. And by rights, when my eyes opened again, the apparition should have vanished like every time before. But this time I was transfixed and I didn't even move when it spoke.

"So good of you to concede that Christi might actually care." His voice was his own; curt and derisive, and exactly how I remembered.

Then there was a bang behind as Adam reappeared at the top of the first flight of stairs in a rush.

"Hello," I heard Adam say and felt the floorboard shift as he stepped forwards to join me in the doorway. He came closer. He eased himself sideways into the gap between me and the wall. Touching mine without really any thought for it, his body was alive with that energy of tension while his voice was extraordinarily measured as he surveyed the vision behind the door.

"I was wondering when you would show up," he said to Rhys. "Tell me; was it the policeman's body you sent tumbling into the waterfall?"

# Chapter 30

All things being equal, being discovered hiding in a bathtub when you'd supposedly committed suicide should have been enough to dent anybody's confidence, but of course it hadn't. Rhys was lounging in his office chair with as much grace as if he were giving a press interview. Jim had fractionally tipped the balance of power in his own favour by selecting the throne-like desk chair. Rhys had naturally claimed the better seat usually reserved for his clients, Christi had the other and Gregory was propped against the far wall on a stool usually employed as a plant stand. Only Adam was standing. He was leaning against the wooden doorframe before a mass of black uniforms peering through from the main gallery room behind. Adam's gaze was roving idly across the papers stacked on top of the cabinet near his side. He wouldn't look at me.

I was perching awkwardly on a hastily collected stack of crates near the foot of the stairs. I was shivering a little and trying very hard to hide it. I would get it under control but then Rhys would pivot in his seat, forcing me to risk a glance that might make contact with him and then it would start again.

He wasn't looking at me anyway. No one was. Perhaps it was just shock that did that; made me feel isolated again – or perhaps the expectation that somehow these people would ensure it. But I wasn't really feeling like that. Adam was just there across the room from me; with me as always, and yet deliberately not diminishing me by standing over me as my guardian.

The rest of this group weren't remotely sharing my unease. They were practically performing caricatures of themselves – the policeman, the art collector, the new wife and the artist back from the dead. In fact, the only thing that seemed to be being presented in real, honest colour was the room itself. But even this wasn't authentic. Christi's system of packing had left a stack of blue books on the desk as if they were in daily use but they were merely old logs of orders and client contacts; and the box beneath me was labelled very clearly *Archive Accounts 1935–1940*. The books had all been old before I'd even left this place.

At first, my former husband seemed to belong to that old world too. He was his usual stocky, rugged self. More than ten years older than me, his eyes had that same intensity and he still had that pure nervous energy that could dominate the room. Christi was the only one who seemed to absorb it and become greater herself. I thought they deemed Adam to be firmly out of the play-acting by virtue of his habitual stillness. It was taken for insignificance by those who didn't know him but, for me, it carried its own kind of strength.

Rhys was saying loudly and slightly scathingly, "Your missing policeman wasn't cast into the waterfall in my stead.

No one was. I take no responsibility for the assumption that I died because—"

He was interrupted by Gregory. His loyal friend was the oldest man in the room and he was looking like a child in the dunce's corner in his schoolboy blue blazer. He was supplying in a tone of deep distaste, "— It's not your fault we thought you'd died because all your note expressed was apologies, it didn't indicate what for."

He'd been surprised when Rhys had descended the stairs. He'd been very surprised. And I think quite deeply wounded that he hadn't been in on the secret.

Jim wasn't surprised. He was unemotionally recording the details as Rhys told him with a rushed sort of arrogance, "We did it in the evening. There'd been heavy rain so the place was pretty wild. I took Christi's camera and a bundle of old clothes and dropped them both over the edge. I needed to leave some traces behind. I waited for some people to walk by, let out a great yell, and then ducked into the back seat of our car while Christi staged her screaming fit." I didn't know if Rhys noticed that he'd just contradicted his own statement that it wasn't his fault that we'd thought he had died. "The police arrived at the waterfalls, my wife gave her statement and that was it except she had to give her name. She wasn't supposed to but the constables there were determined to see formal identification. Luckily, she had an old card for Anthea Christel floating around in her purse. It was fortunate since it was the only identity that wasn't traceable back to me."

Jim's eyebrows lifted as he made a note but he didn't speak.

From his large comfortable chair in front of me, Rhys was oblivious to the fact that he was quite cheerfully implicating his wife in the crime of perverting the course of justice and saying, "Christi and I have been in Richmond ever since. No one would have any reason to find us there. No one knew where we were moving to. No one even knew that we were married, not even our local friends."

Here Rhys inclined his head towards Gregory. His patron acknowledged the regret from his stool. As Rhys turned, I saw his face more clearly for the first time and I realised I'd been wrong when I'd thought he didn't mind this. Rhys's eyebrows were drawn low over fine black eyelashes and deepset green. The familiar arrogance was an act. I knew him. I could see the restlessness that burned beneath; the strain that didn't quite belong to the old world of this gallery; the fear that had aged his features dramatically and the anticipation that, after weeks of cruelty, it might at last be drawing to a close.

Unexpectedly, Adam broke into the silence. He paused in the midst of leafing through one set of old commissioning letters and the next. He remarked idly, "Christel. Germanic in origin, isn't it? I suppose the name stood you in good stead in Italy?"

Christi turned her head. We all did. Her lips curved. "I hope, Mr Hitchen, you aren't about to start accusing me of being a Nazi sympathiser? Perhaps you think this is the great secret Detective Constable Black uncovered while he was masquerading as a journalist? Perhaps you think I killed him?" The smooth tones were mocking, but only just.

Gregory intervened wearily. He said soothingly, "I'm sure

Mr Hitchen is just trying to build a clear picture. We all are. He doesn't mean to be sharp."

"Adam Hitchen," stated Jim dryly, "would do well to remember that he is not here as an investigator. Otherwise he can go into the front room and wait with my constables."

Not all the constables were in the exhibition room. There were still three outside in the courtyard.

I saw Adam jerk his head in a manner that passed for agreement and began leafing through one of the client order books he'd drawn off the top of the cabinet beside him. Its companion was in the collection that lay on the desk before Christi. That one would presumably bear the details of his portrait session with Rhys recorded by my own neat hand. I stared at it for a moment only to be distracted by Jim remarking, "Mr Williams, you said no one would 'find' you in Richmond. We've established that today you took the precaution of slipping in discreetly though the courtyard so that no one could witness your arrival. You hid in the linen cupboard when your good friend Gregory Scott knocked on the door and moved later to the more spacious accommodation of your bath once I and my team had undertaken a quick search of the building." His gaze narrowed. "Have you been attempting to hide from the police?"

My former husband dismissed the implication. "If you're meaning to ask whether I followed that journalist-cum-policeman, confronted him and then disposed of him, I have to tell you once and for all that I haven't seen that man since he supposedly discovered something at the racecourse that day and came scurrying back here alone. And if I really had been responsible for his disappearance, why should I then need to send those men tearing after my ex-wife?"

"But you *did* send those men tearing after your ex-wife." Adam spoke very quietly from his corner. The comment brought my head round. He caught my eye at last; he caught a glimpse of the worry in my mind that had nothing to do with Rhys's behaviour to me. Adam's answering look was designed to be reassuring albeit it with a faint query on his lips. He didn't understand these people and this place as I did.

Jim chose to pretend that Adam hadn't spoken. "What happened that sent Black racing back here?" the policeman asked Rhys. "What did he discover at the racecourse?"

Jim was adopting what I took to be his calm and methodical style of questioning. He didn't try for friendship with Rhys. Obviously he saved that sort of nonsense for people like me.

Then, it came to me with a bolt; he saved it for people he was truly investigating.

Christi was oblivious. She was disturbed I think by the lack of room that was being left for the account of their suffering. She told Jim shrilly, "I can't go on like this. We only came back today to pick up a few last things. This is the first time I've been back to this place and I hadn't been here more than half an hour when dear Greg let himself in without so much as a knock on the door and then you and your ragtag herd of constables and *assistants* did the same only an hour later."

Across the room, Adam stirred restlessly in his lean against

374

the doorframe. He'd already discarded the client order book and reset it upon its pile. Now he demanded, "What things? The gallery is practically empty. These stacks of books and all these boxes; they're just old records, aren't they? What should you wish to retrieve? And why today?"

I thought he wanted to know what was so different now that today they'd felt safe enough to return.

Rhys didn't like this manner of speaking to his wife. With his gaze fixed on the policemen who fidgeted just outside the windows, he remarked, "Why are we doing this here? Why aren't you putting your men to the task of cataloguing this place like I think you're supposed to? And why aren't we taking a little walk down to the police station away from all these *bystanders?*"

His frustration was reasonable enough but there was something that jarred in the way Christi reacted. She wasn't distressed now. She elegantly adjusted her position so that one trousered leg crossed neatly over the other. She made it look like it was accidental but as soon as Rhys made the point about leaving the policemen to search this place alone, I saw her toe give his shin a very little nudge. Bringing his temper to heel. It made me straighten with a bolt on my awkward pile of boxes.

"Adam. Enough." Oblivious to the silent exchange between Christi and her husband, Jim's reprimand was mild. He was examining his notes again. He read aloud, "You last saw Detective Constable Black at the race meeting on Saturday the eighth, is that correct?"

Rhys had his hands resting on the arms of his chair. There

was a cut on the back of his thumb and a faint smear of blood where the barely healed nick had recently received a knock. It looked sore. Some things were not an act.

His tension certainly wasn't for show. He was looking like he considered these questions about the missing policeman were a waste of his time. Irrelevant. Now he confided grudgingly, "As I recall, we were talking about research. We always were. I think he'd imagined it would be a few weeks' work and then we'd have a launch party and that would be it. He hadn't quite anticipated that each collaboration *starts* with several months of study and then the real work begins. It makes sense now I know he was a policeman all along." A faint smirk. His head twisted towards his old friend. "He was a very convincing journalist, wasn't he, Greg? He certainly rivalled you on his power to produce bad sporting jokes. I suppose you think there's no chance of finishing that project now."

Gregory's retort was dry. "It would be a shade tactless."

His disapproval was only a token. He was still Rhys's friend.

"I had no idea he'd even let himself in." Rhys was moving onwards now, steadily approaching whatever it was he wanted to say. "I had no idea he'd been here until some tall carrot of a man pitched up on the doorstep early on the Sunday morning—"

"Clarke?"

"Yes, Clarke." The policeman's interjection was met a shade wearily. "And he told me quite cheerfully that this journalist fellow had been nosing about here the day before and unearthed something he shouldn't only to inconveniently

376

misplace it. Clarke thought I knew what it was. But I didn't. I couldn't even tell that Black had been in here that night. Did you, Sergeant, find any evidence yourself that your man Black had been here?" This was a challenge. The policeman gave a noncommittal shrug.

Satisfied, my ex-husband added, "I said as much to this brute who was standing on my doorstep but that just made him wonder if whatever it was hadn't actually left the prem-ises at all – with Black, I mean. And then our orange-topped beanpole informed me that I should be very clear about the consequences of not handing it over. His turn of phrase was, let's say, a little choice."

"It was for Miss Ward too." This was from Adam. Gregory flicked him a dark little glance. He'd noticed the use of my maiden name. For the first time Jim looked irritated.

"Mr Hitchen," he said severely. Once he was sure the point had been observed, the policeman asked Rhys, "And had he?"

Rhys looked blank. "Had he what?"

"Left you anything?"

"No, of course not. You're missing the point—" Frustration flared. I thought for a moment temper was going to make Rhys explain precisely what his point was. It was clear that as far as he was concerned Jim wasn't following the right path. Then Christi quietly put out her hand to lightly touch his and Rhys calmed abruptly. It was like a light dimming. This woman really did stand out for Rhys as different from all the rest.

Rhys added rather too blandly, "All your sly policeman left me when he disappeared was a big aggressive man standing in my doorway. They hounded me for two days before I got desperate. I think they were waiting to see if anything came in the post to Black's house or mine, or was exposed in a newspaper headline or wherever; but of course it wasn't. So then they got impatient. Threats of limbs lost, dependents scared – you can imagine the sort of thing – and it suddenly occurred to me that they might think to turn on Christi. I had to protect her. You can understand that, can't you?"

He didn't say it but he might as well have done. He had to protect her at the cost of my safety.

Jim tilted his head in acknowledgement. I found that my fingernails were digging into my palms. I caught Gregory watching me with an expression on his face of fascinated revulsion. His lips parted and I knew suddenly he was going to speak to me; to play his usual part as the sympathetic friend and draw me in as the neglected outsider. I recoiled and found Adam's gaze on me instead. This time his look carried a real question and all I could give him was a shake of my head. I didn't know what was wrong.

It wasn't Rhys's admission that he'd knowingly sent Clarke after me at any rate. It was almost funny really how long I'd spent dreading the revelation of precisely this, and fearing what it would teach me about the value of my life. Because now it was here and it was the truth, all I felt was a vague surprise that I'd bothered to think it would teach me anything at all. After all, Rhys had never shown much concern for my welfare before.

Now I was expecting Rhys to give a plain narrative of his troubles that would lead us finally into an appreciation of just how much he had suffered. I was certainly prepared to find myself being tipped into guilt when he proved I could never quite sympathise enough with the terrors that had driven him to give Clarke my name. But shame wasn't his ambition here. The patterns were following their habitual course in that the insignificance of my wishes barely even rated an acknowledgement, but none of this was being laid out for me. And this time I really didn't think the target could merely be his old wife's dreary self-esteem.

Rhys was saying blandly, "They wouldn't believe me, you see, when I said I didn't have it; that I didn't even know what *it* was. I didn't have many other options left. So we hatched a plan."

Jim shifted in his chair to lean against the soft rounded arm. His face was relaxed but abruptly I saw the depth of his concentration. He was aware of the dance Rhys was leading. He was letting Rhys do it. Jim was waiting to learn if he was being ranked like me as a bystander. The realisation carried relief for me. Jim said, "Let me summarise this swiftly. You let these people – Clarke and his fellow – think you were running scared to your parents in Aberystwyth. Then you staged your fall and planted a convenient witness on the bridge in the form of Miss Christel, now Mrs Williams. Then you went into hiding and re-emerged here today. Were you going to use this return as a chance to declare publicly that you were very much alive after all?"

"Ultimately, yes, but not like this."

This made the policeman pause. For me it affirmed Adam's observation that something had changed to make Rhys abruptly feel less afraid. Jim asked, "Did you come straight here from London this morning?"

"No. We stayed with friends last night. Yesterday I was in Aberystwyth. I'd been in Aberystwyth for the better part of three days."

As he said it, Rhys appeared to know he was at last conceding something valuable; something that would be noticed. Rhys said it roughly. Almost defiantly.

Then he added with rather less excitement, "I felt it was important to lay my mother's grief to rest. And tell her about Christi at long last."

"Good of you." This was terse, surprisingly, from Gregory.

Rhys didn't hear. He wasn't laying this out for his old friend's benefit. He gave me a jolt when he abruptly turned to me and addressed me boldly, confidently, unapologetically. He told me, "You know, you gave me the scare of my life when you appeared on that street in Aberystwyth."

My voice was strange, I hadn't used it for so long. I had to swallow twice to get it working. "Outside your mother's house?"

He conceded the point with a faint tilt of his head. "I very nearly bolted. You looked like a ghost."

My heart was suddenly beating. I said, "So did you."

I was remembering the hundred other times when the ghost had haunted me just because some stranger had turned his head in such a way that my beleaguered mind had been able to match the movement to some vague memory. I remembered the real sound his mother's front door had made as it had clicked shut.

It was Christi who snagged at my memory now. She was watching her husband like she was anticipating something thrilling. It was then that I noticed that the exhibition catalogues that rested in piles on the desk before her were old ones from the year before the war. The small pile of catalogues in the stack by Adam's side were all from Rhys's first collaboration and comeback exhibition.

The majority of the exhibition catalogues here were those that had been created for the two launch events Adam had attended.

Across the room, Gregory's voice suddenly drew all eyes to my face. He said clearly, "Are you unwell, Kate? Do you need some air? Come and sit with me by the door. You've gone as white as a sheet."

# Chapter 31

For a moment Gregory was absolutely determined to infuriate me with attention that I certainly did not want. Then in the next I think he'd realised I had absolutely no intention of joining him on the perch adjacent to his seat nearer the door, and he was now occupied with checking the time on his watch and then distracting Adam by asking him in a whisper to confirm his watch was correct. I could feel the strain of Adam's concentration as his mind strayed and fought to return to me.

It snapped back to my face when I asked Jim clearly, "You said that little had been removed since your last visit but how many of the books in this room have been placed into new arrangements?"

Jim ignored me with such intensity that it had teeth. I blinked, stunned. He was examining his notes again. His head lifted to focus firmly on Rhys. "There are just two things I still can't quite grasp in your account. The first is where in all that did they get the idea to go after the former Mrs Williams?"

Rhys approved of this question. His head turned, grey hair

flecking black. His manner had that old confidence that had once been used to tell me he had a new model. "I told them. I had to do something to protect Christi. It didn't take a genius to guess that these brutes knew enough about the workings of the gallery to have seen Christi going in and out, even if they didn't know the rest. But it's also *her* gallery." A tip of his head back over his shoulder towards me. "It wasn't hard to arrange a sly telephone call to that russet-haired lamppost to hint at last that our missing journalist might have been dealing with her instead. By the time they'd thought of a few more questions to ask me, I'd disappeared and *she* was the only link left."

Jim leaned in. His manner was more friendly now. "This whole thing, the suicide, the trail that led to the former Mrs Williams; it was all because it was the only way to conceal the new Mrs Williams. You weren't afraid for your own life." It was tinged, inexplicably, with respect.

I stared. I'd expected Jim to rise on the point of injustice where Rhys decided it was a good idea to send Clarke and Reed after me. I expected him to demand to know how Rhys had known to do that if he had no idea what it was that Black had found. And I certainly didn't expect Jim to persist in referring to Christi and me as the *new* Mrs Williams and the *former* Mrs Williams like it was important that he adhered to the form of our legal names. All I knew was that it credited neither me nor Christi with much of an identity to set us apart. It reminded me that he'd never played the part of my friend except when it was needed to placate Adam.

Only, at the same time, I was recalling that the policeman

was very much in the habit of harnessing the foibles of others for his own ends.

He was using us; he was using us all as tools to unlock his investigation. At least I desperately hoped he was. Adam was staring at my face. His brows had furrowed while my heart raced. He could see the distrust.

Jim was now saying coolly, "My second question, Mr Williams, is how, having been so terribly afraid for your wife's welfare, did you subsequently decide it was safe for you both to come out of hiding?"

Across the room I heard a sharply drawn intake of breath followed by a soft note of realisation, "So that's what it is."

It was Adam. He caught Jim's flickering glance. "He saw me take her."

His comprehension was relayed across the room to me on a note of nauseated disbelief. He told Jim incredulously, "He saw me take her from the harbour that last night in Aberystwyth. That's how he decided it was safe to come back."

Jim sat back in his chair. I'd seen the brief glint of excitement but now his expression was inscrutable. He asked Rhys, "Did you?"

"What? No, of course not!" Rhys sounded appalled. His swift sideways glance implied otherwise, deliberately I think.

Adam's voice still held that slow note of incredulity. He'd seen my anxious fidget that was curbed as he spoke. His eyes were on me, doubting, as he told Jim, "He saw me take her. He was there that day in Aberystwyth. He confessed as much just now when he admitted that he bumped into Kate as she passed before his mother's house on her final gasp. He knew what she was facing and he let her go without a word. Then he saw me close in and he thought he'd just witnessed the villain of this piece fixing his claws on the ex-wife at last. And he didn't call the police. He didn't raise the alarm. He went quietly into his mother's house and waited. He waited until the coast was clear and then he came here today to see what Black might have found on me. And he's been leading you into this story, not because he's a liar and it's a convenient way to justify his own cowardice, but because he actually believes I'm guilty."

He rounded on Rhys and asked with sudden curiosity, "Haven't you noticed that I like Kate?"

Rhys only stared. I suppose he was seeing a capable-looking man whose posture bore none of the uninteresting reserve that had coloured all their previous encounters. Rhys was now seeing a stranger who abruptly really did rank amongst all the Sirs and Titles of his acquaintance, whereas I was only myself.

If the sight puzzled Rhys, it absolutely shook his wife. I saw her eyelashes lift and the stealthy glance that swept upwards to Adam's face only to retreat as soon as she caught his eye. Now the eyelashes dipped to fix her gaze upon hands where they lay clasped in her lap. Then her gaze drifted left, wide-eyed to her husband. Something had changed for her. He didn't see because someone was saying with quiet certainty:

"Rhys has proof."

The certainty belonged to Gregory. He had his diary in his hands, checking the details of his missed doctor's appointment. He grew braver when he saw that he had Jim's attention.

He slipped his diary back into his blazer pocket. He asked, "How else would Rhys be so sure? He saw Mr Hitchen in Aberystwyth and came back here armed with a name to see if he couldn't uncover whatever had been found by your missing policeman. And he did. Rhys found it. I just think he didn't quite know how to use it." A brief glimmer of a humourless smile followed, weightily, by, "Needless to say, I don't think my trusted friend was expecting to be interviewed here today."

No, I thought. He meant to slip in, plant this supposed proof and slip away to his own personal hiding place and then quietly, distantly, give the police an anonymous tip that would direct them to search in just the right spot. He would have done this happily, confidently, patiently; knowing that his freedom was waiting only for the day that the case against Adam was concluded.

Across the room, Gregory was adding bemusedly, "Did it matter, Rhys, that all the while you both were leisurely pursuing this plan, for all you knew Kate was still in the clutches of a villain?"

There was something very odd in this last little defence of me. Like the deep moral loathing was merely there for the sake of form while excitement and a profound curiosity about what had been found bubbled beneath. In a way I thought he was finding all this thoroughly enjoyable.

Whatever the feeling was, the policeman was experiencing something similar. Only Jim was hiding it better and the only clue was that his manner wasn't remotely easy any more. The policeman was a big man in an ordinary-sized chair. "Is this true, Mr Williams? You've found what Black found?" A pause. "Mr Williams?"

Rhys turned his head and blinked at him. For a moment I thought my former husband was actually scared, but only for a moment. Then I saw he had the wide eyes of triumph. "No." It was a firm denial. It left an emphatic silence in its wake.

And Christi broke it. For a long time now she'd been content to simply sit silently in her seat beside her husband. The way she did it now had the air of being a pre-arranged entrance. A point marked in a script. But judging from the way Rhys paled like he'd been tipped headfirst back into the horror that had stalked his past weeks, he hadn't expected her to say this.

Christi turned to Adam. She remarked huskily, "I haven't asked you how your daughter is, by the way. How is she now?"

Rhys was startled and, unsurprisingly, Adam wasn't happy to hear this mention of his daughter at such a time. His head jerked up and he demanded curtly, "What do you mean by that?"

I saw her eyelids flutter. It was an innocent expression. Wherever this impulse had come from, it was not meant in the same tone as Rhys's contributions. Rhys stared while her honeyed voice conceded, "When we met last you were puzzling out how to satisfy her interest in zoology."

"I told you that?"

The hard disbelief in Adam's voice was dangerous in its way. It had the depth of a parent's protective instincts.

With an effort to rein in his temper, Adam curtly informed Jim, "Rhys wasn't lying when he said Black took his suspicions with him. But all the same everything he's said has been very carefully scripted to make you disbelieve him. He *wants* you to decide to search. Presumably you'll find something and discover that it incriminates me. And he'll pretend that it's purely coincidental that he's spent all these past minutes getting increasingly frustrated because you wouldn't notice the hints he's been dropping that this thief must know the gallery personally. Only the truth is he's the author of this piece of nonsense about me and he's hidden something that will prove it. Haven't you, Rhys?"

His anger bit. I don't think he knew that Christi's deviation from her script into ill-placed pleasantries about his daughter had been for his own sake; that she hadn't been remotely considering how he would feel to hear his daughter mentioned here. That in truth she'd only spoken like that at all because she needed to convey a coded warning to her husband. She'd guessed the scope of her husband's mistake as soon as Adam had spoken about his friendship for me.

I wasn't sure Rhys quite knew what to do. The strong, independent, arrogant artist stared mutely at his wife as she turned her head.

There was an emphasis in the widening of her eyes. Suddenly, he understood. And somewhere in him there was the beginning of fresh fear.

Behind the desk, Jim's posture had never changed. This was what he had been working us all towards. This was why he'd let this trail follow its course. He knew Rhys's nature. He knew that without the lure of feeling powerful, Rhys might never have been brought to the point of sharing all his findings. The policeman was confident now and yet all he did was ask calmly, "And where is this 'something' now, Mr Williams?"

Then, when Rhys looked a little sick and failed to admit there was anything to share at all, Jim said to me, "Anything to add, Mrs Williams?"

I searched for the right response. I didn't know what to do either. I'd never known Rhys unable to bluster his way out of a mistake before.

"Kate?"

All of a sudden Jim considered me the owner of my name again. It made me jump. It forced my eyes to travel from Rhys's averted profile to the policeman's face.

"The paintings." The words seemed to drag themselves kicking and screaming from the back of my mind.

I caught Adam's glance. He sensed the unease in me. He added uncertainly, "She's right, isn't she, Rhys ... Christi? You never would have hung them otherwise. You always hated them."

"What do you know about it?" Rhys couldn't help the sneer. It slipped in with desperation.

Adam returned his stare. Abruptly for him, it made perfect sense. The placement of my paintings on the wall had been yet another convenient alteration to the order of this place designed to act as a lure. The recent cut on Rhys's hand that I'd worried had been a mark of pursuit merely belonged to

the discarded screwdriver. Hanging works of that size always
was a fiddly job.

Across the room, blindly, stubbornly, honesty won. Adam
told Jim, "It's hidden behind one of Kate's paintings in the
exhibition room."

# Chapter 32

My paintings were attached by mirror plates to the much-patched boarding that lined the walls. The frames were perhaps an inch deep with a little recess at the back to support the tightly stretched canvas and the first one when it was unscrewed from the wall was perfectly empty. Behind me, Christi was lounging against the open door from the office, replicating the pose she had adopted some hours before. Adam was standing just in front of the doorframe on her other side with a clear view past me where I stood against the wall. Behind all of us was Gregory. Rhys, typically, was at the heart of things, acting as though he was concerned they might damage my precious paintings.

PC Downe carefully set the first portrait down on the floor before moving to support the next. It dropped a little as the last screw released, only a short jerk before his hands secured the weight, and it was followed by a decisive little flutter.

In the seconds that followed, everybody moved at once. First of all I looked down at the paper that had landed by my feet. It shone in the electric light. At the same time, PC Downe set the painting upon the floor and naturally reached to retrieve the other fallen sheet. And thirdly, Jim suddenly saw that I had moved.

"Let that paper alone!"

I froze in the act of bending with my fingers still inches from the floor. Then, when the caution was repeated, I withdrew my hand. I straightened and took a step back. I turned my head. I saw the moment that Adam's gaze ran from my wide eyes to Jim's face and lingered there.

Jim reached out his own hand, gingerly, taking care to preserve what fingerprints there might be. It was a photograph. It was a black and white image of that launch event for Rhys's comeback exhibition in October last year. It had been taken by Christi and it was of Adam in the midst of a crowd.

The second sheet was the unexpected addition. Detective Constable Black had left something for Rhys after all. He'd written a note on the last Saturday before he had disappeared – signed under his cover name as Steven Leicester – telling Rhys simply that he'd taken a handful of Christi's event images away to study at home and he hoped Rhys didn't mind.

It wasn't a declaration of his suspicions and it certainly didn't conveniently name his attacker but I thought it thoroughly vindicated Rhys's belief that Christi's life would have been in desperate danger if he hadn't taken a great deal of care.

Jim's gaze flicked up across the brim of the photograph to ask Rhys, "Detective Constable Black left you both of these together?"

He had to know Black hadn't. Gregory stirred in the doorway. He'd been longingly staring at the office telephone, or perhaps the inviting rectangle of the courtyard door, making a quiet but insistent point about his missed doctor's appointment.

Jim ignored him. He asked Rhys, "Did you find this note when you returned today?"

The note was being carefully eased into a waiting brown envelope by a willing constable. Satisfied that it was safe, Jim lifted his head and fixed Rhys with an interrogative glare. "Well?"

Rhys looked sulky, which was hardly surprising given that he wasn't exactly in the habit of giving way to authority quietly.

I said in a hard little voice, "How can he have found it today? He's had it from the start and carried it with him all this time. He knew that Black had found his clue in some images from a launch event. How else could he have guessed that a few old exhibition catalogues would serve as the key connection between someone who knew me and how to find me, and the identity of the man who used this place to meet your dead letter-writing, gallery-visiting middleman to a thief?"

I caught Adam staring at me. A brief flicker of comfort tried to form at one corner of my mouth before it sobered when beyond me, Jim remarked, "As a point of interest, Mr Williams; when you laid your little decoy, did you tell Clarke where to find Miss Ward? Did you tell him precisely where she lived; where she worked?"

"No, of course not. Just her name."

*Just* my name. Adam made an impatient gesture. It occurred to me then that Rhys was still deliberately goading him. I might have thought that Rhys was working a way to extricate himself from this but actually it felt like he was simply being blindly antagonistic because he couldn't quite think what else to do. Concern spurred me into saying hotly, "It doesn't mean anything. Clarke might have asked anyone for the other details. The shopkeeper next door knew I'd moved back to my northern home. He might have mentioned something. Or Gregory might—" There was an outraged splutter that might have been Gregory's and might have been Rhys's. I told Jim, "Gregory's still working here, you know ... At least, Rhys mentioned the end of this latest collaboration just now and the way he did it implies that Gregory too might have reason to regret its passing. And Gregory certainly still has a key. Christi complained that he let himself in today."

"Now listen here—" This was Christi.

"Oh, don't worry that she's accusing your friend," snapped Adam curtly. I suppose for him too it was the pent-up stress of discovering that Rhys had spent three days working out how to affix proof to his name. "Look at Rhys's face. He knows Kate has seen through his fiction. The photographs were of his launch party. Black disappeared from his gallery. Now Rhys is wondering whether Kate will think next to wonder if this note meant to implicate *him* as this thief all along."

Only as soon as he said it I thought: No. I won't think that.

Something had changed. Rhys's familiar features always did tend towards the dramatic but now I could see that it really was terror that had driven him to hide Black's evidence, and it was the relief of discovering Adam's guilt that had made him feel safe enough to reveal it. And now, instead of despising

Rhys, I had to wonder what should have the power to suddenly fling him so desperately back into fear again at the very moment he learned Adam was innocent.

I looked to Jim. He didn't encourage me to explain. From the expression on his face my recent outburst might as well have been chattering nonsense about my sketchbook again. With one look he discouraged me from speaking again.

Now Gregory moved restlessly in the doorway beside Christi. She turned her head and acknowledged him with a thin-lipped smile. And then, with a lurch so sudden that it was almost a mark of hysteria, Rhys abruptly reverted to his ridiculous story that Black himself had hidden these pages and this was the first he'd heard of Adam's guilt.

Rhys turned to Adam and his lip curled. "Something that Clarke said made me think it must be one of my more prestigious clients. I truly never thought he could have meant *you*."

Rhys enjoyed the expression that built on Adam's face. For me, the sudden kick of realisation was so intense that it hurt. No one noticed my flinch. They were all waiting for Jim to dominate the scene. Adam was expecting the policeman to begin interrogating Rhys about the lunatic decision he'd made to play dead when he could have simply handed in Black's letter at the time and let the authorities handle Clarke and Reed. But he didn't.

And when I didn't step in either, Adam was forced to make his own retort. "No?" he asked unpleasantly. "Did he tell you that by way of an exchange when you were cheerfully offering Kate's life as a bargaining chip?"

It made Rhys smile. Not a happy smile. He said in an off-hand way, "Oh, she's all right. I knew no one would get to her as they did me." I thought his dismissal weak. But he wasn't finished yet. The other man's defence of me was obliterated in the instant that Rhys twisted round, sliding nearer to me, emphatically blocking me against the wall and away from Adam. He said, by way of a private aside between old friends, "By the way, Kate, you've regained your Northern accent. You always did like to blend in wherever you were, didn't you?"

It was a reminder of how much more of my past I'd shared with him than anyone else here; it was meant as a bit of tit-for-tat. I'd attempted to undermine his credibility and now he was assaulting mine. It was, I think, a warning that if I didn't behave myself, his next step would be to bring me into his sights alongside Adam. It was a hint that he was prepared to prove I was the sort of person who would develop feelings for whosoever was the most dominant force at the time. Presumably he was then going to claim the reason I was unharmed was that I was blindly in love; and lay the foundations for proving that Adam had coaxed me into coming here today because he needed me to find this thing; and I hadn't got the wit to perceive the true motives of a man who was a thief.

What was worse for me than this blatant threat – and the fact he clearly didn't know me well enough to know it would fail – was that there was something possessive about this first use of my name. It was like underneath it all he was trying to tell me he knew I would be hurt by this, and he was sorry for me.

My lips burned but I said nothing. The desperate need for release was compounded when, at the heart of this crowd, Jim only said entirely unemotionally, "Well?"

That single syllable was like a curb upon my heart. I turned my head. I saw that it was a moment before Adam realised the comment was addressed to him. Naturally he was bemused. It sent a jolt though me. This wasn't what I'd been led to believe. The wall was cold at my back. Impossibly, it carried a single looming whisper of failure.

Adam said a little haplessly, "Well, what?"

Jim held up the photograph that he had retrieved from the floor. In a tone that was so orderly it was an affront, he said, "This is a photograph of you, Mr Hitchen. You're in a crowd at a launch event and looking reasonably happy about it, against all the odds."

"Jim, no!"

He didn't hear the cry that was wrenched from me. Unbelievably, inexplicably, he persevered. In a voice that matched the granite in his core, the policeman asked Adam, "Perhaps you'd like to explain who that man is with you?"

# Chapter 33

Adam wouldn't look at me. He hadn't met my eye since that first exchange of horror. In the one swift glance we'd shared, he'd betrayed a sickening combination of shock, revulsion and, less easily, a kind of shame.

I thought I knew why.

The first two emotions were easy enough to guess at. My failure to stop this; and the realisation that he'd been working so hard to save me when all the time his very participation had been leading him to this. The third feeling was harder to define.

The photograph was one of those typically ambiguous images where the holder of the camera was so intimately engaged with the subject that she was almost part of the shot. I don't mean that she was close to Adam; the second male in the scene was so close to the camera that he was partially blurred. His nose protruded into the photograph and part of his left eye. But he couldn't obscure the fact that Christi had said something that had made Adam smile.

It looked like they were all friends, very intimate friends. We could almost sense her body sashaying behind the lens.

Now Adam didn't know – he cannot have known – that I was the only other person in this room who recognised his response for what it was. His dry, automatic smile that meant he was aware he was being treated like an object of prey.

The other man was very hard to make out. It was the sort of image that might keep the experts for the prosecution busy spending a good deal of time and money measuring the small hint of the man's nose against photographs of the much sought middleman before ultimately concluding that this was the man and this was indeed the vital meeting. The other half of the experts, the ones for the defence, would undertake the same process in an attempt to prove precisely the opposite. It was, to be quite frank, a bewilderingly inconclusive piece of nothing.

Today it made Detective Sergeant James Fleece certain he was about to snare his thief.

Rhys was the first to break the silence. His unrelenting confidence seemed shrill now, fractured, delighted to have won. He told Adam, "You've spent all morning going through my papers. You were looking for this, weren't you? You knew this was here and you were hoping you could find it before anyone else."

Rhys caught the drift of Jim's eyes towards mine. The policeman was about to ask if this were true. Rhys didn't want me to speak. From his place beside me, he gave a derisive snort. "Don't expect her to sign his committal. My wife always did have an absurd inability to remember that my clients were only paying lip service to the idea of being her friends."

Aside from the insult of his prolonged effort to circumvent

the truth, it was a very private, deeply ugly reference to the fantasy that Gregory had wanted me once, and by extension the delusion that Adam should still want me now. It made me angry in a way that might well have left me spewing the sort of hatred that would leave deeper scars in my mind than in his.

Jim didn't give me time to voice it. He broke across me as if I didn't even count. He said to Rhys, "Don't you mean your ex-wife?" And he began organising people into rooms.

I found Jim had swiftly crossed the floor. His hand was suddenly firmly on my elbow. He turned us both round and led me through into the office as if I were a puppet. His brown eyes were grave. He told me, "It was no lie when we heard that Black hadn't left any statements of proof. That scrap of paper was merely a promissory note of sorts, barely more than a library card. There isn't enough yet to hold him for long. I need time to make a record of precisely what has been done here. I need you to stay with PC Downe and his colleague in this office ...?" The instruction dwindled into a hesitation that came like a question before it was corrected with a decisive, "No. Upstairs."

I nodded. What else could I do?

With sudden energy, he began moving through the disordered rooms. He finally gave Gregory permission to telephone his doctor with the instruction to wait afterwards in the exhibition room with the remaining constables. He moved Adam aside without so much as a word. Rhys had followed his wife into the office and stood there in the heart of this place, not even looking triumphant any more and instead a watchful barrier between me and the room, eyes following the policeman and trying to engage anyone who would listen in some kind of formless debate on the price of lies.

Then Jim made a short silencing gesture that cut him off in mid ramble and turned at last to Adam. "Upstairs please." He was still being very orderly.

I saw Adam turn his head and meet Jim's gaze. We were all strangers to Adam now. The past minutes had worn his face to grey. Jim's expression did nothing whatsoever to invite discussion. But still, under the policeman's unfriendly stare, Adam said in a voice that was so desperate that it came out as exasperated amusement, "Jim – Detective Sergeant Fleece – earlier you separated me from my little girl; surely I shouldn't have been worrying about when you'd let me see her again?"

Jim placed a hand on his shoulder. It had a decisive air about it. Then he barked again, "Hitchen. Upstairs."

And he encouraged Adam on his way with a meaningful push.

---

The bedroom was just as we had left it. Adam eased himself down on the edge of the bare mattress in the light cast from the window. He looked utterly numbed. Withdrawn. It had begun the moment his name had first been mentioned as a suspect and become fixed when I'd obeyed Jim's command not to speak. It made me do what I had never done before. I reached out and touched him. I mean, I initiated it. Previously, all those precious moments of contact, all the gestures of comfort had originated with him. The only time I'd voluntarily extended my hand towards him before now had been the one act of impulsive violence I would dearly like to forget. This was the absolute reverse.

Very tenderly, my palm met the corner of his jaw. I was already crouching before him. I felt him jump a little as he registered the contact. He'd been thoroughly lost in the abstraction of his own thoughts. I felt him lean a little into the warmth of my hand. The act brought his forehead very close to mine. I shut my eyes. I think he had too. I said on the merest breath, "I'm so sorry for bringing you here, Adam."

Then I turned away. I had to. He'd put his hand up automatically to cover mine but it was listless and didn't resist when I slipped my fingers clear. His gesture felt horribly like a farewell. A parting of ways. An echo of what Rhys had said. A necessary acknowledgement of the strain that had been placed on him in my name and proof that even the threat of a renewed separation from his daughter – given everything I knew of the years they'd been apart during the war – must leave an injury too deep for forgiveness. A line had to be drawn somewhere and I thought it was here.

I knelt down on the floor beside the box that had first attracted my interest earlier and got to work. My ankle complained – the one that had been bruised in that collision with a postcard seller in Aberystwyth – but I ignored it. The unnamed policeman settled to wait in the window. PC Downe joined me on the floor. He extracted the photograph Jim had given him from its envelope and set first the envelope down on the floor and then the photograph upon it. Downstairs there was a metallic ting as Gregory reset the telephone receiver back upon its stand. Seconds before he'd been exchanging charming nothings with the lady who staffed the office at the other end.

Most of the disordered photographs in the box were old contact sheets and useless. Some were images I had taken. Some were launch events from his newer projects that had been conceived after I'd left. These images were taken by Christi but I discarded them on the principle that these projects could have no connection to me.

A pattern emerged in these records of past parties. Gregory featured often. Adam never. Rhys featured in the series that covered the period before the war. I set them neatly to one side and started on the next handful.

This set contained more by Christi's hand. Hers had more character than mine. She managed to capture people in the midst of a delightful party that oozed laughter. In one I could distinguish the artwork that hung on the walls. This was the launch event for that comeback exhibition; the event in October last year that had been attended by Adam, as Christi had been so keen to remind us of when we'd first stepped through the front door. I began laying them out into a grid.

"Kate."

The flat tone of my name made my heart kick. I twisted to peer round at him. I had presumed Adam had been observing what I was doing but I was wrong of course. He had stayed there on the edge of the bed, illuminated by the grimy glow from the window. He had his elbows resting upon his knees and his hands clasped between them. He'd been sitting with his head down, staring at the brown pair of abandoned gentleman's shoes on the floor. They were Rhys's; taken off when he'd heard his first unwelcome visitor step in from the street and he'd needed to pad silently about his house and into his bath. It was only now that I realised Rhys had passed the entire interview downstairs in his socks.

"I'm not responsible for this." Adam's voice was expressionless, spiritless. It sounded like the last pathetic excuse of a criminal. I should have had more appreciation for the reduced powers of intuition in a person experiencing a state of shock. I should have known he wasn't blaming me. This was something else.

"Yes," I whispered. "Or rather no, of course not."

Silence for a moment, then, "You *know?*" Then, with a little kick of realisation that made me somehow desperately sad, "Of course you do."

I withdrew the next bundle from the box.

And a little later after that, very roughly indeed, "What are you doing?"

He had regained a little colour. He moved closer to the end of the bed so that his knee was suddenly beside my shoulder. The bed creaked as he settled. I didn't pause again in laying out my photographs.

Ten, twelve photographs lay out in a grid before us. Another and then another was added. All showed variations of the same crowded room and most were illustrative of a very good night being had by all. Beside me, PC Downe commented softly, "He's not here, you know."

"No," I said. And since Adam drew breath to ask, supplied,

"This middleman they're all convinced came here to be introduced to the art thief."

I reached out a finger and lightly tapped a photograph that showed Adam from a different angle. He was talking to a man with a very fine nose. This man happened to be Lord Alfred Warren, one of Rhys's other old patrons.

Adam remarked, "I *told* you I'd never met the man."

The images petered out at a count of about seventeen. With an allowance for the number Detective Constable Black had disappeared with, which were presumably the best for illustrating his point, the rest were a singularly uninformative set. I could identify all the usual characters and not one of them stood out. Gregory was in some of them, a year younger but still wearing his favourite blazer. Christi was there too of course, by virtue of being behind the camera. But none of that meant anything without proof that this dead middleman everyone was getting so excited about had even attended.

Adam reached a hand past my shoulder and pointed at the stack of contact prints. I lifted them and handed them to him. After a few minutes while PC Downe and I stared intently at the photographs laid out before us, Adam passed a single sheet back.

It was the contact print of the negatives for the launch. We peered at it. We identified which photographs we had and therefore which photographs had disappeared with Black. None of them contained this missing link. The face that would close Jim's case for him really hadn't been there.

I sat back abruptly with the hard edge of the bed frame against my back. I knew that downstairs Jim was going through the process of taking statements because he didn't dare let anyone leave. But of the photographs Black had taken, only half of them contained the faces of the people who were presently downstairs. It was impossible to explain what it was about these images that might have made a policeman in disguise suddenly so excited or why, subsequently, an art thief should have felt so much in danger that his only means of escape was to make this evidence disappear.

I looked again. It was then that I finally acknowledged the one other presence at the launch party. The artwork on the wall. Just as the collaboration with Black masquerading as a journalist had focused on sport, Rhys's comeback exhibition had featured the personal acquaintances of one of the foremost athletes in the country. Gregory's contacts had been extensive and clearly inspiring. The work was a triumph even by Rhys's usual standard. The best by far of the pieces on show here in these images was the largest of them all. It had dominated the gallery wall that bore the door into the office and it had been a painfully beautiful portrayal of a notable sprinter's failure: the man in second place crossing the line.

Distantly my ears caught the sound of a rap at a door. It was a sharp knock that cut through the general noise outside the window of people going about their shopping and traffic squeezing past.

I sat back on my heels. The weight of knowing the truth was crushing. No wonder Black had been asking that day at the racecourse about the scale of research the artist habitually undertook for any project. Jim's dead middleman hadn't any need to come to the launch party to meet his thief. He could have walked in through the door on any given day of the week right up to the launch of Rhys's first spectacular peacetime project. And the thief knew I was capable of proving that.

It was all so painfully simple, except...

I lifted my face to the constable's. "Why on earth did he come here today?"

This new visitor was at the courtyard door. From the command Jim gave from the depths of the exhibition room below us to one of his constables, he thought it was the long-awaited inspector. Jim sounded relieved. I watched our own constables climb to their feet. One from the floor beside me, the other from the window. They both went to the stairwell. A small amiable man and one slightly taller and greyer. PC Downe was tasked with relaying our findings to Jim. I heard the visitor enter. He was speaking to Rhys.

Adam felt the bolt run through me. Beside me he said, "Kate, who is it?"

I was on my feet and so was Adam. PC Downe had shot down the stairs at a run. I was standing there shaking and my hand was on Adam's arm, half clinging and half wanting him far away from this and it got worse when I heard Jim's shout through the floorboards as he too recognised the newcomer's voice. He bellowed, "Reed?"

And then half a dozen policemen stampeded through the ground floor and out into the courtyard after him.

Now it made even less sense that the thief had come here today. He can't have known that I'd find these things. He hadn't even known what they were, otherwise there would never have been any need to hunt them and me across the country. He certainly can't have hoped that he would get a quiet moment to retrieve these images today beneath the very noses of the men who were trying to uncover him. The very act of trying would be a more conclusive betrayal than these images could ever be. I was scrabbling all of the photographs together. Adam dropped down to help me. His hands were steadier than mine. The distant sounds of pursuit grew louder as Reed dived out on the street below our window. He must have charged away through one of our neighbouring shops. That must have been how he had reached the courtyard in the first place. I didn't know what the policemen who had been posted there had been doing. It barely mattered. Adam was crouching beside me and now he was sliding the prints into the envelope. The unnamed policeman was still on the stairs. I didn't have a right to be so scared.

My ears were straining to build a picture of who was left down there. I didn't get very far. The house had a hollow sound of desertion. But perhaps that was just what I was feeling. I heard the clump as our unnamed constable tramped down the stairs. Rhys's voice rose up the stairwell to drown him out. Rhys was bellowing at PC Downe to go and recall Jim. I think PC Downe wasn't moving quickly enough for him.

I was on my feet again. A funny little sound like a rugby ball being passed thudded up from the street outside. It was Reed being brought to the ground. We needed to warn Jim. He still didn't know what we'd learned from the photographs. I went to the window. He wasn't there.

Adam had followed me. He wasn't leaving me now. He peered past my shoulder. Reed was face down beneath a crush of about four policemen. Another was holding an ancient charabanc at bay that had nearly run the lot of them down. I couldn't help wondering what madness had prompted Reed to attempt this little stunt. It wasn't two o'clock so he didn't even have the excuse of walking blindly to our meeting.

Below, a man gave a frightened squawk about the whereabouts of the key for the courtyard door. The door was designed to withstand burglary and fire and everything in between if only it could be locked. The man was Rhys.

The impulse that moved me towards the stairs was purely instinctive.

It came as a complete surprise when Adam's hand flashed out to check me. He caught me at the hip and urged me to turn back. I did. I turned a full circle against his arm, fingers clinging to his sleeve, lifting my gaze to his at the same time as still feeling that desperate impulse to go. There was something very strange in the set to his jaw. Something like a rough shadow of suspicion. Something like a requirement to choose sides. Adam observed in a hard undertone, "He's very good at making you take his part, isn't he?"

I know now that I misunderstood him. In hindsight I know this wasn't about Rhys, at least not directly. Adam didn't believe I was obediently answering Rhys's call. Adam was referring to our conversation about the sacrifices Rhys habitually inspired the women in his world to make; and now Adam was asking me not to attempt another, this time for him. I didn't even know at that time that this was what I was meaning to do.

At the time the impulse to go down the stairs overwhelmed everything. I thought Adam was jealous and he was warning me that my ex-husband was Jim's idea of a murderous thief. I gabbled, "It's not Rhys. Rhys thought it was you, remember? He guessed he was wrong when you … when he realised you hadn't kidnapped me. He tried to stop what had been started with his and Christi's insinuations. He didn't want to give up the photograph of you. That was my mistake. He was as frightened as we were. What would you have done?"

"I wouldn't have begun by sending those men running north after an unsuspecting ex-wife, for a start."

I was still imagining this was jealousy. The edge to his voice stopped me in the midst of trying to reach the stairs in mind if not in body. It brought my attention back to his face. I faltered. I wanted to say I agreed with him. Of course I did. If Rhys wasn't guilty of intentional cruelty, he certainly was blindingly, appallingly in the habit of doing whatever happened to be most convenient for him, which unfortunately had lately run to the extent of using me as a shield. But still I begged a little desperately, "Adam, please. I don't want to have to hate him."

It was an echo of what I'd said to him on that trip to the castle with Mary and Jim. Back then I'd claimed it was one of my last inviolable rules. A few days ago it would have had awful connotations for my sense of self-worth. Hating Rhys would have meant admitting I was his inferior and that I'd been powerless back then because he really had controlled me. Those fears had passed but the rule still stood, even now, even to the point of stupidity. For me, hating Rhys wasn't part of my liberation. For me it was the last trap laid by that marriage. It would mean letting my ex-husband define who I was after all, when I intended to just be me.

I was afraid Adam would misunderstand. I was afraid he would take it as weakness and a sign that my ex-husband still had a hold on me.

But Adam's hands were suddenly firm upon my shoulders. "It's all right, Kate," he conceded peaceably. "You told me once that you strive for harmlessness. I suppose this is it. And he did, I will admit, say at the very beginning that everything he's done has been for her."

A pause, a hesitation while he drew a short breath. "Only," he added tentatively as if he were risking something that might come out very wrong. He tried again in a surer voice, "While harmlessness in itself is very commendable, I think you're misunderstanding its meaning. I don't think you realise how much you're still measuring yourself by another lesson he taught you. I don't think you want to admit that to any other reasonable male ..."

He held me there while those grey eyes transfixed me. He emphasised each of the next words with a little bracing pressure from his hands upon my shoulders as he finished, "... You're very dangerous indeed."

He didn't quite smile.

The effect was electrifying. I've never known anything like it. A shiver went through me. There was more than a glimmer of mockery there. Superficially it was a compliment. He knew the effect a comment on my person like that would have and yet his gaze was utterly serious. It carried, beneath the confident assertion that he'd dressed in a teasing note for my sake, a bewilderingly intense confession of his vulnerability.

I could feel his pulse pounding against my skin. It was running even faster than mine. For a moment I'd been about to wonder if he really thought I might have the power to hurt him. This stopped me as nothing else would. I said with a fresh awakening to my own fear, "Adam ... What's wrong?"

He didn't get to answer. There was a clatter of the courtyard door swinging open downstairs, the creak as it shut again and the click of a key turning in its lock. There was a fresh cry from Rhys in the throes of terror. It sounded like he was in the desk chair. I could say that with some confidence because I'd heard him yelling for more tea from there often enough over the years. Then Christi screamed my name in a choking sort of way and there was a thump in the corner, presumably as she sat down. She'd meant it as a warning. Somebody moved from the exhibition room into the office. It was all sound. I had nothing but sound. Adam still had his hands on me and he used them to turn me behind him so that he stood first in the doorway. With a single look he issued a reproof and asserted his willingness to defy me in this. This was the moment I realised that I would have put myself before him.

My view was of the shabby wallpaper and the carved newel post at the foot of the next flight of stairs. The next sound made me think PC Downe had been trying to recall policemen from the street outside. There was the groan of the front door swinging and the hasty clump of his feet across the exhibition room floor. He was stepping forwards to control the scene.

But it was Gregory who moved before him into the centre of the office and was meeting the man who stepped in through the unguarded back door. And it was Gregory's voice that raced as a wild yell of disbelief up the stairs, *"You're going to hit me?"*

And then Gregory screamed. A scream of real pain and all the evidence collapsed again. All the theories of who had done what and why disintegrated. And were rebuilt in an insane new pattern a moment later.

A painfully familiar voice hallooed up the stairs.

It belonged to Clarke. He was calling out clearly, "Mr Hitchen, sir? Are you up there? What do you want me to do to help? Because whatever you do to silence her it had better be swift. Reed was a bad choice for the part of decoy. He's a simple brute and it won't take them long to unpick his tale. They'll soon realise they don't have anything on him except the crime of playing a child's game of knocking on doors and running away."

Before me, Adam turned his head. I was close behind him, gripping his sleeves, cheek brushing the tip of his shoulder.

"Adam," I whispered desperately. "No, no, no."

413

# Chapter 34

Adam's gaze was burning on mine when he turned to me. He handed me the envelope. He raised his voice and answered, "It won't work, Clarke. The police know your names. And she's already established what Black took. We've got the evidence we need."

I hoped Clarke would run. He ought to have run. I heard the creak as he set foot on the stairs and Adam stepped out to meet him. I had Adam's hand. I knew the truth. This was what Adam had anticipated. This was the cause of the hesitation that had prompted him to snatch me back just now when I'd moved to step past him. Adam knew I would feel called on to stand between him and something like this. It was my fault he was here after all. But, unlike my ex-husband, he absolutely knew he was not going to let me.

The decision he'd made was terrifying. He was not a physical man. He was strong, yes, and fit and beautiful and generous and brave, and perfectly capable of dealing with any normal challenge. But violence came to him as naturally as selflessness came to Rhys. It was possible, but only in times of war.

This wasn't war. Clarke was mounting the short run of the stairs at a sprint. Adam's hand urged me onwards. And then corrected me when I moved towards the bedroom window. "No." There wasn't enough time. "Up."

I barely had time to react before Clarke reached the landing. I'd been wondering all along why PC Downe and the other constable hadn't pressed close and it wasn't as I feared. It wasn't that Clarke held a gun. He only held a metal crowbar. It was still an intimidating sight but it wasn't the reason why no help could follow him. That was because no one could get through the office door from the exhibition room. When Gregory had fallen he'd crushed Christi into the corner by the door and PC Downe was both trying to climb over the combined mass of two unwieldy bodies – one shrieking and one quiet and innocent – and trying to not commit murder himself by further injuring anyone. PC Downe was fighting his way through with the other constable just behind but he wasn't going to be quick enough.

Clarke was moving swiftly. He was wearing his crisp pinstriped suit. He looked gaunt in this light and young too. Barely out of his teens. Clarke had his hand extending towards Adam's sleeve; reaching, seeking that first moment of contact and fending off the probability that Adam would attack first. For good reason. There was a scuff as Adam's feet adjusted their position. I was on the lower steps of the stairs to the attic. Below I heard the policeman curse as his foot was snagged by the mass. Downe wasn't being so gentle now in his efforts to break clear. Clarke stepped closer.

And then he hesitated, considering.

Clarke's lightly formed fist was only inches away when he said to Adam, "I did my basic training on National Service too. But unlike you, I'd already been doing this kind of thing for years. What were you going to do? Catch my wrist and put me on the floor?" His smart businesslike exterior disintegrated as the crowbar glinted. "Think again, you ..." And he lashed out with the small wooden block he'd held concealed in his other hand.

---

For a moment I actually thought Adam was dead.

There was a scream – probably mine – and a crash of limbs on wooden floorboards. Adam dropped; the force of his fall flung me sprawling upon the next flight of steps. It was agonising for me. I'm not sure how much Adam was able to feel. For about five awful heartbeats I thought Adam had hit his head on the newel post. If he had, it would all have been over then.

His body ended up at the foot of my stairs with his head turned awkwardly to one side. In one rapid snatch, Clarke bent in to touch Adam's hands to the metal crowbar. His fingerprints. It was all done in a matter of seconds. I could hear my heartbeat. Clarke's gasping breath. Pure passionate horror made me reach out to strike him with my foot – I'm not sure what it would have done if it had landed, left a small bruise perhaps – when he stepped back and let the crowbar slide from Adam's grip to the floor. He kicked it away so that it skittered across the wooden boards to meet the doorframe

416

into the kitchen. He didn't even notice that I was still crashing about there above them both on the next rise, clinging to the banister rail struggling to regain my balance after that abortive idea of attack, still waiting to feel eternally grateful when Adam moved. He *did* move. I saw him turn a little onto one side at the foot of the stairs. I saw him tentatively touch a hand to his head. The hand came away bloodied and he swore quietly under his breath. Repeatedly.

Then Clarke lightly nudged his foot and Adam winced and jerkily turned his gaze. He didn't move again. Satisfied, Clarke finally lifted his head to acknowledge me.

I was much closer than I ought to have been. I think I'd forgotten that Adam had done this purely in the hope of giving me time to get away. I had been gearing up for my next attack in the forlorn hope of intervening. What sort of woman would I have been if I hadn't? Now I remembered. I was sickened. Ashamed. I turned on my step, slithered, lost my grip, recovered and fled.

The stairs to the attic seemed steeper. I heard the thump behind and the nasty curse as Clarke stepped over Adam and was tripped instead. But even as I reached the turn once more that led to the darkroom door, I felt him drawing close. Hands, legs and everything kept my body moving upwards. I plunged for the handle. The door swung. I fell in and took the key with me. The door slammed. Bulged again with the slap of Clarke's hand flinging itself at the last step, then my shoulder engaged with the wooden panel of the door and the key rammed home its bolt.

The door rattled but held. I reached a shaking hand for

the place on the wall where I knew the light switch would be. The room shone blood red. It was a terrible colour to lighten my gasping retreat to the heavily shuttered window. If I had wanted to disappear in here, I might have done better to have left it off.

But I wasn't here to hide. I was already at the end of the attic in the steep triangle of the gable and running fumbling fingers around the frame to find the uppermost bolts that secured the ancient shutters.

Behind, that wiry villain was clawing at my door. This door was stronger than the one at my hotel room but still I heard the lock splinter. Clarke roared something – something like, "*I haven't got time for this.*" It was followed by what sounded roughly along the lines of a description of what happens to a person when they get cornered like a rat.

The shutters had been painted many times. I didn't have the barest hope that even the force of my panic would be enough to move their crusted fastenings. But I had to try. I set myself at the first of the bolts that were Rhys' accursed obsession. The photographer's whole life depended on denying light and now he was having his way just when I needed it most. I hung my whole weight from my hands.

And almost hit the ground when the bolt slid cleanly along its groove. The shutters had been opened recently – Jim really hadn't exaggerated when he told me he'd been over every inch of this place.

I didn't need a reminder of that policeman's determination to magnify mine. Willingly, the second bolt gave and the third, taking several pieces of fingernail with it. Then the fourth began to yield. It stuck, leaving me hanging from its high niche, cursing and scrabbling for extra leverage while behind the door splintered and Clarke shot across the room.

The bolt moved; and with the blinding glare of daylight came the crash as the shutter smacked back against the wall. A distant echo sounded somewhere below. It was smothered by Clarke's breathless snarl just behind.

He held out his hand. "Give that envelope to me."

His head was low so that he was peering at me from beneath sweating brows. His breath was roaring in his throat. Sweat glistened. Ready in his other hand was that hateful block of wood. He'd planned this perfectly. The bloodied weapon downstairs held Adam's prints. This weapon would be unidentifiable and burned just as soon as it could be. Perhaps he believed he would only injure me. My previously battered mind shied from the improbability of it.

This high window was divided prettily into many dimpled rectangles. Jim wasn't down on the street many, many yards below. He still was nowhere to be seen. I had achieved nothing. Clarke was there and this wild attempt to ensure that Jim was armed with the truth was failing. I did what I hadn't imagined possible. I swung the heel of my hand at the old thin glass in the window, a little rectangle amongst a dozen or so more smeared with grime. Then I flung my left hand through the sudden maze of splintering glass. With it went the envelope and the precious proof that must with a mind like Jim's ultimately exonerate Adam, regardless of what came next for the rest of us now.

I opened my grip and, praying that the policeman was at

least somewhere within the range of sound, screamed Jim's name for all I was worth.

I didn't get to see whether anyone down there on the street heard.

Clarke snatched me back. Another cry escaped as the jagged edge of shattered glass traced a fine line across the back of my wrist and drew blood. Clarke's rapid breath grazed my cheek as he peered out past me at the street below, at his prize lost somewhere on the busy tarmacadam and the old grey-haired man in a long raincoat who was peering curiously upwards.

I was nursing my wounded wrist. I heard Clarke curse and felt him release his grip. He strode away from me across the bare attic floor and out of the flare of bright sunlight and left me standing there leaning back weakly against the casement.

Then he turned back. The combination of daylight and the red light bulb cast him in a rosy glow. And flung the room into dust and leaping shadows.

I gasped out, "You murdered him, didn't you? The policeman Black. The journalist." I cringed as Clarke closed the few yards between us.

Clarke hissed something vicious through bared teeth and snatched me aside to swing the shutter closed only to shove me back again onto the rigid black panelling. It made me rebound with a teeth-rattling crash. Then, seemingly satisfied by this startlingly childish act, he simply snarled at my pathetic little shrinking form as it sank against the wooden board.

He said, "It wasn't me. I didn't kill him. I thought *you* were a thief."

Suddenly looking very much like a frightened youth who had stepped into something far beyond his scope of experience, Clarke span away towards the tempting rectangle of the gaping darkroom door. He ran straight into the arms of the four plain-clothes policemen who were pounding up the stairs.

# Chapter 35

I hadn't realised the distant echo had been the shattering of my office windows as the policemen broke in. I learned later that they had been smashed from the inside with the plant stand that had been Gregory's stool. Clarke must have had the foresight to take the key from the lock when he had secured the door.

The attic darkroom abruptly contained a heaving mass of policemen. After so many desperate seconds of desertion the gallery seemed full to bursting, with Clarke buried beneath the majority of them. I didn't recognise any of these plain-clothed policemen except for PC Downe who had led the charge. He'd taken one look at me and turned tail almost instantly to race back down the stairs again carrying the news that I was fine and on the same breath calling for Jim. Someone gave me a clean handkerchief to press over my bloodied wrist and ushered me towards the darkroom door. This was a scene of an arrest and rapid interrogation and judged no place for bystanders, particularly female ones with a vacuous stare.

None of them knew who I was. They hadn't been here, they hadn't even seen Jim. None of them had time to think why I should have been near Clarke at all. The inspector was here now and a new team was in charge. I slid drunkenly step by step down into the gloom of the stairs. I missed the comfort Adam would have brought. Somehow I'd expected him to arrive with them. I had to use my elbow as a brake against the banister rail because my right hand was clamped over the wound on my left. Someone marched up the stairs past me. Two more of them. Orders were being discussed, a confusion between detectives about whether Jim's men were handling Reed's interrogation or the inspector's were. They slid past with barely a glance for a lone woman on the stairs.

It was then that I learned someone had come with me after all. I thought they hadn't but a hand was on my elbow and it steered me left across the vacant landing on the first floor into the kitchen. He was gone before I turned. I think he had spoken to me but my ears were full of the tramp of many feet on the bare floorboards above and the cacophony up there of male voices all talking together.

Quite automatically I drew out a drawer and assembled all the bits and pieces I needed to patch myself up. Luckily Christi's method of packing hadn't valued any possessions of mine and since it was still my kitchen, I knew where everything was: scissors, dressing and a fine roll of bandage.

The landing outside my door was empty. It had only just dawned on me what that meant. He was there, in the bedroom opposite me. The relief of it almost finished me off. Through the angle of the two doorways, I could just make out one half of Adam where he was sitting on the foot of the bed. Someone who rated themselves as a bit of a doctor was trying to do something along the lines of a clean-up of his temple. Adam couldn't see me. He was thoroughly crowded by two of the newly arrived policemen who seemed oblivious to the fact that he might be finding it rather hard to concentrate on their questions with fingers poking at his head.

My wrist was barely bleeding. I managed to brave a quick examination to ensure that there was no glass in the cut. There wasn't but it was hard to look.

Several more policemen raced up the stairs and dived briefly into Adam's room while another paused on the threshold of mine with their hand on the brass knob of the open door. They asked me how I was. I think they were looking for someone. This newly arrived inspector perhaps. Whoever it was, it wasn't me in my tiny space of the little narrow kitchen. In the next blink, the stairwell was empty again and all I could see was Adam through the crowd of his policemen. They had moved aside a little so that I could see Adam's face. His eyes were downcast, gaze resting on the carpet while they spoke to him. I saw the dark line of his eyelashes flicker as he gave a faint nod.

Then Gregory's voice close by murmured, "Looks like he's well surrounded, doesn't he? Is he under arrest?"

I could understand why he should think that. Then the kitchen door was pushed shut and cut Adam off from view.

Gregory had been hiding behind the door. He'd kept his hand on the handle to form a dark little triangular hiding place against the wall. He had his hand on it now, barring any attempt of mine to drag it open again and escape. After my first attempt to dive through the closing door had been rebuffed and flung back against the countertop, I didn't try again. The stifled cry had been involuntary but I didn't scream. I didn't think it was wise. It would push him into immediate action. He and I stood there in an impasse of rapid breathing which finally he broke.

"Don't try to pretend that you haven't guessed." It was a low murmur, daring me to lie.

He looked, odd to say it, almost charming. His steel wire hair was ruffled from his play-acting downstairs. His face was the sort that was rectangular – broad brow and jaw grained with grey – but made robust rather than fat through a lifetime of enjoying exercise. Now his lips were curving through concentration and a certain delicious anticipation of what must come next.

I don't think it had struck me before that this was a man who knew me, and in knowing me had sent violence after me.

"I can't get out, Kate," he told me ruefully.

There seemed to be an awful lot of noise going on in the office beneath our feet. The men who had been searching the house for Gregory had trooped back downstairs again and now they seemed to be moving furniture about. Perhaps they were working to open the bolted courtyard door.

Gregory said, "There's an injured policeman down there."

"Ah," I agreed conversationally, as if I understood.

He told me, "The first one got past me but I got the second. I think he tore a vein."

Gregory reached a hand past my left hip for the roll of bandage from the counter top. A few inches unravelled as he lifted it and I watched his fingers absently smooth the finely textured band of fabric.

"I was about to give the other a little accident too but that man of yours lurched drunkenly into him off the bottom step and then the pair of them set about making a way in for the rest. Your man had to break the office window since Clarke had pocketed the key. I think Hitchen found it quite therapeutic crashing about with that wooden seat. It woke him up enough that he thought to notice me."

A few more delicate inches were rolled free. In the close confines of this kitchen I was standing propped against the hard edge of the counter top with my stinging wrist still cradled in my other hand. The window in this room was small and damp and stained with mould and the dim light caught the sweat standing out on Gregory's brow. There was a thin film there that was threatening to form a bead. His eyebrows still retained some chestnut amongst the grey and they were damp as well. The eyes that glared beneath were deep-set with weathered creases at the edges, and his pupils were strange.

They flicked up to briefly to touch upon mine. "He noticed when that constable left to lead the swarm that had come in through the front door and took them racing up the stairs. No one knew me. No one else would have noticed if I'd joined their stampede to your side. No one else cared about me." His hands moved, miming out the actions that must have inevitably followed if he'd found me upstairs I think. He gave a rueful shrug at the thought, an unfocussed stare that hardened. "Unfortunately, he was determined to stick to me like glue. I could see it in his eyes from across the room when he moved to keep pace with me. It was at the same moment that you screamed for the ineffectual sergeant who was bashing the last of the glass from the vacant window."

He seemed to be waiting for me to respond, so I said slightly hoarsely, "You saw that?"

"Yes. He wasn't stupid enough to close the distance between us."

It was said briskly, regretfully. After a moment of contemplation, Gregory recollected the bandage. He had twisted a length around two fingers from his left hand. I saw him give the thin band a little tug to test its tension. He seemed to think it would do. I watched as he eased the loop from his fingers and uncoiled a little more from the roll.

Outside the door the house was briefly quiet. Like an intake of breath. For a moment I considered screaming and attacking before he unravelled any more but I didn't think it would do any good. Even in the time it took for someone to cross the landing he could have conclusively silenced me. The scissors were just there and there were drawers full of knives and tools and it wouldn't matter in the slightest if I got to them first. Quite simply, I didn't dare to depend on anyone being able to save me from this tiny cage of a room if I tipped him into panic.

Gregory was calmly telling me, "I was running up the stairs and Hitchen was there too. He meant me to know I wasn't going to get up to you without him. Then I was stopped at the foot of the next flight by the sound of that constable coming clattering back down again. I knew it would be a mistake to be seen there. Luckily a second wave of policemen came crowding past and they collided with the rush from the courtyard and then someone started bellowing orders about and jostling everyone further and I dived in here and Hitchen lost me. I think he thought I'd bolted back down the stairs again. In hindsight, that might have been better." He gave a staged sigh. "But your man didn't find me behind the door. He didn't get a chance to because some of those new fellows spotted him in the crush and dragged him out and started trying to organise him down the stairs. They told him you were safe. They told him they had questions. I'm not quite sure they were as ready to believe his account of things as you are. Only with uncanny timing he suddenly felt the effects of the wound to his head and needed to sit down so they had to take him into the bedroom."

Gregory leaned in to confide on a very intimate note, "I think he did it deliberately."

There was a glimmer of a smirk. "Perhaps he thinks he's mounting a guard. Perhaps he thinks I can't sneak past with him watching from there. Shame no one else will believe him."

And I thought suddenly, he really didn't know that Jim had been playing out Rhys's game all along. He didn't know that those men who had run up and down the stairs a moment after I'd walked in here were looking for him. I kept my unsteady lips pressed tightly together as if the realisation might escape.

Gregory was concentrating on his bandage. He had it trailing to a length of about a yard. He cut it off with the scissors and then set about twisting it around his fist and then rolling the other end about his other hand. Over and under his wrists turned to leave some slack between them of about a foot or a little more.

Gregory was fascinated by his own creation. He told it, "I thought I was trapped. Until you walked in, I was beginning to think I was going to have to attempt an exit through that window." My eyes followed the point of his bandage-wrapped hand. He was making a small joke. The kitchen window was tiny. I'd have struggled to fit and I was barely more than half his size. It was a good job too because otherwise I believe he'd have tried to tip me out with a view to slipping away while they all ran to pick me up off the courtyard floor. It would have been a long drop. The descent by the metal ladder from that hotel window in Aberystwyth would have had nothing on this.

Gregory moved towards me a little. His breathing rate had increased. "Of course," he confided, "until you walked in to the gallery today, I didn't have any exit at all. For weeks now I've been trying to retrieve what Black took. You have no idea what it's been like living under a threat like that. I thought he'd handed it on but I guessed after a few days that you didn't have it either. But then I realised that I didn't *need* to retrieve this thing. I knew it had to be something vaguely connected to my work at the gallery. But there's nothing here from my other business. I've been very sure about that. No one knows the people I've worked with all these years. These policemen can make guesses about the bonds and ambitions that rule the life of a sportsman. They can read my patronage of Rhys's career and judge me on my talent for forging connections. But no one could dream of the scale of ambition that was working away inside this body, quietly, discreetly until war conveniently opened up the field again. There are races that don't involve the glory of leading a rowing crew to the finish like I did before. And other ways of winning."

There was something desperately bitter about the way he said the word *winning*. It hinted that, for all the ambition, the bond that ruled him now was torturous. His lips were curling into a leer. "None of that matters. I knew that all Black could have found was a hint of the role I've had in this gallery over the past two years. I knew that without him, there really would be nothing to set me apart from all the other people who've had the opportunity to exploit the contacts of this place. Which means that in reality almost any of your clients might do for a suspect now. And that in turn means that all *I* have to do to put myself firmly out of the running in the eyes of the police is cast myself as an innocent bystander. And discourage the only real witness from betraying me if I can." A dry hint of mirth. Then an automatic step to close the distance between us when he noticed I'd slid backwards, carefully moving away from him along the counter edge. I didn't dare tell him that the last time I'd seen the surviving part of Black's evidence, it had been plummeting towards an old gentleman on the street outside who must surely have been a policeman.

"As soon as your name was mentioned I knew you would use the same foolishness that made you attempt to dissuade Rhys from letting me share his office two years ago as the excuse to betray me again now. I was going to engineer a little accident when Clarke came in. All I needed to make it work was for you to come and take the air by the courtyard door ..."

A tense moistening of his lips with his tongue confirmed the thwarted plan. We both froze as a clump of regulation footwear went past the door. It sounded like they were bringing Clarke down. For all of Gregory's confidence that Adam was still their main man, he didn't think to retract the tip of his tongue or close his mouth until the sounds had reached the ground floor.

In a whisper, Gregory added, "I let you think I brought you here today to find this thing for me. But you're here because I knew you'd bring along a suitably respectable audience for the attack when Clarke burst in supposedly with the intention of destroying the evidence. They were watching when he conveniently bungled it and turned on me instead. You've made me the next innocent victim here."

His hands were testing the tension of his little garrotte. The bandage stretched a little but it wouldn't break. I think he was using the suspense of telling me this to convince himself he was capable of using it. I could almost feel the rhythm of his heartbeat in the air. It matched mine. I think he could see my pulse beating in my throat. I found myself wishing that my frock had a high collar because then my neck wouldn't be feeling quite so exposed. He was staring at my heartbeat, hypnotised.

I put up my hand to my throat. He blinked like a man coming out of a dream.

Then those peculiarly flecked irises flicked up to meet

mine. I don't think he knew he'd stopped speaking. He continued, "The funny thing about today is that it never occurred to me to paint someone else as the suspect. I'd got Reed primed to clear the path for Clarke's entrance on my command; my part here was going to be firmly fixed; and I'd got you, of course ... But then my very good friend gifted me Hitchen when he decided he'd found himself a clue and I thought I could use it too."

He was dreaming of that soiled crowbar; of the opportunity Adam had represented. Of the misfortune of timing that had left Clarke trapped upstairs and Gregory with the choice of either attempting guilty flight or ensuring that he had at least silenced the worst witness by coming after me.

A floorboard creaked somewhere outside, harmlessly enough I think but frustration coloured Gregory's face. He had me now and yet he was being forced to worry about the possibilities of what else might still go wrong. He was worrying about the closed door and about how it was both a shelter and fuel to paranoia. He couldn't be sure now that hordes of policemen weren't silently assembling outside the door waiting for my cue.

I saw it in his face. He didn't dare make me scream. While I was safe and well, logic dictated that they – whoever and however many they were – had to wait out there in the hope of a peaceful resolution. Like all of us, they too couldn't risk moving prematurely in case their own action caused him to tip into that extreme of desperation.

I felt Gregory's concentration sharpen upon my face. He seemed to be seeing me anew. It was like he'd barely considered me as a real presence in here before. For a moment I stood there before him in vivid, glorious living colour.

Then he told himself softly, "And I still can use him, you know. I still can."

Breath stilled. The hands lifted. Slowly. His thumbs were braced upon the taut strip of cloth, ensuring its tension. They were strong hands, weathered from years on the water.

Gregory whispered rather wistfully, "He is only in the next room. They'd think he found the chance to slip across ..."

I think he wanted me to give him my permission. To tell him I agreed and to promise to go quietly. Very slowly, I put out my hands, the clean and the bloodied, to softly meet his.

Very gently I intercepted the steady approach of those tangled fists towards my throat. "Don't you think," I said very carefully indeed, "that you should use me to get away?"

For a moment I didn't think he'd heard. The lips were slightly slack. His hands were warm beneath mine. Trembling. Then I saw a spasm twitch across his mouth. I think his initial emotion was overwhelmingly disappointment.

I said very gently, "You're trapped in this room. You said so yourself. But you can use me to get away. These new policemen don't know you. They don't know your face. We can walk out while they're still talking to Adam. Look at my wrist." He looked. "You can tell anyone who asks that you're a doctor and you're taking me to your car where you have your bag so that I can be patched up properly."

The hands hovered beneath mine. The bandage was a tight band. It was making the skin pucker on his fingertips where it cut into the flesh. I could see he was running the argument through his mind, but still inclining towards action. I'm not sure how he thought he'd escape if he strangled me now. At this moment I wasn't sure he had much capacity for thought left at all.

I guessed he was still fixated on managing the one unplanned element in his day. He was thinking about Adam.

I said softly, dismissively, "What's Adam going to do? He won't dare say anything if I'm with you."

It was the mention of Adam that made Gregory blink. His posture changed. Instead of braced and ready for a physical struggle with me that, while it would be difficult, he must surely win, his head lifted. His hands drew back from mine, though I kept mine there just in case.

With a grim sort of resignation, he abruptly set about unravelling the bandage onto the countertop before using it anew to bind that dressing onto my wrist.

---

After all his worries, when we cautiously opened the kitchen door it was onto a silent and deserted floor. The bedroom was empty. Someone was pacing about upstairs and there was a reassuringly insubstantial murmur of voices from the space downstairs but, essentially, our way was clear.

Gregory's efforts to bind my wrist had been extraordinarily thorough. He'd even taken the time to test that the bandage hadn't constricted the flow of blood by giving a little pinch to my thumb. Now he had his hand on my elbow, keeping me close and steering me slightly ahead of him as we hurried down the stairs.

I went easily, willingly. This was my escape from the terrifying claustrophobia of the kitchen too. There was blood on Gregory's sleeve that wasn't mine. Clarke's blow with the crowbar had not been kind. There was a tear on the blazer at the point where the sleeve met his shoulder and a smear of blood streaked the shirt beneath. I suppose it had seemed important that Clarke's attack was convincing.

He was rushing me along. The office was a mess. My client books were everywhere and so was the furniture. Rhys's client chair was in my path. I put out a hand to ease it aside. The windows were busy rectangles of daylight and so was the door. There were people out there. There were people in the exhibition room too when Gregory swept me through the door. Three of them were new, unidentifiable plain-clothes policemen. They were only casually interested in us. They'd been tasked with cataloguing the contents of the boxes in this room. I drew breath to tell them about Gregory. He thought I was going to tell them he was a doctor. His hand was still on my arm.

And it was then that there was a brief telltale flicker of shade behind as several people moved all at once.

Unfortunately Gregory's reactions were quicker.

A mass of people had been standing with their backs pressed against the wall that ajoined the office. Their plunge for me came at the same moment that my companion gave a startled little gasp of realisation and lashed out instinctively to catch my hand as it thrust against his chest. I was suddenly fighting, and I think I surprised him how much. For a brief moment my free hand flailed and unexpectedly met his face. His cheek smudged beneath my palm. I heard him grunt. I was almost dragged clear by reaching hands. Painfully. But then the disorganised boxes tangled amongst our legs and now I felt the pitch followed by the contraction as many fingers scraped my arm, the one with the dressing, and the sharp crush as they bore me down. A faint cry was forced out by the impact. It was joined by a confusion of other voices that huffed and snarled above me and for a few short seconds I was trapped beneath them; and pinned by all of them amongst the boxes in a writhing tussle that must surely end in only one way. Then, through it all, I heard Gregory's shout.

"I'll do it, you know. I will."

They let him up. He was panting. Everyone was. He took me with him with a grip that wrenched a sob from me. He had my arm, my injured wrist turned cruelly behind me in a twist that he tethered to my waist by hooking a finger through the belt to my dress. It was agony. The grip was too much. I couldn't draw breath. I hadn't anticipated anything like this. It wasn't the sharp pain of violence. It was a slow breaking of my wrist and it was an agonising kind of restraint that got worse with each raging second. And there was a fresh shock too. The explanation of why the policemen hadn't pressed home their attack. There was a needlepoint of metal against the softer flesh beneath my ribs.

It made every muscle shiver in a spasm of revulsion. Through it all, I heard Gregory's desperate command.

"Stay back! Get back I say!"

I could see it now. He'd had the screwdriver in his pocket all this time. Now he had the handle firmly gripped in his palm. Its tip was engaged with my side. It was an odd sort of threat because in some way I wondered just how fatal its two inches of blunted metal could really be. Obviously dangerous enough. I remembered his confession that the injured policeman had torn a vein. Presumably this was how.

PC Downe picked himself up from a sprawl against the boxes that had brought him face to face with me and stepped back, breathing hard. I'd thought Adam was there but he wasn't. There was a vacuum in this room as if hope and help had both suddenly left very abruptly by the back door. PC Downe's frightened eyes scanned the few faces in the room and found himself cast as the spokesperson. It was fear that made him say in a high shrill voice as we made for the front door, "Did you really imagine she wouldn't tell us? That the first words she spoke after realising what Black had found within those photographs wouldn't be your name? She told me upstairs just as soon as she laid out the remaining prints."

Gregory was shaking violently. The shock of the near miss had him twisting jerkily about to check where the next danger was coming from. There was none outside. The policemen out there were retreating in a respectful arc. For me, this was a repeat of the terrors that had haunted me since that doorway in Lancaster; the one where I was made to accept the utter inferiority of my strength when set against another's sheer physical will. But Gregory always did like to give the illusion of choice; so now I had to choose between going with him and the indescribable agony of the hold he had on my arm.

PC Downe was saying, "I hope you noticed that Sergeant Fleece let you incriminate yourself with your telephone call? Because I'm sure when the telephone records are checked, we'll find that you didn't telephone your doctor at all, won't we?"

I didn't know that it was a police policy to enrage a violent man. Perhaps it wasn't. At long last PC Downe seemed to dredge up some old memories of negotiation training. He was now saying something worthy about mistakes and not hurting anyone and how none of this was necessary. It might have sounded more persuasive had Gregory been prepared to listen.

Gregory was snarling at me, "You shouldn't have done this. You should have helped me get away. Your husband would have known to keep quiet. He *did* know. He was only too delighted to lay out Hitchen as a quarry but when he guessed his mistake he swallowed it because he knew that doing *this* to an old friend would mean corrupting himself and the beauty of everything we'd done together."

His urgent steps turned me in the doorway to the street outside. The move tangled my feet. The stumble made Gregory drag painfully on my wrist to snatch me onto a different path. I was gasping fiercely, "It wasn't *friendship*. It was fear because he knew you well enough to know what you were capable of. And he couldn't quite comprehend that you'd really do it."

Gregory wasn't listening. By my ear he was already adding, "I suppose I should have known you were only pretending in the kitchen. You never were very," a pause, "loyal."

The venom in that single word was matched by the cruelty of his drag upon my wrist. It made me cry out. He always

438

had made me feel at fault if I disagreed with his point of view. But this one was just for now. It was absurd, I thought, but Gregory really did blame me for the inconvenience of wishing to preserve my own life.

The realisation finally put an end to the odd battle I'd been fighting lately between retaining a sense of who I thought I was and reinventing myself as someone who was – how had Christi put it? – a little less insipid. Gregory's behaviour now proved the truth. I'd always spoken my mind; it was just that my husband had never seen much reason to listen. But Gregory had. He knew better than anyone that no claim of friendship had ever shaken my resolve before where I knew I was right. He called it disloyalty. And now I understood precisely why I was so dangerous to him.

There was black nearby. The police cars were still waiting beside the kerb. Beyond there was the hum and rattle of traffic by the church. Gathering close were Wednesday shoppers on the far side of the street milling in a horde around the widening fan of policemen. They were staring at me. But I still couldn't find Adam.

I'd been sure he would be out here. I'd guessed easily enough that it was his eyes that had been wrenched up to catch my movement beyond the closing door. It was his mouth that had quietly raised the alarm. But all I had was PC Downe bearing a distant promise of intervention with the bitter truth etched upon his face, and Gregory huffing in my ear.

Gregory was gasping from the exertion of fighting me for the screwdriver and dragging me onwards. I'd managed to fix my free hand over the fist that gripped his weapon. My arm was aching from resisting his but he wasn't athletic after all. Beneath his smart blazer he was overweight and unfit. Which only made it very frighteningly clear just how easy it was for even an ageing man to bring a woman who was fighting every inch of the way into the heart of the road.

Because he meant to take me with him. Of course he did. This was his way of ensuring his control, of demonstrating his power, of exacting his revenge on me for daring to know the truth about him. This was murder; to him I was already dead, he just had to get me in through the passenger door of the waiting police car.

That step might take only a few more seconds. The unimaginable dread of how much longer after that it would take me to accept my end made me use the only weapon I had left. My voice. I gasped out, "Ask him about Detective Black. Ask him to explain how he killed him."

It wasn't easy to speak. I was a spectacle laid on for the endless fascination of the gawping mass of people. The crowd was shoppers and policemen. I'd expected the policemen to pounce. Adam had called me brave enough for anything, but he must know I couldn't do this on my own. He must know. But they all seemed to abruptly give Gregory room; the policemen, everyone.

We were near the waiting car. I could smell Gregory's sweat. Beyond us the watchful public had abruptly stopped retreating. Something had changed and it wasn't my question. My attempt to goad him into betraying that one last secret was irrelevant. Ludicrously, the weight of not knowing what this fresh strain meant very nearly made me trip into taking that last step to the side of the car. Only I knew I mustn't. If I did I knew I would scream. Purely from this nightmare of frustration of fighting him every inch of the way and still finding myself at last brought up against the handle of this blasted car door. I could feel the scream growing. It waited, bubbling in the depths of my soul like a madness, ready to consume me.

*"I didn't kill Black."* By my ear, Gregory was spitting the words. Somehow the injustice of the accusation enraged him. "I didn't start all this. It's his fault it's escalated. He acted like a petty thief. If only he'd surrendered what he'd found when I stepped in off the street to meet him dashing out, or even told me he was a policeman, none of this would have happened. Instead he demanded to know the scale of my involvement in Rhys's projects. He knew I'd have to act. He deliberately *made* this into something big."

Gregory was trying to work out how to hold me and the screwdriver and reach for the car door all at the same time. But then I saw Adam. We both saw him.

He'd stepped in a hasty stumble out of the ugly warped door of the shop next door, only to slow abruptly as soon as he fixed his eyes on us. He was moving through the wavering policemen and onto the road. He was a matter of yards away, that was all. He was breathing hard. I thought he'd been running. I couldn't quite read his face but he had a hand out, like Clarke had done only placating and without the concealed block of wood, ready to make a play for that wavering screwdriver. Relief was like a wash of cold water. Debilitating. His approach bewildered Gregory.

Behind Gregory, another voice pierced the chaos. This was

why they had fallen back. This was what they had been waiting for. This was why Adam had held our attention for these last few precious seconds. Jim had been stepping through from a different doorway. His voice wasn't breathless. It interrupted with sickening calm. "I've just been enjoying a little chat with one of your erstwhile assistants, Mr Scott. Apparently Reed isn't a professional criminal at all. Apparently he's a private eye with a weakness for gambling and you sold him a part in the race to retrieve Black's photographs on the principle that you were the innocent party. And now it seems your attempt to complete the lie has proved singularly ill advised too. A word to the wise if I may; if you're truly determined to close this deal by abducting my friend, you really should have checked first whether the keys to that car had been left in the ignition."

There was a sudden stinging rush of blood to my arm. I kicked back hard with a foot. A zing went by as the screwdriver was flung at Adam's head, forcing him to flinch aside. I felt the thump of liberation as Gregory Scott swung round, roaring for Jim, to land a punch. He twisted, ducking and ready for a fight and in doing so flung me away, spinning. Right into the path of the approaching bus.

# Chapter 36

I crawled back to life to find my face pressed into the wool of his shoulder and an arm flung tightly about his neck. His own arms were holding me close. One hand was warm against my hair and the other was a safe curve about my body. Although for a time there had only been the precipice of the deep abyss and absolute silence, now suddenly I could hear myself repeating over and over again in a pale shadow of hysteria, "*The bus, the bus, the bus …*"

There was the faintest whisper of amusement. I felt of the warmth of his jaw against my temple. I heard him say with a fierce kind of relief, "It wasn't a bus, sweetheart, it was a car. It was a car being driven by a very gentle old man at about three miles an hour and I think you terrified him even more than he did you. He wobbled to a halt, you screamed at him loudly enough to rattle all the windows in the street and took off."

A small movement of his fingers where they tangled in my hair. "It was all I could do to catch you and get you to sit down here."

*Here.* Wherever here was, it felt hard and cold where it met the skin of my calf and it was probably wood. I didn't think I had been crying. I couldn't remember anything between the moment when wild reasoning had abruptly vanished and this slow dawning of thought however many minutes later. Even in a blind panic I must have known who he was and permitted him to guide me. Now I could feel the persistent throbbing of my poor bandaged hand as a steady metronome to my heartbeat. My pulse was more regular than it had been for a long while. The bandaged hand was sandwiched awkwardly between us. We were both twisted towards each other; his right to my left. Hips, thighs and knees pressed close as a sort of barrier to comfort. He was probably deeply uncomfortable. I was too. Like a switch had been thrown I could suddenly hear the noise of traffic very close by and people talking.

I began to sit up. He loosened his hold to allow me to draw away enough to blink at him and begin to look about but he didn't let me go. He kept me in the curve of his arm and his free hand met mine as it drifted down from its stranglehold to rest upon the neckline of his jumper. We were sitting on one of the crude wartime benches in front of the war memorial with its wreaths and tokens left to commemorate the recent Armistice Day. The parish church towered over us all and Royal Wedding bunting was everywhere. It was cold and we were both without our coats.

Adam briefly extended his hand to point out a little old man in an equally tiny Austin 7 who was shakily taking the turn out of Cricklade Street. He said gently, "There he goes. He got quite a ticking off from PC Downe for his part in it as well, because he bowled in straight through the police line without even looking."

"Serves him right," I said darkly. "Silly old fool." Then I gulped and said unsteadily, "I'm sorry. I didn't mean that. I don't think I like people very much at the moment. But—"

Adam supplied lightly, "— But you do like me?"

I don't think I grasped that his humour was a mask for his own worry. I sat up a little straighter and turned and looked at him. Beneath the marks of strain, that familiar faint curve was touching one corner of his mouth. It made me blink at him as though he were being particularly stupid.

I told him, "I love you. I thought you knew."

Then, because he only stared at me utterly, heartshakingly blankly – he really hadn't known – I lifted my hand to his cheek and leaned in and kissed him. His skin was warm beneath my palm where I drew his head round to mine. His mouth felt perfect, just like the rest of him. As I had suspected it would be. This was a man who had been firmly on my side from the very beginning, even when all my actions were incomprehensible. It felt like I must have loved him for a very long time. For a moment this felt like the natural expression of it.

And then I realised what I'd done at a time like this.

I drew away enough to put a shaking hand to my mouth. The tumult of emotions rushed back in and I was too tired to work out what any of them meant. Rejection, hope, guilt, shame and elation. "Oh God," I said desperately. And shuddered into disintegration again.

I say 'again' but actually it was pretty clear to me then that I really hadn't been weeping into the curve of his neck before.

I'd been too shocked for any normal release. No wonder he'd been relieved when I'd spoken. Now I felt his relief again because he drew me into the safety of his arms once more and held my grief so fiercely tight that he might drive it all away. And then his voice murmured by my ear, "Now what on earth is there to cry about in that little statement?"

I felt his smile. An affirmative touch against my hair. And then after a moment or two more, while I fought a hard battle to regain control of my breathing and nearly slipped into giddy giggling, he added in a rather more serious undertone, "Hush. You're fine now and I'm fine too, you see?"

Then suddenly Jim's voice made me jump. He was very close by. "Has she spoken yet?"

I felt the nod of Adam's quiet reply.

"And?"

Through the residual bubbles of mirth, I caught the hesitation as Adam considered just how much to say; and the private conversation that would be kept just for me. I felt his hand move in my hair, smoothing it a little where it tickled his jaw and quietly establishing that I was in the process of regaining control. Then he stunned me by lifting his head and telling Jim in an odd voice, "We're very lucky, you and I. It'll be a long while before I forgive myself for this even if she apparently has."

I heard Jim reply dryly, "Because you didn't catch her before she entered that kitchen? If that's your guilt, what's mine? I suspect the inspector'll have me back in uniform for this fine bit of chaos and that's the least of it. But she's done it, Adam. She's really done it. She found proof of what Black took away with him. She delivered it to the inspector. Gregory Scott is our man. And we've got him now."

I found my voice. "Is your injured policeman all right?"

Jim paused while I rejoined them and sat up once more. He discreetly ignored me while I got myself into some kind of order and pushed the ragged tangles of my hair back from my face. He told Adam, and me too without directing the information at me, "He'll be fine. He's got a bit of a hole in the flesh of his arm and is enjoying making a great deal of fuss about it."

I squinted up at Jim. He was hard to see against the uniform grey of the afternoon sky. "You guessed from the first that it was Gregory, didn't you?"

Jim smiled down at me. He might be set for a sound telling off from his superiors but he looked elated. He also looked entirely unruffled by the day's adventures. He still had his coat and he looked crisp and clean. I knew Adam and I looked utterly ragged. He told me, "It seemed pretty convenient that Mr Gregory Scott should be there today. I thought he was hoping you'd find Black's evidence and he'd get a chance to destroy it or adulterate it, or even capitalise on the tangle your husband, sorry, ex-husband got himself into while he was working us up towards entrapping Adam. I thought we only needed to apply a touch more pressure and we'd have our man in the bag. It was just unfortunate I didn't make any allowance for the insane logic of a man like Gregory Scott. I still can't quite believe he was operating solely on the fantasy that he could stage irrefutable evidence that would put him in the clear."

Beside me, Adam said accusingly, "I actually believed you, you know, when you all but placed me under arrest."

Jim laughed. He looked gratified. "So did Mr Williams. And now," he added with satisfied smirk, "he's going to tell us precisely who else has been coming to that office to pay special visits to Mr Scott. And Mr Scott is going to have a fine time explaining precisely what *did* happen to my friend Detective Constable Black. And this time I won't be playing along with anybody's charade, or giving anyone's ex-wife the nudge to play weak and stupid either."

Then, with alarming abruptness, Jim grew very serious indeed. He dropped into a crouch before us. He said gravely to me, "Thank you." His brown eyes were steady on my face. "I'd already thought you'd made our man desperate, Kate. I should have gauged more seriously just how desperate. The terrifying thing is that he might have actually achieved at least part of his plan if Adam hadn't shaken off his guard and come and found me."

I felt Adam shift uneasily beside me. Jim's mouth briefly fixed into a rueful line. "We broke for cover when we heard you were going to come out. We were there in the exhibition room when you came hurrying in. We were there right up to the moment that Gregory Scott started brandishing his screwdriver. I gave PC Downe the cue to distract him as much as he could and dragged Adam away to slip round by way of the courtyard to intercept your procession outside. Adam didn't want to leave you, you know."

He adjusted his position as his knees complained from the prolonged crouch. "I didn't mean to either. I hadn't, you know, left Gregory Scott unguarded for a moment, not even when the excitement of Reed's appearance proved too tempting a lure. PC Downe and his fellow were there. When Clarke stepped in and I heard my name being screamed from the rooftops, I was already in the process of pounding back in with a handful of fellows." Jim looked decidedly uncomfortable at the memory. Then his gaze returned to my face. He smiled. He told me, "This sounds terribly like I'm trying to escape accusations of negligence but I want you to understand that when the inspector arrived with the full team from the Cirencester station, they took charge of everything upstairs. I thought Scott must have slipped away while my lowly Gloucester constables were being relegated to crowd control. All the time that our man was waiting to find you on your own, I was chasing about trying to fill the gaps in our search. It's not an excuse for leaving you unguarded, but it is what happened. I'm sorry. And," he added on a rather darker note, "I have to tell you that I'm still blindingly grateful you came today, and it's not as you might think because I'm willing to sacrifice everything just for the sake of catching my man."

I must have looked disbelieving because he smiled. "It's true, you know. If you hadn't been there today, I don't believe he would have been satisfied with the collapse of our investigation. He still would have come for you. He would always have come for you. I don't think he knew until today precisely what form the evidence against him took but as soon as your name was thrust into his mind he knew you weren't the sort to be bribed or bullied into silence, and he certainly believed

449

you really were the woman who could undo him. I don't think he was ever going to bear it."

And if Gregory hadn't attempted to finish this with the full benefit of witnesses, he wouldn't have done it in the presence of the only policeman determined enough to be capable of putting a stop to it. It seemed I too had to be thankful for some parts of today.

Needless to say, Jim left a little hard chill behind when he climbed to his feet again. He shook his own regrets off abruptly. With his customary cheerfulness that meant that it was impossible to know whether he agreed with the next part of his inspector's actions or was just too well disciplined to contradict them, he said bracingly, "Enough of that. What I really came over to say is that the inspector's already tasked someone with telephoning your sister. Apparently she's just got to ask the neighbour to manage the children and then she'll be here to pick you up. Her husband's away so she said it's not too much trouble to put you up for a few days while your parents travel back from Paris, then she supposed you'll be keen to head back north as soon as possible. Time to leave this accursed town behind once and for all wouldn't you say, Mrs ... Miss ..." A pause while he stumbled between the choice of titles he had for me and forgot that 'Kate' would have done perfectly well, and then finished inconclusively with a lame, "eh?"

I saw his gaze flicker between me and Adam. I know the policeman saw my brittle smile. By way of a tactful exit, he abandoned the effort of saying farewell to me and instead put out his hand. "Mr Hitchen."

After the smallest of hesitations, Adam extricated his right arm by lifting it carefully over my head before reaching out and taking Jim's hand. Jim gave it a firm shake then he nodded at us and turned to go, and that was it. He went to wrap up his next loose end.

Adam and I watched him go. We sat quietly side by side while the clock tower struck a quarter past the hour. I had no idea which hour. It felt like midnight but it probably wasn't on account of the sun still being in the sky. Beside me, Adam observed calmly and quite unexpectedly, "You've been fighting my corner from the very beginning, haven't you?"

For a moment I didn't understand his meaning. I'd thought his gaze was fixed on the bustle outside my gallery but then I realised his attention had dropped to his left hand where it lay across his thigh. Mine had passed across my lap and was closed over his very firmly. I must have sought his hand when Jim had been describing their efforts to entrap Gregory by using Adam. I was gripping him very tightly indeed. I loosened my fingers. "Sorry."

"Whatever for this time?"

His tone might have made me give a little laugh but something in the way he turned his head caused my breath to catch. I made him turn a little further and saw the ragged little cut above his ear. It was largely covered by his hair but there was still a faint trace of dampness where the doctor had tried to clean it. Very lightly, I touched the limit of his hairline with my fingertips. He flinched a little but then let me find the bruise on his cheek. "It looks sore."

"It is sore," he agreed. He reached up a hand to drag mine down to his lap again.

Then he resumed whatever he had begun to say before by remarking, "If the sense of desperate isolation I encountered for a while in that place is even half of what you must have been dealing with lately, this is just one more bit of proof that I've never quite been doing you justice."

I grinned as I was supposed to, only for my humour to fracture a little and I suddenly found myself in the curve of his arm again. His grip was tight. His cheek was warm against my hair. Then he broke across my thoughts by saying roughly, "When you came to me in that room upstairs after Rhys's unpleasant revelation about that photograph, I thought you were saying goodbye. I thought you were going to help them. I thought you were sorry, but you were going to help them build their case against me all the same."

I was very still. My hand was clutching at his jumper somewhere about his middle. I knew now what he was feeling; what he had felt. Of course I did. For years he and I had shared the same fear – the one where loneliness tried to consume everything. I think he knew full well how it felt to be perceived as something other than he was.

And if today I hadn't known instinctively that he was honest. If today I'd shown that the distrust that had haunted my dealings with him over the past week still lay dormant ready for the first hint of accusation ... It would have proved at last that he had to fear that even the people who loved him could define him and teach him that what he believed about himself wasn't really true at all.

His hand moved upon my arm. Restless. He hadn't even

been certain at the time that I did love him. I could sense the exhilaration running beneath his skin and the uncertainty even now.

He drew a sharp little breath and said quite calmly, "Will you let me come and visit you in a couple of days? After you've had a bit of time to recover?"

And then just as abruptly he seemed to come to a decision.

It took an extraordinary degree of courage for him to say fiercely, "No." It was a hard correction. "I know that informing your family was a perfectly reasonable thing for them to do. But I don't want you to let them organise you into going to your sister's. And I don't want you to go back to Lancaster with your parents. I know it's not remotely the done thing but I want you to come back to my house." A pause, then, "Will you come back?"

Without moving from my place in the curve of his shoulder I knew those serious grey eyes were fixed intently on the only bit of me he could see. His hold on me tightened. He said blandly, "Please? I need you. I love you."

I think he knew he was going to make me cry again. He said quickly, "I promise I'll encourage you to paint any subject you like."

His words were for my ears alone. My fingers had moved jerkily upon his jumper and he lifted his hand to cover them. Then he added persuasively, "And I won't make you use any brown ..."

There was a smile in his voice. I drew a little calming breath.

"And," he added very seriously indeed, "you can organise

the garden; that is, just so long as May doesn't claim the wilderness as a vital wildlife habitat."

That made me turn my head and find his smile. He was there at the moment I rediscovered happiness. He was there when the sense of who we were and what we wanted to be was laid out and put in its proper place for both of us, and stayed there beneath that cold November sky.

His grip grew fierce. Crushing. I could feel the fire pounding through his veins and it was echoed in me. A while later he drew an unsteady breath. Across the market place, the shop windows were becoming blazes of light.

With his gaze on them, he admitted in a rueful whisper, "You might have to change your name." I laughed when he asked as an automatic afterthought, "Can you bear it?"

# A Letter from the
# Author to the Reader

Thank you for reading *The War Widow*. The original idea for this book came from the discovery of a pre-war Aberystwyth guidebook in a Cirencester charity shop window. I'd just finished writing my first novel *In the Shadow of Winter*, and the discovery of the Aberystwyth guidebook came at the crucial moment when my mind was toying with a new idea about linking an old life with a present one. The guidebook united my memory of life as an art student in the Welsh seaside town with my new life in Cirencester. It made me think about how much a woman might try to reinvent herself after the end of a relationship and how certain elements of the past might quite simply refuse to let her go.

The part of me that was inspired to set this story in the post-war period came from my sense that to me it all seems a very long time ago and yet it still has a significant impact on the world I live in today. There are, after all, quite a lot of people alive who remember that time. And actually that's part of why I have loved doing the research for this novel. I haven't needed to learn what life was like after the war from a historical record. Someone could tell me. They could tell me how the nation had to heal after the years of hard conflict. They could share their experiences of the shortages and the worries of the time. And they could describe the sense some people had that the new peace was the opportunity to shake off the old ties from a former life and build instead the new life they had always hoped for. It was the perfect, dynamic, challenging time for Kate, the heroine of this novel, to arrive in Aberystwyth.

Kate's account of her story unfolds in November 1947. She's working hard to save herself from a crisis that is threatening her independence and it happens at a time when a woman's power of making her own judgements is at best uncertain anyway. For me there's no more proof of Kate's bravery than in the way she faces her most personal challenge of all - the question of who she thinks she is, set against the way other people perceive her.

I have loved helping Kate to learn to trust her judgement of these people in her turn. She has to choose whether to cautiously get to know Adam in the midst of danger and through that rebuild her confidence in her own identity, or to admit that her ex-husband's opinion of her is still powerful enough to define her life even after she's left him.

I know she's brave enough for the task. I'm really glad you've joined her.

# Acknowledgements

There are many people who have been a wonderful influence on me in the course of writing this book but my particular thanks must go to my editor Suzanne Clarke. Her guidance has been invaluable.

Thank you also to Charlotte Ledger at HarperImpulse for her enthusiasm.

The Ceredigion Museum Service kindly provided access to historic photographs and information on locations within Aberystwyth. Details of other Welsh tourist entertainments and destinations from the period were taken from the Cambrian News Illustrated Guide 'Aberystwyth: What to See and How to See It' (c. 1928).

The appearance of buildings and streets in Cirencester during the post-war period was drawn from the photographic record in 'Cirencester Through Time' by David and Linda Viner (Amberley Publishing, 2009) and 'Cirencester in the 1930s and '40s' by Jean Welsford and Peter Grace (Hendon Publishing, 1990).

## Lorna Gray

Finally, a special thank you goes to my husband Jeremy for discovering my treasured Cambrian News Illustrated Guide in a Cirencester charity shop. Through that single act, he bears responsibility for gifting me the idea that grew into this novel.